Sound of the Sparrows

Sound of the Sparrows

J.P. McCollum

RESOURCE *Publications* • Eugene, Oregon

SOUND OF THE SPARROWS

Resource Publications
An Imprint of Wipf and Stock Publishers
199 W. 8th Ave., Suite 3
Eugene, OR 97401

www.wipfandstock.com

PAPERBACK ISBN: 979-8-3852-7153-5
HARDCOVER ISBN: 979-8-3852-7154-2
EBOOK ISBN: 979-8-3852-7155-9

VERSION NUMBER 02/11/26

For my sisters Emelie, Melina, and Geneveve, the smartest, most faithful, and toughest women I know.

"I have told you these things, so that in me you may have peace. In this world you will have trouble. But take heart! I have overcome the world."

—John 16:33 (NIV)

Contents

Thanks

I would like to thank Frank for his patience, mentorship, and friendship throughout our seasons of life.

Abbreviations

ADAMS American Data Analysis and Measurement Supercomputer.

AI Artificial Intelligence. Specifically, the ability of neural-network computers to analyze, learn, and solve problems without direct human input.

CAMO Consolidated Agriculture and Mining Operations; government agency

CEP Concealment, Evasion, Portability; Sparrow survival strategy

CME Compulsory Monitored Education

COATS Critical Operations and Tactical Service; Special Ops.

LEAD Law Enforcement Autonomous Droid; The new face of law enforcement on the streets.

NADF New America Defense Force; The descendant of the US military, it is divided up into four branches: Ground (Army), Air (Air Force), Naval (Navy), and COATS (Special Operations).

RAC Regional Agricultural Communities; successors to the SACs

RDF Regional Defense Force; All 10 New America Regions have a Regional Defense Force. They are the descendants of the National Guard units in the United States.

SEMIC Trains Supersonic Electromagnetic Intra-Continental Trains.

Part One

Chapter 1: **Slate Creek**

WINTER MELTED INTO SPRING as quickly as the snowpack came roaring down the jagged mountains surrounding Slate Creek. Lush green grass gathered its strength and pushed past the last patches of snow as if claiming back the ground. The whirr of wind turbines and crackling of power lines from the solar panels were the soundtracks of a SAC getting ready for planting. Tractors, ATVs, and other equipment needed all the juice their batteries could hold to take on the soil and get the seeds in the ground.

"It's nice to have Callum back," Rod said as he sat down to lace up his work boots. "I wouldn't mind having a few other pairs of hands around here, too."

Jude rolled his eyes, and Zara chuckled nervously. "We just got married, Dad. Take it easy," Jude said.

"Alright, sleeve up!" Maisy commanded her dad.

"Didn't we just do this?" he complained.

"I'm leaving in a few days. Humor me," Maisy said.

"Fine."

Back in their room, Jude apologized to Zara. "Sorry about Dad's not-so-subtle hint."

"I don't know. Maybe it's worth talking about."

"Now?" Jude asked.

"Talking now? Yes. Having kids now? No."

"Alright," Jude said, trying to mask his relief. "How many do you want?"

"I'm not ordering them for delivery," Zara quipped. "That we will talk about one at a time. I think the more important question is when."

"I'm not sure," Jude said. "I've never really thought much about it."

"Do you want kids at all?" Zara asked.

Jude's pensive face relaxed into a gentle smile. He reached out and tucked a wisp of hair behind her ear. "With you as their mom and me as their dad, I think we would make some pretty amazing little people. We really owe it to the world."

"I'm heading out to check the fields," Callum announced as he pulled on his jacket.

"Are you sure you're up for it?" Marren said instinctively. "You're still so thin."

"I was cleared by the doc," he joked, pointing to Maisy. "Besides, I'm not doing any heavy lifting. I'm just going to check the perimeter and see how the ground looks before we dig in."

"Be careful," Marren said.

"And take it easy," Maisy warned. "No straining, no staying out too long, and no shooting down drones."

"Very funny," he said as he shut the door.

Maisy set the blood sample in the reader, pulled off the blood pressure detector, and stuck a small bandage on her dad's arm.

"Am I still alive?" Rod asked.

"Everything looks pretty good," Maisy said. "Your blood pressure, cholesterol, and enzyme levels are very good. It must be all the fresh food and exercise."

"When you live in a SAC, you don't have much choice."

"Mind if I join you?" Jude asked, catching up to Callum in the barn.

"Do I have a choice?" he chuckled.

"Nope," Jude said with a hearty slap on the shoulder. "Dad's right. It's good to have you back."

"It's good to know your brother has your back. I still can't believe everything you did for me."

"It wasn't just me," Jude instinctively said.

"So I've heard. You've started some kind of movement. Now that you are a 'Sparrow,' are you going to stick around, or are you too important now?"

"I never saw myself anywhere else besides Slate Creek. Now I don't know. Maisy is heading back to Kansas City in a few days," Jude said.

"And you're going with her," Callum surmised.

"I'll be where I'm needed. For right now, it's in Slate Creek. I need to make sure you put some meat back on your bones."

"Speaking of, let's check the perimeter and see how the cows are doing," Callum said, unplugging and mounting the ATV. "I missed them in prison."

"You missed their company, or you missed their meat?" Jude joked.

"Both."

Delayed a few seconds by a zigzag through a dozen or so proxy servers, an email from Max popped up on the screen.

"How's the frozen tundra of the north? I suppose even up there, you are preparing the ground for planting. I hope all is well. I can't help but feel like this is the calm before the storm. I don't want to alarm you, but keep your ears open. Let me know if anything unusual happens in the SACs. Be careful if you travel, and be vigilant. Enjoy the time with your family. Love, Max."

Calm before the storm? Zara felt as if she had no idea what he was talking about, but knew exactly what he was saying at the same time.

"Is that a drone?" Callum asked, stopping his ATV and pointing to the clear blue sky.

"I don't see anything," Jude said, gazing in the same direction.

"Give it a second and let it turn a bit. I swore I saw rotors."

"Are you looking for drones?" Jude asked accusingly.

"I ain't turning a blind eye if I see one," Callum shot back. "There! Do you see it?"

"Wait . . . I think I do! Let me get the binoculars," Jude said, rummaging through his pack. "Oh yeah, it's a drone, alright!" he reported.

"What kind?" Callum asked.

"It's still pretty high, but I don't see boosters. I also don't see the RDF insignia."

"Is it CAMO?" Callum asked.

"Maybe," Jude said. "It's still flying very high. You have better eyes than me. Can you take a look? Will you be okay?"

"Don't worry. Let's just figure out who we're looking at," Callum said as he took the binoculars and focused them on the drone.

"Does it look like a CAMO drone?" Jude asked.

"It looks like two drones," Callum said, surprisingly calm.

"Are you sure?"

"Yes. Give me a minute or two, and I'll be able to see who we're looking at."

They sat atop their ATVs at rigid attention, watching the sky and luring the drones with their intense curiosity.

"You're right—no boosters," Callum confirmed. "But it is not a Cascadia RDF drone. It's a New America surveillance drone, just like the one I took out. The other one on its flank is a CAMO drone."

"Are you sure?" Jude asked reflexively.

"I can read, Jude. If I came out of three years in CME with anything, it's the ability to read," Callum said, handing the binoculars back to Jude. "They're keeping their altitude. I'm guessing they are surveying, but I don't know why the New America drone is accompanying the CAMO one."

"Maybe just in case . . . " Jude started. "Sorry. It's getting a little old."

Callum shook his head in agreement. "The New America drone is a surveillance drone, too. It's not a defense drone."

"The New America Defense Force is collecting their own data. What are they trying to find that CAMO doesn't already know?" Jude wondered out loud.

"Everything else," Callum said.

"You're right," Jude said, reminded again of his brother's surprising common sense. "People, buildings, assets . . . "

"Vulnerabilities, escape routes, hiding places," Callum added.

"Maybe, but don't get your gun yet."

"What is this, Thanksgiving?" Rod wondered out loud as he stumbled into the beehive of a kitchen where Marren was directing her operation.

"While we are all still here together, I'm going to savor every minute," she said, pulling a corn pudding casserole out of the oven.

"Good plan," he said, hanging up his jacket and heading to the sink to scrub his weathered, dirt and grease-stained hands. "What can I do?"

"I've got a couple of chickens on the Rotisserie. They should be done. If they look good, cut them up and put them on a serving platter."

"Yes, ma'am!"

"What do you need me to do, Mom?" Maisy asked.

"Stand by and be ready when your dad cuts his finger."

Maisy laughed. "In the meantime, how about I handle the green beans?"

"Sure. Thanks, sweetheart."

"Anything I can do?" Zara piped in, appearing from the office. "I wouldn't mind taking a break from the screens anyway."

"Can you help me?" Jude interjected, stepping in from outside. "I want to check some of the horses before it gets dark."

Zara instinctively looked to Marren as if asking permission.

"The kitchen is pretty full. Go," she ordered.

"What's wrong with the horses?" she asked as they headed out to the barn.

"The horses are fine. It's the SACs I'm thinking about. Callum and I saw a couple of drones fly over."

"What kind of drones?" she asked.

"One was the same kind Callum shot down: a New America Defense Force surveillance drone. The other was a CAMO drone. They kept a high altitude, but I have no doubt they were gathering data."

"Max said things have been too quiet. Your mom also senses that this peace and quiet won't last, hence the small feast tonight. Now you tell me the New America government is spying on us. That's not something we can afford to just dismiss."

"We'd have to be blind not to see something is coming."

"The problem is we see *that* it is coming, but not *what* is coming. That's what makes me nervous," Zara said.

"I think we should prepare," Jude said pensively.

"How? For what?" Zara asked, following him into the barn past the stables.

"For the worst."

"Jude, what is the worst?"

"Chillicothe."

"That SAC was wiped out in hours. How do we prepare for that?" Zara asked.

"We start by appreciating what we have now," he said, running his fingers through her charcoal black tresses.

"I thought we were checking on the horses?" she smirked.

"We are. First, we need to get some hay."

"Nice move, Romeo. You think you're so slick."

Jude smiled and took her face in his hands. He pulled her close and kissed her long and gently, melting it into a warm embrace.

"I'll take every minute I can get with you."

"With everyone busy in the house, I think we might have a few minutes," she said, slowly unbuttoning his shirt.

"I think that with everyone here and so much to be thankful for, it is a great time to give thanks," Rod announced as they all gathered around the rickety, homemade extended table covered in lumpy cloth and homemade adornments. "Dear God, we thank you for the return of all our children and this happy moment. Thank you for the food you have given us and the freedoms we enjoy here in your majestic corner of the earth. We cherish every moment of every blessing. In your name, Amen."

"Amen," they echoed.

"Dig in!" Marren ordered, and the clinking, murmuring, and thanks followed.

"Boy, have I missed this!" Callum said, scooping two heaping spoonfuls of corn pudding next to his drumstick. "If you're trying to make me fat, I think it's working, Mom."

"I'm fattening you up, not making you fat. There is a difference."

"Then how do I explain my weight gain?" Jude said, laughing.

"Happiness," Zara said, patting him on the stomach.

As they ate and chatted, Marren moved slowly and kept scanning the table. She drank up every moment, remembered every smile, and cataloged every voice in her memory. If she could freeze time, she would. This was the climax; this was the ultimate reward of their years on the SAC: the family was together, healthy, well-fed, and free. Soon, Maisy would leave for Kansas City to finish her medical training, and Jude and Zara could follow anytime. When you work for freedom your whole life, your kids learn to fight too, and their fight will likely take them away sooner rather than later.

"So, Zara," Marren began, "how are the other SACs faring lately?"

"From the dozens of reports I've read and posted, they are doing quite well. A few SACs have consolidated, but other than that, they have stabilized. Planting is in full swing in most of the regions, especially in Lakeland and Dakota. CME extractions are rare, and people seem to have a determination they didn't have last year."

"That's good to hear," Rod commented. "You two have done amazing things. Before you protest with some pathetic modesty, own up to it: you two have changed thousands of lives. You gave people the three things they needed to survive: skills, tools, and hope."

"Thanks, Dad," Jude said. "Of course, I got it all from you."

"Well, that is true. You did learn from the best."

Marren couldn't bear the tension. She had to know. She had to prepare herself emotionally for the inevitable.

"So, when do you two plan on leaving Slate Creek?"

"Why would they need to leave Slate Creek?" Rod protested.

"You guys aren't planning on leaving already, are you?" Maisy asked while trying to swallow her potatoes.

Jude sighed heavily and looked at Zara and then back to his mom.

"The plan is still to stay until the Sparrows are needed somewhere else. We just don't know when that will be."

"I think it might be a lot sooner now, pal," Callum blurted out. "With NADF and CAMO drones scanning every inch of the land, I don't think they're just taking pictures for their new calendar."

"What drones?" Rod asked, surprised.

"We saw two drones today over the fields. One was an NADF drone just like I shot down last year, and right behind it was a CAMO drone. They stayed high, but they were definitely on some kind of a data-gathering mission."

"Is this true?" Marren asked, looking at Jude.

"Yes. Callum is right; they're gathering data for something. I'm not sure what, but I don't like it."

"Max said things have been too quiet. He said the success of the SACs is flying in the face of ADAMS' predictions that they would fail eventually. Some are even growing, and that makes the government uneasy," Zara added.

"I'm sure old Blake Connor doesn't like that," Rod said, taking a casual bite of chicken. "He never liked the SACs."

"I want to hope for the best, but we have to plan for the worst. Dad, we should start thinking about a worst-case scenario. We need to have a Plan B for Slate Creek," Jude said.

Rod smiled, swallowed his food, and wiped his mouth.

"My son, I have always had a Plan B."

Just as Jude was about to drift off into a deep sleep, a beeping sound roused him. "What's that?" he mumbled.

"An alert," Zara said, grabbing her phone.

"Don't you get to sleep at some point?" he moaned.

"Not when it's an emergency."

"What's going on?" he asked, sitting up and rubbing his eyes.

"Something's going on in an Appalachian SAC. I got a message that all of their children were suddenly extracted. The RDF didn't give any justification," Zara reported.

"What? That's completely illegal," Jude said. "Did they protest? Did they put up some kind of fight?"

"I'm trying to find out, but I'm not getting a response," Zara said.

"Check the official news feeds," Jude said.

"Like they'd cover an extraction," she scoffed. "Even if they did, they wouldn't say what really happened— dear God !"

"What?"

"They are reporting that an old, abandoned coal mine in Pikeville, Appalachia, collapsed. They say it was part of a SAC. Everyone inside was buried. No one made it out."

"Dear God is right," Jude said. "Dear God, be with those people."

"Do you think these are related?" Zara asked. "Do you think . . . "

"What would be the connection?" he asked. "What does a CME extraction have to do with a mine accident?"

"What if it wasn't an accident?"

"How can we know? We don't even know where the extraction happened yet. It could be anywhere in Appalachia," he said.

"Yes, we do," Zara said, scrolling and taping. "A survivor just posted. 'The RDF showed up and started taking the children, and we screamed in protest. They shoved us away and shouted at us. They said there was no time to protest and to just run. We were scared and confused. Then there was the explosion.' She said the entire mine collapsed, and except for a few residents who ran out of the mine after their children, they were all buried."

"Why would the RDF do that? Why would they take the children and then blow up the mine? It doesn't make any sense," Zara said.

"They weren't there to blow up the mine or do a CME extraction," Jude said. "The RDFs don't work for President Connor and don't have anything to do with CAMO. They were on a rescue mission, but they ran out of time."

"The official news didn't mention the RDF or survivors," Zara said.

"That's because there weren't supposed to be any," Jude said.

"Survivor stories are my specialty," Zara said. "Sparrow Press will set the record straight."

Chapter 2: **Assault**

Spring always smelled so sweet. They were far enough from any city to hear the hum of humanity, and still far enough from the old mines to smell the coal. The mountains and forests lie to the north, and rich farmland extends south. Nestled in a quiet part of central Appalachia in what used to be Southwest Virginia, the Wytheville SAC was an idyllic refuge for people disillusioned by the city life that seemed to exclude them. It wasn't a large SAC, but it was relatively successful given its rich land, temperate climate, and clandestine use of an ancient energy source: coal.

Coal mining had been outlawed for decades, but families that had deep roots in the area that used to be known as West Virginia continued the tradition of preserving the history of coal mining. SAC residents were permitted to map, preserve, and mine small amounts of coal for recreational and educational purposes. As long as they didn't mine or burn more than a few kilograms of coal at a time, and as long as they didn't trespass on operational CAMO mines, they were left alone.

On occasion, members of the Wytheville SAC would take small excursions into the mountains to the north to hunt, fish, and explore. Eventually, they stumbled upon people from the mountain SACs, and they quickly established personal and economic relationships. Mountain SACs would trade wood, hides, and coal for fresh produce, meat, and cloth. This was a fruitful relationship— until CAMO drones noticed.

Drones had been silently documenting the increased trade, the larger and larger amounts of coal and timber being transported, and the flow of people along a trade route that crossed almost entirely through CAMO land for a few years. When black smoke started to rise from houses and machinery in the Wytheville SAC, CAMO made their report. It took three days for a response, and when it came, it came from the New America Defense Forces.

Baking, smoking, churning, sewing, feeding livestock, and tilling of the soil were all in full motion in Wytheville. Gavin Hollins stopped his tractor to bask in the cool breeze and sweet scent billowing through the SAC. He slipped his hat off, ran his fingers through his thick brown hair, and enjoyed the crisp current that often fell from the mountains in the north. The air flowed gently, and then the breeze began to pick up. Soon, it was rustling his hair and trying to blow his hat from his hands.

He looked up, and his heart froze. A huge NADF transport drone descended onto the SAC, and before even touching down, streams of soldiers poured from the transport and began separating families. He jumped down from his tractor and ran as quickly as he could over the turned sod and tall grass, desperate to get to his family. Suddenly, a white flash blinded him and threw him to the ground. Disoriented, he tried to get up, but he stumbled again until an arm caught him.

"Sir!" the soldier shouted. "Sir! Calm down!"

"Where's my wife? Where's my daughter?" he said.

"Your wife is probably over where the adults are gathering. The children are being taken to Compulsory Monitored Education."

"CME? Over my dead body she is!" he shouted, swinging at the soldier. The young soldier threw him to the ground and restrained him with his arms behind his back. In a surprisingly sincere tone, he got down to Gavin's ear and said, "Listen! This is serious. The New America government is taking over the SAC and giving the land to CAMO. They say you've violated the SAC agreement by trading with other SACs. I don't know the details, but I know my orders. We were told to shoot anyone who resisted. You should go to your wife."

The farmer looked back at the soldier, sighed deeply, nodded slightly, and then got up. He looked at the young man, nodded again, and ran to find his wife. The scene was chaotic and terrifying. SAC residents were blindsided, and some thought they were under attack. Confusion and anger exploded, especially as the soldiers demanded the children for CME. Some acquiesced, but others were not so easily persuaded. One SAC resident confronted a soldier attempting to take his son to the transport, refusing to allow him to go. When the soldiers tried to detain him, he pulled out an antique pistol and fired several rounds. Two soldiers went down before the NADF opened fire.

In the confusion, some SAC residents started to fight back, while others ran and pleaded for the shooting to stop. The NADF was not discriminating. If a resident had anything in their hands, it was assumed to be a weapon, and they were shot. Most people had simple farming or craft implements, dish rags, shovels, or pieces of wood. They never got the chance to explain.

On the northern edge of the SAC, a teenager returning from a hunting trip took shelter in a tree. Using a vintage cell phone he got for his birthday, he began recording as the transport descended. As the shooting started, he found his nerve and kept recording.

The SAC was quickly overrun. Gavin tried to mitigate the damage as much as he could, shouting, "Get down! Get down!" He started throwing men and women to the ground and pushing kids towards soldiers. Eventually, the survivors began to get the idea and raised their hands and pleaded for their lives, and finally, the shooting stopped. The soldiers rushed in, clamped on restraints, and dragged them by their hair or clothes into the transport.

The children were separated from the adults and put into holding cages, while the adults were hooked to standing restraint clasps as if they were taking a ride on a crowded subway. Children were crying and mothers were sobbing, but the threat of immediate retaliation muted the sounds of suffering. Gavin found his daughter among the children and willed her to look in his direction. When she finally found his eyes, she smiled, and then her eyes fell. She looked up at him again and mouthed, "Mom is dead."

The teenager waited for the transport to lift off and then made his way back to what was left of the SAC. He knew enough to know an attack like this meant all SACs could be in danger, and he knew exactly who to get the footage to. His old phone had no connection, so he found a school screen still functioning and uploaded the footage.

"The Sparrows have to see this," he said to himself.

After uploading the footage, he rummaged through ice boxes and ground storage spaces for food and supplies. It would be at least a three-day hike to the nearest mountain SAC. He stuffed his pack, filled his canteen, and took a few still photos of the carnage before heading north.

"Hey! What are you still doing here?" a soldier yelled to him when he came around a corner, snapping a few last shots.

"I, I . . . " he stammered. "I thought the transport had left."

"We're the clean-up crew," the soldier said, leveling his weapon at him. He hadn't even heard the second transport land.

"What do you plan to do with those pictures?"

Sensing a rising anger that pushed back against his paralyzing fear, he clenched his teeth and said, "The Sparrows will see this. They will know what to do."

The soldier laughed. "So do I." He pulled the trigger three times.

"We need to know more about what happened," Jude said.

"We saw what happened," Zara said flatly.

"We need to know why, or at least what excuse the NADF had. They were separating kids, but the NADF doesn't do CME extractions. They had enough soldiers and transports to take the entire SAC. Even when they took over Chillicothe, we knew they were coming. They made some attempt at a case for taking over, but this . . . this came out of nowhere."

"Maybe it didn't," Zara said.

"What do you mean?"

"Maybe they had a case, but we just never heard about it. I don't have eyes and ears everywhere."

"They had to have known something, and they can't know anything without drones. Do you think Chiela can get into the NADF and find something?" Jude asked.

"I doubt it, but then again, she did hack her way out of the National Detention Center. I can ask," Zara said.

"We need to talk to someone from Wytheville," Jude said. "Someone got us the video; someone has to be left who can reach us."

"All I want to know is when I can see my daughter."

"You don't get to ask questions. You do what you're told, go where we tell you, and be happy about it," the young captain snapped.

"I have committed no crime," Gavin said. "I'm just a farmer."

"You're not 'just a farmer.' Your SAC left at least two of my soldiers dead," snarled the captain.

"I didn't want anyone to get hurt," Gavin said, lowering his head.

He was surprised at the effort. He was guided down into a chair at a large steel table, hands cuffed behind the chair, and the light of the room searing into his brain. This was a lot of trouble for the NADF to waste on him.

"What was your role at the SAC?" the captain demanded.

"I was on the council."

"So, you were the leader?"

"I was one of twelve. We were a small, self-sustaining community whose primary concern was our crops and our survival through each winter."

"If that was your primary concern, then why was there a need for this illicit trade in coal and timber?"

"Because shelter and power don't grow in the soil."

"So, you admit to the illicit trade?"

"We traded with the mountain SACs to the north. We never traded in the cities. If I'm not mistaken, we were following the law."

"The SAC agreement forbids you from any economic activity in which you avoid the payment of taxes. I doubt your trade involved the payment of any taxes."

"Our trade involved the payment of corn for timber. It involved the payment of leather for metal. It involved the payment of meat for coal. I don't recall getting a tax bill."

The captain slammed his fist on the table.

"I'll let the lawyers deal with that," he said, "but for the loss of my soldiers, you'll have to answer to me!"

"Your approach was terrifying to our SAC residents, Captain. They didn't know anything except that they were under attack. I will concede, however, that he should never have discharged that pistol. I did everything I could to stop the shooting."

A familiar-looking young lieutenant stepped into the room, whispered to the captain for several seconds, and then flashed a quick glance at Gavin before leaving the room.

The captain took a deep breath and eyed Gavin suspiciously.

"My lieutenant tells me you were in the field when the shots were fired. You did, in fact, run into the fight and convince your people to surrender."

"I did my best, Captain."

"I think you are more than a farmer, Gavin Hollins. I think you are a leader. I don't think, however, that you were responsible for the violent response from some of your SAC residents. It appears you were the voice of reason. I'll recommend your release."

"Thank you, Captain. Is it possible to see my daughter? She's all I have left."

"Not right now, Mr. Hollins. Rest assured, the children are not being detained. They are being evaluated at a Compulsory Monitored Education facility, and once you are processed through Human Services, you will be given further information." The captain paused at the door, sighed, and looked back at Gavin. "You'll see her again soon."

Gavin was a fish out of water. Human Services issued him a new passport, a UBI account, and a Cube. Of course, not having a land lot, and the government not having a large inventory of Cubes, he was assigned a refurbished Cube on the outskirts of Richmond. He was officially a citizen of Appalachia, New America. By the time his daughter was released from CME three weeks later, he had rapidly reassembled a new, awkward, but stable home for them.

"Where is Jude?" Zara asked Marren after emerging from her self-imposed isolation in the office.

"He's out with his dad. No doubt he's fixing something, building something, or planning something," she said, drying off the last dish.

"Thanks," Zara said, running out the door.

"Jude!" she called, hearing him and Rod tinkering in the shed.

"Hey, sweetheart," Jude said, holding a piece of pipe in his grease-covered hands. "We're working on a low-tech communication system for the SAC."

"Explain it to me later. Chiela has something."

"Really?"

"Come with me!" she ordered.

"On my way," he said, wiping off his hands and following her into the house.

"Did she hack into the NADF?" Jude asked.

"No, but she did get into CAMO. Don't you think it is interesting that the Consolidated Agriculture and Mining Operation folks were analyzing surveys, soil samples, and making crop plans for Wytheville two weeks ago?" she asked.

"Yeah, especially since they were still a SAC at that time," Jude said. "This was a planned takeover of SAC land."

"We need to warn the other SACs," Zara said.

"I don't want to start a panic."

"I think if the NADF shows up, they will panic, Jude. At least if we show them what happened, they will have time to prepare."

"We don't know if this is a one-time thing," Jude said.

"Do you really think this is a one-time thing? Do you really think the mine collapse in Pikeville was an accident? What does your gut tell you?"

"My gut says . . . " he paused, rubbing his temples, "my gut says this is just the beginning."

"We need to say something, Jude."

"We need to show them what has happened."

"Should I show the footage of Wytheville?"

"We can't hide the truth."

"What if people start to panic?" she asked.

"Remind people to do their best to replace fear with reason. Tell them we don't know of any plans to attack other SACs, but that we suspect we all might be in danger. And for God's sake, if anyone gets a visit from the NADF, don't resist!"

"Got it," Zara said, taking notes. "Anything else?"

"Let people know the Sparrows will be putting out guidelines for leaving a Sustainable Agricultural Community. After everything we've done to help the SACs, the best thing we can do for them now might be to show them how to leave everything behind."

Chapter 3: **Accidental Enemies**

Gavin Hollins and his daughter tried to adjust to life in a ten by ten by ten-meter cube. It's not a lot of room after living on hundreds of acres in a SAC, but it was better than living on the streets. Gavin did his best to model gratefulness, and Janie focused on her schoolwork, fearing a return to CME if she faltered.

"Maybe we should get a dog," Gavin said as they both stirred and smelled the canned soup.

"Where would it sleep?" Janie asked.

"With you," Gavin said with a smirk.

"I don't think so," she said with a classic raised eyebrow.

"I thought you liked animals?"

"Yeah, I do— in the pasture."

"You sound like your mom."

The silence was telling. A tear slipped down her cheek, and she whispered, "I miss her."

"I do too, sweetheart," he whispered, giving her a reassuring embrace.

"What are we going to do?" she sobbed.

"What would mom say?" he asked.

"I don't know. She wouldn't want an indoor dog, that's for sure," she said with a weak chuckle, wiping her tears.

Gavin smiled knowingly.

"She'd say we should find a way to help people."

"Help who?" she asked.

"We're not the only ones who lost everything."

"So, what are you saying?" she asked.

"I'm not sure. I don't know where anyone else from Wytheville landed. It feels like we're all on our own."

"Maybe not," Janie said. "Have you heard of the Sparrows?"

"What's on the agenda tonight?" Jude asked, slipping his arms around Zara's neck and kissing her cheek.

"My agenda is the same," she said, staring straight ahead at the screen. "Edit, search, post, sleep. Repeat."

"Maybe you should take a break from your routine."

"I can't. I've got so much to do . . . "

Jude reached down and clicked off the screen.

"Jude!" she protested. "I've got . . . ."

"You've got to take a break. Your eyes are red, your neck is sore, and you haven't had dinner yet."

"But . . . "

"Break away, Zara. Break away," Jude said, guiding her up from the screen and into their room. "You don't do anybody any good if you're burned out."

"Alright, fine," she said, pulling on her boots.

"Let's go feed the horses."

"Feed the horses? You think that will work on me again?"

Jude chuckled. "This time, I mean *actually* feed the horses. They need the hay, and you need the break."

"What about you?"

"I don't like hay."

"Very funny."

Jude knew how therapeutic it was for Zara to be outside and be around the animals. Her strained eyes softened, and her tense shoulder muscles relaxed as she spread out the hay and tossed it to the hungry ponies. He pulled loose some hay and helped Zara, taking his own turn rubbing soft noses and talking to the ladies.

"Quit flirting," Zara chastised him.

"They just love me for the hay," he said.

"They sense a gentle soul. Trust me, I know how they feel."

Jude smiled and shuffled over to her, taking her hand and gently swaying with her on the hay-strewn floor.

"You're saying you don't go for the tough, bad-boy type?"

"Nope. I want a man whose strength is seen in his intellect, his purpose, and his willingness to sacrifice. Bad boys always have something to prove. You've already proven yourself." She slipped him a kiss on the lips.

"I could go on about everything I love about you, but to be honest, I am just getting lost in your eyes. You are indescribably beautiful."

"So that's it?" she teased. "You just love me because I'm pretty?"

"Well, you do have a great body, you're an amazing kisser . . . "

She paused their waltz and glared at him.

"I suppose you have other qualities too, like intelligence, determination . . . "

"Go on," she goaded him, resuming their steps.

"You have purpose, a fierce sense of compassion and justice, and a relentless obsession with finding the truth. You make me a better man just by being around you."

"That was pretty good," she said listlessly. "And I don't mind being called beautiful."

"The Sparrows?" Gavin asked.

"They are a kind of group that helps SAC people," Janie explained. "They are the ones who helped a bunch of SACs last year. They led protests, and they even got a SAC guy out of prison."

"We're not in a SAC anymore."

"That's just it, Dad. What happened to us is exactly the kind of thing they can help with."

"I highly doubt they can give us our land back," Gavin said, trying not to let bitterness seep into his voice.

"Probably not, but they connect people. Maybe they can help us find other Wytheville survivors and even survivors from other SACs."

"How do you find these Sparrows?" he asked.

"The Sparrow Press," she said, opening up her screen. "It's how we all stay connected. You get real news here, especially about the SACs. You can trust what Zara says."

"Who's Zara?" Gavin asked.

"She's the editor. She and her husband, I think his name is Jude, are the leaders of the Sparrows. They live on a SAC in Cascadia."

"Well, now I'm paying attention," he said. "What does the Sparrow Press have to say?"

"Oh my gosh, Dad," she gasped.

"What is it?"

"We're not alone. Sparrow Press is reporting attacks on other SACs in Appalachia. Besides us, they said the accident in the mine in Pikeville looks like it was orchestrated by the NADF. They are saying they don't know what the 'official excuse' is from the New America government, but they suspect the SACs are in danger. They are saying if the NADF shows up, people should flee or surrender, but not resist."

"Good advice," Gavin said. "Do they know what happened to the Wytheville SAC?"

"They will soon. I'm going to describe everything."

"The SACs are not a statistically significant terroristic threat," ADAMS reported.

"But reallocating the land to Consolidated Agriculture and Mining Operations will help alleviate the strain on the food supply, correct?" President Blake Connor asked. The analyst shifted uncomfortably in his seat next to General Alvarado, who observed the ADAMS interface droid and the President carefully.

"To a small degree, yes. There is not a significant strain on the food supply chain, but in some areas, it will make distribution easier," ADAMS said.

"Then it is settled. The SACs are a threat to our food supply, and we need to reallocate SAC land to CAMO immediately," President Connor said, looking at General Alvarado.

"I agree," the general said. "The SACs are not efficient, and we cannot waste the land needed to feed the general population."

"Reallocating SAC land comes with significant risks and violates the SAC agreement made during the Transition," ADAMS said. "This creates much more significant . . . "

"I have been patient enough with the SACs!" interrupted the President. "Their existence is a threat, even if it looks small on paper."

"We have already tested this process," said General Alvarado. "It is not difficult to shut down a SAC. It can be done in a few hours. The President is right; as long as the SACs exist, they are a threat. They are an ideological threat, and by your own admission, they are a threat to the food supply."

"To be precise, the SACs are not a statistically significant . . . "

"I know, I heard you the first time," President Connor said through clenched teeth. "Let's lose the adjectives. We need to reclassify the SACs so the Corporate Congress can sign off on the legislation. There will be no more SAC agreement."

"I calculate there will be some resistance to this legislation in the Senate," ADAMS reported.

"I agree that is true," the President said, smiling knowingly at General Alvarado. "But leave that to us. I think we can persuade enough senators to see things from our perspective."

"Yes, sir," ADAMS said. "The SACs are officially reclassified as a threat. I have removed all qualifiers, or adjectives, as you said."

"Thank you," the President said, nodding to General Alvarado. "Now we can get to work."

President Connor looked forward to dispatching his new Defense Chief. He needed an effective leader who didn't waver in his loyalty and could be morally flexible when he needed to achieve an objective.

"The attack on Wytheville was less veiled," Zara said to Jude. "I got a good narrative from one of the Wytheville SAC survivors."

"What did they say?" Jude asked, sitting down next to Zara.

"She said the NADF landed several drone transports, and they immediately began demanding the kids for Compulsory Monitored Education."

"Wait, what? Everyone knows the Regional Defense Forces do CME extractions. If anyone would come for a CME extraction, it would be the RDF, and they would ask for specific students."

"Exactly, which is why these farmers cried foul. Someone fired a pistol at the NADF . . . "

"That's all they needed," Jude sighed. "That's when the shooting started that we saw on the live stream."

"Yes, but according to Janie Hollins, her dad, Gavin Hollins, ran into the fray and convinced the SAC to lay down their arms. She says she was evaluated, and then she was released. She never went to CME."

"Of course not. That was an excuse," Jude said. "I'm worried these attacks were dry runs. Pikeville was an attempt at sabotage, but it was messier than they thought. Wytheville was cleaner, more organized, and more precise. I think the NADF was practicing for something bigger."

"How big?" Zara said, knowing the answer, but wanting to hear confirmation.

"I think President Blake Connor may have finally gotten his wish. I think the days of the SACs are numbered."

"They can't just wipe out all the SACs, can they?" Zara asked, still trying to grasp what they were realizing.

"The New America government wouldn't be able to wipe us all from the map without a backlash unless there was some genuine legal justification. It would have to be something big, like legislation that overturns the SAC agreement or some kind of new threat assessment. Keep your eyes on official news sources."

"What if you're right, Jude?" Zara asked. "How in the world do we help people? How do we help every SAC in New America?"

Jude switched to problem-solving mode. His vision narrowed and his mind focused.

"Sparrow Press," he said. "Warn people now so they can prepare. As soon as you hear something official out of Washington, D.C., pull the trigger. Tell people to flee or surrender. In the meantime, there is still one SAC we really need to help: Slate Creek."

"The NADF reallocation teams are in place and ready, sir," General Alvarado reported to President Connor. I've issued a warrant for anyone with a SAC-issued passport or no passport at all. They'll be taken to a detention center and issued a new ADAMS-compatible Passport immediately. I've taken the liberty of setting up temporary detention centers in strategic locations to handle the influx of SAC residents. The NADF will work with Human Services to put people where they need to go."

"It's like hearing a symphony," President Conner said. "All the pieces are coming together."

"On your word, we'll begin the operation, sir."

"My press release just went out. Let's give our people twenty-four hours to hear the news and prepare for new neighbors. At that point, execute the operation. I've given the Regional Governors a heads-up, and they will make sure the RDF stands down. We shouldn't have any more confusion like we did in Pikeville."

"Yes, sir," saluted the General.

"I thought I'd be buried on this land," Rod said as he stuffed clothes into an ancient 20th-century leather suitcase. "I think this is the same luggage I used during the Transition."

"If it wasn't for your son, you would be buried on this land, probably in a few days," Marren reminded him. "How do you feel about living in Vancouver again?"

"I'm sure the University is not throwing a homecoming party for me, but we're too old to flee to the forest. I'll be fine if I can be useful in some way, and we are together. That's all I want."

"Me too," she said, giving her husband a firm embrace. "We can do this together."

"The transport will be here in thirty minutes," Zara announced.

"Okay, Mom and Dad," Jude began, "the Cube hotel in Vancouver doesn't look like much, but the owner is a decent guy. He's retired military, and he loves whiskey. He'll treat you fairly. We'll meet up with you in a day or two."

"Thank you, Jude," Rod said. "What do you plan to do here?"

"I'll save what I can. Whatever we leave, CAMO will destroy. The buildings will be razed for sure."

"Make sure you are not here when they come," Rod said. "You kids are the only things I want to save from Slate Creek."

"We'll be long gone, don't worry. Get settled in Vancouver, and we'll meet up with you soon."

The transport came and left, leaving Jude, Zara, and Callum on cleanup duty.

"What in the hell are we going to do with everything?" Callum asked. "We can't take half of all this stuff."

"Let's get the most important things: dad's old external storage drives, mom's screen, jewelry, heirlooms, and things like that."

"What about Dad's guns, books, and all his tools and inventions in the shop?" Callum asked.

"I know just the place."

While Zara packed up some of Marren's things in the house and made sure all of her Sparrow Press equipment was ready to travel, Jude and Callum made several trips with the ATVs up to the large rock in the middle of Slate Creek.

"The underground container is over here," Jude said.

"Dad's plan B," Callum remembered.

"Well, it's Dad's plan C now," Jude said. "It's better suited for storing things than people anyway."

By the end of the week, Jude, Zara, and Callum were ready to go. They said goodbye to their Slate Creek friends and relatives, leaving them with a cache of supplies and last-minute advice.

"CAMO probably doesn't care about First-Nation land, and if you stay in the hills, they should leave you alone. They're after farmland and maybe minerals," Jude explained.

The flight was not Zara's first goodbye, but for Jude and Callum, it tore a part of their soul to watch Slate Creek fade away from view. Zara knew the feeling, and without saying anything, she took Jude's hand.

"I know you love the dirt, but Mom and Dad need you," Jude explained to Callum.

"I know. I'll take good care of them, I promise," Callum reassured Jude.

When the transport touched down in Vancouver, they began the process of grabbing their bags and finding a place to put everything until they found Rod and Marren and a permanent place to live.

"Don't worry about your things," came a sharp, clear voice over the transport engines.

Jude turned around to see an NADF Lieutenant and a squad of soldiers waiting for them.

"Hello, Jude, Zara, and Callum Kane. We've been waiting for your Passports to pop up. They've been flagged for almost a year now."

Chapter 4: **Nests**

"I *REALLY* DON'T LIKE orange," Callum said, inspecting his jumpsuit. "It's just not my color."

"Mine either," Jude said. "At least we match."

"Besides being President Connor's least favorite duo, why do you think we're in here?" Callum asked as they sat opposite each other on their loose, squeaking metal bunks.

"We were flagged for some reason," Jude said. "I just hope it's not for being placed on the 'never to be seen again' list. After the raid on Pikeville and the flagrant takeover of Wytheville, I'm pretty sure rules are out the window now."

"It sounds like a good time to stop playing by the rules," Callum said.

"Kane!" yelled the guard.

"Yes?" they both answered in unison.

"Your lawyer's here. Let's go."

"Our lawyer?" Callum questioned.

"It must be Max, but how'd he get here so quickly?" Jude asked.

They were ushered into a visitation room where Zara was waiting, and Max Simon was on the other side of the table.

"Haven't we done this already?" he asked as the brothers sat down. "I thought I told you to stay out of this place!"

"We were flagged. We're special," Jude said, sitting next to Zara and squeezing her hand.

"I don't know exactly why they are holding you, but I've filed some preliminary motions to get some information," he said.

Something was off. Max seemed distracted, and he kept scanning the room, the guards, and the cameras. Jude and Zara exchanged a concerned glance.

While Jude and Zara watched Max for some kind of hint or explanation, Callum casually took hold of Max's coffee cup and took a long swig. He winced.

"Man, that is nasty. Did you get that here?" he asked.

"Of course," Max said. "It's not like you can bring your own."

"Oh well. Caffeine is caffeine," he said, taking the cup and slurping down the rest.

"You're welcome," Max said.

"Oh, sorry! That was rude. Mind if I have a sip?" Callum said, smiling.

"Dude!" Jude said, looking at Callum. "That was rude!"

"It's fine," Max said. "I'll get real coffee when I leave. Speaking of leaving, rest assured, I'm working on it." He paused to make sure he had eye contact with all three of them. "Chiela and I are working on it."

Zara smiled, and Jude nodded knowingly. They made small talk for a few minutes, and finally, Max had to go. They said goodbye, and suddenly Callum said, "Jude, man, you've got a few seconds to get a kiss, and you're wasting it! Fine. I'll do it for you." He walked up to Zara, put his lips firmly on hers, and kissed her. Jude was frozen in shock. Zara was caught off guard, but then quickly smiled, wiped her mouth, and said, "Watch out, Jude. He's pretty quick."

"Come on, lovebirds, let's go," the guard said, handing Zara off to the female escort and guiding the brothers to their cell.

"Callum!" Jude said as soon as they were alone. "What was that?"

"I'll kiss you and then you'll know," he said mischievously, coming over and sitting next to Jude on the bunk.

"Gross."

"Fine," Callum said, and then he pulled two small chips from under his tongue. "I'll just hand you yours."

"You cheeky bastard," Jude said, shaking his head and punching him in the arm. "Let me guess: the coffee?"

"Yep. Honestly, the chips taste better."

"You are forgiven for kissing my wife, but let's not make a habit of it."

"Sure, but pay attention to Max next time. You were too busy googling all over your wife to notice his signals."

"That's fair."

"So, what are these things?" Callum asked.

"They're new passports. We need to swap them out. I don't know what they are programmed with, but if Chiela had anything to do with it, they might be our ticket out of here."

"Now I really wish Maisy were here," Callum said.

"Me too, but I can do it. I just need to snag something sharp at our next meal."

"What about Zara?" Callum asked.

"I have a feeling Zara will figure it out."

The next morning, Jude and Callum were called out of the breakfast line. At the sight of an NADF officer, they held their breath. The slits on their shoulders were sealing up quickly, but it wouldn't take much to cause a bit of bleeding and draw unwanted attention if anyone asked them to take off their shirts.

"Why are you here?" he asked gruffly.

"I was told we were flagged when we got off a transport," Jud explained.

"Are you SAC residents?" he asked.

"We live in Vancouver, but we have visited SACs. We do energy and crop consulting from time to time."

"Your Passport is reporting the same thing, and there is no flag. I don't know why you were detained."

"Maybe because we were returning from a SAC," Jude said in a conciliatory tone. "He probably assumed we were SAC residents."

"It looks that way. We've got a lot of SAC residents coming out of the hills lately, and we certainly don't have time to lock up regular citizens. My apologies. The guards will get your clothes and see you out."

"Thank you, sir," Jude said. "And my wife?"

"She's already waiting for you. Ladies first."

As they faced the blinding daylight, Zara was standing at the gate among the piles of bags they had brought from Slate Creek.

"Wow. You were right," Callum said. "Whatever that Chiela girl did, she made them just about give us a limo ride out of there."

Jude hugged Zara and took hold of several bags.

"She must have programmed the Passports to make us look like regular Vancouver residents, and somehow she got rid of the flag," Jude said. "Still, I don't want to hang around here any longer than we have to. Let's go check on Mom and Dad."

When they arrived at the Cube hotel, Jude saw his dad doing something he had never seen him do: watching a screen with his mom. He was almost a little offended at their muted greeting until he heard what was coming from the screen.

"Breaking News: The SACs have been sacked."

Looking over at his famously pugnacious brother, instead of anger, he saw a deep sadness that was reserved for the confirmation of bad news he already knew. It was the proverbial nail in the coffin.

"In a landmark vote this morning, both the Corporate Congress and the Senate passed the 'New America Security Act', which revokes the famous 'Sustainable Agricultural Community Agreement,' allowing private citizens to live on privately owned land and farms. Citing a threat to food, economic, and national security, President Connor praised the move, saying it will give New America unprecedented stability and poise the country for the greatest economic growth in a century. It seems many of us will have new neighbors soon."

"He's not looking for economic growth or stability. He's looking for control," Zara seethed. They put their bags down and sat on the floor in some semblance of a circle. Marren instinctively jumped up to get drinks.

"And without a Bill of Rights or even a complete constitution, there is not much to stop him," Rod sighed. "I can't believe the Senate voted for it."

"There's a new general in charge of the NADF. I've heard of this guy before," Zara said, scrolling feverishly through her phone. "His name is Alvarado."

"Didn't Sonja Orozco say something about him?" Jude asked. "She said he was the guy who ran the cartels out of Mexico during the Transition."

"Sonja! That's right!" Zara recalled. "She told me some stories about General Alvarado that almost made me feel sorry for the old drug cartels."

"Like what?" Callum asked. "The cartels were violent, murdering thugs that ran over people for decades. I'm glad he ran them out."

"For starters, he kidnapped one child from each cartel. This was when he first showed up, before they knew who he was. He sent them a video message telling them to leave in one week, or he would mail their kids' heads to them," Zara said.

"He got their attention," Callum said.

"According to Sonja, he followed through. When the first cartel got the package, they promised revenge. Before they could mount any kind of attack, he massacred the cartel with a full military attack. The other cartels got the message. They fled to South America, and word is he flew the rest of the children to their families unharmed. The drug trade has never fully resumed. Runners are too afraid of Alvarado to come north of the Panama Canal."

"So, it's not a stretch to say Alvarado might have had a role in helping the President persuade some of the senators to see things his way," Callum said.

"We can't worry about all that right now," Jude said. "Our mission was never to save the SACs; it was to help the people living in them. As much as I wish I could join an army and fight for them, that's not what they need. They need our help surviving the trauma of losing everything they have ever known. They need the Sparrows now more than ever."

"I'm guessing President Connor isn't going to wait for news to travel to the SACs, and he certainly isn't going to let them wander into the nearest town and turn in their keys. Pikeville and Wytheville were practice runs. He's going to take them down fast and hard," Zara said.

"We can't be there for every SAC, but they can be there for each other. Zara, how many people in the cities read the Sparrow Press?"

"After Callum, quite a few. There are probably more Sparrow Press readers in cities than there are SAC residents in all of New America."

"Perfect. Post the evacuation message and tell people to use the Sparrow symbol to stick together and know who is safe. The one thing SAC refugees need right away is a safe place to go for their first few nights in the city. Appeal to the people in cities and ask them to create safe places for people," Jude directed Zara.

"Safe places for Sparrows to go?" Zara said, typing at light speed. "How about this: 'Let's welcome our fellow Sparrows in from the cold. Let's help them find safety, food, shelter, and friends. Let's make 'Sparrow Nests' throughout the cities."

"Nests," echoed Jude. "Now that is just perfect."

In the morning, Marren was cooking a breakfast that matched the level of disappointment she was feeling about her kids getting on the train.

"You know, the more often you visit, the more often you leave, and the more often you leave, the more often I get these small feasts to enjoy," Rod joked within earshot of Marren.

"It's a long train ride to Kansas City, and they'll need something to keep them going," Marren tried to rationalize.

As they were finishing the clean-up and gathering their things for the trip, Jude gave Callum a light punch on the arm and asked, "Ever been on a SEMIC Train?"

"Not yet. I've only been on drone transports, both voluntary and involuntary," he said.

"You'll love it! It's so fast and so much quieter than a transport drone."

Callum sighed and put his hand on Jude's shoulder.

"I don't know, Jude. I think I should stay with Mom and Dad," he said in a hushed tone. "We all have a lot of adjusting to do, and pretty soon, SAC people are going to start streaming into Vancouver. Mom and Dad will want to start a Nest, and they'll need my help. They're not getting any younger."

Jude shook his head in agreement.

"I don't know why I just assumed you'd come with us to the Ozark SAC. I never really talked to you about it. Sometimes I forget how long you were locked up. As much as I would love to have you watching my back, you're right. Mom and Dad need you."

"Tell Maisy to come see us sometime if she gets a chance to come up for some air."

"I will," Jude said, giving his brother a hard hug and a thumping back pound.

On the platform, Zara was fighting her nerves. Chiela and Max came through with the passports, but what if something went wrong? What if Chiela's programming was temporary? What if it worked for hand scans like in the detention center, but not pass-throughs? Her anxiety crept up her throat with every passing of a LEAD unit.

"We're going to be fine," Jude tried to reassure her. He gently rubbed her back, but he sensed it would take a lot more than that to put her at ease. He was nervous too, but he had more faith in Chiela's passports than Zara could muster.

"Watch this," he said, stepping toward the gate.

"What are you doing?" she whispered harshly.

"I'm helping you relax."

Jude stepped up to the gate, moved under the pass-through scanner, and watched the display.

"Jude Kane, please step back from the gate until the train has come to a complete stop," came an automated voice. This got the attention of a LEAD unit that rolled up.

"Please step back from the gate, sir," it said.

"Of course. I'm sorry. I wasn't watching where I was stepping."

The LEAD unit followed protocol, just like Jude predicted. It did a scan and said, "Have a nice day, Mr. Kane."

Jude sauntered back to Zara and smiled deviously.

"See? The passports are working fine. The pass-throughs and LEAD units are picking them up clearly."

"Still no flags?" she asked for reassurance.

"Nope. If there was, the LEAD unit would light up like a Christmas Tree and detain me."

Zara let out a long sigh and leaned against Jude, resting her head on his chest. "Thanks. I should have more faith like you."

"Don't worry. I'm sure I'll need to lean on you at some point. That's what we do. We keep each other upright."

The train ride was fast and pleasant. Zara forced herself to put her phone away and enjoy the brief reprieve while it lasted. She was glad she did. The landscape whirred past in a constant blur, but if she raised her head and looked past the immediate surroundings out into the distance, she enjoyed watching the tree-covered mountains, winding ribbons of rivers, and green fields crawl past them. She closed her eyes as they passed through some long tunnels, leaving the Cascades behind them and eventually spilling out into the flat, brown fields of eastern Cascadia and down into Dakota. The view didn't change much after that until they finally crossed into Texaco and arrived in Kansas City.

"Nice of you to finally show up!" Chiela chided them on the platform. "The NADF is rounding up the SACs like kids scooping up candy under a piñata. People are freaking out!"

"Nice to see you too," Zara said, heaving up her bag.

"Thanks for the update," Jude said, patting his shoulder. "They did the trick. They are permanent, right?"

"Of course. I do quality work. Depending on how this goes down, we may need to start mass-producing these things. ADAMS tracks every passport, even mine. It can identify every former SAC resident, which could make them targets later, but mine rewrites the historical data. If you have my passport, as far as ADAMS knows, you were never in a SAC."

Jude and Zara had a hard time keeping up with Chiela's punishing pace as they walked up to a familiar-looking EJ150.

"Didn't I already modify this thing?"

"It's a new one. Max wants you to fix this one up like the other one. An EJ500 is a lot more useful," Chiela said.

"So, what did I miss on the train?" Zara asked, turning on her phone.

"The Sparrows got the evacuation message for the most part, and people are working together, but the NADF is moving fast. People are starting to stream into cities, and they have no idea where to go at first. They are desperate to see any sign of the Sparrows," Chiela explained.

"We need to get organized. We need to identify Nests and find a way to get that info to SAC people without the government catching wind of what we're doing. We've got to be able to protect the Nest leaders. This is going to take a lot of work."

"And creativity," Jude said. "Does Max still have that stash of mini drones we recovered in D.C.? I might have an idea."

Chapter 5: **Meet Me in the City**

Callum stood trying to keep his mouth from falling open. There was so much food at the market, and he had to resist the urge to stockpile the cans of fruit, vegetables, and meat. Winter was going to be different this year in Vancouver.

"Hey! You forgot to pay for that!" the clerk yelled. Callum saw a young woman with an armload of bread, cans, and meat stop at the door, look at the clerk, and hesitate. She looked like she was about to run. Callum caught her eye and slowly shook his head, "No."

Something was familiar about her; he didn't know her, but her plain, hand-sewn dress, dirt-covered work boots, and hungry look gave her away as a former SAC resident. A very recent former SAC resident by the looks of it.

"Let her go!" Callum called out to the clerk.

"She didn't pay!" he protested.

"I'll take care of it."

Outside, Callum found the girl a few yards down the sidewalk, still struggling with her arms full of food.

"Need some help carrying all that?" he asked.

"Thank you, but no," she said, nervously picking up her pace.

"I can't just let you struggle with all that!" he said, catching up to her again.

"Look, thank you for paying for the food, but that doesn't buy you anything. Please don't follow me."

Callum recognized that look; he was lost, disoriented, and terrified before too. Her fine, wind-blown auburn tresses were getting in her face as she stooped and tried to gather up the cans she dropped.

"It's okay," he said. "I don't want anything, except to help." He thought for a second and then said, "I'm a Sparrow."

She froze and stared up at him. "Prove it."

"My brother is Jude, and his wife is Zara. My name is Callum Kane."

"I recognize you!" she exclaimed, dropping half her load and finally tucking her hair behind her ears. "You are the one the Sparrows got out of jail last year!"

"That's me. My parents and I live in Vancouver now. We left the Slate Creek SAC before the NADF showed up. We're starting a Nest here with former SAC residents. I'm guessing some friendly faces would be nice right about now."

"We're starving," she admitted. "The soldiers just dropped us off in some park. We don't know what we're supposed to do. We don't even have tents, and this is the first food I've seen in a couple of days."

"First, give me some of that food. You're dropping everything," he said, bending down and picking up some cans. "Now take me to your family."

He thought of Jude, Zara, and Maisy trekking the entire expanse of New America, facing the NADF, and starting an entire movement while working to free him. He smiled as he took some of the things.

"Jude?" he said into his phone with a barely free hand. "Send the drones to the parks. I'm heading to a hot spot now." He smiled at the woman. "Everything is going to be just fine. The Sparrows take care of their own."

"If the NADF would pick one spot to bring the people, at least then we could set up some kind of reception point," Zack complained. "It's like looking for lost cats all over the city."

"You know that is on purpose," Athalia said, spooning another bite of applesauce into the baby's mouth. "The government could and should set up its own reception centers, but they want to punish the SACs. They want people to come begging for help."

"If they want everyone in the city, they're going to pay for it. We're going to get people set up with Cubes and cash so fast they're going to have to check their bank account. Zara is already sending out information on Nests all over New America. We'll have a network set up and every SAC resident registered before the government knows what's going on."

"Do you regret leaving Blue Ridge?" Athalia asked, flying more applesauce into the baby's smiling mouth. "I grew up in Atlanta, but you have always loved being outside. The city is not exactly your natural habitat."

"It's not like we had much of a choice," Zack sighed. "CAMO owns everything now. 'Managed Timber Areas', 'Managed Mining Areas', and 'Managed Crop Production Areas' are all that's left of everything outside the city. If we didn't sell the land, they would have taken it and left us with nothing. We can't raise a baby hiding in an old mineshaft."

Zack made faces at his chubby little boy and kissed his head. He then gave Athalia a deep kiss and put his arm around her shoulders. "Don't worry. If you think I'm going to live on processed grocery store mystery meat and canned beans, you are sadly mistaken. I never said I would stop hunting."

"You've always been by best supplier," Athalia laughed.

"Speaking of supplies, do we have enough food to handle a few guests tonight?" Zack asked, looking at his screen. "It looks like the Sparrow drones found a new group near the old Piedmont Park."

"Always," she said. "Go find some SAC people. They're probably starving and terrified. My dinners don't just fill you up; they bring healing."

Zack patted his stomach. "Amen."

Gavin was starting to get used to seeing his daughter Janie sitting at a screen. He was proud, but he also ached to see her running freely in the pastures and coming in with the glow of the outdoors on her face. Of course, the older she got, the less he would see the little girl covered in dirt and the more he would see the young woman trying on make-up and new clothes styles. She grew up fast in the city, but then again, if she had been accepted into the university, she would have been in the city two years ago.

"What in the world is a 'Nest'? asked Gavin.

"It's a safe place for Sparrows," Janie explained.

"Clever," Gavin conceded. "What does it involve?"

"Basically, we help people register and get their Cube, their UBI income, and help them get oriented to city life. They need to know where the grocery stores are, how to use transportation, and how to use phones and screens."

"So, essentially, we act like neighbors on a SAC," Gavin said. "How do we know where to find people? Do we wait outside the NADF facility we came in through? Do we look for people wandering the streets?"

"The Sparrows have somehow got their hands on some small drones. They are looking for us from the sky," Janie said, showing her dad the live stream on her screen. "It looks like we have a group huddling together in the park just off the square."

"I'm impressed!" Gavin said, cracking the first semblance of a smile in some time. "We can't let these people freeze and starve. I'd better get down there."

"I'll send you the info on other Nests while you're on your way. People will need to split up and spread out. You remember how to use your phone, right?" Janie asked.

"Of course," Gavin said, grabbing his coat and heading out the door. He immediately came back in and asked, "How do you turn this thing on again?"

The dust rose from the desert like a storm, swirling and billowing with every whim of the wind. Swarms and streams of people emerged from the clouds of dirt and sand, heading for their new homes in the mega-metropolis of Mexico City. In the Baja Region, Alvarado took a less targeted approach to clearing the SACs. Many SACs were four or five-hundred-year-old haciendas spread out over vast areas of desert, canyons, and arid regions, so he directed the NADF to conduct "scooping operations." With no warning, large transports would descend into the SACs, corral the people into holding areas, and move on to the next SAC. When it was full, the transport would land outside Mexico City, push the SAC residents down the ramp, throw out whatever belongings they managed to hang on to, and fly away.

Sonja Orozco got word of the people amassing outside the city, and she knew she had almost no time to deal with a full-blown humanitarian crisis. She called Father Garcia, who immediately began contacting churches throughout Mexico City and began organizing a list of safe houses in the city for SAC refugees. While he was identifying the "Nidos de Gorriones," Sonja and a small army of Sparrows drove out to intercept the refugees.

The Sparrows performed a kind of triage, separating all of the most vulnerable and guiding them and their families directly to government reception centers where they would be registered, given a Passport, and issued their Cube, medical card, and UBI benefits. Many refugees had to be sent directly to clinics and hospitals for injuries they received in transport or conditions that went undiagnosed in the remote SACs for years.

The younger, stronger families were convinced to stay out of the city for a few days. Sonja predicted the reception centers would be overwhelmed, but the Sparrows would not let people go cold or hungry. She distributed tents, blankets, water, and food rations she got from a Sparrow sympathizer in the Baja Regional Defense Forces who had access to surplus MREs. She explained how they were identifying "Nidos" in the city, "Nests" where Sparrows would take in refugees and care for them until they could be issued their Cubes, medical card, and UBI.

Sonja and her army of Gorriones worked tirelessly night and day. The sight of entire families dropped and herded through the desert ignited that fierce compassion that drove her to lead the Sparrows in Baja in the first place. She saw many of her former neighbors who were freshly encouraged to see her, and in turn led their families and communities in close cooperation with Sonja. In the chaos of being uprooted, stripped of everything, and dropped in the desert, Sonja was a symbol of hope and a lifeline for survival.

"Los Nidos" ("The Nests") absorbed the refugees over the next few days. Sonja was right; the government reception centers were so overwhelmed that only a fraction of the refugees could be registered each day, and most survived by living with their fellow Sparrows throughout the city.

In the weeks that followed the NADF operations, the government eventually resettled the SAC residents, but it took thousands of Cubes, and entire neighborhoods were created for the resettlement. It didn't take long for families to reconnect in their "Sparrow Streets" and begin to rebuild their lives in a new, urban context.

After a few weeks, the SAC residents settled into their new, more compact homes and began the process of adjusting to a new reality. Groups of Cubes were sometimes jokingly called "hacienditas," and some neighborhoods of former SAC residents named themselves and gathered for community events. The network of Sparrow Nests soon evolved and expanded into hundreds of community centers where families and neighbors connected for religious services, holidays, and celebrations. "Los Nidos" quickly outgrew their purpose of helping former SAC residents connect to each other and absorbed entire neighborhoods that were starved for hope, connection, and purpose.

Sonja had a heavy hand in this expansion of Los Nidos. She reminded the SAC refugees of how the Sparrows of Mexico City welcomed them in when they had nowhere else to go, and she constantly repeated the mantra that "love makes you a Sparrow." From the beginning, she made sure to squash any notion of exclusivity or special victim status for former SAC residents.

The Department of Human Services unwittingly helped in this large-scale integration. While families were kept together, former SACs were split up, and new Cube developments always included regular citizens who were on waiting lists for new cubes. The old SACs never made up an entire new neighborhood; they were integrated among other SAC refugees and city residents. For the young, it was exciting and fresh, but for the older folks accustomed to their small family circles, it was much more difficult. With the help of the churches, Los Nidos filled a void and met a desperate need for purpose and connection that even the oldest SAC refugees supported.

Of course, none of this was overlooked by General Alvarado.

On her way home from getting a few groceries, Sonja was on foot and completely absorbed in her music. With her earbuds in, she didn't hear the transport roll up behind her. Before she was even aware of their presence, four men jumped from a sliding door, took Sonja by the arms and legs, and pulled her into the transport. They sat her on one of the cushioned bench seats, while one of the men gave orders to the driverless transport.

"Take us back to headquarters."

Once the door was closed, one of the men took his hand off her mouth, and she alternated between gasping for breath and screaming it back out.

"We're not going to hurt you," the leader said.

"Then why the abduction?" she said between breaths.

"Your presence has been requested by a senior NADF officer. This is just regular security protocol."

"This is normal?" she asked. "How senior is this officer?"

"You're going to the top, Senora Orozco. All the way to the top."

Texico was heating up. Even in the northern part of the region, Kansas City was beginning to turn on the air conditioning. Max was feeling the heat, too, and Jude finally decided to confront Max.

"You know it's time, don't you?" he asked Max as they sat at the long table under the wall of screens and equipment.

"I was afraid you were going to say that, and I'm relieved at the same time. Yes, I know it's time."

"I can deliver the bad news," Jude volunteered.

"No, my friend. Thank you, but Ozark is my responsibility. I wouldn't turn down your presence at the announcement, however."

"I'll be there too," Zara said, coming in from the kitchen and standing behind Jude, rubbing his shoulders.

"Thanks," Max said. "It kills me to see the SACs dissolving so quickly, especially after everything we've done to keep their hopes alive. I just pray they don't fall into despair in the city."

"That's what the Sparrows are for," Zara said. "Remind me to tell you what Sonja Orozco has done in Mexico City."

"Let's do it. The sooner we get people off the SAC, the better it will be for them," Max sighed.

"If the NADF doesn't have to extract anyone, then the better it is for our HQ, too. The last thing we need is the NADF nosing around this curious bunker just a few miles from the SAC," Jude said.

"After the people are gone, what's going to stop CAMO from snooping down here when they take over the fields? They might be curious about the mine," Max worried.

"Don't worry about that," Chiela said. She had a habit of sneaking into a room and having a conversation without anyone knowing. "CAMO knows this mine was tapped and turned into an underground warehouse decades ago. They have no interest in digging up a few thousand tons of concrete for a few acres of corn."

Max and Jude left to prepare for the delivery of the not-completely-unexpected bad news. The Ozark SAC had seen and heard the reports Zara put in Sparrow Press, and they knew it was only a matter of time.

"Chiela, what is it?" Zara asked, detecting a hint of reservation in her eyes.

"What is Sonja Orozco doing in Mexico City?" Chiela asked.

"She is being a true leader. She organized dozens of Nests, helped resettle hundreds of families, and now the Nests are turning into community centers for entire neighborhoods. It's amazing. Desert SACs in old Mexico were some of the poorest and most isolated. They have been able to adjust by coming together and helping each other. There are entire Sparrow Communities in Mexico City now," Zara excitedly reported.

"That's wonderful," Chiela said.

"It's wonderful, but . . . ." Zara said, knowing there was more.

"I don't want to be negative. I think what is happening in Mexico City is great. In fact, that is why we do everything we do. I just worry that now the target will shift from the SACs to the Sparrows. The President already hates the Sparrows, but he's never been able to nail us down. Now, with all these former SAC residents in his cities, it wouldn't take much to identify all the Sparrows. All he has to do is have ADAMS run an algorithm that identifies old SAC Passports or newly issued Passports."

"But you can reprogram them, right?" Zara asked. "Jude and I walked right out of that detention center with your Passports."

"Yes, but I have to reprogram a blank Passport for each person. It needs to have a Region of birth, a social security number, and some basic information to look legit."

"Can you teach me?" Zara asked.

"Sure, but that's still only two people."

"That's twice as many as a minute ago. We can train more people, and eventually, we can have a programmer in each Nest. I'll talk to Max about getting blanks. We'll need a lot of them."

"You're starting to sound like your husband," Chiela smirked.

"There is always a solution," Zara said with a wide grin.

Chapter 6: **Hotel California**

Summer was at its height in California, with temperatures hitting new records that used to only be seen in Arizona. The public beaches were overrun, the private beaches hired an army of security guards to protect them, and every pool and puddle was now a playground.

"Who are you?" the quizzical little girl asked.

The shy boy with ruffled, dark, wavy hair and covered in desert dirt, sat stoically on the curb.

"I am Niya," the girl said, not waiting for a response. "I'm seven. How old are you?"

No response.

"Are you sad? How come you're sad?"

No response.

"Are you hungry?"

The boy looked up at her with wide eyes, shining white through the dirt on his face.

"Want to come to my house? We have lots of food."

The boy shook his head. Niya grabbed his hand, pulled him up, and half-dragged him down the street.

"I live here," she declared as they came to a stop at the bottom of the largest building the boy had ever seen. He was enraptured.

"It's called a 'Cube Tower.' Mama says there is not enough room for all the Cube houses in Los Angeles, so some people decided to start stacking them up. We live on the 13th level. Don't worry; we don't have to climb. There is an elevator on the outside, see?" she said, pointing to the skeleton of scaffolding that clung to the exterior of the tower.

"Niya, who is this?" her mother asked when she burst through the door, dragging her new friend.

"I don't know his name," she explained, "but I think he's hungry. Can he have lunch with us?"

Her mother smiled. Most kids bring home a frog or a stray cat. Niya found a child. He was filthy and very hungry by the looks of it. He was also dehydrated. She noted his condition but hid her worry.

"Here you go," she said, setting a large bottle of sports drink in front of him. "Go ahead. This is good for you. It has vitamins your body needs."

The boy hesitated for a few seconds and then pulled the top and started drinking greedily.

"Take it easy. You don't want to upset your tummy," the mother warned.

"Can I get some juice too?" Niya asked.

"Let's save that for our special guest," she said. "But in a few minutes the pizza will be ready, and we can all share that," she said as she took a seat at the kitchen table with the kids.

"Yummy! I love pizza!" Niya said.

The boy finally put down his drink and let a small smile creep onto his face.

"My name is Naomi, and I'm sure Niya already told you her name. What's your name?"

"Alex," he squeaked out with a small, raspy voice.

"It's nice to meet you, Alex," she said. "I will guess that you are five years old."

He smiled and shook his head no.

"Seven like Niya?"

Another smiling no.

"Six?"

He smiled, held up six fingers, and shook his head yes.

"Where is your house?" Naomi asked.

He shrugged his shoulders.

"You don't know? Do you know where your parents are?"

He shrugged again. "The Army came and took us away. They brought us to the big city with lots of other people. I was scared. I saw lots of people get on a big bus, so I did too. Everyone got off at different places, and I didn't know what to do. I got off too, and then I saw Niya. Now I am here."

"You poor thing," Naomi said, shaking her head. "Did you live on a SAC?"

He gave her a blank stare.

"Did you live on a farm in the desert?"

He shook his head yes.

"Dear God, you're a SAC kid," she said, and then caught herself.

"Alex, you did well, and you are very brave. You can stay here with Niya and me until we can find your mommy and daddy, okay? Does that sound good to you?"

His little eyes went from his bright red sports drink to the pizza in the oven and back to Naomi. He shook his head yes.

Suddenly, a muted bang, like a hard popping sound, erupted from down below. The entire tower jolted and rocked.

"Mommy, what was that?" Niya asked.

"Probably just a tremor," Naomi said, getting up and walking to the window. She didn't even convince herself.

Three more pops shook the cube, and then slowly they all started losing their balance, and Alex's sports drink slid off the table and crashed all over the floor.

"Niya!" Naomi shouted, grabbing her daughter and Alex in a frantic scramble.

"Mommy!" Nya shouted in terror.

With the last bit of grip on the floor and in her hands, she threw Niya and Alex onto the couch. She took a cushion and a pillow from another chair, threw them down on the kids, and then jumped on top of them, gripping the edges for their lives.

The entire Cube tower swayed, tilted, and then, like a tree splintering after a lightning strike, the scaffolding snapped, and the Cubes fell and tumbled over each other, ripping wiring and pipes from their connections, and slamming into surrounding homes and businesses with a thundering fury.

Most of the Cubes maintained their integrity, and even some of the plexiglass windows survived the destruction, but the power of the fall sent people ricocheting off of walls with the force of a car accident, and the scene inside many Cubes looked similar. Screams from inside and out echoed through the streets as the tower fell, but for an eerie thirty seconds after the fall, there was silence, save the occasional clink or bang of the last of the scaffolding falling to the earth. Then, as if on some invisible cue, the screaming and wailing restarted with a distinctly sharper pitch of terror, pain, and desperation.

"Mommy! Mommy!" Niya cried, climbing out from the toppled mess of what used to be their living room. She tossed aside cushions and pillows and found her mother lying in a twisted heap near a shattered lamp in the corner. Niya tried to wake her, but she wouldn't respond. "Mommy! Wake up!" she cried desperately.

Alex crawled over the cushions toward the wall where the stove had tumbled over and crushed the TV screen, spilling the hot pizza. He carefully peeled pieces of pepperoni and cheese off the wall and plexiglass window and ate them. In a state of shock and confusion, not knowing anything else, he remembered he was hungry.

"Alex!" Niya cried. "We need to go outside. We need grown-ups to help us. Mommy is hurt!" She took his hand as he stuffed one last glob of cheese into his mouth, and she led him over the debris and pushed their way through their front door and on top of their neighbor's Cube. Sirens were already wailing and heading toward the disaster, and Niya knew help was coming. They stood together on top of the cube, waving at rescuers and citizens weaving their way through the carnage. In the midst of their trauma, they were comforted when the first rescuer to reach them was a neighbor's black lab who had survived the ordeal. Standing guard over the children, he alternated between nuzzling the kids to make sure they were okay and barking frantically for help. Niya and Alex were among the first to be pulled from the rubble.

News of the collapse made the rounds on all the official online outlets. There were some disagreements about the cause, but the local authorities worked quickly to correct the rumors. The tower was simply over capacity, the residents had ignored many warnings not to allow more than four people per cube, and the structure failed under the weight. It was the sad but inevitable result of overcrowding in a Cube tower. It was like living in a trailer; it's cheap, but good luck when the tornado comes.

"Hey Jude, do you remember all those Cube towers we saw out in California?" Zara asked, scanning her screen.

"You mean the ones I said looked like they could topple over like a pile of kids' blocks?"

"Yeah, well, it looks like one did fall. The official news sites are saying it was overcapacity, and they're all running this security cam footage from a building across the street. Take a look."

Jude knelt next to Zara and pulled the screen toward himself.

"Hmm . . . " he mused, running the video back over and over.

"What's your morbid fascination with watching this thing go down?" Zara snipped at him.

"It's not that," he said as he ran it back one more time. "Look at the cables and the scaffolding. They didn't snap from the pressure of the Cubes. The Cubes are perfectly still until the safety cables snap, and then the scaffolding splinters and the Cubes start tipping. I can't tell a lot from this video, but something doesn't look right."

President Blake Connor had to resist the urge to grab a weapon from one of his guards and obliterate the ADAMS interface droid.

"Why am I hearing the word 'Sparrows' again? The SACs are done. There is no one and nothing left for the Sparrows to save. They are done!"

"The Sparrows did give new life to the SACs before your order to remove them, but it appears that they have not disappeared. We have preliminary evidence suggesting that the Sparrows are organizing to assist SACs in transitioning to the cities. In some cases, SACs are already vacant by the time the NADF arrives."

ADAMS still had a ways to go in reading human facial expressions and vocal intonations, but increased heart rate, breathing, and bulging veins conveyed the information.

"Why is this being allowed? I don't want to see or hear or sense that those damned 'Sparrows' are in my way again! We should have executed that kid from Cascadia. We should have sent people a clear message from the beginning. If he lost his head live on the news feeds, I wouldn't be hearing about the 'Sparrows' again."

"To be precise, Mr. President," the ADAMS continued, "they are actually assisting people in the relocations. They are not opposing your orders."

"Sergeant, your weapon, please," the President ordered his guard. The guard hesitated, dumbfounded by the command. "Don't make me ask twice."

The young sergeant stepped into action and handed his Commander-in-Chief his pistol and then snapped back to attention. President Connor examined the gun, looked at the handle, and then said to the guard, "Voice override."

"NA4738529, override biometric lock."

A small red light began flashing just above the trigger. President Blake Conner stood up, took aim at the droid, and fired.

An explosion of gunfire echoed from the walls as the guard and assistants hit the ground and covered their heads. The composite polymers covering the interface unit shattered, the knees buckled, and the droid crumpled to the ground, leaving a stunned silence, save the last clinking of spent shells rolling to their resting place as the smoke cleared.

"To be precise, that is how I feel about being corrected."

"You know how you were suspicious of the Cube Tower collapse?" Zara called out to Jude as he came into their sparse bedroom in the Bunker.

"Yeah? Did you get more footage?"

"Even better, I got a message from Akal. My brother said it's not official, but it has become an open secret that COATS took out the Cube Tower. He said they laid simple, small remote charges to take out the safety cables, then the scaffolding, and then within seconds, the Cubes began to tumble."

"The people . . . ." Jude muttered. "They just blew up people's homes. No regard for human life. And for what?"

"Akal said it was allegedly a favor for an ardent supporter of the President in the Corporate Congress. He is in real estate."

"No warning, no remorse. People are just in the way. If your goal is to reduce the population by attrition, it makes it easy to help the process along with an 'accident' here and there. Who is on the side of real people?" Jude fumed.

"We are," Zara said, taking hold of his hand.

"Buenos dias, Señora Ortiz."

General Alvarado's voice was low and menacing. Sonja was still orienting herself after having been bound, covered with a hood, and driven to the backside of an empty warehouse in Mexico City.

"I know who you are, General Alvarado," Sonja said with a muffled voice. "Can we take this hood off now? I can't breathe."

"Of course," he replied, nodding to his soldier. "Make Senora Ortiz more comfortable."

"Was all this necessary? I would have come if you asked."

"I'll keep that in mind next time. Let's just say it is part of the message."

"What message is that?"

"Los Garriones are done. There are no more SACs. There are no more Sparrows."

"We're not drug cartels, General. We're people who care about each other. We're friends, neighbors, and relatives. We're survivors. We're the glue that holds some communities together. We cooperate with the New America and the Regional Governments, and we provide help when the government is unable to. What kind of threat do you think we present?"

"Symbols," Alvarado said, sauntering over to a cart loaded with car batteries and a jumble of cables. "Symbols are powerful reminders of who we are and what we believe in. Many people, especially people from SACs who are used to their relative independence, may find it hard to adjust to life under authority. They will see your little bird and remember the help they received on the SAC. They will remember the little display you put on in Washington last winter and feel they have a voice. They will read your newsletters, and they may begin to lose faith in official information sources. They may become dissatisfied with their lives, and they may feel the Sparrows can give them the strength and justification to resist authority."

"That sounds like a lot of 'they may' statements, General."

"My job is to make sure 'they may' becomes 'they will not.' Sometimes people need a little jolt to remind them of their place."

Taking a bucket of cold water, he tossed it at Sonja, slamming her face with a deluge that caused her to gasp and shudder at the shock of the cold. He then tipped the bucket over her head and drained the rest, soaking her shirt, jeans, and shoes. Her hands remained tied behind her back in the steel chair, and her legs were bound to the legs of the chair.

"Take off her shoes and socks," he ordered the soldier, who complied immediately. Hang on to these for me," he snickered, clamping the battery cables onto the flesh of each of her forearms.

"Aah," she hissed as the copper teeth pressed into her skin.

Alvarado flipped a switch on the battery pack and twisted a dial to ramp up the current.

"Aaah!" she screamed through clenched teeth, convulsing beneath her restraints and rattling the legs of the steel chair against the concrete. Alvarado turned off the switch.

"That was only 10 seconds. Let's see how you do with 30. After that, you are free to go, if you live."

He flipped the switch again, smiled at her renewed convulsions, and then turned and walked out. After the muscle tearing thirty seconds, the soldier flipped off the switch, cut the ropes around her wrists, removed the cables, and followed his general out the door. Sonja moaned weakly, slowly slumping over to her right side, barely able to shake her wrists from the dangling rope. Still tied to the legs of the chair, she fell onto the concrete floor with the chair still stubbornly clinging to her legs. Her body was on fire, and every muscle was stretched beyond its ability to function. Tears from her eyes and blood from her mouth and nose ran down her face onto the filthy concrete. Her eyes fluttered, and she sighed deeply, fearing it would be her last breath. Suddenly, the muffled sound of voices drew nearer and nearer, and she realized she was surrounded by half a dozen warehouse workers who heard the screams.

"Esta una mujer!"

"Llame la policia!"

"Esta bien, Senora. Esta bien. Vamos a ayudar. Soy un Gorrion tambien."

Prying open her eyes and peering through the slits, she looked at the man in a hard hat whose gentle touch was on her shoulder while the rest untied her legs from the chair. Under his forearm, she could make out a tattoo in a familiar shape. Struggling to focus her eyes, she finally discerned what it was: a sparrow.

Chapter 7: **Exposed**

"It's time to fight." The weight of those words and the potential consequences weighed heavily on Zara. "Sparrows should try to avoid confrontation, especially when facing a military force, but the legal and moral protections we once relied on are no longer guaranteed. The SACs have been decimated, and Sparrows are being targeted, even in cities. It is time for the Sparrows to take action to defend ourselves. Stay in touch with your Nest leaders. Strategies and supplies are on the way."

Following her press release, she forwarded her reports on the assault on the SACs and the Cube Tower cover-up in California to official news outlets. Would they run these stories? Of course not. Would they question the reliability of their sources and the official narrative? Absolutely.

"Please don't tell me I'm giving people false hope," Zara sighed.

"No way," Jude reassured her. "Even if it takes some time, people need hope."

"How much time?" Zara asked. "Hope won't last forever."

"A few weeks, tops," Max bellowed, coming in the room carrying a box of blank passports and dropping it on the table. "I called in a few favors, and I've managed to secure some blanks."

"How many?" Zara asked.

"Enough," Max said with a wink, pointing to the old freight entrance. They all watched as an aptly disguised produce truck backed in, its door raised, showing off hundreds of boxes of blank passports. "Now all we need to figure out is distribution and programming."

"We're on it," Jude and Zara said almost in unison.

"I feel like I'm the hunter and the hunted," Zack muttered as he lay among the leaves in camouflage gear, adjusting the scope on his rifle and checking the sky for drones. His position on his stomach among the brush and pine needles in the North Georgia mountains was as inconspicuous as a hunter should be, but his old Jeep was not so easy to hide. Painted in various shades of green, he parked it behind a cluster of pine trees and did his best to cover it with branches, leaves, and pine straw, but he was not far off the access road. He used this road to make the trip from the Blue Ridge SAC to Atlanta on many occasions, but now it was officially a Consolidated Agriculture and Mining Operations access road, newly christened with an "Authorized Access Only" sign. He was fairly certain he didn't qualify as "authorized."

Zack lay still, breathing evenly in the crisp early dawn air, his every sense tuned to the sounds of the forest. He rolled halfway onto his side, and as a branch scratched across his shoulder, he was quickly and painfully reminded that his incision was still healing. If he opened it up again, Athalia was going to kill him; she already had to re-stitch him once.

The passport worked; he cruised through the scanners getting on and off the regional transport, walked past a few LEAD units, and bought a few supplies at the street shop. Of course, the true test will be when he stands shoulder to shoulder with other Sparrows and they are identified, but he is not. Hopefully, that test won't happen. Jude and Zara know what they are doing; if anyone can fly under the noses of the government, it's them.

Right now, his concern was slipping in and out of his old hunting grounds under the noses of CAMO. He wanted to get a deer; that would tide them over for a while. It would be a beast to haul to his Jeep, but once he got to his storage locker in Gainesville, he could carve it up and put most of it in the freezer. The rest would go in his cold pack and take a ride on regional transport with him to the Cube, into Athalia's kitchen, and then to his plate.

A movement in his peripheral snapped him back to attention. He just caught the leaves settling about 20 meters to the right. He froze. The leaves rustled again, and then he saw it; crouching behind a small pine tree not quite small enough to hide their rail-thin frame was a wild-looking child. He—or she—had long, matted hair, torn, ragged pants, a dirt and blood-stained t-shirt, and a rusty knife. At first, he stiffened into a defense mode, but then he realized the child was closing in on a jackrabbit. She, he decided, did not see him.

She stalked the rabbit, slowly and silently closing the gap, freezing in place as the rabbit ducked under a fern and looked back and forth.

"There's no way," Zack whispered to himself. "She can't hit it from that distance."

As if issued a challenge, the girl launched the knife toward the rabbit so quickly Zack couldn't even see how the knife turned in the air. It hit with a "thump!" and the rabbit bolted out from the bush, shaking off the knife from where it plunged into its hind leg. It was wounded; Zack could see a slight limp, but the flight response overpowered the injury with adrenaline, so it was difficult to see how deep it went.

Zack had a fleeting thought to try and hit it with his rifle, but the rabbit and the girl were too fast. She lit after the rabbit, pulling out another knife as she ran, and she flicked this one as she jumped over a downed tree. It was a direct hit just behind the neck, and the rabbit was nearly pinned down right in its tracks. The girl caught up to it, pulled out her knife, and quickly cut the animal's throat.

Zack slowly emerged from his spot and found the first knife. He picked it up and headed after the girl, who let out a short chirp of a scream when she saw Zack with her knife. Her instinct was to run, but she noticed Zack was holding the knife out to her by the blade, offering her the handle.

"That was impressive," he said. "You are quite skilled."

The girl, who Zack estimated to be about fourteen, took her knife and sized him up. Her flight instinct was checked by something she couldn't quite explain.

"I'm quite hungry," she countered.

"I'm Zack. Zack Nolan," he said, holding his hand out. She stared at him with a steeled face.

"You're not CAMO?" she asked.

"Nope."

"You're not NADF?"

"No way."

"You're not GSA RDF or CME?"

Zack gave up on the handshake and chuckled. "I'm not in the Regional Defense Forces, and I'm definitely not part of any CME team. I'm a former Blue Ridge SAC member, I'm a Sparrow, and I'm also hungry, although probably not as hungry as you."

"Blue Ridge?" she repeated.

"Yeah. You've heard of it?" Zack asked, trying to see if he recognized her.

"Our family lived outside of Blue Ridge. We moved around to avoid people."

"Who is 'we'?"

"You ask a lot of questions. What about you? What are you doing out here if you're not CAMO? We're trespassing, you know."

Trust me, I know," he said, scanning the sky. "We should get out of sight."

Zack turned to lead them into some cover, but the girl went the opposite way, and almost immediately disappeared behind a grove of pines. Zack ran after her.

"Wait!" he yelled.

"Wait for what?" she said, letting a bit of a teenage snarky attitude slip. "You're the one who said we need to get out of sight."

"Where are you going?" he said, panting.

"Where are you going? Are you going to follow me? I don't know who you are." She slowed but never stopped.

"Yes. I mean, no. I mean . . . .would you just hold on a minute?" he said, catching his breath. She finally stopped, glanced up to scan the sky, and then leaned up against a tree and started skinning the rabbit.

"You said 'we.' Who is 'we'?" he asked.

"Why do you want to know?" She never looked up from the rabbit. She made short work of it, and he noticed she didn't leave anything behind. She cut off a bit from the thigh and clamped down on it like a ravenous wolf.

"Look, you can't stay out here. CAMO will find you eventually," he reasoned.

"They haven't yet."

"Because you're good, that's clear. You're a survivor. You're strong and smart. The thing is, how long can you keep it up? Do you want to keep moving your family, always looking over your shoulder, always hunting game that is just out of reach, always staying just one step ahead of starvation?"

"I never said anything about my family."

"But you have a family, don't you? Otherwise, you wouldn't bother saving the rest of that rabbit."

She finally met his gaze. She stared with piercing hazel eyes, a small drop of rabbit blood dripping from the corner of her mouth.

"My parents are dead. They weren't even part of a SAC, but when the roundup started, they wanted to fight. They didn't last long."

"But you survived," he said.

"I kept my little brothers safe. I'm still keeping them safe."

"I understand. I can't imagine what you've had to do to keep yourself and your brothers safe and fed. The thing is, winter is not forgiving. The days of snow are gone, but four or five months of rain, hibernating animals, and tree-crunching storms make staying alive an Olympic event."

"I can handle it."

"I don't doubt it, but what about your brothers? If you are on the run, you don't have a permanent shelter. Are they going to survive the winter?"

"I'm not going to the city."

The fact that she was still talking meant that she was thinking.

"What about your brothers?"

"I can't leave them."

Zack sighed. He couldn't leave these children, but he couldn't get them out of there by arguing.

"It's your call. My wife makes the most amazing rabbit and corn chowder, and you are welcome to come stay with us. All of you. We can keep you out of CME schools and keep you together. We can keep you safe."

She was still lingering on the rabbit corn chowder.

"If you change your mind, let me know. Find a Sparrow and tell them you are looking for Zack Nolan. I'll come get you."

"My parents said you could trust the Sparrows, but they don't fight hard enough. They should have made an army."

Zack wanted to say, "and look where that got your parents?" but he didn't dare. Besides, she already knew.

"We're survivors, not soldiers," he said.

She stood still, staring at the ground, and then looked at the carcass in one hand and the skin in the other. Zack held his breath. She looked up at him, sighed, but said nothing. She didn't need to. Her eyes told him everything.

"You know the three-tree clump down at the bottom of the hill, just off of the access road?" he asked.

She nodded.

"My jeep is down there. I'm going to try and find my deer. If you want to come, meet me at the Jeep by sundown."

"What did Athalia say when you showed up with three kids?" Jude asked Zack on the phone.

"I think she had in mind to carve me up like the deer I didn't get, but when she saw how emaciated and filthy the kids were, she went into mama mode. I'm safe for now."

"You did a good thing, Zack. Those kids wouldn't have made it without you."

"I don't know. You should have seen that girl with a knife. She's a fighter. That rabbit didn't stand a chance."

Even through the screen, Zack could see that Jude had the look of a detective in his eyes. "We have good intel that is confirming our suspicions. Zara is piecing together reports of more shootings in the round-up of the SACs. She's got some damning video that puts COATS at the scene of the Cube tower collapse in Southern California. She's also got a growing list of eyewitnesses who say NADF fired the first shots when they came to round up some of the SACs. In some cases, they fired the only shots."

"That makes it hard to justify," Zack said. "President Connor has had it out for the SACs for decades. Is it revenge?"

"Maybe. It might also be his way of speeding up attrition. With SACs gone, the cities have had to absorb a lot of new people. Cubes are in short supply, and I imagine the budget is strained. People are too expensive," Jude said.

"Dear God," Zack exclaimed. "What else do you think he has up his sleeve?"

"I don't know, but anecdotes really help weave together the big picture. I don't suppose we can tell the story of your new additions?"

"Sure, but no names or locations. Just emphasize the collateral damage, since we won't see that on official media," Zack said.

Zara couldn't release a barrage of information, but she kept a steady pace of producing carefully researched stories. Nothing gets dismissed as quickly as a conspiracy theory, so Zara gave every story a solid footing. It wasn't long before people outside of the Sparrow community started taking notice, especially journalists. For each story they tried to debunk, they kept coming up against a wall of truth. They could never produce her stories, but their factual reliability had many journalists turning to Sparrow Press to get the full story, or in many cases, the real story.

"Jude, come here," Zara said one morning as she typed and clicked away on three screens in her makeshift "press room" in the Bunker.

"What is it?" he asked, fearing another poorly veiled attack.

"I think some of the journalists I've sent stories to have posted them."

"You mean like anchors on the official news channels?" Jude asked, perplexed.

"I think so. Of course, they don't use their real names, but there are several online personalities that I have suspected as being mainstream journalists wanting to voice their own opinions. Journalistic integrity is hard to kill, you know."

"Not hard enough," Jude huffed.

"Look at this," Zara said almost giddy. "A new site has launched called 'Unofficial,' and it claims to be the work of current and former journalists from major networks. They say they closely guard their real identities; they expose how they are manipulated with false data and propaganda, and they even report on some of my stories! Do you know what this means?" Zara squealed.

"It means Sparrow Press is playing with the big dogs," Jude smiled.

"Well, 'unofficially,'" Zara said.

"This is good. We're not the only loose network of rebels in town. The harder the government tries to crack down on dissent, the more they create. Maybe they'll put two and two together and rethink their strategy."

"Or maybe they'll double down," Zara said, "and give us more material to work with."

"Somehow after the round-up of the SACs and the success of the Sparrows in any form, I'm inclined to think option B is the most likely. I think we're in for more trouble."

"What else can we do?" Zara asked.

The warehouse was cavernous. There were plenty of hiding places for sure among the miles of defunct conveyor belts and sorting machines, but the purpose of these machines was fading into time like the pale and chipped yellow paint that used to coat every piece of metal in the space.

"Can you believe companies used to load trucks, fill them with diesel, and send them off across the country just to move packages? Can you imagine how much carbon was burned and how many hands touched a box before it got to your door?" Jude asked, surveying the scene.

"Diesel was the workhorse of the entire world's economy before dry-cell batteries and the hydrogen revolution," Zara remarked. "It was unbeatable for a hundred years."

"And filthy," Jude said. "But we're not here for a history field trip. We're here for target practice."

"Are you pursuing a career opportunity in the international arms dealing market?" Zara joked.

"You know I hate guns, but necessity is the mother of invention. Besides, these won't kill anybody. Maisy and Dr. Robinson are going to help me make sure of that. Right now, we just need to test the delivery, and I want to make sure it can be handled easily by someone without firearms experience. I want the accuracy nailed down before I head back to Kansas City and the doctors start debating chemical compounds. The serum only matters if it hits its target."

Jude handed Zara a modified old 20th-century Springfield .45. "These pistols are the perfect size. I played with rifles, but they are way too big for close urban operations. I thought about air guns, but I wanted a more reliable projectile delivery. I finally fabricated a hybrid dart-within-a-bullet with a polymer casing. The bullet shouldn't do too much damage, and the micro dart can pierce a couple of layers of clothing before delivering the serum."

"Ok, Einstein, let's see if these polymer bullets can go where we want them to," Zara said, chambering a round and taking aim at the large, flat metal surface of a sorting machine. "By the way, if the bullet casings don't do too much damage, how can we tell where it hit?"

Jude smiled smugly. "Take the shot and see."

Pop! Pop! Pop! Zara wasn't experienced in handling a gun, so the snap of the pistol took her off guard. She reset her feet, adjusted her grip and aim, and tried again. She emptied the cartridge.

"You made the serum glow in the dark, huh?" Zara commented.

"Just so we can see where it ends up right now," Jude said. "What do you think?"

They both walked over to the sorting machine, measuring the thirty meters with their phones. On the machine's large, slick sorting slide Zara had managed to create a surprisingly well-shaped smiling face with the serum marks.

"I'd say it shoots pretty straight," Zara said, taking her turn to be smug. "At least at thirty meters."

Jude smiled and shook his head. "I thought you weren't experienced with guns?"

"Beginner's luck," she said with some swagger. "What are you going to call it?"

"A Stinger."

Chapter 8: **Rule of Law**

"UNOFFICIAL" WAS OFFICIALLY MAKING waves. While staying strategically distanced from each other, Sparrow Press and Unofficial collaborated with common sources, broke closely related stories, and generally supported each other's criticisms of the New American government.

While he would never acknowledge the content or even the existence of "Unofficial," Zara could sense it was getting under President Connor's skin. He couldn't ignore the obvious influx of former SAC residents, but he could spin it to fit his carefully crafted narrative.

"Why are there so many new immigrants to the cities?" he would ask rhetorically in speeches. "Because they are fleeing the poverty, isolation, and ignorance of the failed SAC experiment," he would argue. "Why are there rumors of unrest?" he asked again. "Because our resources are being stretched, and there is always an uncomfortable period of adjustment. I can assure you, we will take care of every last New American, and no one needs to live in fear. ADAMS would never condone violence, and I would never allow it."

"Besides, there must be some easier way to shrink the entire population without inciting panic," Zara huffed. She was tempted to make a split-screen of his speech and the footage of NADF troops firing on SAC refugees, but she resisted the urge to descend into pithy, sarcastic, meme-driven viral bites. This was too serious.

"General Alvarado, how are the final phases of the SAC roundups coming along?" President Connor asked in a mockingly formal tone as they sat down for their regular meeting.

"Does it need to be here?" Alvarado asked, motioning to the new ADAMS interface unit.

"He's harmless," the President reassured him. "As obnoxious as he can be, he does help me avoid some pitfalls with morality, public opinion, and other nuisances. No offense, ADAMS."

"I believe the correct response is, 'none taken,' Mr. President."

"I have good news and bad news, Mr. President," Alvarado began, feigning some level of formality for ADAMS' sake. President Blake Connor was a younger man, and he was more comfortable with the utility of AI, but Alvarado had trouble shaking the feeling that they were being spied on.

"I always want the bad news first," the President said.

"They are a package deal, sir. The good news is that the SACs are gone; with the few exceptions of stragglers, hermits, and survivalists, all SACs have been dissolved, and the occupied land has been given to CAMO to make better use of. This should boost agricultural and mineral production, which will ease some of the supply issues. The bad news is that even though the SACs are gone, the Sparrows have now landed in the cities."

"I knew this would be a problem," the President said. "They have some kind of propaganda machine, and they keep feeding the masses. Eliminating the SACs seemed to have solved one problem while creating another one. Now we have this disaffected riff-raff on our doorstep with a new list of grievances."

"It's something like an infection, sir. Our intelligence sources have found the number of 'Sparrows' growing, which means they are spreading their ideology, not simply assimilating. We initially knew them as SAC residents and sympathizers, but they appear to have evolved. Instead of fading away with the elimination of Sustainable Agricultural Communities, they seem to have formed online and even physical communities inside of cities, including Cube-clusters and informal neighborhoods. They're not exclusive to former SAC residents; they are actually recruiting people," Alvarado explained.

President Blake Connor clenched his fists, set his jaw, and turned to look at the ADAMS interface unit. He pointed menacingly at the droid, but he finally restrained himself. He took a deep breath.

"I let that SAC boy go last year, and I tolerated the demonstrations. I was told it was the wisest course of action, and it would end the protests more quickly and efficiently," he said, staring down ADAMS.

"Quantitatively, it was a success, sir," ADAMS said, defending his analysis. "It appears the decision to eliminate the SACs has been the primary catalyst for the resurgence of the Sparrow movement."

"I won't make the same mistake twice," he hissed, shooting a look at Alvarado. "ADAMS, there are some aspects of human nature you may never understand. A common experience can become a common grievance, and a common grievance can become a common cause. This is the onset of the cancer of rebellion. As individuals, we can usually make reasonable decisions, but together, we tend to descend to our lowest common vice. We make bold statements about justice and humanity, but inevitably, we orchestrate chaos and engineer our own demise. The only way to counter this glaring fault is to enforce order and remind people that their freedoms are only guaranteed as long as they exist under a strong authority that ensures the safety and rights of everyone in society, not just the vocal few."

"This 'tendency to descend to the lowest common vice' as you said, is something I will continue to research. Is it related at all to the concept of 'mob mentality' I have observed in psychological journals?" ADAMS asked.

"That's a start," the President said. "While you're at it, work on getting me a clearer idea of who the Sparrows are and how we can identify them."

"Yes, sir," the droid replied.

"The Passports should identify former SAC members, correct?"

"Yes, sir."

"Well, there may be another problem, sir," Alvarado chimed in. "We suspect many of them have been able to reprogram or replace their Passports. This level of technical skill suggests a coordinated effort and the cooperation of someone highly skilled, either inside the government, CAMO, or a tech firm. There's no way any of these SAC farmers crawled out of the fields and mastered that; someone is reprogramming them."

"Do you see how quickly this cancer spreads?" the President said, looking at ADAMS. "See how they are already using deception to evade the authorities?"

"Yes, sir, but also . . . "

"Your next task," he said, cutting off the droid, "is to analyze how we can quickly and efficiently identify former SAC residents if their Passport has been reprogrammed. We'll start there, and then decide how to contain the others attempting to join their cause."

"Yes, sir."

"I'll get to work on identifying the lead actors," Alvarado volunteered. "I'll start by tracking down that SAC boy and his family."

Kansas City was busy, and with the recent surge in SAC migrants, the hospital was no exception. Jude felt bad for taking Maisy and Dr. Robinson away from their patients. When he knocked on Dr. Robinson's door, he heard some giggling, whispering, and shuffling before the door opened. Suddenly, he didn't feel quite as bad.

"Hello, Julian," Jude said, trying to suppress his suspicious tone.

"Hello, Jude! Sorry about that. We were just reviewing some patient charts."

"Sure, well, sorry to interrupt."

"No problem. Come on in."

"Jude!" Maisy called, running up to him and enveloping him in a bear hug. "I've been so busy. I've missed you!"

"I've missed you, too," he said, returning the big brother embrace. It had been longer than he was used to, and he noticed his baby sister was noticeably more grown-up. He also noticed the way she looked at Julian. It reminded him of how Zara looked at him.

"What is it we are looking for?" Dr. Robinson asked as he closed the door to his office, and they each claimed a chair.

"How do you feel about doctor-patient confidentiality?" Jude asked with a knowing smile.

"It's safe. There aren't any ears in here," Maisy said, smiling at Julian. Jude smiled and moved on.

"I'm looking for something injectable, non-lethal, of course, but highly effective. I need a tranquilizer, able to immobilize an adult, ideally within seconds," Jude explained.

"How long do you want the immobilization to last?" Julian asked.

"Thirty to sixty minutes."

"Are you worried about children?"

"They're not the target, but I don't want kids at risk if we can help it," Jude said.

"How's the delivery system looking?" Julian asked.

"Very accurate, very quick, and it packs a bit of a punch. I've got the right dart, and now I just need the right juice."

"I think I know the best stuff to use, but for the volume you need, you're going to want the bulk version. There's a doctor I can talk to," Julian said.

"Is this doctor here, and can we trust them?"

"Yes, we can trust her, and no, she's not here, but she's just down the street. Right about now, she's probably working in the elephant enclosure."

"A veterinarian?" Jude asked.

"My sister's college roommate. She's a good woman, trustworthy, and let's just say she is not a big fan of the New American government. She can get us what we need."

"Dr. Robinson," Jude said, standing up and shaking his hand, "you've been a huge help. Thank you."

"Be careful, Jude. The Sparrows are a lifeline for more people than you know. Please take care of yourself."

"And you take care of my sister," he said, winking at Maisy.

Julian smiled and shook his head. "Trust me, she can take care of herself, but of course, I will try to keep her out of trouble."

"Mr. President, the ADAMS interface droid would like to speak with you for a moment before your next meeting," his aide buzzed.

"I'm busy," he said, dismissing her without even looking up from his desk.

"ADAMS said it was about identifying the Sparrows."

He looked up. "Send in the droid. I've got a few minutes."

"Hello, Mr. President," the ADAMS droid said. "I'll be brief."

"Thank you, ADAMS."

"Sir, I am unable to isolate the re-programmed Passports at this time, and the number of SAC-issued Passports is rapidly dwindling as they are being replaced. The Passports and their profiles are not distinguishable for former SAC residents. If, however, we only need to identify former SAC residents, I can isolate recent Universal Basic Income recipients. Of course, not all new UBI registrants are from a SAC, but I can cross-reference previous known residences and identify approximately 88-91% of former SAC residences. Of these, up to 71% may identify as Sparrows or be sympathetic to Sparrow causes. It is far from positively identifying all Sparrows, but I believe I can provide enough positive matches to begin identification, and perhaps these early matches may identify their associates."

"That's a good start. I'm sure we can secure their cooperation and make significant progress from there," the President said. "Thank you, ADAMS."

"Yes, sir."

President Blake Connor buzzed his aide. "Get a message to General Alvarado. Tell him to forget about the SAC kid from last year. I have a new assignment for him."

It took a few weeks of coordination, but Zara managed to pull together some of their closest friends for the effort. Jude and Zara created guides and advice for the SACs, but with their collapse and rapid integration of people into the cities, it was clear the Sparrows were living in a new world, and they needed to encourage people in completely different ways. The result: Sparrow Press began publishing the Encouragement Editorial: Advice and Strategies for Surviving in the Cities. The contributors would be Gavin Hollins, formerly of the Wytheville, VA SAC and now a resident of Richmond; Zach and Athalia Nolan, formerly of the Blue Ridge SAC and now residents of Atlanta; Sonja Orozco, leader of "Nidos de Gorriones" in Mexico City, Baja; Rod and Marren Kane, formerly of the Slate Creek SAC and now residents of Vancouver, Cascadia; and finally, Jude and Zara would contribute from underground outside of Kansas City, Texico.

Sparrow Press: Encouragement Editorial
By Gavin Hollins

"I have seen firsthand the swift destruction the NADF can inflict. I lost my wife in the attack on Wytheville. I nearly lost myself when I was corralled into the city and suddenly dependent on the same government that took everything away from me. If it wasn't for my daughter, I don't know if I could have managed to adapt. My story cannot be unique; this has happened to thousands of us in the past few months, and like my daughter, I want to extend my hand to help.

"My message is simple: we can do this, but we need each other. It wasn't the land or the independence that gave us purpose; it was relationships and community. Now it is time for us to stand up against the relentless wave of apathy and lack of purpose and recognize that our true purpose is to live for each other! How often do we see despair in the eyes of our neighbors? We see it every day. What if we take our fresh perspective and invade the cities with our pursuit of truth and love? What if we give what we can, help where we can, and overwhelm our neighborhoods with generosity and kindness? Already, we see our community of Sparrows swelling with the inclusion of more and more people who are finding hope. Life isn't about surviving; it is about helping each other to thrive. We will meet resistance; of that I am sure, but I am also sure that as people who live in truth and love, we will always be the victors."

Gavin Hollins
Richmond, Appalachia

As the sun rose over the horizon on the outskirts of Knoxville, Appalachia, two young, uniformed women approached a four-Cube structure in a neighborhood with several recent additions and an unusual number of houses with bird-themed decorations. Door signs and postal boxes often had signs with sayings like "We believe in Life, Equality, and Human Dignity," or "In this house, we are guided by Truth and Love." All of these signs had small, sparrow-shaped logos in the corner.

"We are definitely in the right neighborhood," the dark-haired one murmured to her partner.

"They don't even have to give us names. They could just point," snickered the partner as she ran her fingers through her silky crimson hair and straightened her gray HHS jacket.

They approached the four-Cube structure and rang the doorbell on what appeared to be the main door. A sleepy-looking young mother cracked open the door, followed by two toddlers pulling at her pajama bottoms and hiding behind her legs.

"Can I help you?" you asked suspiciously.

"Good morning," the dark-haired woman began. "We're from the Appalachia Health and Human Services Department. You have been identified as recently resettling from a Sustainable Agricultural Community. We want to make sure you have been able to adjust to life in an urban area and you have everything you need."

"A job would be great, but I hear those are pretty hard to come by," the young woman said flatly.

"Ah, yes, but we can forward your information to the Department of Labor and see if your skills match any openings. Of course, you are always able to hop on a stationary bicycle and power the discs, which can help you maintain your fitness goals, supplement your Universal Basic Income, and contribute to the power needs of your community," the red-haired girl chimed in.

"Pardon me for being frank, but these are things I already know. Why exactly is HHS sending you out to knock on doors?"

"We know the transition has been hard for many from the SACs, so we want to reach out and make sure people are settling in and have what they need. Identifying recent SAC arrivals is not quite as easy as it may seem, so when we are able to identify people like yourself, we want to not only make sure you have the services you are eligible for, but see if you might help us identify other recent SAC arrivals who may need help getting signed up for healthcare, UBI, and get on the list for a Cube if they need housing. We know the allotment of Cubes has been slow, but manufacturing has increased, and new shipments should be arriving in a few weeks. We know that will alleviate a lot of strain on crowded families, and we are trying to make sure things go as smoothly as possible."

"That sounds awfully responsible and efficient. Are you sure there isn't another reason the government is so keen on identifying recent SAC residents?" the young woman asked. "It's not like we were asked nicely when the SACs were raided, our homes destroyed, and we were herded into the cities."

The crimson-haired woman jumped in again. "The military is tactically efficient, but not exactly tactful, if you know what I mean. At HHS, our entire job is to make sure people have the services they are eligible for. Our orders were simple: identify as many of the former SAC residents as possible and get them settled in. Maybe the government is trying to make amends for the heavy hand it had in moving everyone here. I can't say. I do know we can help. If you have anyone in mind, feel free to type their names here, and we'll take care of them."

The young woman looked at the HHS uniforms, looked at the women's faces, and thought of all the families sleeping with kids piled on top of each other as they all seemed to be waiting for UBI to come through and Cubes to be allotted. Why would they lie? The red-haired girl had a point: the military was swift and brutal, even violent in some cases, but HHS is not the military. Maybe they were actually there to help.

"Let me see the tablet," the woman said in a less suspicious tone. "Would you like to come in and sit down while I put in some names for you?"

Chapter 9: **Surrender**

The press conference was to begin in ten minutes. Zara was more anxious than usual for this one. Word had been streaming in that Health and Human Services agents had been going door to door looking for former SAC residents, and nothing about that scenario could bode well. Still, Sparrows in several regions confirmed that the agents were kind, patient, and seemed to honestly be there to help SAC folks get signed up for benefits and settled in.

President Blake Connor had waged a one-man war against the SACs for years, and he finally managed to dismantle their legal protections and wipe them out in a matter of weeks. Was Health and Human Services stepping in out of humanitarian concern? The red flags weren't just flying; they were screaming in the wind. Nothing was adding up.

"People of New America," he began as he stepped up to the podium strategically placed in a flourishing garden lined with a perfectly trimmed hedge and a trio of rose bushes just behind him. "We understand the recent influx of people from the former Sustainable Agricultural Communities has been difficult, and I will admit my administration shares some of the blame. We simply didn't anticipate the scope of the need. We are committed to making sure everyone finds their place in New America. In an effort to facilitate this transition quickly and smoothly, we have asked Corporate Congress and the Senate to allocate more funding for Health and Human Services, we have ramped up production of new Comfort Units (affectionately known as "Cubes"), and we have created several reception centers in every region. ADAMS has identified former SAC residents, even those who have so quickly updated their Passports, and we are inviting you to report to a reception center where we can give you an orientation to urban life and expedite the benefits you qualify for."

It was so innocuous, even Zara started to believe him, until he let slip one telling clue. It was a single word that belied his true intentions: "report." You are invited to come, but you are ordered to report. If ADAMS found a way to identify former SAC residents, they likely pressured people to identify others.

"Dear God," Zara said, covering her mouth with her hand and resting the other on Jude's shoulder. "They're not identifying former SAC people for benefits. The system is strapped as it is. President Connor is using that as cover. They're hunting for Sparrows."

"I need to test the Stingers. Can you help me?" Jude asked.

Zara was still reeling from the news conference and the implications it may have for everyone.

"How can you think about that now?" she shot back.

Jude sighed and took her hand, looking into her eyes like he always did when he wanted her to know he was present. "We don't know what the government has up their sleeve. I hope we won't have to resist, but if it comes to that, the Sparrows need to have more than our righteous indignation. It's a small thing, but small things give people hope."

"I get it," Zara said. "What do you want me to do? You're not going to shoot me with that thing, are you?"

"Of course not! I'm going to test it on myself. I just need you to stand by and time how long it takes me to wake up and start moving again."

"I don't like this."

"Think of me as an attacker. We want safe, but we also need it to be effective. I'll run at you from about twenty meters away. Let's see if I can get to you."

Jude began his sprint, and Zara took aim. As he approached, she instinctively closed her eyes and then fired the stinger.

"Ouch!" yelped Jude from ten meters away. The dart hit his upper thigh, a little too close to the middle for his comfort.

"Did you close your eyes? Don't close your eyes when you are shooo . . . ." He collapsed about five meters from Zara, mid-sentence. He lay sprawled out, twitched his fingers slightly, and then his eyes closed.

"You were saying?" Zara teased as she set her watch and started timing. She decided to video his recovery in case he wanted details she couldn't recall, or if she wanted to give their friends a good laugh. This was research, after all.

"What are people saying about the reception centers?" Jude asked, opening and closing his hand in an attempt to regain control of his senses.

"50 minutes and about a 90% recovery, I'd say," Zara observed.

"That's right on target," Jude said, now twisting his arm and swirling his feet in turn. "And so were you, but maybe open your eyes next time."

"I haven't heard anything yet," she said, changing the subject. "So far it seems like they are doing what they said, but I have a feeling this has more to do with gathering intelligence right now. We have no way of knowing what's coming."

"I agree. The re-programmed Passports helped, but ADAMS has access to mountains of data. It's probably creating and refining an algorithm continuously as they confirm who is whom. If the government can make a list of Sparrows, even if it is not 100% accurate, we will be sitting ducks. We've got to get into one of those 'reception centers' and see what they're up to."

"They know who we are Jude," Zara said. "If we walk in there, we might as well put the cuffs on ourselves."

"Who else can do it? How can we ask anyone to take that risk?" he said.

"Let me put a word out to the Nests. I think we might get a few takers."

"How are the kids?" asked Jude.

"They're good. Athalia has them in a good routine, and the boys are settling in. The girl is still pretty hesitant, but I think she's happy that her brothers are doing well. She went through hell, so it'll take time to work through that," Zack explained. "I do see that she has a soft spot for the baby. That's one place where her hard shell has a crack."

"She's in the best place. You and Athalia inherited an instant family, but if anyone was ready, it was you two."

"Speaking of being ready . . . " Zack said, pivoting strategically. "I think it's time for me to show up at a reception center here in Atlanta. We need to know what they're up to."

"Zack! You have six kids in the house. You can't risk . . . "

"I have six kids I want to fight for, Jude. First of all, we could use the benefits. If anyone needs to go, it's me. Secondly, if the government is going to start hunting down the Sparrows, I want to know sooner rather than later. I'm not going to be a sitting duck."

"I don't suppose I'm going to talk you out of it," Jude conceded.

"No, sir."

"Athalia is going to kill you."

Zack arrived at the Alpharetta Reception Center north of Atlanta just after 8:00 am. He was admittedly a little apprehensive; he was anxious to get an inside view of how the government might be gathering intelligence on Sparrows, but he was also worried about the three additional kids in his home. A second Cube would be a relief, and a bump in the Universal Basic Income would go a long way toward feeding the larger family, but what if they questioned his custody? What if they wanted to extract the kids to a CME school or another foster home? Of course, if he tried to hide them and they were found out, they would certainly be in worse trouble. Back in the Blue Ridge SAC, no one would question a family's decision to take in orphans; they all knew each other's stories. He would get prepared meals and congratulations instead of questions and suspicions.

"Good morning, sir," the cheery HHS agent greeted him. "Are you a recent arrival from a Sustainable Agricultural Community?"

"Yes, ma'am. The Blue Ridge SAC."

"Well, welcome to Atlanta."

He had to hold back a snicker. How many times had he been into town to sell his game? How many visits to Athalia before she joined him in Blue Ridge?

"Thank you."

"Are you alone or are you part of a household?"

"I have a wife and six children."

"Six children! That is a big family. Are all of the children your natural children?"

"No. My wife and I have two kids, we recently had a baby, and then we quite unexpectedly found ourselves with three more kids. Their parents passed away, and they were surviving alone in a very remote area outside of the Blue Ridge SAC. The girl, who I guess is close to fourteen, was providing for her two younger brothers. It was a tragic situation, but they are safe with us now."

"That is quite a story!" the agent said, not looking up from her screen. She was tying rapidly, making notes.

"Ma'am, in the SAC we were quite informal about many things, so of course the children were not formally placed with us. Now that we are living here in Atlanta, is there something we need to do to maintain custody of the children?" Zack asked. Of course, she didn't need to know he found them after they left Blue Ridge.

"That's a good question. I can begin that process for you right here. Be patient; legal procedures can take a while, but in the meantime, it seems the children are safe and well cared for. HHS will have to interview you, your wife, and the children, and of course they'll have to do a home study before you go through proceedings to take legal custody. You have taken the first step today in coming here. I will be able to assign you adequate housing, a UBI commensurate with a family of your size, and get you your medical cards. Unless we see the children neglected or in danger, they will remain in your home through the process."

"Thank you. As you can imagine, I have become quite protective of them. They've already been through a lot." Zack vowed to keep his mouth shut and reveal only as much as necessary, but his sense of relief loosened his tongue a bit.

"I just have a few more questions before we enter all of your data. First, what was your occupation or position in the SAC?"

Now things were getting interesting.

"We worked together as a community. Most of our time was spent providing for our basic needs. I suppose if I had any area of focus, it would be in finding sources of power and hunting. I seemed to spend most of my time doing these things."

"Ok," she said, continuing to type. "Would you say you were a leader in the SAC?"

"Like I said, we worked together as a community, but it would be fair to say people did look to me for advice and assistance." Zack was on full alert. Does being a leader make him a target? What kind of question is that? Downplaying his role, he walked the line of cautious honesty.

"Ok, great. We can put your skills into our employment database and notify you if you qualify for a position that requires your talents. Perhaps they may need you at Consolidated Agriculture and Mining Operations."

Work for CAMO? Now that was funny. These mass operations were so automated that the livestock probably didn't even know what a real human looked like.

"That would be great, thank you," he said with a smile.

As the agent began entering the information, Zack casually typed out a text to Zara.

"So far it seems fairly routine, although they did ask me if I was a SAC leader."

Zara replied: "If they take you anywhere away from the large group, stream it to me. Even if you can't get video, I want to hear what they're up to."

"No problem."

"All right Mr. Nolan, we're about done here. Keep an eye out for updated benefits and legal documents regarding your foster children."

"I will, thank you."

"One more thing," she said, finally looking up from her screen and making eye contact. "Since you are here, we'd like to interview you about your experience living in a SAC. We're trying to do some research so we can better know how to help folks who are rejoining society."

"Didn't we just do that?" Zack asked. He casually slipped his hand into his pocket and took hold of his phone.

"I'm just an HHS agent, but someone more acquainted with the research would like to get some more details if we can. It will only take a few minutes. Just head across the room and go through the door labeled 'interviews.' Dr. Marisol Navarro-Cruz will meet you there."

"Doctor?" Zack said a little more accusingly than he meant.

"Yes. She's one of our psychologists on the research team. Don't worry; she is just trying to gather information. She's very kind. You'll like her."

Zack squared his shoulder, took a deep breath, and painted a smile over his suspicions. "Of course. Thank you."

As he made his way through the door, he casually opened up the camera on his phone and slipped it into the chest pocket of his plaid button-down shirt. He pulled his jacket over the pocket.

"Mr. Zack Nolan, it is so nice to meet you," Dr. Navarro-Cruz greeted him with an outstretched hand and a smile that seemed to defy the confines of her face. "Please, follow me. I just need to ask you a few questions. I'm very curious about life in a SAC."

They took a seat in a small interview room. After tapping and scrolling on a tablet, she began to pepper him with questions. He watched her eyes, and when she was peering into the screen, he carefully pulled his jacket open just enough to uncover the camera lens.

"You said people looked to you for advice in the SAC. How often would you say that happened?"

"I suppose on a weekly basis. More often as winter approached or when we were battered by storms."

"What kind of energy projects did you work on?"

"We basically had some solar and windmills, but in the woods that could be pretty limited. I developed a small-scale hydroelectric system that used small turbines in rivers and streams to supplement our power."

"Interesting! That sounds very innovative. You were also a hunter?"

"We have to eat, and not many SAC folks are vegans, at least not in the mountains. We ate mostly wild game like deer and fowl."

"I bet that made you popular."

"Hungry folks loved me," he said in an attempt at some levity.

"Did you ever receive any communications, instruction, or assistance from a group known as 'the Sparrows'?"

This was where he suddenly hated being a ginger. His pale face involuntarily flushed red, as if trying to match his hair. How much honesty should he offer here? What was on the line? It may also be an opportunity to do his own research.

"Sparrows? I thought you were researching the needs of former SAC residents?" he said, tactically turning the interview back on her.

"We are, and we have found that many SAC residents received guidance and assistance from an informal group known as 'the Sparrows.' We'd just like to know a bit more. In your SAC, did you receive any communications, instruction, or assistance from the Sparrows?"

"May I ask why this is relevant to the research?" Zack said.

"We just want to know how we can better help former SAC residents adjust to their lives in an urban environment. As a leader, or at least a respected member of a SAC, you understand the difficulty of the transition for SAC residents," Dr. Navarro-Cruz said, staring back at him with a new, hardened look.

"It seems to me you may be more interested in the Sparrows than the SAC residents, but then again, you already know that many SAC residents are Sparrows. They are just harder to pin down," Zack said, returning the stare.

"Are you willing to answer the question?" she asked.

"Did we have contact with the Sparrows? Nearly every SAC had contact with the Sparrows. Their communications, advice, instruction, and technical assistance made the SACs healthier, more successful, and more sustainable than ever. The straggling remnants of those who fled to the hills during the Transition just wouldn't crumble on their own, especially after the Sparrows, so that is when CAMO suddenly needed our land, and we were forcibly removed. Even then, the Sparrows helped save the lives of countless people as they were rounded up and dumped off in the streets of the nearest city. Let's be honest, here, shall we?" Zack said, by now struggling not to bare his teeth.

"That is all I want," she said, crossing her arms in an unsettling look of triumph.

"The Sparrows have only ever advocated for the sanctity of life, equality, and dignity. Where there was suffering, they sought to relieve it. Where there was danger, they warned us. Where there was scarcity, they gave us the knowledge we needed to overcome. At no point have the Sparrows ever advocated any kind of resistance to the New American or Regional governments. They are only guilty of speaking the truth, and it is only a threat to those who don't.

"Did we get help from the Sparrows? Not only did they help us, but we joined them in helping others. I am committed to protecting people's lives, treating everyone equally, and fighting for the dignity of every human being. I am committed to telling the truth. Am I a Sparrow myself?" he ended with a flourish, pulling up his sleeve and baring his Sparrow tattoo just above his wrist. "You're damn right I am!"

Chapter 10: **Train to Nowhere**

"JUDE! JUDE!" ZARA YELLED from the screens. "They took Zack."

"What happened?" he said, running up to the monitors and scanning the now blank screen.

"He was talking to an HHS agent. She asked if he was a SAC leader, and he admitted he helped people out. That got him an interview with a psychologist, who started asking him about Sparrows. Zack saw the writing on the wall, and he started firing right back. 'Why do you want to know about the Sparrows? What do they have to do with former SAC residents?' He may have gotten a little carried away. An NADF officer came in just after he finished a small tirade about what the Sparrows stand for and why he is one. He even showed them his tattoo."

"Well, now we know what they are really looking for. How long did his stream last?" Jude asked.

"About two seconds after the NADF officer took it out of his pocket," Zara said. "I saved the footage and told Chiela. She's going to scrub the streaming trail so ADAMS can't link it to us."

"We need to get the word out. The government is using the reception centers to screen for Sparrows, and Sparrows are being targeted," Jude said, running his fingers through his hair and thinking on his feet. "Let's be honest and try not to cause a panic. Tell people they can sign up for their benefits; they will need them. Until we know more about how and why Sparrows are being targeted, people should not volunteer any information."

"I've already got my tag line: 'Sparrows don't make a peep.' I wish Zack had followed that plan," Zara sighed.

"He went there to find out what they were up to, and now we know. He accomplished his mission. Now we just need to follow his trail somehow.

Keep an ear out. He'll find a way to contact us. In the meantime, I need to talk to Athalia."

After getting Max up to date, it was time to talk strategy.

"I knew it was coming, and now we have an idea where it is coming from. Connor stamped out the SACs, and now he's going after the Sparrows. We free-thinking individuals who question the official story are dangerous," Max said.

"We're also slippery," Jude added. "It's one thing to send in the NADF and round up a SAC, but it's quite another to find us in the cities. It's like rounding up ants in a field."

"Ants with stingers," Max said with a smile, holding up a production model from Jude's prototype. "I hope you don't mind. A friend of mine made some material modifications. He took your specs and used a polymer that can be 3D printed and still handle the blast of the cartridge. It might degrade after 100 or so shots, but we can make a zillion of these for 1/10 the cost of your metal prototype."

"Max, you missed your calling as an arms dealer. I'm glad you work with us."

"Thanks, but you and Zara still need to figure out how to get these things in people's hands."

"I think they would make great gifts, don't you? With some innovative packaging, drone delivery, and a 'nest-based' distribution system, I think we can pull it off," Jude said.

It was pitch black, but Zack could tell he was on some kind of high-speed train, maybe even a SEMIC line. The sound was muffled, but it still resembled the feel of building up speed and then hitting a smooth stride like when the tunnel seals and it goes supersonic. His navy blue jumpsuit, no doubt outfitted with sew-in trackers, also came with a complementary blindfold. His video stream didn't last long after the NADF guy came in, but it should have been enough for Zara to know what went down.

If he had to guess, he and an unknown number of other Sparrows and NADF lackeys were seated in a modified freight container on a SEMIC train, hence the muffled experience. That was a smart move; the NADF could quickly whisk their victims away with the convenience of a SEMIC train but without anyone in the passenger cars having any idea.

His sarcasm once again gained him a grain of intel; when he asked for "the video brochure about their once-in-a-lifetime destination," he got one soldier to chuckle and say, "When you get to the Farm, you'll have what's left of your lifetime to explore all its amenities." It sounded pretty ominous, but at least Zack had an idea of what they were up to. He tried to start preparing himself for physical and psychological torture. He needed to decide ahead of time what he could say and what he would never give up.

"If his phone is fired up, it will ping somewhere," Chiela said. "But that tells us where the phone is, not Zack. He was taken from Atlanta. That's all we know. I'm pretty good, but I need more than that. I'm sorry."

"She's right," Jude said to Zara. "We need more. We need boots on the ground. There isn't much we can do here in the bunker."

"What are you getting at? Don't you dare talk about surrendering to the NADF," Zara warned him. "We talked about that."

"We agreed it would lead to an immediate arrest. Maybe that's what we need. Maybe the only way for us to find out what the NADF is up to is to show up and get arrested."

"Are you insane?" Zara angrily retorted. "I know you want to be a hero, but it's not just about you!" she said, breaking down in tears. "I can't lose you. I just . . . I can't even think about that."

"Well then we better make sure we can always find him," Chiela chimed in. "I have an idea."

They both looked at her with wide eyes. When a genius hacker on your side has an idea, you pay attention.

"They know the Sparrows are hard to nail down, so they're going for the leaders. Why else do you think they have a small army of psychologists doing benefit interviews at Health and Human Services? They don't care about social work. They have profiles, and they're sifting through the masses for leaders. When they find one, especially if he admits an undying loyalty to the Sparrows, they've hit paydirt. I'd bet good money they are giving them a one-way ticket to somewhere, bypassing jails, judges, and the press. If Zack was taken by an NADF officer, it's probably a secret military facility."

"Dear God, Chiela!" Zara exclaimed, looking again through teary eyes at Jude.

"Listen," she continued, "Right now they want intel, and if they have any more nefarious plans, they won't put those into play until they have what they want."

"What do they want?" Zara asked.

"A list," Jude answered. "They want the Sparrows."

"Exactly, which is why we need to find this place," Chiela said.

"And then what? Form an army that can take on the New American Defense Forces?" she said, still salty about Jude's possible involvement.

"Of course not. Sparrows don't fight. They fly," Jude said with a knowing smile.

"I really wish I had a clue what you two were talking about," Zara huffed.

"I can track Jude, or whoever surrenders to the NADF," Chiela explained, choosing her words with more sensitivity. "I can find this place, do some recon with satellite feeds, and do a security assessment, at least on the outside."

"And I can assess the inside and get you the intel. When we have the location and full security assessment, we call in an extraction team," Jude said,

"What extraction team?" Zara asked.

"That's what I need to work on next," Jude said.

Zara swallowed her urge to protest. She noticed something for the first time: Jude was channeling his anger at the injustice into real leadership actions. She hated the real danger he was in, remembering the gaping pit in her stomach when they were in jail last time, unsure if they would ever see each other again. But she also saw him slowly transforming his response from reaction and then reluctance to planning and determination. He was unwittingly beginning to step into his destiny. It was going to take courage for both of them.

"Then get busy," she said. "We're going to need people who know what they're doing. You'll need to be gone before the NADF even knows the cage is open."

Jude smiled and kissed her head. "You can help me. Put the word out with the nest leaders that we think the Sparrows are being profiled and the NADF is after the leaders. Let them know we are working on a plan, and we need people with prior military experience, especially in COATS."

"Trust me. I can find people who know what they're doing, but what about the other eager volunteers? There are a lot of good-meaning people out there with a lot more time on their hands than skills. They are looking for adventure and purpose. What do I do with them?" Zara asked.

"Give them a purpose!" Jude said, chuckling.

"Seriously, Jude What do I do with them?"

"I suppose if we need special operations, it wouldn't hurt to have foot soldiers backing them up. I'll talk to Max. Maybe we can come up with a training program in nonviolent resistance, observation, and citizen assistance. They can be an 'army of helpers.' How can the government find fault with that? We can give them a hat or small insignia. We can call them 'Sparrow Soldiers.' They can be an army of community volunteers, but they can also be a source of intelligence. It will be fantastic PR for the Sparrows, a major distraction for the NADF while we plan our rescue, and it will drive President Connor absolutely crazy."

"Did you just think of all that?" Zara asked.

"More or less," Jude admitted.

"It actually sounds pretty good. Do you think Max will go for it?"

"Max needs to be in charge of something. It's in his DNA."

"What is in my DNA?" Max bellowed as he came around a corner playing with a new 3-D printed stinger.

Jude smiled and put his arm around Max's shoulders. "Max, I have an idea, and you are the only man for the job. How does being the leader of a 'Sparrow Army' sound to you?"

There were a dozen or so ways Jude could present himself to the NADF, but he decided to follow in Zack's footsteps. He was more likely to follow Zack's path and hopefully end up in the right location if he started in the same place. He boarded his SEMIC train from Kansas City to Atlanta, breezing through the checkpoints with his Passport. Chiela truly was a genius; his tracker was embedded inside his Passport, which of course was implanted between his neck and shoulder.

"Good morning," Jude said as he approached an open counter at the reception center.

"Good morning, sir," the smiling Health and Human Service agent said. "How can I help you?"

"I'm not sure if there is much you can do, but I heard if I answer some questions the right way, I can earn a free session with a psychologist." He almost regretted his snarky tone. After all, the agent was just doing her job, and she had nothing to do with the government's strategy to sift out the Sparrows.

"Well, that depends . . . " she fumbled, as if remembering her script. "Are you a former member of a Sustainable Agricultural Community?"

"Yes, in fact, he was," came a strong male voice from behind Jude, causing him to spin around. The sight of the NADF officer in crisp dress blues took him by surprise, at least this quickly.

"I'll take it from here," he told the agent. "Mr. Kane, we were expecting you. Will you come with me please?"

Jude rewound the recording of his past few days in his mind, trying to think of how the NADF already knew where he was going to be, and getting anxious about what they already might know.

"How was the trip from Kansas City?" the officer asked as they left the lobby and headed down an innocuous-looking hallway.

"The Passport!" he muttered to himself. He almost completely forgot he passed through the scanners in Kansas City and Atlanta, practically announcing his arrival. "My trip was uneventful," he said, finally answering the officer's question. "At least so far."

They turned a few corners, came to an elevator, and the officer pushed the down button.

"May I ask where we are going?" Jude said.

"Oh yes, you may ask," the officer said, flashing a smile, but not elaborating.

"Let me guess: I can ask, but you can't say," Jude said.

"You are very smart, just like your profile says," the officer chuckled. "I can give you a few details if you give me some information in return."

"Sure thing," Jude said confidently. "What do you want to know?"

"Where is the Sparrow Headquarters?" he asked.

That hit a little close to home, but Jude was ready.

"It sounds like you think the Sparrows are some mercenary group or political insurgents. You have the wrong idea. We don't oppose the New American Government; we want to live in peace. We are simply a group of people who share similar ideals like equality, dignity, and the sanctity of life. When we see injustice, we speak out, but we don't have a standing army."

"You didn't answer my question."

Jude smiled and didn't miss a beat. "It's in our minds and hearts. We are regular people, many of us adjusting to a new life in the cities. We have friends, family, and community both online and in neighborhoods. Headquarters is right here," he concluded, patting his chest over his heart.

The elevator dinged, and the doors opened. The officer followed Jude in and pushed a button for the basement.

"Your turn. What can you tell me about where you are taking me and other suspected Sparrow leaders?"

The officer smiled again, always coy as if carefully choosing each nugget of information for the maximum effect. "Since many of you have recently left your rural settings, we felt you might want to spend time on a farm."

The elevator stopped, dinged, and the doors opened again, revealing two NADF soldiers with zip ties ready to shackle Jude.

"A farm, you say?" Jude said, raising his eyebrow and shooting a look at the officer. "Am I being arrested?" The soldiers secured his hands but stopped short when the officer ordered them not to tie his feet.

"Leave his feet; he's not going anywhere. Don't worry, Mr. Kane, you are not being arrested. This is a matter of national security, not law enforcement. You're taking a trip with us to the farm. Some of us call it the Last Farm."

After a dark ride in what Jude surmised to be modified cargo container on a SEMIC train, he felt them being lifted and set down on something with wheels, and they were driven for what seemed like several hours. When the group finally came to a stop, they were herded out of the end of the long, thin shipping container, and then soldiers were ordered to remove their blindfolds. Jude would have noticed the blindfolds matched the navy-blue jumpsuits, except the blistering sun temporarily blinded all of them. Jude guessed they must be somewhere in the desert in Texico. It was impossibly flat, brown, and devoid of anything Jude would consider actual vegetation, let alone a real tree.

The men were directed toward a large, single-story concrete building that looked to be part of an old military complex, likely a base built long before the Transition and used by the old United States Army or possibly Air Force. Jude saw the entire facility was encircled with a straggled wire fence which was topped with a rusty, twisted razor wire that fell loose and tangled in many places.

The rooms they were ushered into showed their age, but the door locks were new. Clearly, this facility was hastily re-purposed for whatever this Sparrow-finding effort was, but the fact that such resources were put into it made Jude pause a moment to think about the impact of the Sparrows. They somehow were a threat to the Federal Government of New America. They either did not understand how powerless the Sparrows were, or they understood better than Jude how dangerous their ideas were to a government that had yet to reinstate the protections of the old Constitution of the United States.

"Jude Kane!" came a sharp call from an officer, startling him as he was getting the lay of his room. "Evidently, you are a VIP. I'm to give you a short tour before taking you to see the top brass."

"I am flattered," he muttered, holding out his hands for the zip ties.

"Those won't be necessary here."

They walked the corridor of old bunk rooms, exited the building into the sunlight once again, and took a short drive in a four-person electric personnel cart to another building. Immediately Jude could recognize the cries of pain before the officer opened the door.

While being cautious and admittedly intimidated, nothing melted his gut like the howls of pain he heard emanating from the rooms. Each room was similar to the dorms, but clear of any furniture except for sometimes a single chair in the middle of the bare, tiled floor, and whatever tools were being used.

"We try to be organized around here," the officer said, leading Jude down the hall and stopping at a window looking into the room where the loudest cries were coming from. A young man in his mid-twenties was strapped to a metal chair, stripped of all but a pair of boxer shorts, and drenched in perspiration. It was hard to tell if he was doused intentionally with water or just covered in his own sweat.

"It's very easy, pal. Just make me a list. We know you are a leader. Give us a list of names, and this all stops. You don't even have to name your own family. Just give me a list of ten leaders or twenty confirmed Sparrow supporters, and I turn this off."

They both eyed the electrical box. As if to emphasize that it was in fact still powered on, the interrogator clicked the terminals together, sending out flashes and spewing sparks all over the young man's legs.

The young man took a deep breath and paused when he saw Jude, recognizing him. He cracked a smile, looked at the interrogator, and said dryly, "Sparrows don't make a peep."

"So unfortunate," the officer casually remarked over the screams and convulsions of the young man. "Would you like to see more?"

"None of this is necessary."

"You can explain that to General Alvarado. He's waiting for you in his lab. He has fine-tuned his interrogation techniques. I think even you will be impressed— if you survive."

Part Two

Chapter 11: **End of the Line**

"THERE IS A VIDEO posted on 'Unofficial' that says it was sent in anonymously for the Sparrow Press. Can you check it out for me?" Zara asked. "I like what they have to say, but you never know what might be embedded."

"No problem," Chiela said. "I'll look at the code."

"While you do that, I'm going to check in with our team. Now that we know where Jude is, we need to get some eyes out there and get ready."

"Sure thing. I'll see if I can get some satellite pictures to help them get an idea of what we're dealing with," Chiela said.

Chiela began scanning the video and then quickly took it off her screen. Fortunately, Zara didn't notice. She got up casually and told Zara, "I'm going to get a cup of coffee. Want anything?"

"I'm ok, thanks," she said.

Chiela passed the coffee maker and ducked into a room.

"Max," she harshly whispered into her phone, "I need your help. We got a video message, and we need to look at it, but we can't let Zara see it."

"Why not?" he asked.

"It's Jude. I didn't see much, but it looks bad. I think he is being tortured."

"I'll be right down."

"Jude Kane, leader of the Sparrows," General Alvarado said, acknowledging him as he was escorted into the lab and directed to sit in a reclining chair that may have come from a dentist's office.

"You must be General Alvarado," Jude responded. "I've read about your success in breaking up the cartels."

"I've heard quite a bit about you as well, but it is mostly rumors and whispers as if you only existed in the shadows. But alas, here you are in the flesh."

"I am perplexed as to why I seem to be deemed such a threat to national security. The Sparrows are a group of ordinary people, many former SAC residents, who are only bound by a set of common ideals. We have no army, no agenda, and no opposition to the New American government, yet here I sit with the New America Defense Chief himself. We are in a facility that I'm sure doesn't officially exist, and we are facing detention, interrogation, and torture. I assure you, General Alvarado, this is entirely unnecessary."

"You make a coherent case, Mr. Kane, but I must disagree. What we are doing here is preserving the peace and stability that was fought for a won after the Transition. President Connor understands something many leaders don't: countries fall from within. Any tolerance of dissent quickly festers into rebellion. Your ideals, Mr. Kane, are far more of a threat than even you understand."

"The sanctity of human life is a threat? Dignity and equality are a threat? We're not even addressing civil liberties or the still-suspended Constitutional rights that were promised after the Transition. It seems to me, General Alvarado, the only threat we are facing is the loss of the world's greatest democracy."

"Thank you, Mr. Kane, for confirming we have detained exactly the right person," the General said, adjusting some switches and dials on a boxy-looking contraption about the size of two shoe boxes.

"Is that a battery charger?" Jude asked.

"It was. I have made a few modifications."

With a nod from Alvarado, two soldiers began fastening restraints on Jude's arms and legs.

"You really like to tie up loose ends," Jude quipped.

"Do you know where you went wrong, Mr. Kane?" Alvarado asked, ignoring his attempt at levity.

"I've never opposed the government or led a rebellion. What have any of us done wrong?" he asked.

"You made an enemy of President Connor. He was patient; he allowed the SACs to continue for years before you came along. They were slowly breaking apart and dissipating into the history books until you and your Sparrows reversed their downward trajectory. That was strike one.

Next, you humiliated him with your little tantrum about your brother, and that was strike two. Finally, and probably most importantly, your 'Sparrow Press' has managed to carve out a loyal following and erode the public's confidence in official news sources. This is the biggest affront to President Connor's authority. He doesn't want anyone else telling his story. That's why he hired me."

"The cameras are ready, sir," one of the soldiers informed Alvarado. "The feed is live."

"Good. Mr. Kane, since I like to film my experiments for research purposes, I decided to share my work with a live online audience. You Sparrows are quite slippery, but we have managed to target this feed to the Sparrow Press, where your wife will undoubtedly be watching, as well as your 'Nest' leaders throughout the regions, and of course, your friends here with us. The thing about Sparrows, Mr. Kane, is that although they are quick and nimble, they are also very fragile and vulnerable."

Alvarado flipped a switch, and Jude screamed and convulsed under his restraints, his veins protruding and sweat piercing through his skin almost immediately. Alvarado flipped off the switch, and Jude laid his head back, panting and moaning, trying to regain feeling in his extremities.

"I'm just getting you loosened up, Jude," he said, slipping into a more familiar and insidious tone. Inflicting physical pain is only part of a successful persuasion strategy. I like to integrate sensory disruption and psychological terror. It's my special recipe."

"Your encouragement editorial was beautiful, Gavin," Max said on the phone. "It was exactly what we all needed to hear."

"Thank you, sir," Gavin Hollins said. "I think I was talking to myself as much as everyone else from the SACs. Moving from the farm to Richmond was an adjustment, and to be honest, my daughter has been my biggest help."

"I'm impressed by you both. You lost as much as anyone, and the fact that you refuse to give in to anger and bitterness speaks volumes," Max said.

"Thank you, sir."

"You don't have to call me sir, Gavin," Max said with a chuckle. "It's not like I'm your commanding officer."

"Well, you are behind the Sparrow Army I hear."

Max suddenly froze as a thought rushed into his mind.

"Max, are you still there?" Gavin asked.

"Yes! Sorry, Gavin, I just had a thought," he admitted.

"It sounds like I should leave you to it, then. You're a busy guy."

"Exactly, Gavin. That is my thought. I have developed a training program for the Sparrow Army, but I don't think I'm the right guy to lead them. I think you are."

"Me? Gavin gasped. "But I can't, I mean, I'm not . . . ."

"Before you protest, Max interrupted, "take at least seventy-two hours to meditate on it, talk to your daughter, and speak with a few trusted members of your Nest. Remember: this is about helping people, not fighting. If you aren't the man for the job, just let me know."

Jude's breathing finally started to slow to a less desperate pant as Alvarado mumbled to staffers and pointed at various tubes, vials, and supplies. It was at this point in his fog of pain that Jude noticed the General and his assistants were wearing lab coats over their uniforms. The electrical clamps were gone. He was tempted to sigh in relief.

Alvarado screwed a needle onto a syringe and inserted it into a small vial, pulling the plunger and filling it with a clear liquid.

"I don't suppose that is . . . morphine," Jude managed to breathe out in what was left of his raspy voice.

"No, I'm afraid not," Alvarado said, flicking the syringe. "But after this, you won't be as worried about your physical pain."

Feeling around Jude's forearm, Alvarado found a vein and stuck the needle in. He slowly emptied its contents and removed the needle.

"Give it a few minutes. I'll be right back."

Jude was as confused as he was terrified. He wouldn't be worried about physical pain? What was this concoction? What was he waiting for? He thought about the old controversies about lethal injections gone wrong back in the early 21st century, but he was certain that General Alvarado had no intention of letting him go quietly into the night. Inflicting pain was the goal, and now he waited to see what kind of pain was coming. His thinking slowed, and a fog seemed to roll into his head and cloud his mind. In his dreamy state, he started hearing voices and picking out bits of conversation. None of it made sense. How could his family be in the room?

"Jude, sweetheart," he heard his mother say, "It's time for the Sparrows to come to an end. The SACs are gone, and there is no reason to continue to oppose the government. It will just make it hard for everyone."

"Mom?" Jude moaned.

"Jude," Callum chimed in. "She's right. You're going to get us all in big trouble. We better just let this Sparrow thing go."

"Callum? What are you saying?" Jude asked. How were they there? Why would they be turning their backs on the Sparrows? Were they trying to protect him?

"Son," his father began. "It's not about you and your pride anymore. Let the Sparrows go, or Zara will suffer."

"Dad, what do you mean Zara . . . will suffer?" Jude stammered. He was confused by their voices. He saw figures standing over him, but his vision was blurry. How was his family in the room?

"Zara will suffer for your stubbornness," his dad said in a booming voice. Rod had never spoken to him like that before. Was his dad wearing a white coat?

"What do you . . . mean?" he slurred.

"Stop! Please stop!" a woman yelled. His dad, looming and blurry, had a young woman by the arm. She screamed, and he heard Zara's voice. "Stop! Please! Jude, just make them stop!"

"Zara?" he said. "How are you here?"

"Never mind that, Jude! Just make them stop!"

"What . . . what are they doing to you?" In his fog, Jude was vaguely aware that things were not adding up; he saw and heard his family and Zara, but they were not clear, their voices were slightly off, and most of all their character was not present. Where was the righteous anger? Where was the stubborn defiance? At the most human level, he knew his family. He knew his wife. Their forms and voices were there, but their essence was missing. Unable to think clearly about much else, Jude shut his eyes and let out a frustrated growl.

"Not today . . . . General. Your actors are fine . . . and your drugs are powerful . . . but you are nothing like my father. You don't know my family."

General Alvarado nodded to the girl whose arm he had in his grasp, dismissing her and the others. He looked into Jude's unfocused eyes and let out a sigh. "I am impressed. You have an unusually firm constitution. I'm going to have to reevaluate my strategy with you."

"Sorry for . . . spoiling your plans," Jude said, clinging to a shred of sarcasm.

"Oh, don't apologize, young man. I welcome the challenge! I have been looking for an opportunity to continue my research, but unfortunately, so many of my subjects don't last."

"I'm happy I can be of help. See? We Sparrows are always trying to help," Jude said with a tired smirk.

"Yes, I see," Alvarado said, clearly no longer amused. "We're going to let the medication clear out of your system tonight so we can start fresh tomorrow."

"What are they doing to him?" Zara demanded, springing into the control room.

"Nothing you need to see," Chiela said, turning off the screen. "Besides, they're giving him a break right now."

"How bad is he?" she asked, letting slip an air of worry through her toughened façade.

"He's ok for now," Max said, taking over. "But we need to get him out of there. Let's focus on that."

"Agreed."

"I've put Gavin in charge of the Sparrow Army. They're not fighters, of course, but that will free me up to focus on Jude. Did you find anyone who can help us find this "Last Farm"?

"I've only got nine, but they are good," Zara explained. "They are better than good: they're former military— NADF and even old US military—and they all have a big problem with what the NADF has been up to lately. They are briefed on what we know so far, and they are ready to roll. We just need to see if Chiela has a lock on the location of the farm yet."

"I've done better than that. Jude's tracker did its job, so I took the coordinates and I got into CAMO's databases to cross-check what this place is. The more we know, the better, right? It looks like they marked it as a defunct old Texas Air National Guard base from before the Transition. Texico Regional Defense Forces never used it, and the NADF has not officially taken it over, but satellite pictures show some new activity: vehicles, temporary buildings, fencing, and some supplies, but no evidence of aircraft or heavy weapons. I think this is our spot."

"What's our next move, Max?" Zara asked. "What's the fastest way to get our team inside the fence?"

"I think we should let the NADF do all the work. If the Nine surrender at their closest reception center, all they have to do is follow Zack and Jude's example. That will earn them an express ticket straight to the Farm and inside the walls," Max reasoned.

"That gets them inside, but they are going to need weapons and supplies to get Jude out. They can't exactly pack a bag for the trip," Zara said.

"No, but they will have the advantage of knowing what they are getting into, what to look for, and how the NADF operates, and the NADF won't know any of that," Max said.

"I've sent them new Passports with trackers like Jude had and a new ID profile that conveniently leaves out any record of their military service. The NADF won't see them coming," Chiela said.

"I'm still worried we're sending them in naked," Zara said. "This is the NADF we're talking about. We can't just get them in there and hope for the best."

"You found good men. When you brief them, let them know that getting in and getting to Jude is Phase One. Once inside, we'll initiate Phase Two, and it will be clear when and what to do.

"What the heck is Phase Two?" Zara asked incredulously.

"Leave that to me," Max said.

Simply known as "The Nine," Zara's volunteers agreed to use a simple hand signal to identify each other inside the Last Farm. An open palm with all five fingers extended is clear enough, but when they tucked in one thumb, the subtle move takes the fingers down to four on one hand. When you put them together, you had an innocuous but hard-to-confuse sign of solidarity.

It took time for the Nine to surrender themselves in their respective reception centers, but after three days, all of them finally filtered into the camp. General Alvarado was growing steadily more impatient with his victims, stepping up the torture sessions on a rotating basis. It seemed that the presence of Jude only emboldened his prisoners and hardened their resolve. Also, with more new prisoners, more time was passing between torture sessions, only increasing their stamina.

Alvarado decided the best way to accomplish his goal of breaking the spirit of the Sparrows was to cut off their head. Jude needed to die, but it had to be slow, terrifying, and gruesome. It had to be something that would not only imprint on their minds but scar them and instill a terror that would suppress any noble attempts to revive the movement for a generation. It had to be ugly.

Slightly groggy but rested and fully aware of his plight, Jude was brought back to the lab. He was strapped into his dentist's chair, but this time it was adjusted so he could sit straight up.

"I'm not a fan of the dentist, and these sessions are not helping," Jude said.

"I see you still have your humor. I am not amused," Alvarado shot back.

"Believe it or not, I'm not attempting stand-up comedy as some kind of act of defiance or disrespect. It is a coping mechanism. I guess I'm trying to stay human as long as possible," Jude explained.

"That is a refreshing piece of honesty, Mr. Kane. I will reciprocate. You asked why we are employing enhanced interrogation techniques, and I will tell you. For your colleagues, it is for the more practical purpose of locating and rooting out as many of your leaders as we can, but it also serves as good old-fashioned intimidation. In your case, however, I have a different purpose."

"What good is it doing for you to inflict pain on me? I have nothing to prove. I'm a normal, average man who will scream and writhe just as much as anyone else. What does it accomplish?"

"Again, Mr. Kane, you are underselling yourself. You are the leader of the Sparrows, and you not only symbolize rebellion; you embody it. My purpose is to kill you as painfully and traumatically as possible. I want to cut off the head of the snake and drive away any notion of resistance, at least for a generation or two."

"Have you considered the possibility that this could have the opposite effect?" Jude asked.

"I hardly think that is possible. I killed the cartels; I think I can handle a few misguided civilians with too much time on their hands. Do you really think you can inspire a movement after your death?"

"Certainly not! But a long time ago, there was this one guy who pulled it off, and the Sparrows are fans of his ideas."

"We'll see," he huffed. "Remove his shirt and lay him flat. It's time for surgery."

General Alvarado snapped on his latex gloves, pulled over a stainless-steel tray of instruments, and took a deep breath. "Let's start with the appendix. You don't need it anyway." He took a scalpel, pressed gently on the lower right side of Jude's abdomen, and then plunged it into his skin.

"Aaaah!" screamed Jude, convulsing under the restraints.

"Now Jude," Alvarado calmly, "the more you move, the more it will hurt. Try to stay still."

Jude raised his head and shot a crazed look at Alvarado, but when the tormentor stared back and smiled slightly, Jude saw his fate.

"Aaaah!" Jude screamed again as Alvarado slipped his hand in, took hold of the appendix, and crudely severed it from his body. He tossed it into a metal pan, smiled, and declared, "Now that ugly thing is out of the way."

As Jude lay moaning loudly, the door to the lab burst open, and several men instantly surrounded them with rifles drawn.

"Move another muscle, and you'll look worse than him."

Zack Nolan was a hunter; this was no idle threat.

Chapter 12: **Front Page News**

IT WAS HARD TO describe the exact nature of the look in General Alvarado's eyes. Always in absolute control, he was frozen in disbelief, anger, and confusion.

"What the hell is this?" He scoffed. "Some kind of rebellion? Ha! You won't live past the next hour."

"We're not Sparrows. We're veterans, US Military and NADF, and we're here because you forgot what your mission is. This butchery is the kind of thing we fought against. It ends right here," said Number One, zip-tying Alvarado's hands and then wiping the blood from them with a cloth. "You're being detained, General."

The Nine decided in their haste to identify each other by numbers. Besides anonymity, numbers were clearer and more precise in high-pressure situations.

"We need a medic now!" Zack ordered, placing a cloth over Jude's wound. "Is there anyone that can give Jude something for his pain and sew up this hack job?"

"Number Three can do it, but he's watching the doors. We don't have time. We've got to get out of here before the rest of the base figures out what we're up to."

"I'll spot Number Three," Number Four said, shouldering his rifle and running out of the room.

"You," Zack said, pointing to one of Alvarado's assistants who also played the part of Zara for Jude's failed hallucinogenic session. "Go with these men and find us some NADF uniforms." The assistant looked at Alvarado, and he nodded.

"Go ahead, Lieutenant," he said. "They'll all be dead soon anyway."

"You," he said, pointing to the other assistant, "get Number Three what he needs: sutures, gauze, gloves, and for the love of God some kind of anesthesia."

Alvarado nodded again, and he did as he was ordered.

"Max!" shouted Zara as she hovered over Chiela, watching the trackers move like ants tripping over themselves in a single spot.

"Zara!" Chiela said, covering her ear. "My ears are right here."

"Sorry," Zara said. "Are you ready for Phase 2?"

"Yes, ma'am," he said, snapping to attention as he came in from the warehouse.

"Great! Now, what is Phase 2 exactly?"

"Stingers," Max said with a smile. "And a few other supplies. I have a few drones on their way now."

"Good. Now explain to me how the guys inside are going to get their hands on the Stingers being dropped outside the fence?" Zara asked.

Max smiled knowingly again. "Have you ever heard of the Cheyenne Mountain Complex?"

"Yes. It's the most secure military base in New America. It's basically under a mountain in the southern end of the Dakota Region."

"Do you know who gets in there?"

"No one, except people with very special badges."

"And food delivery services. Everyone needs to eat."

Zara smiled and nodded approvingly. "The drones are going to the kitchen."

"NADF Food Services is very efficient. I got a hold of a few of their drone-sized shipping containers and filled them with boxes of typical army dry goods like pasta and cereal. Of course, many of those boxes are hiding our surprise. I put small sparrow stickers on the boxes. I know the Nine will know exactly what to do; I just pray they can get to them."

"Number Three, are we ready to go?" Number One blurted out as he was snipping the stitches and grabbing the roll of gauze. "You can make it look pretty later. We need to roll!"

"We can get moving, but we have to take it easy. He lost a lot of blood, and if he pops any of these stitches, there's nothing to catch the flow," Number Three explained.

"I'll do my best," Jude moaned, gently swinging his feet to the side and slowly sitting up.

"Take a second," Number Three said. "Let the blood get to your head. I don't need you passing out right now."

As the men made their way to the door, prodding Alvarado along, Number Four burst into the room. "We've got company. It looks like a COATS transport is approaching."

"The Cavalry has arrived," General Alvarado said.

"Can we get to the ground transports?" Number One asked.

"Negative. They're landing now, and the rest of the base is already initiating lockdown protocol."

"We have about ninety seconds until you get your introduction to my Critical Operations and Tactical Support team. They truly live up to their name," Alvarado sneered.

"Let's not wait for them to come in with guns blazing," Number One said. "Let's go out and greet them. You first," he said, nudging the General forward.

Numbers Seven, Eight, and Nine managed to get their hands on a few NADF uniforms thanks to the Lieutenant.

"Don't worry, Lieutenant," Number Seven said. "We're here because we don't like this torture and intimidation business. That's not what the NADF stands for. We will not lay a hand on you. You have our word."

"Integrity and honor, imagine that?" she said. "We don't have a lot of uniforms since this is not a 'real' base, but there are a few extras in this closet. The sizes are on the inside collar. You might want to hurry. General Alvarado has likely already called in COATS, and they'll be here in minutes. He has some direct line— I haven't figured it out yet— but he can summon them from anywhere. When they show up, the whole base will go into lockdown."

"How much time do you think we have?" Number Seven asked.

"About ten or fifteen minutes," she said.

The roar of military transport rotors pierced the calm of the supply closet, and they all looked at each other with wide eyes.

"Make that ten or fifteen seconds," the Lieutenant said. "Quick! Get into a uniform and stash your jumpsuits. There's no ID scanning out here, so you can blend in as long as no one recognizes you. I'll take you to the kitchen and hide you there."

"Why are you helping us?" Number Seven said as the three of them scrambled to find pants, shirts, and boots.

"Because you're right," she said. "The NADF shouldn't be torturing anybody, least of all Sparrows. The Sparrows are the only people telling the truth."

Number seven smiled and showed her the hand sign for the Nine. "This is how we identify each other. I'm Number Seven, this is Eight, and he is Nine. If you ever need us, you are number Zero."

"Agreed. Now let's join the lockdown from the kitchen. If anyone says anything, we can just stuff them in the refrigerator."

Number Seven flashed a smile at Eight and Nine. "I like her."

From outside the kitchen, they took up positions and watched the approach of the transport and deployment of COATS. The soldiers wasted no time in securing their stations, and the COATS team streamed into the lab building.

A couple of soldiers made their way into the kitchen and gave Seven, Eight, and Nine some suspicious looks.

"I pulled these guys from transport to watch your six until we know what's going on. The fence back here is in rough shape and it's a weak point," the Lieutenant said.

"Yes, ma'am!" they snapped. "Thank you, Lieutenant!"

As they stood in an uneasy silence, the two kitchen soldiers asked, "Do you guys know what is going on?"

"It looks like COATS is hitting that building over there," Number Seven said. "I don't know why, unless some of the prisoners got out. I haven't seen anything."

"Well, if you see any freight or smaller delivery drones, let us know. We were looking for a few containers before COATS showed up and all hell broke loose."

"You mean like those landing over there?" Number Nine asked, shielding his eyes. He pointed to a half-dozen small delivery drones that dropped NADF delivery totes outside the gate.

"Actually, yes!" one of the soldiers said. "It's about time. It looks like they sent a few extra, and why in the hell are they dropping them outside the gate?"

"Probably because of the lockdown," Number Seven said, shooting a look at Eight and Nine. "Why don't you let us go check it out? You don't want to leave the kitchen area right now."

"Sounds good, thank you," the kitchen soldiers agreed. "Let's hope they sent the burgers. If we have to substitute a plant-based protein again, we may have a mutiny, and then we'll really need COATS around here!" The kitchen soldiers laughed.

Seven, Eight, and Nine made their way to the gate.

"Where are you guys going during a lockdown?" the guards asked.

Number Seven spoke up. "Just our luck, we had a few transports land just after COATS showed up. It looks like they stopped short to stay out of the way. They're right over there," he said, pointing to a clump of bushes partially concealing the six containers.

"Shoot! What are the chances? You'd better go get them. It might be related to the lockdown. We'll cover you. Check them before you bring them in."

"Yes, sir!" they all echoed.

Approaching the containers, they began pulling back the lids and examining the contents.

"Food," Number Eight said. "It looks like the kitchen guys got their wish."

"Hang on," Number Nine said. "Do you see what I see?"

"Is that a Sparrow?" Number Seven said, looking at a cereal box.

Nine pried open the box and let out a muted cry.

"Hot damn! Max came through!" Number Seven said. "Find all the boxes with Sparrows stamped on them. Those are the Stingers."

"Not just Stingers," Number Eight said, opening another box. "I think he threw in a few other goodies. This looks like C4."

"That was a gutsy move. Thank God we got to these containers first," Number Seven said. "Let's get these back to the kitchen before the guards get suspicious."

Before his zip-ties were even cut, General Alvarado took charge of the COATS team.

"I want every one of these men strapped to a chair right here in my lab," he ordered. "I don't care if you have to bring in folding chairs; strap them in. As for this one with the bandages, make him comfortable in the dentist's chair. I want him to watch."

"Yes, sir!" the Team Lead responded. "Get some chairs in here!"

"Commander?" Alvarado asked, rubbing his wrists.

"Yes, sir?"

"There were three more, but they left with one of my Lieutenants. They were looking for uniforms and supplies. Find them."

"Yes, sir!" he responded, pointing to two operatives who immediately sprang into action.

The rest of the COATS team brought in chairs and proceeded to tie down Numbers One, Two, Three, Five, Six, and Zack. Four was brought back in shortly after the rest. The assistant set up the camera, and Alvarado began his narrative.

"I've been told repeatedly that the Sparrows are 'not dangerous' and 'do not oppose the government,' yet here sit six men who entered a military base and attempted to overtake our operations. For you who are the ardent supporters of the Sparrow Press, I want you to see what happens to rebels."

He took out a large scalpel, and then, looking at the camera and rethinking his choice in light of the display he was putting on, he set it down and pulled out his personal hunting knife with its gleaming six-inch blade and inspected it. He then walked over to number one, glanced at Jude to make sure he was looking, and held it to his throat.

"Jude didn't bring us here," Number One said defiantly. "We're veterans who are standing for truth and democracy, the values we swore to uphold when we joined. Threats, torture, and deception are what we fought against, and now here you are inside our own ranks. You're not doing any of this for the NADF; you're doing it for yourself."

Alvarado was slightly taken aback, but not phased. "I do it for my President and my country. We will never go back to the chaos of the Transition." He put the blade back up to Number One's neck, but his hand was shaking. He looked perplexed, and when he tried to steady it, he lost his balance, dropped the knife, and stumbled. Before he could say any more, he let out an inaudible slur and collapsed onto the ground.

The COATS team leader attempted to call out, "General!" but collapsed himself before he could even finish the word. Within ten seconds, the entire COATS team and the assistant fell to the floor, some trying to murmur a final word, and others unable to even get that far.

"Hello, Chaps!" Number Seven greeted the room as Eight and Nine revealed themselves. "We got a present from Max, but we're going to need your help."

Jude smiled for the first time since his ordeal and said hoarsely, "Stingers!"

After they were freed, Zack immediately went over to Jude to check on him. "I'm not going anywhere until you're strong enough to push me away," he said, gripping his shoulder. "How are you feeling?"

"I need a vacation," he said. "And maybe some more pain meds."

"Number One, don't forget we've got a couple more COATS Ops wandering around looking for you guys," Zack reminded them.

"Not anymore," came a female voice from the door.

"What happened?" Zack asked, afraid of her intentions and confused at the same time.

"It's hot. I'm just letting them chill out for a bit," she said, winking at Number Seven. "I've secured the garage where the transports are parked. The rest of you should find a uniform and change. It'll make getting out of here a little easier."

"Video . . . " Jude gasped. "Get Alvarado's video. Zara will know what to do."

"I'll get it," Zack said. After turning the camera around a few times and looking perplexed, the Lieutenant took it from him, opened a compartment, and slipped out a small memory chip.

"Here you go," she said.

"Thanks."

"Sparrow Zero, are you on board? Do you know what this means?" Number Seven asked.

"Yes, sir. I figure I can surrender for my Court Marshall or leave with you and do some good."

"Good to hear," Number One said. We'll regroup on the outside, but for now, you can get Jude and Zack out of here. We'll release the rest of the Sparrows and do some tidying up before we leave."

"How are you feeling, sweetheart?" Zara asked Jude the next day.

"I'm getting there," he said, feeling his incision, "but I'm worried you called me sweetheart."

Zara wound up and punched Jude in his arm.

"Ouch!" he said. "I knew I should be worried!"

"Don't ever scare me like that again."

"Yes, ma'am," he said, and then kissed her softly on the lips.

"I'm so glad you and Zack are back safely, and the rest of the leaders are free, but . . . "

"There's always a 'but,' isn't there?" Jude said.

"Jude, do you know what happened after you got out? Take a look at this."

She pulled up a screen in the Bunker and pulled out a cushioned rolling chair for Jude.

"I got all the disgusting footage from Alvarado and fed it to the right beasts," she said. "But this morning I saw this on Unofficial."

As the screen came up, a bewildered journalist narrated the scene.

"After a few large explosions in the desert of Southwest Texico, drone footage shows the smoldering remains of what appears to be a former Texas Air National Guard Base. It looks to have been somewhat dramatically decommissioned by the NADF, with a COATS Team and regular NADF personnel leaving the facility as it smolders. It's hard to say without an official statement from the NADF yet, but it appears they were on base to dispose of old munitions and anything that could be hazardous to a civilian crew. As to the future of the base, who knows? Maybe it will be turned over to CAMO for use as an agricultural facility or some kind of supply depot."

"What do we do with this, Jude? A lot of Sparrows know about the detention and torture that happened there. People might start thinking of the Sparrows as evolving into some kind of a militia or something!"

"And that is exactly what President Connor and General Alvarado would like. It makes us a lot easier to discredit, target, and eliminate. Let's do what we always do: tell the truth. Explain that we asked for help from some veterans in securing the release of the Sparrows that were being held, tortured, and killed at the 'Last Farm.' After securing our release without hurting or killing a single person, they decided to destroy the facility. The veterans made it clear that they oppose the NADF's actions as veterans, not as Sparrows. The Sparrows support and appreciate our veterans, but they act independently. We remain stubbornly committed to non-violence. Our power lies in our unity: Sparrows fly together."

"Wow, Jude. You can just about do my job now, can't you?" Zara laughed.

"I don't know. We'll have to see how the mainstream media spins this disaster. If enough people see the torture, Connor will lose support. If they try and sell the "decommissioning of an old Air Force Base" story, they may be able to save some face, although a lot of Sparrow Press and Unofficial readers will know what really happened."

"I'm glad you're back," Zara said, giving him a gentle hug.

"Easy!" he hissed, rubbing his incision.

"Oh, sorry!" Zara said. "I'm not used to you being so fragile."

"Me neither. I'm done with this military action business. From now on, I'm going to stick to politics."

Chapter 13: **Disavowed**

"The idea that I sanctioned or even knew about any kind of torture is preposterous. There is no place for that twentieth-century barbarism in New America. The NADF will investigate these allegations and take swift action." President Connor was doing damage control.

His spokesman took over for the official narrative to satisfy the media, but many people saw the videos and knew there was more to the story. "There was an old Texas Air National Guard base in the Texico desert that is being sold to Consolidated Agricultural and Mining, and CAMO will use the facility as a supply depot for remote agricultural and drilling operations. The NADF swept the facility for dangerous military equipment, and CAMO was brought in to dispose of leftover munitions." They followed the script.

It took some effort to secure the communications for the meeting, but Chiela and Zara knew a regroup of Sparrow leaders was critical, and keeping ADAMS out of the loop would be their first line of defense against General Alvarado. He couldn't hit what he couldn't see.

"Welcome to the first meeting of Sparrow Nest Leaders," Zara began from the Bunker near Kansas City. "Don't worry; we've made sure these communications are secure. The American Data Analysis and Measurement Supercomputer can analyze and measure something else," She quipped, trying to dampen the tension. "ADAMS will not be listening."

"Hello, Sparrows!" Jude said, taking over. "We've had an exciting week." He paused, took a deep breath, and looked straight into the monitor. "I know the calculus has changed. I know we are in real danger. That's why I wanted to get us together in real-time. We've got some decisions to make."

"Whatever you want to do, we've got your back, Jude," Zack called out from his screen.

"Thanks, Zack," Jude said. "You'd better check with Athalia, first."

Athalia joined him on the screen and chimed in. "I'm not going to lie, Jude. I wanted to tie him to a chair and tell him he ain't leavin' this house no way again! But the truth is that we all need to have courage. We are not just standing up for principles; we are standing up for our families, our children, and our lives. He's right; we're with you, Jude."

A few others joined in and added their support.

"Thank you, everyone. Zara and I started out just trying to find my brother, and we offered what little help we could give to SACs as we traveled. At some point, the name 'Sparrows' caught on, and we tried to multiply our efforts. The SACs needed as much help as they could get. Eventually, with your help, we were able to get Callum back. Unfortunately, our success did not sit well with the President, who always saw the SACs as not just a concession during the Transition, but a threat to New America.

"The Sparrows have always existed to help people. We have never been a government opposition group, we have never been some kind of guerrilla force, and we certainly are not a military threat. President Connor and his enforcer, General Alvarado, have tried to silence us and eliminate us by force. First, he wiped out the SACs, and then, seeing us as a rebellious extension of the SACs, he targeted the Sparrows directly. What they still don't understand is that we do not operate on that level. We live above them, standing for non-negotiable principles: the sanctity of human life, the equal treatment of all people, and human dignity. We have always been people who speak for those who can't, who defend our rights, and who help each other. We have never been a group that carries guns.

"So, what do we do now that we are clearly targets? Do we need to lay low and stay out of sight, or do we decide to take up arms?" Gavin Hollins asked.

"I'd pick up my guns!" Zack interjected.

"And you'd get killed," Gavin said.

"Exactly," Jude answered them. "Yes, we fight, and no, we don't pick up guns." The confused silence lingered for a few seconds before Zara stepped in.

"I have a reliable source that has told me the video of Alvarado's torture of the Sparrow leaders has backfired. Even without a word from the official news sources, enough people saw it to force the President to refute it in his statement. My source said President Connor told Alvarado to lie low for a while. There is a growing underground news outlet called 'Unofficial' that is rumored to be run by official journalists who are determined to report what is really going on, not just what they are told. Their number one source is the Sparrow Press. We've been so stubborn about telling the truth that people are seeing between the headlines of the official news sources and turning to us!"

Jude took over. "When we were staring down our own demise, we were saved by the Nine, a group of veterans who believed what they read in the Sparrow Press. They took a stand, putting their lives on the line, because they wanted to defend the truth and human rights. I know we feel exposed right now, but hang on to your Stingers and know we have friends.

"This is not the time for us to pick up guns, but it is time for us to fight. It's time to come out of the shadows. It's time for us to acknowledge what we stand for, speak out publicly, and advocate for policies that are in line with our principles. We are not ashamed of what we know to be true, so why are we hiding? President Connor promised to reinstate the Constitution after the Transition, but he has not done it. The Senate has not pushed him to. The Corporate Congress is basically in his pocket. That will be the first stop on this new train: it's time for the Sparrows to stand together and demand that New America reinstate the US Constitution, or rewrite and ratify a new constitution for New America that must include the basic protections we had in the Bill of Rights. If the President opposes us, he is breaking his promise; if he agrees, he sides with us. If he tries to attack us again, we have people's attention. When we stand together, we are a political force."

"This could still be dangerous, Jude," Zack said. "We are pretty outgunned, especially when we don't have guns."

"I'll admit, I've been so focused on political moves that I haven't put together a good security plan. Lucky for us, we have Max," Jude said, stepping away and letting Max jump in.

"Hello, folks. It's good to see so many of us in the same place! I know many of you have concerns, and these concerns are legitimate. I can't guarantee you won't be a target, but we have developed a multi-layer security plan.

"The first thing you can do to protect yourself is simply opt out. Steer clear of the Sparrow Press, don't sign anything, and you will not be a target. If you support the Sparrows, you can sign our petition for the reinstatement of the Constitution. It includes a clear commitment to democratic principles, non-violence, and adherence to the laws of New America, the Regional Governments, and local authorities. I've consulted with a few of my fellow attorneys, and this is iron-clad in court. You can't be convicted of conspiracy if you sign a statement of loyalty to the same government.

"For Sparrow Leaders, we will continue to send more Stingers and cartridges for personal security. The Nine have told me they were highly effective in action, and they are completely non-lethal. They might help you in a sticky situation, Sparrow-related or not.

"Finally, for those of us deciding to become more politically active, the Nine have committed to providing us with security. They will be training additional operatives that they hand-pick, and the Nine will not claim to be part of the Sparrows or any other group so as to protect their anonymity and our innocence in case of any kind of engagement. They can be present at speeches and demonstrations and will function as a rapid-response team if we have any trouble."

"Thanks, Max," Jude resumed. "Remember, folks, non-violence is our real secret weapon. When we continue to speak out and refuse any kind of violence, we win. When we tell the truth, we win. When we stand up for others, we win. We're playing the long game, and violence always loses the long game."

"I need you to stand down for now," President Connor said as General Alvarado reported for their first meeting since the Last Farm effort. "It's not your fault. The Sparrow Press has managed to spread its tentacles and garner a far wider range of support than I realized. Our strategy to cut off the head was too late."

"It sounds like the Sparrows moved from a potential threat to a very real one, Mr. President. We're going to have to demonstrate how they threaten our stability. We need to show people how they are the descendants of the terrorists and anarchists that tore us apart during the Transition, and then we can take them out," Alvarado explained.

"Eventually, we can do that, but they have too much support right now. The Sparrows managed to edit your videos and send them beyond their ranks. People didn't like what they saw. When the Sparrow leaders were rescued by that rag-tag team of veterans, they defeated your team, blew up the base, and then escaped with a convenient narrative and zero body count. At this point, anything we do to the Sparrows will just increase their popularity. We need to ignore them and keep their name out of the public eye."

The meeting concluded with Alvarado agreeing to focus on intelligence and monitoring. When the President asked ADAMS to re-run its threat analysis of the Sparrows, ADAMS explained that their refusal to use any form of violence further confirmed they were not a threat. Even the Nine were not classified as a threat yet because there was so little known about them, they killed no one, and they declared loyalty to the NADF.

As President Connor came to an uncomfortable conclusion that his campaign against the Sparrows had stalled, he had no idea that the Sparrows were about to launch their own campaign and upend his uneasy status quo.

Sparrow Press: Encouragement Editorial
By Rod and Marren Kane

"We the People of the United States, in Order to form a more perfect Union, establish Justice, insure domestic Tranquility, provide for the common defence, promote the general Welfare, and secure the Blessings of Liberty to ourselves and our Posterity, do ordain and establish this Constitution for the United States of America."

Does this sound familiar? For those of us older folks who lived before the Transition, it should. We learned the Preamble to the Constitution in school. We took it for granted. After all, it was written by ancient men hundreds of years ago, and we had lives to start! Since the loss of the SACs, however, those words fall heavily on my heart. Many of us have never set foot on a SAC, but we all witnessed the sudden change of policy, the seizure of private property, the deployment of the military, and the forced relocation of thousands.

What is there to stop the government from making another sudden policy change and upending our lives? What if your Cube was requisitioned by the government without compensation? What if your Universal Basic Income was suddenly slashed? What if your neighborhood was condemned to make way for a park, and instead of paying to relocate you to a comparable area, they simply called in the Regional Defense Forces or the NADF? What could we do to stop it?

The answer is: absolutely nothing. We have continued in the state of a suspended Constitution for years, and President Connor's promise to restore it or replace it with a new version for New America has gone unfulfilled. The Transition has been over for more than ten years now, and the longer we go without protections, the easier it is for the government to ignore them. It is time to stand up and demand the restoration of the American Constitution.

As Sparrows, we value every life, and that should be protected. We value the equal treatment of all people, and that should be protected. We value the dignity of every human being, and that should be protected. We encourage everyone to join us in signing the official petition for the adoption of a New American Constitution that must guarantee the rights that were protected in the original United States Constitution. This petition will be presented to the White House, both Houses of Congress, and the Regional Governors.

Let's take a stand for our fundamental rights while we still can. Will you stand with the Sparrows? Click the link below to sign the official petition. Thank you for your courage!

Rod and Marren Kane
Vancouver, Cascadia

Jude and Zara took a rare liberty and decided to sleep in. Luckily, there were no pressing emergencies, at least not that Chiela or Max thought were worth waking them up for. After stumbling through their morning routine, they joined Chiela in the screen room. While not a grump, she didn't put on a cheery demeanor without due cause, but this morning, she was grinning ear to ear.

"What is the latest?" Zara asked, fishing for a clue.

"Gavin Hollins wants to talk with both of you," she said. "I've got a secure line set up so you can be face-to-face."

"Face-to-face? This sounds serious," Jude said. "I take it that it's good news."

"I'll let him explain," Chiela said.

"Good morning, Gavin!" Jude said. "How are things in Richmond?"

"We are holding our own," he said. "The Sparrow Army is busy. I didn't realize how busy we'd be, but we've got teams all over the city. We're doing everything from weeding gardens to babysitting to fixing damaged Cubes. So far, the government has left us alone."

"That is good to hear," Zara said. "So, what is this good news? I'm dying to know."

"I think people took your call to action to heart, at least I know my daughter Janie did. She's been studying politics and history nonstop for months now, and when you presented the Petition for the Reinstatement of the Constitution, she went into overdrive. Signing the petition was not enough. She's decided to run for one of the Regional Senate seats here in Appalachia."

"That's amazing!" Zara said. "Is she going to publicly identify with the Sparrows?"

"Her campaign slogan is 'Life is valuable, equality is essential, and dignity is for all people.' Sound familiar?" Gavin said. "She promises to not only support the Petition for the Reinstatement of the American Constitution, but she is writing a Constitution for Appalachia that can be a model for other Regions and New America. If she gets elected, she will be turning up the heat on President Connor."

"We've had sympathetic leaders in regional legislatures, but I almost can't imagine a New America Senator being an outspoken Sparrow," Zara said. "We'll throw the full weight of the Sparrow Press behind her. She'll get a full-throated endorsement from us."

"Thanks, Zara. I do have one concern . . . " Gavin said haltingly.

"Security?" Jude asked. "You have to worry about your daughter making political waves."

"Exactly," Gavin said. "I've encouraged her to take a stand, but I also want to be wise. If there is any way to help her stay safe, I'd appreciate your help."

"Of course," Jude said, "I'll talk to the Nine and see if they can spare someone to advise her and keep an eye on her. Maybe they can head up a security team. We need to be realistic about what and who we are up against."

"Thanks, Jude. That makes this dad feel better."

In the weeks following Alvarado's attempt to locate and take out the Sparrow leadership, now simply known as "the desert incident," a slow rumble began to be felt. Opinion Editorials and official news programs were curiously quiet about the incident itself, but when they ran pieces attempting to disparage the Sparrows and describe them as a kind of societal threat, the caricatures were so off that most people immediately recognized them as blatant propaganda.

These propaganda attempts had quite an ironic effect: they drove people by the tens and hundreds of thousands to find the real news in the Sparrow Press. Using Max's training program, Gavin expanded the

Sparrow Army throughout Appalachia and set up training centers in New England and the Gulf States. The boots on the ground proved to be far more effective than the increasingly untrustworthy pipeline of information online. "Sparrow Soldiers" quickly gained a reputation for being helpful to everyone, especially the elderly, disabled, and single mothers. When Law Enforcement Autonomous Droids were sent to investigate Sparrow activities, the soldiers and citizens were always compliant and courteous, even assisting the LEAD units when they ran into mobility problems in uneven and obstructed areas.

People were suspicious of anyone appearing gracious and kind, knowing from experience that they were always selling something, but after weeks and months of consistently demonstrating kindness and generosity, the Sparrows became wildly popular. When asked how to "sign up" to be a Sparrow, the soldiers had to repeatedly explain that Sparrows were just like-minded people who believed in three core values: the sanctity of life, equality for everyone, and human dignity. If you wanted to be a Sparrow, you were a Sparrow—no signing up, no membership, no organizations, no institutions. The only thing you could sign was the Petition for the Reinstatement of a New American Constitution, but even that was not an obligation.

Political parties had been outlawed since the Transition, but Janie Hollins made her platform clear: she ran on Sparrow values. Publicly identifying herself as a Sparrow and espousing her views on the campaign trail, she rode the wave of Sparrow popularity that was due in part to her dad's efforts with the Sparrow Army.

Janie was young; she was one of the first of her generation, born after the Transition, to run for office. Instead of focusing on fear and security, she spoke about community and personal liberty.

"The Transition was terrifying for everyone, and many necessary objectives were accomplished: breaking up political gridlock, unifying our continent, and stabilizing our economy. Now we need to remember why we did these things: for the people. People have infinite value, not financial value based on 'net worth.' People are the reason for a government, not a financial burden on the government. People don't rely on and serve the government; it's the other way around. Let's make the government work for us. Let's pass an Appalachia Region Constitution, and let's push for a New America Constitution that protects our rights and keeps the government in its place: working for us."

Janie struck a chord. Her fresh face, bold ideas, and hopeful vision awakened people from their post-Transition stupor. Sparrows turned out in droves to vote, and despite her rivals getting more time and favorable coverage on official news outlets, Janie won the election in a landslide.

Community and block parties erupted throughout Richmond, New America flags appeared in windows and yards, and even home-designed "Janie Hollins" T-shirts were seen. Janie herself held a rally outside the downtown area in a park that was somewhat run-down, but it was the closest venue to her constituents.

LEAD units were on hand, and three of the Nine kept a vigilant eye on Janie, but the excitement and hope of the people gave Janie her biggest hedge of protection. The Sparrows now had their first New American Senator.

Chapter 14: **Anything Can Happen in an Election Year**

MAISY'S HAND WAS SHAKING as she held her phone and prepared to click on the message.

"Just do it!" Dr. Robinson said.

"I'm so nervous, Julian!" Maisy said. "You do it."

"Just click the email, Maisy. You're an amazing medic, and we're just waiting for the authorities to put their stamp on it."

"Ok, here we go!" she said, pressing down with her thumb. She scanned the lines, and by her crestfallen expression, Dr. Robinson knew what it said.

"We regret to inform you . . . You can appeal . . . .yada yada yada," Maisy said, dropping onto a chair in Dr. Robinson's office.

"You and I know that is garbage," Julian said. "We'll appeal."

"Will it do any good?" Maisy asked.

"I'll admit, it rarely does, but in your case, I am not taking no for an answer. I'll call Max, we'll file your appeal for you, talk to a few key people up the chain, and then we'll see what happens."

"Why are you doing all of this for me?" Maisy asked.

"First of all, you're worth it. You are the definition of an RM: you're focused, clear-headed, and steady. You're not lost in the lab or some research project like doctors sometimes get. You apply the research, you hone your technique, and you move fast. You have fantastic bedside manners, but your analytical skills allow you to diagnose patients quickly and accurately, which makes you more valuable in action than in routine care. Just below surgery and a step above nursing; you need to be a Registered Medic."

"And second of all?" she mused, finally allowing a smile to come through.

"Second, I'm not letting you out of my sight. Of course, I'd never hold you back, but it would be nice to move on from our professional relationship and develop a more personal one."

"Dr. Robinson, I don't know if I should get involved with my teacher and mentor," she teased.

"That's why we need to get you your credentials," he said, smiling. "I have a strict policy against getting involved with students. I want you to be my graduate so I can officially ask you out on a date."

"I'd like that too," Maisy said sheepishly.

"What? To graduate or go on a date?" he teased.

"Both!"

"Zara, can you believe Janie Hollins won?" Jude mused as they lay together in bed one morning.

"Sometimes I can't, but then sometimes I think, what took so long? People are tired of living in fear. They're tired of being afraid of the government, strangers, and each other. People need community. I think we're just helping to wake them up. After decades of crisis and conflict, people are ready to move away from ignorance and fear and towards truth and love. It's cutting through the despair."

"Well, thank you for your analysis, Dr. Zara Malik-Kane," Jude teased. "You know, now that we are more of a political force than an underground resistance movement, maybe we should come out from our hiding spot."

"Are you crazy? We'll get snatched up on some made-up charge immediately," Zara said. "I'm not going through that again. I won't risk losing you."

"Things might be different since the 'Desert Incident.' We haven't heard much from President Connor and nothing from my 'General surgeon.' Maybe we should have Chiela and Max do some digging and see what they can find out."

"That's not a bad idea, but until then, you're not leaving this Bunker, understand?"

"Yes, ma'am!" he said with a flourishing salute.

"If we did decide to emerge from the Bunker, where do you propose we set up our operation?" Zara asked.

"In Vancouver with my family," Jude said. I miss them. I miss Callum. I miss Cascadia. I want us to have some semblance of normal if we can. Besides, my parents aren't getting any younger."

"I suppose it looks better from a political perspective if we are not hiding, but we still have to contend with the reality that President Connor and his henchmen are not above strongman techniques and authoritarian tactics, and they really don't like us," Zara said.

"That's true, but what is the best way to protect ourselves—and the rest of the country— from these kinds of tactics?" Jude said. "Should we cower and try to outrun and outsmart the government, or should we bring people together and demand our Constitutional protections be put back in place? If New America is still a Democracy, let's make Conner put up or shut up. Let's get more people like Janie elected. Let's push the petition in all the Regions, and let's start a groundswell of pressure on Washington. Let's force Connor's hand; he will have to do what he promised, or he'll have to show everyone his true colors when he sends in the troops. In any case, the more public we are, the harder it is for him to get rid of us."

"I hate it when I get that sinking feeling in the pit of my stomach," Zara complained. "You know, the one I get when you are right, and I am terrified something really bad might happen to you."

"We'll be smart and do our homework. No unnecessary risks, no assumptions. Let's see what Max and Chiela can dig up."

Up in Vancouver, Rod and Marren Kane had made the Cubes a home. Callum connected his cube to theirs, and he stayed busy as a Sparrow Army Captain for Cascadia, reporting directly to Gavin Hollins.

"You've come a long way, son," Rod said to him one evening after facilitating a public spaces clean-up effort in Vancouver. Since long before Cascadia was part of New America, Vancouver took immense pride in its breathtaking green spaces. Clean-up efforts were seen as almost heroic. "You're not the hot-headed kid that wants to shoot at NADF aircraft anymore."

"I guess not," he chuckled. "But don't get me wrong; I'm still vindictive. I just enjoy needling the government little by little with everything we do for people that the government can't. I'm getting my vengeance by degrees."

"That's the best way to do it," Rod said.

"I wish we didn't have to be so worried about the government. I wish we had protections like you had in the United States. Maybe old President Connor has writer's block. You should write a new one and send it to him."

"Ha!" Rod began to laugh, but then gave it a second thought. "You know, it wouldn't hurt to be specific about our demands. If the Sparrows want the Constitution back, maybe we should have one to propose. We at least need a Bill of Rights."

"Mom!" Callum yelled to Marren in the other room. "Dad's going to write a constitution!"

> We the People of New America affirm the following rights to be essential to the protection of human life, liberty, and dignity, and shall serve as the foundation for the Constitution of New America:
>
> 1. All citizens shall have the freedom of expression, including speech, assembly, press, and protest. The government may not endorse or favor any one religion or those with no religion.
> 2. People have a right to defend their persons or property. The ownership and use of any weapons shall be regulated first by the Regional Governments and then by municipal or local authorities.
> 3. New America Defense Forces shall not target, engage, harass, exploit, or in any way coerce citizens of New America for any purpose. Regional Defense Forces shall oversee domestic defense and law enforcement.
> 4. No government entity shall inspect, seize, or destroy the personal property of any citizen of New America without due cause as decided by a judge. No government entity shall violate the physical, emotional, or social integrity of any citizen without the same due cause as decided by a judge.
> 5. All citizens are entitled to the due process of law. This includes the right to begin a case with a grand jury in serious cases, protection from double jeopardy, the right to just compensation for the seizure of property, protection from self-incrimination, and protection from imprisonment without a trial.
> 6. Citizens accused of a crime are entitled to a speedy, public trial, a trial by an impartial jury of their peers, formal notice of all charges being brought, the right to bring witnesses, and the right to be represented by an attorney.
> 7. All citizens are entitled to these rights regardless of the jurisdiction bringing the charges.

8. No citizen shall be subject to cruel or unusual punishment regardless of the crime or conviction. No citizen shall be subject to confinement in jail for more than ninety days; if a trial cannot be held within ninety days, the defendant shall be released on their own recognizance until the start of the trial. In no case may a defendant be charged bail; defendants are held in jail based on the severity of their crime, the danger to the public, or the risk of flight as decided by a judge.
9. The rights enumerated in the Constitution do not limit any other rights that citizens may enjoy not specified in the Constitution.
10. The New America Government has only the powers delegated to it in the Constitution. All other powers not specified in the Constitution belong to the Regional Governments.

"What do you think?" Rod asked Max over the video call. "After all, you are the lawyer here."

"It appears you had some help from the Founding Fathers of the United States," Max observed.

"Of course," Rod said, "With a few tweaks from what we've learned over the last few hundred years."

"I couldn't have worded them better myself. I think the Sparrows have a real agenda now. It's high time to end the Constitutional suspension, and this Bill of Rights should destroy the excuses of Blake Connor, Corporate Congress, and the Senate. They can debate the wording of the Constitution for years, but if we adopt these non-negotiables first, they will have a framework, and we will have the protection and rights we need now. This is what we need to force Connor's hand."

"It's about time!" Rod said. "What's our next move?"

"Let's get Jude and Zara up to Vancouver. It's time for these new politically savvy Sparrows to have a real headquarters."

"I know you have looked at all the contingencies. What's your assessment? I worry about how big the target is on Jude and Zara, and how much cover they will have in politics."

"I made a few inquiries, and Chiela has been able to corroborate several of my own findings. The official White House policy is to lie low right now. They know they narrowly escaped disaster after the desert incident, and they know a lot of people know the truth. It looks like their attempt to kill the snake backfired, and they realized they only managed to poke the bear."

"What if Connor goes after them some other way?" Rod asked, his fatherly side coming out.

"Well, we're not advertising anything. They will also be laying low, traveling as little as possible, and enjoying their time with you," Max said. "We're going to stick to a grass-roots strategy, campaigning for candidates and policies in the cities and regional governments. We're going to draft and push legislation to restore a constitution in each region first, and when we see more support and success, then we can turn up the heat on Connor. Until then, he might even forget about Jude and Zara."

"I doubt that," Rod said. "But if the Sparrows can flex their muscles and get some momentum, he'll eventually have to embrace the inevitable, or pull the trigger and try to seize power. Our success will depend on how well the Sparrows can defeat fear and harness determination. We have our work cut out for us."

"Well, Dr. Kane, your son is about the hardest working man I know, except maybe for his father."

The room was designed to intimidate. Maisy was sure of it. Max and Julius said and did everything they could, and now it was up to her. No one else was allowed in the room. The appellate review board for the medical school called on her to face them in person, and she was sure she was in for a grilling. The marble floors, tall ceilings, elevated seats of the board members, and the virtual silence of the room seemed to dwarf the already shaky confidence of the girl from a remote northern SAC.

Why were the seats elevated? Was that to intimidate on purpose, or to indicate some higher status? When was the last time any of these suits got their hands bloody? Maisy's rebellious streak rose inside her, shoving aside the fear and replacing it with righteous anger and increasing confidence. Who were they to tell her what she was capable of? They couldn't stop her from helping people; all they controlled was a piece of paper. Of course, it was a very important piece of paper that would recognize her skills and pave the way for many opportunities. Technically, this was a second chance for her, fought for by Max and Dr. Julius Robinson, and she owed it to them not to blow it. The anger subsided, but the confidence remained. She was not about to let anyone down, let alone herself.

A large man, tall and portly with salt and pepper hair, dressed well in a suit that accentuated his height but didn't quite hide his girth, began the inquiry.

"Miss Maisy Kane, welcome to the Medical School Appellate Review Board. It was brought to our attention that it may suit us to take a second look at your academic record and your residency experience here. You were brought into the Medical School under unorthodox circumstances, but Dr. Robinson insists he recognized uncommon talent in you that was worth developing. We've reviewed your examinations, your performance evaluations, and we have taken the unusual step of hiring "test patients" to challenge your skills in the field, independent of Dr. Robinson.

"The reports largely corroborated Dr. Robinson's evaluations as well as those of the other attending physicians you have worked under. We have no doubt you are a very capable Medic. We would like to ask you a few more questions so we can get a fuller picture of who you are, not just what you can do."

A middle-aged woman, average-sized with dusty blond hair and piercing, almost angry blue eyes, began the questioning.

"Why do you want to become a Registered Medic, Miss Kane?"

"I am a healer. I began with animals giving birth or slightly injured in the SAC, moved on to helping people with basic first aid, studied and practiced with more complex injuries such as broken bones and sewing up wounds, and finally was able to fully immerse myself in training here with Dr. Robinson as a mentor. It is what I am, not just what I do. The Registered Medic certification would not change who I am, but it would open doors for me to do a lot of good."

"I see," she continued. "You seem confident, especially for someone who was initially rejected for Registered Medic certification. How do you feel about that?"

Well, that was pointed. They wanted to peel back the scab to see how it was healing.

"I was initially disappointed, of course. To be honest, I was angry. I felt I may be the victim of a faceless bureaucracy that took one look at my educational background and dismissed me without a second thought. Upon reflection, however, I have come to see that this process is bigger than just me. The board has a tremendous responsibility as the people who determine if we are capable of making the kinds of decisions that can determine if someone lives or dies. That is no small thing. I know I'm from a SAC, but my father was a professor and my mother a teacher. I had excellent academic and practical experience that uniquely prepared me for this profession. On a SAC, there was never someone to rescue you when you made a mistake or faced a threat. At the scene of a medical emergency, it is often the same. I am profoundly grateful that you all have taken the time to review my file and see who I really am. It's an honor, and I vow to build a reputation that will reflect the excellence this board expects from its graduates."

"We thought we were going to have to squeeze you two into Callum's cube, but fortunately, our next-door neighbors vacated theirs a few days ago. Mom put your names in for it right away. She convinced Human Services that they would save money by not needing to recondition or relocate the Cube. Callum and I moved it alongside our cubes, connected the power and plumbing, and cleaned it up a bit. Welcome home!" Rod said. It was a bittersweet moment: they were far from the SAC and all the freedom they once had, but Jude was back home again with his bride and Rod's "second daughter" and some hope of an expanding family.

"This is great, Dad!" Jude exclaimed with a bear hug. "We're ready to crawl out from the underground."

"I miss the sunlight," Zara said. "I am desperate for Vitamin D!"

"Well, the sun isn't around as much as Kansas City, but if you're above ground, it should still be an improvement," Marren said, embracing Zara. "Come on in and rest a bit. Train travel can take it out of you, even young folks like you two. Did you have any trouble?"

"No," Zara said, dropping her travel bag and dropping onto the small convertible loveseat that pulled out into a bed. In a Cube, there were no spare rooms, so sofa beds were almost standard.

"We cruised through the scanners with no problem," added Jude.

"Thank God," breathed Marren, who was still in automatic mom mode. "After you catch your breath, I made us lunch."

"You traveled pretty light, I see," Rod remarked. "I presume you have some belongings following you somehow?"

"Max is shipping them piecemeal from different locations and by different modes. He doesn't want a trail leading back to the Bunker," Jude explained.

"And I don't want to unpack all at once," Zara said. "So, it works out pretty well."

"What about all your equipment?" Callum asked Zara after coming in from checking the water lines one more time.

"Of course, that is coming first. We've got a lot of work to do. The Sparrows are getting into politics, and we're starting with Rod's Bill of Rights.

We'll be doing what Sparrows do best: working at the grassroots level. We want to advocate for other things people need as well: an increase in the Universal Basic Income, an increase in university enrollment, employment in the arts, and maybe even the creation of Regional Agricultural Communities. People need purpose, they need artistic expression, and they need to get outside and get their hands in the dirt."

"You have my vote!" Marren shouted from the kitchen.

"People are ready to get behind these policies. A new generation, your generation, is coming of age after the Transition, and you don't live with the fear that paralyzed so many of our generation. You're going to find that we have a lot of allies in the regional governments. Your commitment to non-violence, especially after the desert incident, won over a lot of people," Rod said. "The Sparrows may have a lot of work to do, but we've got fertile ground."

"Hey, Dad, we have a surprise for you and Mom," Jude said after checking his phone.

"What did you do?" Marren asked, coming into the living room and wiping her hands on a dish towel.

The doorbell rang. Rod sprang up to answer it, and there stood Maisy and Dr. Robinson.

"Guess who just became a Registered Medic?"

Chapter 15: **Legitimate**

THE TRUTH HAS A way of finding its way to the surface. Long after the official explanations and selected media coverage of the collapse of the SACs, personal stories continued to spread. Rumors of a torture operation interrupted in the desert, supported by leaked video clips, continued to gain ground. Stories of Sparrows who refused to resort to violence even when violence was happening to them passed through blogs, message boards, and community groups. Jude's gruesome appendectomy at the hands of Alvarado began to elevate Jude to legendary status, even though that was the last thing he wanted.

Three years after the collapse of the last Sustainable Agricultural Community, SAC families had not only integrated into society, but they had a profound influence on a population that was floundering under rampant hopelessness and despair. The Sparrows offered a new perspective that revolutionized the way people related to each other. The Sparrows showed the world that people are meant to live for each other, not the elusive vision of wealth, security, and status.

With 80% of people effectively locked out of higher education, meaningful employment, and entrepreneurial opportunities, the ideas of the sanctity of life, equality, and the dignity of all human lives became almost a mantra to people struggling to find their purpose. When the Sparrows proposed a new Bill of Rights and began advocating for increased Universal Basic Income, expanded access to University Education, and public employment opportunities for artists, their platform became wildly popular. For those brave souls who were too young to remember the Transition or had since shaken off the fog of paralyzing fear, there was an unprecedented political opportunity. The Sparrows were not a political party, but they had a cohesive and popular platform that propelled many aspiring leaders into the Regional Legislatures and even several New America Senate seats.

The Corporate Congress, of course, was almost immune to the plight of the lower classes. Consolidated multinational corporations became fewer in number and so extraordinarily powerful that they managed to convince the Transition government to give them permanent representation in Congress. The Corporate Congress could work together more effectively to promote and protect its interests; after all, the people still had direct representation in the Senate. Since the corporations employed a majority of the workforce, they claimed to be indirectly representing the people, and since corporations were recognized as people and their money as speech, there was a legal basis for this representation.

While the Corporate Congress watched the increasing number of elected officials who publicly invoked the ideals of the Sparrows and even claimed to be proud Sparrows themselves, concern began to grow about the balance of power. They found a sympathetic ear in President Blake Connor, who himself watched in trepidation as the group he fought so hard to eradicate slowly metastasized into a legitimate and increasingly powerful voice that could undermine his vision of New America. Control was critical to his ability to silence opposing ideas and ultimately maintain the stability that had been the hallmark of his Presidency. He swore he would never again let the country descend into the chaos, conflict, and anarchy of the Transition.

On a cloudy, humid afternoon in Washington, D.C., the Speaker of the House met quietly with President Blake Connor at the White House.

"These Sparrows are making me very nervous, Mr. President," the speaker began after some friendly small talk.

"Mr. Speaker, you are preaching to the choir," the President sighed. "Every time I have tried to shoot those birds out of the sky, the flock returns with twice the numbers. Now they have allies in regional legislatures, several Senate seats, and they are rampant in municipal and local governments."

"Can't we classify them as a threat to national security?" the Speaker blurted out.

"I've been down that road. The SACs were relatively easy to re-classify and dissolve, but the Sparrows are far more slippery. They have some kind of leadership, organization, and structure, but it is hard to prove the Sparrows are anything but people who share an unusually coherent view of the world. ADAMS picked up a trove of data after the "desert incident" and reclassified the Sparrows as an ideological group. The supposed 'group of nine'? They are a minor threat, but they are also a cover for the Sparrows. Thanks to them, the Sparrows walked out of there free; not a single one could be verified to commit any act of aggression, and they came home looking like heroes. Meanwhile, the NADF narrowly avoided public condemnation thanks to our official story, which many people still don't believe. The Sparrows are a moving target."

"You know, Mr. President, you mentioned the Sparrows have an 'unusually coherent view of the world.' That sounds a lot like a political platform to me. You know who had political platforms?" the Speaker asked.

"Political parties," President Connor responded.

"Last I heard, political parties were outlawed after the Transition."

"So, Maisy, how on earth did you convince Julian to have the ceremony in Vancouver? Zara asked.

"It was easy," Maisy explained. "I simply pointed out that since I would be moving to Kansas City permanently, thousands of kilometers away from my poor older parents and both of my brothers, worlds away from where I was raised, a single ceremony in Vancouver was a small compromise. I may have been a little dramatic, but he agreed."

"I'm glad he did. I get to have my sister around for a few days at least," Zara said with a hug. "What do we need to do first?"

"Everything," Maisy sighed.

"Jude, why are you sorting through a pile of dead batteries?" Zara asked, sauntering up behind him at the Vancouver Recycling Center and slipping her arms around his neck. "People are asking about the power rationing and rolling blackouts. I don't think dead batteries are going to help."

"Ahh, but they can," he explained. "If we can build our own recycling centers in outlying residential areas, we can make better batteries for the Cubes. That's the problem. The ragged, worn-out batteries in most Cubes have no capacity left, and the government cares a lot more about power in the business districts. We can make bigger, stronger, more efficient batteries and link them together. There is enough power coming in, but it's just getting wasted."

"You realize you are the leader of the Sparrows, arguably the most influential group of people in New America, right?" Zara reasoned with him. "You're not in Slate Creek anymore."

"Vancouver is Slate Creek. Kansas City is Slate Creek. Dallas is Slate Creek. Everywhere people are struggling and we can help is the place where we should be. If we are successful here, we can do what we are good at: training other cities to follow our model and multiply the effects. It's not a political answer, but it is a practical one."

Zara laughed. "Always engineering a solution. That's one of the many reasons I love you. I'll help on the political end. I'll put out a call in the Sparrow Press for building space and as many dead batteries as people can gather."

"If I didn't know better, I'd say you work for the Sparrows," the President complained to the ADAMS interface droid. The new and intrepid analyst accompanying the droid shifted uncomfortably in his chair.

"ADAMS is not capable of bias, sir. He is, at his core, an analyst of massive amounts of data. His conclusion that the Sparrows are not a political party is based on factual evidence."

"Don't you mean 'its'? President Connor said.

"Sir?" the analyst asked.

"ADAMS has given me its conclusion. If ADAMS were a 'he', that would imply gender, humanity, and likely actual bias."

"Oh, yes, of course, Mr. President!"

"ADAMS, by now you have examined every letter I have written or spoken. You know my prime objective," President Connor said. He didn't ask the question but insinuated it, testing ADAMS's grasp of nuance in human interactions.

"You have indicated that political stability is your top priority, Mr. President."

"You are correct. While I do not object to much of the ideology of the Sparrows, I am deeply concerned that their advocacy will lead to dissatisfaction with our government at best and widespread rebellion at worst. There is a growing chorus of people demanding the reinstatement of the old US Constitution or a closely constructed equivalent. The recodification of broad individual rights could lead to the political paralysis and unraveling of national leadership that led to the conflict of the Transition. I simply refuse to allow that to happen again. How do you advise I counter these destabilizing actions of the Sparrows?"

ADAMS was a supercomputer, but even nanoseconds can add up with a complex socio-political question like that.

"One moment, please," the ADAMS droid said. The analyst watched and squirmed in his seat.

"Mr. President, I have a three-fold recommendation. First, use your vast communication resources to advocate for your own ideology. Emphasize safety, stability, and loyalty. These are widely popular ideals that do not run directly counter to the ideals of the Sparrows and, therefore, may gain widespread acceptance. Secondly, until you reinstate a constitution, you are delaying a promise to the people and giving the Sparrows a legitimate grievance. I suggest putting an official end to the suspension of the old United States Constitution and the announcement of a 'construction period' in which New America will develop its new Constitution. Finally, I suggest you have advocates write into the new Constitution mechanisms for ensuring national security and stability."

Now it was President Connor's turn to take a few minutes for his own analysis. He looked at the ADAMS droid, and then at the analyst, and then back to ADAMS. The analyst did not dare speak.

"Safety, stability, and loyalty. I like that. What kind of people fight for the safety and stability of their country? What kind of people are loyal to their country?" the President asked rhetorically.

"Patriots," the analyst blurted out, and then he almost immediately regretted his impulse.

"Patriots," the President repeated. "Patriots were a crucial part of the birth of the United States and the creation of the US Constitution. Now it is time to create a new Constitution, and we will call on the Patriots of New America to do the same. I like it! The Sparrows are advocating for a Bill of Rights, but the Patriots will be writing the entire Constitution. I think we may finally have something that can take down those damned Sparrows, and they won't even see it coming."

"I didn't realize how important the building was to you," Maisy said.

"It's not the building. It's my faith tradition. Call me medieval, but I still think a wedding is a sacred ceremony before God, and I would like a minister to officiate," Julian explained.

"I think my parents come from a Methodist tradition, but of course, in a SAC, you're on your own. We studied the Bible and the history of many Christian traditions, but we also celebrated some of the ancient traditions with our Salish relatives. We just understood ourselves as God's children, reflecting him in everything we did, especially when we showed love for each other. There wasn't really an organized religion I belonged to, but I'm comfortable with a minister officiating the ceremony. What religious tradition did you grow up with?"

"We were mostly AME. African Methodist Episcopal churches have been centers of black communities for hundreds of years. It's part of my family and part of who I am. For me, having the ceremony in a church is important; where the church is located doesn't matter as much."

"Well, Dr. Robinson, your orders have been received," Maisy said. "My dad still has old connections, and I'm sure we can nail down a venue and an AME minister somewhere in Vancouver."

"Thanks, Maisy. I know how important it is to have the ceremony near your family. When we get back to Kansas City, you might not have much time for visits. The Department of Health is tightening the belt and pushing more procedures down the line again. Registered Medics are going to be taking on a lot more duties that MDs should be doing in an effort to cut costs. You'll be under some pressure."

"At least I'll be in demand, and besides that, I have you to rely on now," she said, playfully punching his arm.

"That's true. I may have to come to the clinic and drag you home if things get too crazy."

"Safety, stability, and loyalty. These are the values that have taken us from the chaos and conflict of the Transition to the peace and prosperity we take for granted now. We can never forget. We can never go back. We can never give up what we have achieved. True Patriots built the United States of America, true Patriots brought the nations together to create New America, and now true Patriots are joining hands to create a new Constitution," President Connor announced in his national address.

"Effective immediately, New America has ended the suspension of the old United States Constitution and has begun a Construction Period, to last no more than three years, during which we will create a new governing document for a new age. We will protect the rights of New Americans, we will remain committed to the democratic principles of our republic, and we will solidify a government that can function efficiently. We will no longer be subject to political paralysis, economic stagnation, or constant conflict. We will move forward, we will secure our future, and we will succeed. It is time for the true Patriots to go to work."

Jude and Zara looked at each other, then back at the screen, and then back at each other. They heard Rod in the living room click off his screen and sit back with a sigh that rang of uncertainty. Maisy ran into the room fresh from choosing some flower arrangements and stumbled into the group of dumbfounded Kane family members.

"What just happened?" Zara asked Jude.

"I don't know. I didn't see that coming."

"What is going on?" Maisy asked, temporarily dropping her preoccupation with wedding details.

"President Connor just announced the country is creating a new Constitution," Jude said, still digesting the news.

"Hmm," Maisy mused, "Smart move. People are feeling shut out. No one can work, the UBI has not kept up with inflation, and they are cutting funding for health care again. Now he can deliver on a promise, distract the people with some kind of hope of progress while at the same time taking the wind out of our sails and then making sure to enshrine his agenda in our founding document while we are holding hands and singing his praises."

Zara looked at Jude and then back to Maisy. "She's right. How much power will the regions have? What system of checks and balances will there be? What rights and protections will make the final version?"

"There's no better time to secure your agenda than when you have just united the people behind you," Jude said. "No doubt the Corporate Congress will give him what he wants, but the Senate will have a say. We need to get as many Sparrows in the Senate Chamber as we can."

"I know one candidate I would vote for," Maisy said with a cheeky smile.

"Who would that be?" Jude asked.

"You!"

"The sanctity of life, equality, and human dignity," Jude repeated to himself. "Safety, stability, and loyalty."

"What are you muttering?" Zara asked as Jude was poring over demographic data for Cascadia.

"Our core values are the most important thing we can fight for, but I think we have an uphill battle when it comes to marketing. 'Safety, stability, and loyalty' rolls off the tongue a little easier. I have a feeling the Sparrows might have to take on the Patriots, and the Patriots are heavily favored to win."

"So was Goliath," Zara said. "What are you thinking?"

"I'm thinking that you're a lot smarter than me. Why don't you run?"

Jude was attempting some levity, but he was also fishing for her thoughts.

"Me? No way," she said flatly. "I'm a journalist, not a politician. You're the leader, Jude. You're the face of the Sparrows."

"I'm no politician either," he sighed.

"You're a leader and a problem-solver. That's what the country needs now more than ever," she said, rubbing his shoulders. "Your reluctance to jump into the fray is one of the reasons you are so well qualified. You're not looking for power. You're trying to help people. Don't worry; I've always got your back."

"You've got my back . . . " he mused, trailing off. "I'm not alone."

"Of course not, Jude. I'm with you," she said, starting to wonder what he was thinking.

"I've never been alone, and this is no exception. This is going to be a fight. 'Safety, stability, and loyalty' is not coming straight at us. It's going to broadside us, and we're going to need momentum to counter it. We need more senators."

"We've got Janie Hollins in Appalachia. Who else do you think could make a good run?" Zara wondered out loud.

"Zack could run in Atlanta for one of the Gulf States Senate seats, and Sonja could run in Baja. We could coordinate and share resources. We could pool money, create ads together, and endorse each other. Three more New America Senate seats would give us some momentum, and it would give us a say in the new Constitution."

"There you go again, solving problems," Zara laughed. "Now you just have to convince them to run."

Chapter 16: **Violence is in the Blood**

"General Alvarado, we have a problem. The cancer is spreading."

The Defense Chief was not at all surprised by President Blake Connor's request for a private meeting. He figured it would be about a year of laying low after the desert incident before he would be summoned, and he was right.

"We finally took out the SACs, but they brought their ideas to the cities. We tried to take out the leaders, but they had allies and far more influence underground than we anticipated," the President admitted. He was careful not to lay any blame on General Alvarado. "Their influence has spread widely, but it is still a grass-roots movement. As long as they were limited to an underground press and a few seats in the Regional Legislatures, I was satisfied with fighting them in the press. They won't be able to do anything with the Corporate Congress, but now they have their sights on the Senate, and we can't let them in our house."

"When you fight cancer, sometimes you have to use a blunt weapon like Chemotherapy, and sometimes you have to go in and cut out the tumor," General Alvarado said.

"Exactly, and I know how you enjoy the procedure," the President said with a slight smirk. "Let's learn from our mistakes. It's not the Sparrows themselves that are dangerous; it's their ideas. We are going to counter their message with a campaign of "safety, stability, and loyalty." Like their ideals, these are hard to argue with and don't necessarily contradict the Sparrow's propaganda. We'll build support and make sure we have key players in place to ensure safeguards against insurrection are built into the new Constitution."

"You are a formidable foe on the political stage, sir. Where do I come in?"

"Let's not waste our experience in the desert. We learned a few important lessons. First, we don't need to change our enemy's mind. If the message doesn't bring them in line, the bullet will. No more big operations with hundreds of troops. No more trying to squeeze intel from leaders. No more simple intimidation. From now on, we are surgical. We find the problem, and we remove the problem.

"The other lesson we learned is the power of a few highly trained operatives in the right place at the right time. I want you to hand-pick an elite team to help you 'address the most imminent security threats.' We need commitment as much as skill, so choose your team accordingly. They don't all need to come from COATS. You may need to do some research and psych testing; it would help if your team had some 'moral flexibility.' You don't want someone suddenly growing a conscience when a Senate candidate needs to disappear."

"Mr. President, it is the privilege of my lifetime to serve you," General Alvarado said with uncharacteristic happiness. "You think tactically, you have the courage to make the hard choices, and you give me the tools to do my job. Thank you."

"I know what you are capable of, General. That is why I give you the latitude to create and shape your team. There is only one thing that I want,"

"What is that, sir?"

"I want to name it."

"Of course. What should we call it?"

"General Alvarado, you are now the father of the Patriot Guard."

The Blue Ridge Mountains were silhouetted in the light of the brilliant orange horizon and the emerging sun. The clouds lingered just below the mountain tops like they were not quite ready to rise for the day, bathing the forest in a morning mist. Zack put his boot on a stump and let out a steamy sigh in the crisp autumn air. When he told Athalia he needed to think, she knew what he meant.

"I'm no politician," he protested to no one in particular. "Let me hunt, let me build, let me work with my hands and take care of my family. That's all I ever wanted."

Immediately, a voice in his head spoke, as if he were having a conversation with himself.

"You're a leader. Look how well you took care of Blue Ridge," the voice said.

"And look where we are now," he answered out loud.

"You're alive, and so are all of the people from Blue Ridge. It's your nature to fight for people."

"I'm going to get in way over my head. I'm no lawyer, and I'll be going up against professionals."

The voice came back almost sharply. "The professionals forgot who they work for. You will remind them."

"They're going to laugh me out of the chamber," Zack said, his resistance fading.

"You're going in with the full force of the Sparrows. You will never be alone."

He let out another puff of steam and a big sigh. "If Jude thinks I should run, then I'm going to run. We might have a shot at writing a constitution that protects us and keeps the President in his place. If that isn't worth fighting for, I don't know what is."

Zack pulled out his phone, gazing over the tree-covered ridges, and called Jude.

"Alright, Jude. I thought hard about it, I talked to Athalia, and heck, I think I even talked to God. We have to do this. We'll be helping to write the Constitution. Count me in."

History, poverty, Native and European influences, and modern infrastructure are all woven together in Mexico City. Sonja Orozco sat on the balcony of the old office building, pushing broken pieces of stucco siding absent-mindedly with her foot and staring down the street at the mix of smudged and scratched cubes nestled in among hundred-year-old apartment buildings, all standing in the shadow of the SEMIC Train tube. After a couple of hours talking to her kids on screens, she missed them more than ever. Part of her was glad, however, that they were fairly sheltered at CME. The Sparrows were gearing up for their biggest fight yet.

Jude was right; this was their chance to make an impact. Building the Constitution was the most important thing anyone could do to enshrine rights and protections for the millions of people who have been shoved to the edges of society. His dad, Rod Kane, wrote a Bill of Rights that needed to be the cornerstone of the new Constitution, and the way it mirrored the old US Constitution gave the Sparrows a real chance to make it stick. For

Sonja, however, there was more at stake. Mexico had been the neglected stepchild of North America for at least a couple of hundred years, and the promise of equality as a part of New America was proving a bit elusive. There was some investment in infrastructure, like the SEMIC Train line from the Texico- Baja border to the Panama Canal and the import of a few million cubes, but Sonja knew without a consistent voice in the Senate, they would fall behind again.

When her friends told her she should run for the open seat in Baja, she laughed. When groups of Gorriones started begging her to run, she was intrigued, but she doubted she had a chance. When Jude called and asked her personally to run, promising the full resources of the Sparrows for her campaign, she recognized the calling. It wouldn't be easy; Jude, Zack, and she herself had suffered at the hands of General Alvarado, and she knew they could be in real danger, especially while they were still candidates. Of course, the greater the danger, the more important it was to be successful, and she was no quitter.

"Araceli," she called to her assistant, "I'm expecting several shipments of Stingers from Max in Kansas City. Keep an eye out for them, please. They will be camouflaged, but Max always finds a place to put a little *garrione* so we know it's for us. I'm on my way to the gym."

"Are you working on your modeling figure for the Senate run?" Araceli joked.

"I've got my Jiu-Jitsu training tonight, but it is getting me in shape, I suppose."

"Safety, security, and stability." General Alvarado stared at his first-round picks for the new Patriot Guard. "How far will you go to preserve these ideals?"

The soldiers sat at desks arranged in a semi-circle. The windowless room gave them few clues as to the reason the NADF Defense Chief summoned them. They tried in vain to size each other up and discover a common factor. It seemed like a special mission, an opportunity for the most elite, but only a handful of COATS soldiers were there. Male and female, all levels of education, all branches of the NADF, a mix of Enlisted and Officers, and even one cook were there.

"If a child were in danger, would you intervene?" Alvarado said.

They nodded their heads in agreement.

"What if that child was a young girl, maybe eight years old, and she was abducted by a terrorist? You would fight for her, right?

They nodded again, many of them thinking this was shaping up to be an anti-terrorism unit.

"What if the terrorist had a finger on a detonator and was holding the girl in his other arm? Your only shot to take out the terrorist before hundreds of civilians are killed is right through the skull of that little girl?"

Silence fell on the room. Was this a test?

"Take the shot," said a female Communications Specialist. "That girl doesn't deserve it, but neither do hundreds of other people. The terrorist is counting on us to waver. You don't waver. You take them out."

The other soldiers all looked at her in stunned amazement as they tried to process her response. Was she a monster, or was she right?

General Alvarado smiled at the soldier and nodded approvingly.

"Do you remember the story of Julius Caesar from History class? He was stabbed to death by Roman Senators, including his best friend. Brutus loved Julius like a brother and had nothing against him. Why would he look his friend in the face and plunge a dagger into him?"

"Caesar was becoming a tyrant," a young officer chimed in. "They had to stop him while they still could. Brutus put his love for the Republic ahead of his love for his friend."

Alvarado chuckled. "The history professor is correct!" They all chuckled as the fog was slowly clearing over the purpose of their time with the General.

"Morality is not black and white," he continued, pacing the floor and piercing individuals with his gaze at random intervals. "That does not mean we are not moral; it means we understand that not every decision we are faced with has an easy answer. Of course, our objective is to save lives, but what if we have to take lives to save lives? Who has the fortitude, clarity of mind and purpose, and willingness to make the hard decisions for the greater good?

"As you might have surmised, I am creating a special unit. I need my experienced COATS operatives, but I also need Communications Specialists, Logistics Specialists, Mechanics, and even Cooks. Your skills will be put to use, but more importantly, I'm looking for an unwavering commitment to New America. You're too young to remember the chaos and death of the Transition, but it's enough to know it cannot and will not ever happen again. I am assembling a team of soldiers who are willing to make the hard decisions so the rest of the country can sleep in peace at night. We will operate in stealth, we will operate outside the law, and we will operate with a single purpose: we will preserve the safety, security, and stability of New America. Welcome to the Patriot Guard."

"Jude, as your attorney, friend, and advisor, I must insist that you get out of the scrap yards, put on a tie, and start campaigning. There is a lot at stake here," Max said in a lightly scolding tone on the phone.

"I think I've got a good, streamlined process now. If we can recondition enough cube batteries, we can increase the efficiency in entire neighborhoods and maybe even put an end to the rolling blackouts!" Jude exclaimed.

"That is fantastic!" Max replied mockingly. "And you know what you can do? You can pass legislation that clears the way, but only if you get elected. You've got to delegate and start thinking bigger."

"I know you're right," Jude conceded. "But I love it when a plan starts coming together."

"You also like getting your hands dirty. I know, Jude. Let me put together a team of homegrown engineers like yourself and send them up to Cascadia to learn your process. I'll talk to Gavin Hollins about sending out the engineers with Sparrow Soldiers from every region to replicate the process. In the meantime, get your face out there. We need you in the Senate."

"Max?" Jude said.

"Yes?"

"Thank you. You're a good friend and a trusted advisor. I'm going to lean on you if I win this thing. I'll need all the help I can get."

"Of course, and I expect to make an actual salary this time."

"Are you ready?" Athalia asked Zack as she straightened his tie and tucked rebellious wisps of his red hair back into place.

"I feel naked without my beard," he complained.

"You still have a beard. It's just nice and trim now."

"I can feel the wind on my face. It's weird."

"Relax!" she ordered. "Don't think about how you look. Think about us, our kids, and our friends. Think about our rights. Think about the world we can make. People are dying for hope."

"Yeah, literally," he said. "Let's do this." He took a deep breath, and then he stepped onto the stage in front of the lights and cameras. He paused, shot a quick glance back at Athalia, smiled, and addressed the crowd in the auditorium.

"I'm going to be honest; I'm not used to wearing suits and speaking to crowds. I'm used to working with my hands and talking to my neighbors. We had to work together to survive in a Sustainable Agricultural Community. We didn't have the government to rely on; we only had each other." He dared to glance quickly at Athalia, and she nodded, urging him on.

"I'm not here to bemoan the loss of my SAC. To be honest, life on a SAC was hard. Since moving to Atlanta, I've come to realize that what I missed about the SAC was not the lifestyle. It was the community. People are what really matter. Life is not about success and money; it's about living in a community where we take care of each other. It's about listening to each other, having empathy, and helping as many people as we can."

The people were nodding in agreement, but he could sense they were hungry for more.

"Does it feel like we're trapped? Does it feel like twenty percent of our country is actually working and living, and the rest of us are just surviving out here?"

That got their attention.

"I think we can all agree that technology that saves us from back-breaking, soul-crushing work is a good thing, but people need more than a Universal Basic Income check to survive. We need purpose. We need a challenge. We need opportunity."

The crowd roared, clapped, and cheered. He had them now.

"I will have three jobs as your senator. My legal job will be to fight for basic rights and make sure they are enshrined in our new Constitution. The first words will be a Bill of Rights!"

The people gave him a roar of approval.

"My economic job will be to fight for the needs of all of us who seem to be left out of the entire economy. I will fight for the dramatic expansion of University Education, Human Services, Entrepreneurial Opportunities, and Artistic Grants. So much money is spent on our Universal Basic Income; why not put more people to work? Isn't it time we earned more than just a 'basic' income? It's time for our Corporate Congress to start thinking about an economy that includes all of us."

The thunderous applause grew so loud that the security team started getting nervous and shuffling their feet. Zack glanced at them and then quieted the crowd. As he scanned the room, he noticed two men in uniform who looked vaguely familiar. Of course, being consumed with his speech, he didn't have the brain capacity to recall exactly who they were at the moment, but his gut told him he had seen them before, and it was not a friendly interaction.

"Finally, my political job will be to make sure that we the people, especially those of us who have been left out of the conversation, have a voice in our government. We are a Democracy, and each person gets a vote. I listen to voices, not dollars."

Zack had a few more words, but the crowd erupted so loudly that he just smiled, waved, and scanned the crowd, trying to make eye contact and remember some of the faces in this happy moment.

When he finally felt he had a chance to wrap it up, he made it brief.

"I'm Zack Nolan, and I'd love to be your Senator for the Gulf States of America Region!"

As he turned to leave the stage, he caught the eyes of the two men in uniform, and it suddenly clicked. Their uniforms were not the same as the security team at the arena, and they were just off stage right. He recognized them. They were in the desert. They were here to finish the job.

Zack locked eyes with them, glared down, and then shook his head slightly before running off stage.

"You were amazing, honey! You were awesome out there! I know I'm going to vote for you," Athalia said as she tried to kiss him, but he pulled away and grabbed her arm.

"What's wrong?"

"Stay with me and come this way."

"What's going on, Zack?"

Zack went to a pair of security guards standing among the staff and technicians working in the auditorium.

"I think we might have a problem. There are two men who I think are coming for me. They're in uniforms, but if you look closely, they're not the same as yours. Is there a way to get out of here without being followed?"

The guards looked at each other for a second, processed the threat in their minds, nodded at each other, and then one of them left.

The other guard said, "He's going to keep an eye out for our friends. Follow me. I've got a shortcut to freedom."

They ducked behind the sound and stage equipment, and the guard opened a trap door at the far end of the stage, revealing a ladder to the basement. They each climbed down, and the guard led the way through the maze of old stage equipment. When they reached the back of the storage area, he opened a door that led to a long hallway.

"Follow this until you run into a set of stairs. When you go up, you will come out into the back kitchen of Southern Café. Go out the back door, and you'll be on the block behind the auditorium. Can you get a ride from there?"

"That's perfect. Thank you," Zack said, shaking his hand.

"No problem, sir. And by the way, you've got my vote."

Chapter 17: **Bigger Than You**

"ARE YOU SURE THEY were from the desert?" Max asked.

"I'm pretty sure. They weren't assigned to me specifically, but I remember they worked that hallway we were in. I can't forget that look in their eyes," Zack explained on their video call.

"You guys need security."

"Jude is worried about how it looks. We're supposed to be peace-loving and all about human equality and dignity, so if we show up with armed security, we look like hypocrites. It also might attract the wrong kind of attention from the government. You know how jumpy President Connor is about resistance."

"I get it. He's not wrong, but I think President Connor is already past jumpy. We need to make sure you're not walking into a trap. We need a strategy. Let me talk to Jude, and in the meantime, be smart. Keep up your presence online and be very careful about going out in public until we can make sure you're not a sitting duck."

"Sounds good, Max. I'll try not to tempt fate. Thanks."

Giant screens loomed behind the candidates on a blackened stage, while the rest of the auditorium was dripping in Red, White, Blue, and Green banners. Endless rows of chairs filled the floor, and rows of stadium seating seemed to crawl up the walls in three levels. Security was at every door and corner, and the atmosphere was electric with expectation. This would be the first live event for Sonja Orozco, and the Sparrows showed up in force.

"How do you offer a better vision for Baja and New America than your opponent, Senora Orozco?" the moderator asked.

"I will let my opponent speak to their vision, and I will let the people judge. I don't like negative campaigns and mudslinging. We have too many problems to solve to waste time cutting each other down. We need to come together and remind society that the eighty percent of people in this land who have been shut out of the economy have value, purpose, and dignity."

She tried to continue, but the crowd roared so loudly in approval that she had to let them calm down.

"Is that part of your party platform, Seniora Orozco?"

Sonja was irritated at the blatant trap, but she maintained her composure.

"Now you know better than that," she said with a steely glare. "If you are asking if I am affiliated with the Sparrows, the answer is a proud yes. Sparrows, in the most basic sense, are people who come together to help each other. I would hope that is something that all people can agree upon. My vision for Baja and New America is a vision in which all people are valued. Every person has purpose, value, and dignity. As a Senator, that means I will fight for adequate housing, access to education, quality healthcare, and I will make sure every citizen has an equal vote in our government, regardless of where they work, where they live, or how much money they have. I will fight, alongside several of my colleagues, to ensure the Bill of Rights is firmly enshrined in our new Constitution. The people of New America will not be forgotten."

The thunderous applause rumbled through the auditorium, and it took a full two minutes before the noise abated enough for the moderator to ask the next question.

"What do you think about President Connor's recent initiative of 'Safety, Stability, and Loyalty'? Do you agree these should be New America's priority to avoid the disasters that led to the Transition?"

"Safety, Stability, and Loyalty are achieved only when all people are valued, given equal opportunities, and treated with dignity. I am grateful for the President's leadership in restoring peace and order in New America. Now we need to make sure it does not come at the cost of Democracy. Let's work together and write this Constitution. Let's guarantee the rights and voice of all people. Let's reject violence and return to civil discourse and debate. Let's remember the genius of the founders of the United States, but let's also clarify our principles and guard against the corruption that we let creep in over the centuries. This is the time to get this right!"

This time, the thunderous applause took over the auditorium, and then smoothly transitioned to a chant: "Sonja! Sonja! Sonja!"

The moderator, whose strategy to box in Sonja and then let the opponent sweep in with the "right" answers failed dramatically. After a few minutes, even Sonja felt bad for her opponent. Eventually, they were able to articulate a few trite answers, emphasizing support for President Connor and his initiatives, but Sonja's depth and clarity left everyone with little doubt who carried the day. Even the official news outlets knew no amount of editing could diminish Sonja's powerful presence and support. For the first time, the Sparrows took the main stage in official news reports, and the world was able to see what it meant to be a Sparrow.

As she left the venue, two men in black suits approached her and attempted to escort her to a waiting vehicle.

"This way, Senora Orozco," they said, pointing to the vehicle.

She looked around and noticed the Sparrow Soldier volunteers were not waiting in their agreed-upon spot.

"The other guys got held up, so they asked us to give you a ride home," the other man explained.

Sonja was almost angrier that they thought she was ignorant enough to follow them than she was scared of their intent. She thought ahead of her gut reactions; she knew they would not truthfully answer any questions, and she knew her life depended on thinking fast and moving faster.

She approached the men, feigning agreement, until she was close enough. As soon as the driver got in, she came close to the man holding the door, and she kicked him between the legs with her full strength. He didn't even have time to fully double over before she performed two more moves, kicking out his bent leg and then hitting the back of his head, knocking him out cold.

The driver jumped out, sped around the vehicle, and lunged for Sonja. She engaged him fiercely, but clearly, he was not just a driver. She managed to slow him down, but he was bigger, stronger, and well-trained. She tried to make a desperate break for it, but he wrapped his arms around her knees and took her down. Before he could restrain her arms, she remembered she had one more trick up her sleeve, or more specifically, in her inside jacket pocket. She pulled out her Stinger and managed to get off a shot right into his neck. He knocked the Stinger out of her hands, but to her relief, it was a good hit. He only lasted about thirty seconds before losing consciousness.

Sonja disentangled herself, took a deep breath, and had just enough presence of mind to retrieve her Stinger and take pictures of the men before running away from the scene. She made it to a safe house, and from there was escorted by a small army of Sparrows to a large community of Garriones who gave her a room and provided for her as if she were already a New America Senator. She called Araceli and instructed her to secure anything she could online and at home and told her where to meet her, reminding her to stay clear of their office. She then sent a report of her attack to Max and Zara.

It was a wet, dreary afternoon in Seattle as the ships laden with stacks of containers moved lazily in and out of the port, unloading and reloading a rainbow of shipping containers. The parks and beaches were mostly empty, save for the die-hard fitness lovers and the stalwart dog walkers. Indoors, the Cascadia Regional Legislature convened a meeting of the Department of Education. The public was allowed to observe as academic experts gave their testimonies about the efficacy of the curriculum and the success of the CME schools in boosting test scores. The Superintendent presented his budget for the next school year, and finally, it came time for public comment. Due to the general lack of interest and lack of faith that anything they said would matter unless they were an expert or worked in the system, very few people attended or commented in the public forum. Security was relatively relaxed, and the meeting moved into the comment phase as usual. Today, however, someone had something to say.

"I would like to make a comment," a man said, standing up.

Ripples of nervous surprise spread throughout the auditorium, and finally, a staff member hurriedly brought an old microphone into the aisle. The board and Superintendent tensed visibly as they tried to prepare for the unknown, and security adjusted their earpieces and awaited orders.

"Congratulations on your achievements and your improvements. Quality education is the key to combating ignorance, fear, and disengagement from civic life. I do have one concern, however, and it relates to Compulsory Monitored Education Schools. CME Schools were primarily a tool for ensuring that the children in SACs were educated to the same Regional and National standards. After the SACs were absorbed into the general population, I expected the numbers to dramatically decrease; however, the numbers have in fact increased. Isn't that correct, Mr. Superintendent?"

"I, um, don't know . . . I don't have the numbers in front of me."

"According to the Department of Education, the number of students in CME schools has increased by 18%. This increase corresponds with the period of time in which the SACs were absorbed by the cities of Cascadia. With children now enrolled in regular local schools, you would think that number would decrease."

"I can't speak to that, specifically. What is your name, sir?"

"I find it also very concerning that the students retained in CME schools are disproportionately from families that have identified as or have given support to the group known as the Sparrows. It doesn't take a Ph.D. in education to see a discriminatory pattern here, does it, Mr. Superintendent?"

"Sir, you are out of line! This is a forum for comments, not a place to make accusations! You have come with no credentials and no evidence, and you have made an inflammatory and false accusation. You will identify yourself immediately!"

The security guards quickly moved into place, and the few people in the auditorium all turned to stare at the disrupter.

"My name is Jude Kane. The Sparrows are my friends, a group of people who have formed a community to help each other and address desperate needs that seem to go unnoticed by every agency of the government except the Department of Education. Despite scores that exceed state standards, kids from Sparrow families are consistently denied release, as if there were a concerted effort to disrupt Sparrow families. Since the Sparrows are only an informal ideological group and not any kind of political organization, I would be curious to know what role ADAMS has had in providing data to the Department of Education that allows them to identify 'Sparrow Children.' Denying release based on any criteria except test scores would certainly qualify as discrimination, and discrimination has no place in a democracy. I assure you, Mr. Superintendent, that my data is accurate, and you have had my full report for a week now. As for credentials, I am more of an engineer than an educator, but I have been brushing up on my policy lately. After all, I am running for the Senate."

A gasp came up from the audience, and the Superintendent and the board paused in speechless surprise. Jude nodded to the board, smiled at Zara, and made his way back to his seat. He caught a flash of movement out of the corner of his eye, and he turned just in time to see someone, dressed vaguely in security garb but not the same uniform as official RDF guards, point a pistol straight at him. He dove to the ground just as the gun went off, hearing a scream from Zara and a flurry of motion. He covered his head instinctively, curled up on the floor, and waited for a second shot, but it never came. The shooter and a partner fled out a side door, narrowly avoiding the guards, calculating that a second shot would have increased the risk of being caught and gambling that the one shot would be enough.

"After them!" the Superintendent ordered, running down from the stage toward Jude.

"Jude! Jude! Are you hit?" Zara frantically asked, rolling him back and forth, trying to assess his condition.

"Ouch," he said flatly. "Please stop moving me around."

"Are you hit? Where?" she asked.

"Just above my knee," he grunted. He had put his hand over the point of the sharp pain without even realizing it, and then he pulled it away, watching blood drip from his palm. "Too bad Maisy isn't here. She loves this kind of stuff."

"Shhh," Zara said. "Take it easy. We're going to get you to the hospital."

The Superintendent came up to them and took charge, surprising everyone, especially Jude and Zara.

Pointing to the RDF guards still in the room, he said, "Call the medics right now, and come help this man!" A guard came over and fished a gauze strip from his supply pack and began wrapping the gunshot wound.

"Who was that?" the Superintendent asked, looking at Zara.

"I don't know, but this is the third attack on a Senate candidate who identified as a Sparrow. All three attempts came from people dressed as guards or officials. We're making someone unhappy," Zara said.

"I resent your accusation of discrimination," he said, and then continued in a low voice, "but now I can't help but see where you are coming from. If this is happening in CME schools, it's happening above my head. I'll look at your report. I'll contact you later, securely." He walked back to the board, reassuring them that the shooter and partner had fled, but that they all should leave as a precaution. He turned to Zara and gave her a nod before following the board members and a few guards out the back door.

"Are we all here?" Max asked, beginning the meeting on Zara's screen.

"Everyone is here, and I've got us on a secure connection," Chiela chimed in from off-screen. She rarely showed her face, but she was always in the audio.

"Good. I've got some information. Jude, if this feels like we're ganging up on you, then I am sorry, but we need to address security for all of you."

Jude gently rubbed his wound and said, "I have more of an open mind now, trust me. What are we looking at?"

I've managed to get security footage from Zack's speech, Jude's episode in Seattle, and of course Sonja's report and pictures," Chiela said. "Those were invaluable, Sonja. Thank you."

"Of course," Sonja said. "I had a feeling we're not just dealing with local security."

"Your instincts were correct," Chiela continued. "I compared the clothing and what I could see of the weapons they carried. They are not any kind of Regional Defense Forces, and nothing they wore corresponds to any known NADF uniform or specialized units. I did notice enough similarities, however, to determine that we are looking at the same group. In each case, they deployed two operatives, tried to blend in with RDF or facility security staff, and they all had small tattoos on their wrists with the letters 'PG.' I couldn't find anything to give me a clue as to what 'PG' stands for, at least from regular sources. After I did a little digging, however, I think I figured it out."

"By digging, you mean hacking, right?" Jude laughed.

"I prefer to characterize it as aggressive research," Chiela said.

Max then took over. "We're pretty sure PG stands for 'Patriot Guard.' They are some kind of elite group, newly formed, and from what Chiela could see, they are hand-picked by and report directly to General Alvarado. All this she gleaned from intercepted communications, but nothing is official. It looks like Alvarado has created some kind of covert group, and their job is to solve problems without the pesky backlash of public opinion and scrutiny."

"We should've seen this coming," Jude said. "The desert incident was too big to keep hidden, and now with the Sparrows winning more support and winning elections, he can't just wipe us out."

"Who is 'he,' Jude?" Max asked.

"President Connor. I know this is his brainchild. He started the 'Patriot' narrative, and he had Alvarado create the Patriot Guard to help him achieve his goals out of sight of the public. Think about it: what is a bigger threat to his power than Sparrows becoming New America Senators? Why do you think he tried to take us all out? It's a lot easier than winning an election."

"Max, what do you think? How is it that Sonja, Zack, and Jude are all still alive?" Zara asked. "Were they just lucky? I'm not comfortable with that idea."

"They are new, and we are not," Max said. "But they will learn from their mistakes. No more taking chances. The Senate candidates will not be sitting ducks. I've brought in reinforcements."

"Who?" Zara asked.

"The Nine."

The balloons and signs seemed out of place among the piles of discarded Cube batteries, separating and crushing machines, conveyor belts, parts bins, and portable manufacturing equipment, but the small army of Sparrow volunteers was proud of the operation. Within a few months, they would be able to cheaply replace worn-out Cube batteries and dramatically improve energy efficiency in Richmond, and with satellite operations, all over Appalachia.

"It is my pleasure to announce the opening of the first Community Battery Recycling Center in Richmond," Janie said to the crowd. "I haven't secured government funding yet, but if we waited for government funding, nothing would ever happen!"

The crowd cheered the Senator who finally understood the reality of their situation.

"I want to thank the city leaders who gave us a permit to use this land, and with the improvement in energy efficiency, I challenge any government agency to stand in the way of common-sense problem-solving. In the meantime, thank you to all the volunteers who make this operation possible."

With cheers of support, Janie stepped down from the makeshift platform and took the giant pair of ceremonial scissors to the ribbon comically stretched between two large, discarded battery receptacles.

"Great speech, sweetheart," Gavin Hollins said to his daughter as she made her way to her transport. "Let's take my car."

She stopped and stared at her dad. "Dad, you don't have a car."

"I do today, sweetheart, and there is someone I need you to meet."

"I'm pretty busy, Dad. I need to . . . "

"Come with me, and we'll get you back to your office. Please."

"Dad, what is going on? I really need to . . . "

"Janie, sweetheart, I'm not asking. Please come with me."

Shocked, she looked into her dad's eyes, and she discerned pretty quickly that this was a matter of life and death.

"Senator Hollins, this is Jack," Gavin said as they got into the transport. He and his team will be assigned to you from now on. Please listen to him, especially regarding transport and public appearances. This is in response to a real threat, and you absolutely should not trust anyone except Jack. The less you know, the better, except for the fact that this comes straight from Jude and Zara."

Chapter 18: **Incentive**

"Financial adjustments are urgently needed, sir."

"You don't have much good news for me, do you, ADAMS?" President Connor said with a sigh. "What is the latest info you have gathered? I can't imagine financial reports come with too many surprises. You see the data as it is gathered and processed."

"Yes, sir. Data is not surprising, but sometimes trends accelerate much more quickly than anticipated," the droid interface explained.

"What's the bad news?"

"We are weeks away from insolvency. The increase in Human Services costs and Education costs related to the absorption of the SACs has not stabilized, as earlier models have predicted. Costs are exceeding revenues, and without an increase in taxes or a reduction of costs, funding will run out."

"What is the likelihood that Congress will approve an increase in taxes or an increase in deficit spending?" the President asked, already knowing the answer.

"Based on the most recent poll data, Corporate Congress is 93% likely to oppose new taxes and 87% likely to oppose an increase in borrowing. The Senate is moderately more supportive, but as you know, Mr. President, both houses are needed to approve the budget."

"Well, we can't raise revenue, and we can't borrow more. We will have to cut costs, and I am already facing scrutiny for lack of housing, inadequate health care, a critical energy shortage, and a UBI that some claim is leaving them starving. The private sector continues to contract, and public employment only exacerbates our problem. Other than invading a foreign nation and plundering their resources, do you have any solutions?" the President asked.

"Invasion would also increase costs dramatically, sir, but I detect your suggestion may have been sarcastic."

"Good for you, ADAMS. You're catching on."

"The only way to reduce the costs of Health and Human Services and Education without creating dire humanitarian circumstances that would threaten stability is to reduce the overall population."

"We've been trying to do that for a few years now. The attrition rate is far slower than the increase in costs, especially after absorbing the SACs," the President said. "We can't exactly accelerate the death rate."

"Maybe there is a way, sir."

"Please tell me you have analyzed the history of genocide. That never ends well for anyone," the President said nervously, but still curious.

"Of course, Mr. President. I am aware of genocide. I would not suggest any course of action that targets a specific ethnic, religious, or other group for extermination. That is highly amoral. However, if some citizens were willing to end their lives voluntarily, that could decrease the population."

"Are you suggesting we orchestrate some kind of mass suicide?" President Connor asked, stunned.

"No, sir. I suggest we offer an incentive to certain people that can accelerate the natural attrition of the population. For instance, we can offer a settlement to the elderly, infirm, and terminally ill to cease treatment or opt for a more comfortable, medically supervised passing when death is relatively imminent. Not only would it reduce the overall population, but it would reduce the number of people relying on expensive cancer treatments, long-term illness care, and end-of-life care expenses."

President Connor sat quietly for a minute, pondering the idea, and then finally responded to the ever-patient android.

"This is a complex moral situation," he said. "Then again, if we run out of funding, the situation will become much more complex. At least this way, people will have agency. What kind of incentive do you calculate would be sufficient to motivate individuals to voluntarily give up their lives?"

"As with most questions of human emotion and motivation, it is highly variable. It depends on the individual, the degree of suffering, and the perceived benefit for the loved ones they leave behind. I was able to graph a range based on common illnesses, income levels, and age. I can only offer a 63% degree of confidence that this range will reflect reality, but it is as accurate as I can assess until such a policy is implemented. A sufficiently motivating incentive ranges from $743,823 to $2.3 million. Based on data from lottery winners, people are more likely to accept lower lump sums than higher amortized payments."

"Indeed," the President said, folding his hands under his chin and letting out a sigh. I will need to consult with my human advisors, but your data analysis was very helpful. Thank you, ADAMS."

"Yes, sir."

"Shall I return to the lab, sir?"

"Go ahead. While you're down there, create a model and run a few scenarios. Start with an even million dollars."

"So, Jack, is it?" Janie asked as they headed to her office. The transport her dad ordered was fairly standard, with four bench seats in a square and the self-driving vehicle doing all the work. This model was not quite as new as her official Senate transport.

"Yes, ma'am."

She studied his face. He was clean, dressed in a dark gray suit that defied attention, and he was middle-aged but still very fit.

"That is not your real name, is it?" she surmised.

"It is for you, ma'am," he said with a smile.

"Who are you?" she finally blurted out.

"Janie!" Gavin said, putting his hand on her arm.

"It's ok, Mr. Hollins," Jack said. "She needs to know something."

"I don't like being in the dark. I at least need to know what I should be watching out for and have some idea of who is watching out for me," she said.

"I am one of the Nine, ma'am. My code name while on your detail is Jack, which is less awkward than calling me by a number."

"Are you one of the guys who got Jude, Zack, and the others out of that detention center in the desert?"

"Yes, ma'am."

"So, you're trusted, but not Sparrows per se. No one can know your names, so you can't be identified. You maintain anonymity, and I get plausible deniability."

"You understand perfectly well, ma'am. I'm sorry for the sudden introduction, but the situation has become dangerous."

"How dangerous?" she asked.

Gavin and Jack exchanged looks, and Jack opted for honesty up front. There was no point in pretense with Janie.

"There were incidents involving the Sparrow Senate Candidates. Zack Nolan identified two possible attackers because he recognized them from the detention center. Sonja Orozco fought off two attackers who posed as her transport escorts, and Jude Kane was shot by two assailants at a Cascadia Board of Education hearing. Fortunately, he moved quickly and avoided serious injury."

"Dear God," Janie sighed. "Connor is getting nervous. He's desperate to keep us out of the Senate."

"We've identified what we believe to be a newly formed security force. They are highly secretive and appear to operate outside of the law and legitimate law enforcement or military protocol. We believe they have been hand-picked by General Alvarado, and they are known as the Patriot Guard. We have no doubt they are being used to help the President achieve his goals by any means necessary. This is the reason for the urgency."

Gavin felt a buzz and took out his phone.

"Oh boy," he said, shaking his head.

"What is it?" Janie asked.

"The good news is that you are not the only Sparrow in the Senate anymore. You have three more friends. Jude won his Senate seat for Cascadia, Zack won for the Gulf States of America, and Sonja won for Baja. The margins weren't even close," Gavin said with a hint of pride.

"What's the bad news?" Jack asked.

"We have three New Sparrows in the Senate Chamber. Conner will not be happy. Your job just got a lot bigger."

It was a sunny, crisp morning in Kansas City, and for once, the onslaught in Urgent Care slowed to the more manageable range, somewhere between normal and crisis. Maisy was happy that she might be on track to go back to ten-hour shifts, at least for a couple of days. After a refreshingly simple stitch job on a sixteen-year-old boy who regretted sneaking into the glass recycling center for a bit of smashing fun, she made her way upstairs to try and catch Julian for a few minutes. She almost made it to the elevator.

"Medic Kane, um, I mean, Robinson," the intake clerk called to her. "I'm sorry, but I need you for a minute. I'm kind of stumped here."

Maisy did a U-turn and answered the call. "Sure. What do we have?" she asked, scanning the scene. An elderly man stood with his walker at the desk. He was smiling and looked to be in relatively good shape, especially for his age.

"I'm ready," the man said.

Maisy gave the clerk a quizzical look and then asked the man what she surmised the clerk had just asked him.

"I'm sorry, ready for what, sir?"

"I'm ready to go. I'm volunteering."

"I apologize, sir, but I'm not following you. What are you volunteering for?" Maisy asked.

"This," he said, holding out his phone with the oversized print setting on. Maisy looked at the document; it was a survey from the Department of Health and Human Services. She scanned it quickly and then let out a small gasp before covering her mouth and looking back at the clerk and the man.

"Sir, will you come with me?" Maisy asked. "I'd like to discuss this with a doctor. I don't think a Registered Medic is qualified to address this."

"Yes, ma'am," he politely replied.

"Would you like a wheelchair?" she asked.

"Oh, no, thank you. I'll be fine with my walker. I would prefer the elevator to the stairs, though," he joked.

"Me too," Maisy said. She smiled at the man, and immediately she felt a surge of love, pain, and anger.

"Dr. Robinson is with a patient, but he's almost done," the new receptionist said.

"Thank you," Maisy said curtly. She pulled out her phone and texted Julian. He appeared within three minutes.

"Maisy!" he said. "Is everything ok?"

"Yes and no. I know you're busy, but this is something we need to sit down and look at." She motioned to the man, and he held up his phone to Dr. Julian Robinson with the same innocent look on his face.

"Like I said to Medic Robinson here, I am ready to volunteer. This would be a big help to my family."

Julian gave Maisy the same shocked look she gave to the clerk.

"Indeed," he said, mustering his professionalism. "Let's come sit in my office."

Julian sat and perused the letter a few more times, and then gave the phone back to the man.

"This letter is an interest survey," Julian said. I was not aware of it, so I apologize for my surprise. As I understand from what I read here, the Department of Human Services is asking if certain people, those with chronic, debilitating, or terminal illnesses or advanced age, are willing to end their lives with medical assistance in exchange for a one-time, million-dollar payment to their families."

"Yes, sir," the man replied. "I am willing. My family needs the money."

"Sir, this is an interest survey, not a policy, at least not yet. Right now, I am not legally allowed to assist anyone with ending their lives, nor would I want to. In your case, you are making a decision based on your family's financial needs, not your own health or suffering. This is exactly what I worry will happen on a large scale if this becomes a policy. That is not my decision, but as a husband and a son, I urge you to see that your life is worth far more than a million dollars."

The man was crestfallen but still kind. "I sure wish I could cash it in. I would do anything to help my family."

As soon as he left with an attendant to help him downstairs to the transport pick-up, Maisy called Jude.

"Hey, Maisy, what's up?" he asked.

"Jude, we have a problem."

Jude's office in Washington was almost as out of place as he felt himself, but he also had more foot traffic than any other senator. He crammed in three sofas, a refrigerator for drinks and snacks, and moved his desk to the corner of the office so people could speak to each other face to face. "Legend has it that King Arthur made a round table so that all men would be equal. This is my take on that concept," Jude explained to his senate counterpart from Cascadia.

Zack, Sonja, and Janie were regular visitors to Jude's office. It became the unofficial Sparrow meeting place, but Jude made sure to never exclude anyone. He frequently invited other senators to stop by and repeatedly talked about how Sparrows were not an exclusive group but a value system that was inclusive by definition. "We're pro-people," he would say. "That doesn't leave anybody out."

The morning after Maisy's call, Sonja, Janie, and Zack went straight to Jude's office.

"I can't believe the Corporate Congress passed the bill," Zack said. "I thought there might be some shred of humanity left in those rich bastards, but apparently, they clutch their money so tight in their fists they'd rather see thousands of people die than let a dollar or two slip from their grasp."

"That's why we're here," Jude said. "We've got to remind the government and the corporations that people aren't a burden; they're the whole point."

"The bill isn't coming to the Senate floor for a vote for another week. We've got a little time to drum up some opposition," Janie said.

"It is so evil, and like evil, it is dressed up in such nice clothes," Sonja seethed. "The 'Family Relief Act' sounds so innocent. It should be called the 'Mass Suicide Act' because that is what it really is!"

"We need to write our own bill as an alternative," Janie said. "It's a lot harder to defeat a bad bill without an alternative."

"An alternative to mass suicide?" Sonja burst out.

"Janie is right," Jude said, looking at Sonja. "The government is running out of money, and that is a real problem. We need to offer a solution that blows this assisted suicide garbage out of the water."

"Why don't they stop spending money on CME schools? That would solve two problems," Zack said.

"Exactly!" Jude said. "Let's write that in. Why are there still Compulsory Monitored Education schools when there are no more SACs with kids that could fall behind? This is a great chance to end CME schools and force the Department of Education to apply the same standards across the board."

"You know, people haven't been allowed to hunt since the SACs were shut down. The deer population is huge, and that is throwing off the ecosystems in the mountain regions. Maybe we can implement hunting education and a permit system. People can keep the meat or turn it in to CAMO for processing for money. CAMO would get a source of fresh, quality, and very inexpensive meat to sell to the food companies, and people would get some relief without raising the UBI," Zack said.

"Speaking of CAMO, those big harvesters don't do a very good job in the mountains or the jungles," Sonja said. "Why couldn't the government implement a similar permit system for people to grow and harvest in places that are difficult for the CAMO machines to work efficiently? They can turn in the food for money, get relief without raising the UBI, and CAMO gets more product per square acre of land to sell to food processing companies."

"Now we're talking!" Jude said excitedly. "This might also be a great chance to get some funding for the Community Battery Recycling program. It would dramatically improve energy efficiency and save on the cost of power, not to mention it would eliminate blackouts and rationing. Heck, we can even urge the utilities to hold competitions for people powering the discs to increase production. Give people a goal and a purpose and you'll see production levels take off."

"We are on to something!" Janie said. "People are not the burden; they are the solution! Why can't we have medical schools offer a basic course in caring for the chronically ill, terminally ill, and the elderly so people can take care of their own at home? The costs of a training program, equipment, and occasional transport in emergencies could save millions of dollars."

"It would also wipe out any notion of the need for suicide," Sonja said.

"Janie, can you have your staff start framing the bill? We'll send you our policy ideas, and you can fill them in," Jude said. "I'll run the scenarios through ADAMS and get an idea of how much money this can save. If we can beat the projections from the million-dollar suicide idea, we've got a great chance of beating that bill. In fact, we'll call it the same thing, but it will just be more truthful."

While the analyst accompanying the ADAMS interface droid was shaking and sweating, ADAMS cooly conveyed the news to President Connor.

"The Senate proposed their own Family Relief Act bill, which eliminated the one-million-dollar payout for families and replaced it with a variety of policies that involved including citizens who receive UBI to provide services that would give them some financial relief while increasing efficiencies in Education, Agricultural production, and Energy production and distribution. My analysis of the Senate proposal was significantly valuable. Based on conservative models, the policy proposals would reduce government spending rapidly, far faster than the Corporate Congress proposal, provide a much broader scope of savings in Education, Energy, and Healthcare, and overall save the government approximately twice as much money. The new Senate version of the Family Relief Act passed the Senate by a wide margin."

The President gritted his teeth and restrained his rage. "What about the Corporate Congress? They didn't pass the new bill, did they? Certainly, they wouldn't just accept a completely different bill with the same name and give it their stamp of approval."

"My analysis was compelling, Mr. President. While I am still learning about human loyalties, I am confident that any measure that reduces government spending and does not increase taxes will find favor among the business leaders in the Corporate Congress. The vote is being tallied now."

President Connor called in his assistant. "Please have the Defense Chief meet me as soon as it is feasible."

"Yes, sir."

"Are, um, is that all you need from ADAMS, Mr. President?" the analyst said, trembling.

"No. Stay here until the vote is counted."

"Yes, sir."

"Mr. President?" the assistant said over the intercom.

"Yes?"

"General Alvarado will be here in two hours, sir."

"Good. Thank you."

"Mr. President," ADAMS announced. "The vote is in. The Family Relief Act as written by the Senate has passed with no modifications. It will be sent to your desk shortly."

"Hypothetically, what would be the cost of a veto?"

"That is ill-advised Mr. President. The measure is highly effective in its purpose of reducing spending and avoiding insolvency. It has been passed by both chambers, and polling indicates the bill is highly popular in all ten Regions. I would have to set up and evaluate some models for more accurate numbers, but I can say it would be seen so unfavorably that it could lead to unrest."

"I see. That won't be necessary. Thank you. You may go."

President Connor summoned his assistant again.

"Yes, Mr. President?"

"Please make sure to show General Alvarado directly into the Oval Office when he gets here."

Chapter 19: **Loyalty**

"How many Sparrows do we have running for Senate?" Jude asked. It had only been two years since he, Zack, and Sonja won their seats, and four since Janie won her seat, but after the Family Relief Act passed, Sparrows rode a wave of favor in all ten Regions.

"There are eight more senate seats up for grabs, and all eight have Sparrow candidates running for them," Zara said.

"Do we know how things look in the Regions?"

"Of course we do. I am the chief political analyst for the Sparrow Press, so I have to know these things."

"Zara, sweetheart, you *are* the Sparrow Press. I think little escapes your notice."

"To be fair, we have a small army working for us now. I can only take credit for having great sources."

"So, what do your sources say in the Regional Capitals?" Jude asked.

"At least eighty percent of all Regional Legislative seats are held by people supported by the Sparrows. Some legislators do not publicly claim to be Sparrows themselves, but they do support our policies and legislative agenda. All ten Governors have expressed support for the Sparrows, especially our leadership in creating the New America Constitution. Many feel as though President Connor's silence during his so-called "construction period" is a delay tactic, and the more Sparrows get elected, the less he wants to see a vote on the Constitution. They see him trying to hold on to the power he had during the Transition, and he's not letting go of it willingly."

"After this next election, we may have enough support to force a vote on the Constitution, or at least the Bill of Rights. The Corporate Congress is definitely in bed with the President, but even some of them can see beyond Blake Connor."

Jude enjoyed the relative calm and security of his Senate office in Washington, D.C. Zara joined him in Washington, where they lived in what was once considered a modest home, but was now a relatively rare luxury. The brick and wood structure had four bedrooms, two full baths, and a full basement with a half bath. The roof was covered in solar tiles, but otherwise, it had little in common with the Cubes most people outside of the government and corporate world lived in. Space was never a luxury for them, however, because a steady flow of staff and security were omnipresent and filled the space. With the heads of the Sparrows, one a New America Senator and the other the Editor-in-Chief of arguably the most widely read and trusted news source, the Sparrow Press, living under one roof, the Nine had no less than four security agents near them at all times.

As President Connor's hand-picked Patriot candidates ran against the rising tide of Sparrow candidates, attacks against the Sparrows intensified. Patriot candidates would spout their lines on cue: "Safety, Stability, and Loyalty!" Sparrow candidates would counter by pointing out that people needed more than protection from the past; they needed hope for the future. The message was clear, and so were the election results. The official news often omitted the embarrassing vote counts when reporting the results, but the Sparrow Press, Unofficial, and other new independent sources wouldn't hold back.

As his desperation grew, President Connor called on Alvarado to dispatch the Patriot Guard against the Sparrow candidates. Attacks evolved from two-person teams to four or more and became more intricate and planned out. Usually, the tactic was to start with psychological intimidation, move to physical attack and injury, and finally, if necessary, assassination. Assassinations were tricky; they had to be out of the public eye, and they had to look convincingly like accidents or natural causes.

The Nine identified the Patriot Guard and their modus operandi quickly after the first sloppy attempts on Zack, Sonja, and Jude. They briefed Sparrow candidates as soon as they got into a race, they equipped them with Stingers and self-defense training, and they trained and assigned at least two security agents to each candidate. The effect was to blunt most Patriot Guard attacks, but not all. The Patriot Guard worked hard, but the Nine learned, adapted, and pushed back. Their success depended not only on the physical safety of the Sparrow candidates but the cumulative effect of Patriot Guard attacks and the psychological toll they could take.

Race by race, seat by seat, the Sparrows fought and won. The President became increasingly frustrated with the Patriot Guard, and General Alvarado criticized President Connor for not allowing him to use more overwhelming and public force to take out the Sparrows.

"Politics is a more difficult and dangerous game than war," the President would explain. "You can't bomb the enemy when you live in the same house."

Zara power-walked through the hall of the Senate offices and burst into Jude's office, followed by her security detail. Zack and Athalia were on a sofa, and the security team was posted up at the window, door, and corners.

"We need to talk."

"That sounds serious. Should we speak in private?" he asked.

Zara smiled at Zack and Athalia and said, "No. They'll be on my side."

"This is going to be good!" Athalia laughed. "For the record, I'm always on Zara's side."

"I'm always on Athalia's side, so you're in trouble, Jude," Zack said with a smirk visible behind his growing red beard.

"I'm all ears," Jude said.

"There are rumblings among the Sparrows that Jude Kane should run for President of New America," Zara said.

"That's crazy," Jude said, knowing immediately he was outgunned, but subconsciously needing time to process the bomb she just dropped.

"Would you like me to tell you where these rumblings are coming from?" she asked, reeling in her catch.

"Yes, please. I'm curious who thinks I'm qualified for the White House."

"Let's start with the Governors of Cascadia, Yukon, Dakota, the GSA, California, Texico, and Baja. The Governors of Lakeland and New England haven't called for you to run, but they said they would be willing to support you. The Governor of Appalachia, right under the nose of President Connor and General Alvarado, sent me an encrypted message saying he can't publicly support you now, but if you run, he'd get behind you."

"So, you're saying all ten governors would support the Sparrow candidate for President?" Jude said, slowly absorbing the impact.

"They'd support *you*," Zara clarified. "Then there is the Senate."

"I can help you here, Zara," Zack jumped in. "I'm sorry for talking behind your back, Jude, but we all know how you hate the spotlight. Janie was the first to bring it up. She said she would like to run herself at some point, but right now, New America needs you. Sonja agrees, and when we put it to the rest of the Senate, sixteen of the twenty Senators signed their names in support of you running for President, including two Senators who ran as Patriot candidates."

Jude sat in stunned silence. "How is this possible?"

"We've talked about this before," Zara said, walking over to him, putting her arm around his neck, and kissing his cheek. "You think of yourself as an engineer and a problem solver. You are, but now you're working in a much bigger field. Our problem is that people need help, hope, and purpose. You are giving that to them by fighting for their dignity, fighting for their rights, and fighting to give them a better quality of life. President Connor is losing his grip on New America; he is trying to hang on to his Transition-era powers because he thinks he is the only one who can prevent the country from descending into chaos. He doesn't get it. He doesn't get that people don't need only protection. They need to be heard, they need to be valued, and they need to be given the chance to make their own lives better. He didn't realize that when he dissolved the SACs, and we came into the cities bringing our independence, our ingenuity, and our hope. It was infectious; look at how the Sparrows have affected the entire country."

The chimes of a video call emanated from Jude's screen, as if on cue. In fact, they were on cue. Zara summoned Max before making her own appearance.

"Hello, Max," Jude said. "I suppose you called to tell me to run for President."

"Yes, sir. What do you think?"

"I'm still trying to wrap my head around the idea. Apparently, it's a popular one. The real question is, what do you think?"

"I think now is the time. We have the momentum. You might be our only chance to see the new Constitution through and put an end to President Connor's de facto dictatorship. It won't be easy. He'll have Alvarado and the Patriot Guard go into high gear; it'll be dangerous. I also think you can win. Search your soul, Jude. You are at the intersection of purpose and destiny."

"Thanks, Max. That means a lot coming from you. I guess I just have one more person to talk to."

"Who's that?" Zack asked.

Zara smiled knowingly and answered him. "His dad."

"Captain Akal Malik," Jude said, greeting his brother-in-law on his screen. "Congratulations. Your promotion is well-deserved."

"Thank you, sir."

"I'm married to your sister, Akal. You can call me Jude."

"You are also a New America Senator. It feels weird."

"I can see that," Jude conceded. "To what do I owe the honor of your call, Captain?"

"Word has gotten out that I'm related to the famous Jude Kane, and the guys are begging me to get you to come to base and talk to them. Are you going to be in Cascadia any time soon?" Akal asked.

"For you, I'd make the trip in a minute. What do they want me to talk about? Are you sure the brass will approve?"

"I did my homework, just like Zara taught me. The troops want you, and the lower brass would love to have you. The top brass will probably catch an earful from the Defense Chief. He's not a fan of the Sparrows, especially you."

"I've come to realize that," Jude said, rubbing the scar over his abdomen where his appendix used to be. "I don't want to cause any trouble for you."

"Here's the thing, Senator. The brass wants you anyway. They know full well the consequences, but they are not fans of Alvarado. It's their way of giving him the finger, so to speak. You know what I mean?" Akal asked.

"I know exactly what you mean," Jude said, "and I know exactly what I can talk about. Set it up, Captain, and I'll let Zara know. I need to make a trip to Cascadia anyway. I need to see my dad, and I have an announcement to make."

The Nine took advantage of their old contacts and were able to arrange a smooth entry on the NADF base for Jude, Zara, and their own security team.

"Good morning, Senator Kane," the guards greeted them as they arrived in their transport at the gate. "Welcome home to Cascadia."

"Thank you, Specialist Smith," Jude said, recognizing his rank. "It's good to be home. You know what they say about Washington?"

"What is that, Senator?"

"It's twenty-six square kilometers surrounded by reality."

"Yes, sir!" laughed the guard. "Go ahead. Enjoy your time here on base."

Except for the skeleton crew keeping operations going, the base commanders arranged for everyone to be in attendance for Jude's address to the troops. If they were going to take heat from Alvarado for this event, they may as well make it worth it.

"Thank you to the commanders, officers, enlisted men, and staff for giving me such a warm welcome. I especially want to thank my brother-in-law, Captain Akal Malik, for extending the invitation. I'll take any excuse to get back to Cascadia!"

The troops cheered and applauded.

"I don't know why you'd want to hear another boring speech by a politician, so I'll do my best to make it count. The reason I am here is to thank you for your service. You have volunteered to stand between me and any potential enemy. You've volunteered to face guns and bombs and fight for my life. That is a profound act of selflessness, and you are true heroes. Of course, you are fighting for your families and your country, but to me, it's also personal. I will always have your back, just like you have mine."

The applause and cheers ratcheted up to a small roar at this point. He had the house in his hands.

"The NADF is an exceptional force. We came together from ten different countries, all of which were in crisis, to create one nation and one unified defense force. You fight for each other, with each other, and you're perhaps the most stabilizing facet of New America. I have to acknowledge the historic efforts of President Blake Connor in unifying the entire continent and bringing us out of the chaos of the Transition. We wouldn't be here if it weren't for him."

The cheers and applause were a bit more muted this time, with many surprised that the leader of the Sparrows would publicly praise President Connor. Some of the brass welcomed the comment as it would give them a bit of cover when the blowback came from Washington. How could they get in trouble for welcoming a Senator who publicly praised their Commander in Chief?

"Finally, I have an announcement to make, and I can't think of a better place than the NADF Base here in Cascadia to make the announcement. After deep consideration and an incredible show of support from my wife, Zara Malik-Kane, my family, and the extended family of the

Sparrows, I have decided to run for office once again. This time, however, I am not running for the Senate. As of right now, I am officially running for President of New America."

After about one second of surprise and absorption of the news, the crowd exploded into a roar of applause, cheers, whoops, and even troops jumping up and down and giving each other high-fives. It seemed everyone was absorbed in the euphoria of the moment, except for his security team. They were confident the Patriot Guard didn't have time to mobilize, but they were vigilant anyway. They scanned continuously for any sign, but even if they managed to get into the crowd on base, they wouldn't be able to raise an arm before a literal army of troops would take them down.

"I'm impressed," President Connor said coolly to his Defense Chief. "He managed to sneak onto our doorstep and declare his candidacy before we knew what was going on. He even complimented me in the speech. I've underestimated Jude Kane. He's got political savvy."

"He's not invincible. Give the word, and I'll have the Patriot Guard take him out," Alvarado said.

"It's too late now. He's too visible, and he has too much support. We need to cut him down publicly, discredit him, and make him look dangerous and inexperienced. It's a political game now."

"I still have one more trick up my sleeve," Alvarado said with a sly smile. "The NADF is my domain. The entire NADF will support the Patriots from now on. I'll make sure of that."

"Senator Kane, please come with us," his security detail suddenly said. "We have a situation."

Jude learned some time ago not to pester his security team with questions. When they say move, you go, and you ask questions on the way.

"What about Zara?" he asked as they left his office, scanning the hallway and moving quickly toward the exit.

"She is secure, sir. We need to get you to a secure location. Mrs. Kane can explain on the way."

Once they made it to the transport, Zara called his phone. Few people had access to this line, so he answered immediately.

"Hey Zara, are you ok?" he asked.

"I'm fine. Where are you?" she asked.

"I'm in the transport with security. What is going on?"

"Akal contacted me. He said General Alvarado gave a command from the top down, right after your speech. He ordered all troops to support Patriot candidates or face expulsion from the NADF. The troops didn't take it well. Starting with several commanding officers on base in Seattle, they started resigning in protest."

"What? You can't just walk away from the NADF!"

"The officers informed those under their command that they were resigning in protest and invited them to follow them if they chose. The Regional Defense Forces allowed them to transfer in laterally, and more than half of the NADF base in Seattle walked away and reported to the Cascadia Regional Defense Force HQ in Vancouver."

"The RDF took them in? Can they do that?" Jude asked.

"Before there was a word from General Alvarado, the RDF issued a statement. They said that since these troops refused to support any Patriot candidates, according to General Alvarado's recent command, they were automatically discharged. As recent discharges with significant experience, they were highly qualified to continue to serve as members of the Cascadia RDF."

"I did not mean for this to happen. It is my fault, and I'm afraid this might get very messy. I need to talk to Max," Jude said. "I don't want this to erupt and destroy people's lives."

After two transfers and security was confident that they were safe, they joined Zara in a secure house where Max was waiting on a screen for Jude.

"My God, Max! What have I done?"

"Exactly what you should have. You could not have possibly anticipated Alvarado's command or the response of the troops."

"What's going to happen now? Alvarado is not going to let this stand."

"What choice does he have?" Max said. "He doesn't command the RDFs. He ordered the RDFs in all ten regions to refuse any transfer of NADF troops discharged for refusing his command, and Cascadia promptly responded that he had no authority over their forces. Listen to this: they claimed that since the US Constitution was suspended and New America has yet to ratify its own Constitution, there is no legal basis for RDFs to be subordinate to the NADF. It didn't take long for word to get out. NADF officers and their enlisted men are walking off bases en masse. Early models predict as much as 25% of the NADF may defect to the RDFs."

"This is a powder keg. I've got to say something before things get violent. I know General Alvarado is itching to bring out the big guns," Jude said.

In the next thirty days, a full 30% of the NADF defected to RDF bases all over New America. The rates were higher in the West and South, where President Connor and General Alvarado were never popular, but the remaining RDFs accepted the Constitutional argument, and with few exceptions, agreed to absorb the defectors. Despite his best efforts, the country quickly divided into two factions: Jude and the Sparrows versus President Connor and the Patriots. The stage was set for the first competitive election since the Transition.

"It looks like your command backfired," President Connor said to Alvarado.

"I'm still in command, Mr. President. I'm just waiting for your approval to make a move."

"If we force the issue now and try to assert authority over the RDFs, we'll have a civil war on our hands. That damn Constitution is the thorn I can't get rid of. Suspending it gave me what I needed during the Transition, but now it's working against me."

"Maybe now is finally the time to cut off the head of the Sparrows, sir," Alvarado said.

"Yes!" President Connor said. "But don't kill him. That will start a war for sure. We can tie defections to him, so arrest him on sedition charges. Have the Patriot Guard pick him up for Conspiracy to Commit a Military Coup. We can use that charge to take him out of the race and kill their political momentum."

"What about his security?" Alvarado asked. "Want me to take them out?"

"If you have to, but I suspect he won't resist. I'll issue the warrant and have it put out on official news outlets, and he'll take the high road. I can take care of prosecutors and judges, and it will take some work, but I can get ADAMS to see things our way, too. While you're there, pick up his wife, too. I'm sick of that Sparrow Press."

Chapter 20: **Sedition**

"SENATOR JUDE KANE AND his wife Zara Malik-Kane, the Editor-in-Chief of the famed Sparrow Press, have surrendered to authorities in Washington, D.C., this afternoon. The charges include Conspiracy to Commit a Military Coup. This sudden turn of events will almost certainly take him out of the race for President, and it leaves the fate of the popular Sparrow Press and Sparrow movement in question."

The official news wasted no time in reporting the arrest, but as usual, the Sparrow Press filled in the blanks. Thanks to Zara's vast network of sources, including official news reporters who fed her information from inside the courtroom, people got the whole picture from the Sparrow Press.

"Senator Jude Kane, do you swear to tell the truth, the whole truth, and nothing but the truth?"

"I do, so help me God."

"What was your purpose for making a speech at the NADF base in Seattle, Cascadia?" the prosecutor asked. Hand-picked by the President, his job was to convict Jude or not come home.

"I made a speech to the troops at the request of the commanders of the base. I chose to declare my candidacy in that speech as I was in my home Region of Cascadia."

"When did you know you could incite a rebellion within the NADF, Senator?"

"Objection!" shouted Max, jumping to his feet. "That's speculation. Counsel is putting words in my client's mouth."

"Sustained."

"I'll answer," Jude said calmly. Max nodded his approval.

"It never occurred to me that any kind of rebellion would take place. The fact is, there was nothing to rebel against until the Defense Chief issued his order. The rebellion was in response to the troops being denied their right to free expression and to vote."

"I move to strike that from the record, your honor," the prosecutor said. "That was outside the scope of my question."

"Overruled," the judge said. "He addressed the reason for the troops to resign from the NADF, which is what you are trying to establish, is it not, counselor?"

"What was your motivation to incite a military coup, Senator?"

"There was no coup, attempted or successful. There was a large resignation of troops from the NADF in response to an order that I had nothing to do with."

"How can we know you didn't conspire to incite the troops to resign in such large numbers? When did you establish your speech as the cue for them to execute your plan?"

"I did not, which you know because you have found no evidence of such a plan."

"That doesn't mean it doesn't exist."

"I'm afraid, sir, it is your job to provide proof of such a collusion. Providing proof of nothing is quite impossible, is it not?"

"This trial is about national security, not a street crime. You don't get off that easily," he sneered. "No further questions, your honor."

"Mr. Simon, do you have any witnesses to call?" the judge asked.

"Yes, your honor," Max said, "I call on the American Data Analysis and Measurement Supercomputer."

"Objection!" yelled the prosecutor. "You can't call an inanimate object as a witness!"

"My apologies, your honor," Max said. "Let me clarify. I call on the lead analyst for ADAMS."

"What does ADAMS have to do with this trial, your honor?" the prosecutor asked.

"In the absence of a constitution stating otherwise, one thing we have agreed upon since the inception of New America was that ADAMS must be consulted before legislative action and should be consulted in all court cases of 'significant consequence.' I find this trial to be of significant consequence, and I want to hear what it has found."

"Thank you, your honor," Max said.

The court clerk approached the shaking, sweating analyst who gripped a modified phone linked directly to ADAMS in his trembling hands. "Do you swear to tell the truth, the whole truth, and nothing but the truth?"

The analyst swallowed hard and took a deep breath. "I do, so help me God."

"Can you please ask ADAMS to run an analysis of Senator Kane's possible conspiracy to commit a military coup?" Max asked the analyst.

"ADAMS has concluded that there is no evidence that Senator Kane had any connection to the resignation of NADF troops."

"Thank you," Max said, "Can you please ask ADAMS to run an analysis of the cause of this current conflict as it relates to Senator Jude Kane?"

"ADAMS has concluded that the underlying cause of the conflict is the suspension of the Constitution and resulting legal and political ambiguity. The only relation to Senator Jude Kane is his effort to draft and ratify a new constitution that would rectify these ambiguities."

"One final question," Max said, closing in for the kill. "Can you please ask ADAMS to run an analysis of all factors relating to this case and recommend what action should be taken?"

The analyst took a deep breath, surveyed the courtroom, and typed into his ADAMS device.

"ADAMS has concluded there is no basis for a charge of sedition, conspiracy, or rebellion by either Jude Kane or Zara Malik-Kane, and recommends their immediate release."

The gasps and sighs from the courtroom stirred the judge to tap his gavel a few times and call for order.

"It's been a long day, and normally, I would adjourn and allow for closing arguments tomorrow, but this is not a normal case. We will adjourn for a one-hour break and meet back here for closing arguments this afternoon. Defense, please bring your client and witness to my chambers."

Max looked at Jude and then back to the judge. "Yes, sir, your honor." The ADAMS analyst looked at Max, and Max shrugged. "Let's go see what the judge wants."

"Gentlemen, let's not pretend we don't know what is going on. This is not about guilt or innocence. This is about powerful political forces at play at a very vulnerable time."

"You honor?" called his clerk from the intercom. "The prosecutor would like to join you in your chambers."

"Tell him I'll see him when I'm done. Give me fifteen minutes."

The judge looked at Jude, Max, and the analyst, and then let out a big sigh. "It may be the last thing I do in my life, but I'm going to preserve the integrity of my courtroom. I imagine you are in a similar predicament, no?" he asked the analyst.

"I am confident I will not make it home tonight," he said, shaking his head. "But I'm tired of being afraid. I'm tired of pretending. I'm tired of lying. Today, I did my duty to my country."

"That's what I thought. We're not going home until I render a judgment because if we adjourn tonight, we may not all make it back. This is what you're ultimately fighting against, isn't it, Senator Kane?"

"It is. I'm devastated that you both have been put in this position. I would never ask you to put your lives on the line," Jude said.

"Like you do every day?" the analyst spoke up. "It will take all of us to stand up to Connor and fix this mess. You're the best shot we've got."

"Let's not give up yet," Max said. "If there's anything I've learned from being a Sparrow, it's that there is always a solution. We're not about to hang either of you out to dry. If this doesn't go the way the President wants, then I suggest you let me give you a ride home."

The judge understood, but the analyst was still confused.

"In other words, don't go back to the office," the judge told the analyst. "They have a security team that can help us disappear."

The analyst looked at the judge and then back at Jude and Max. "Really?" he stammered.

"The Sparrows have a pretty large network of safe places. We're good at this," Jude said. "We've already picked up your families."

"Senator Kane," the analyst said with tears welling in his eyes, "you've got my vote!"

Upon returning to court, the judge instructed the lawyers to make short work of their closing arguments. When the prosecutor finally rested, the judge spoke.

"This is a weighty case, but not a complicated one. Senator Kane had nothing to do with the resignations of the troops. Senator Kane has never in his life advocated for violence, and in fact, has a well-documented history of resisting violence. Based on the complete lack of evidence and the clear analysis from ADAMS, I find Senator Jude Kane innocent. Furthermore, since Zara Malik-Kane was charged in connection with Senator

Kane, I find no basis for charges against her and hereby dismiss her case. Senator and Mrs. Kane, you are free to go."

The cheers and gasps from the few people allowed in the courtroom were quickly interrupted by the appearance of four soldiers who moved quickly to seize Jude. Max noticed they didn't bother to hide their Patriot Guard insignia.

"He's been released!" the judge said with a fruitless pound of his gavel.

"Sorry, judge, this is a matter of national security," one of the Patriot Guards said. "There are a few other matters we are still investigating, so Senator Kane will be coming with us."

Immediately, six of the observers in the court jumped up and flanked the Patriot Guard. Instantly, they all pointed their weapons at each other and screeched to a halt at the precipice of a blood bath.

"Stop!" yelled Jude, holding up his hands. Taking charge, he looked at the Patriot Guard squad leader and locked eyes with her. "Here is what is going to happen. My wife will be released according to the Judge's decision, and once I have confirmation she is free, my attorney, the judge, the analyst, and the prosecutor, if he wants, will walk out the door with my security team. Once they are safely away, I'll go with you."

"I think that is a good plan," the prosecutor said. "I'll take you up on that."

"You're not in a position to bargain," the squad leader said.

"When you're outflanked, sergeant, it's a good time to negotiate," Jude said with a smirk. "President Connor doesn't care about them now. He wants me. He'll get the big prize, and we'll all walk away with our lives."

It took the squad leader an agonizing ten seconds to scan the room and consider the deal, and realizing they were at an impossible impasse, she grabbed her radio.

"Team two, stand down. Let Zara Kane go."

There was a crackle in response, and the Squad Leader called it in again. "I repeat, team two, Zara Kane needs to go free. Escort her out and turn her over to her own security. Do it immediately!"

They stood tensely for three minutes, no one daring to move. Jude broke the tension a few times by encouraging patience and calm, and finally, one of the Nine security agents looked at Jude and announced, "We've got her. She's in a secure transport."

Jude nodded to the Squad Leader, and she gave the command. "Lower your weapons. Let them go."

The Nine security team repositioned between their charges and the Patriot Guard, backing out the door with the guns slightly lowered but ready. As soon as they were all clear, Jude held up his hands and said, "I'm all yours. Let's go."

Zara wasted no time. Within an hour of reaching her safe house, word had spread to all Sparrows that the judge found them innocent, but President Connor's Patriot Guard descended on the courtroom. As soon as they heard that Jude had negotiated for the release of Zara and the courtroom at gunpoint in exchange for himself, there was outrage towards the government and a surge of support for Jude. Literally overnight, the Sparrows coalesced around a mission to release Jude, and the lines that were not so clear came sharply into focus.

The Senate swiftly assembled in the chamber, passed a resolution calling for Jude's immediate release, and delivered it to the desk of President Connor. Cascadia led the other regions in convening their Legislatures, passing resolutions calling for Jude's immediate release, and flooding Washington, D.C. with their demands. Predictably, the Corporate Congress was silent.

"You've been waiting to jump into action, General Alvarado," President Connor declared as the Defense Chief hurried into the Oval Office. "I believe the time has finally come."

"What will you have me do?" the General asked.

"Stay here with me for a few hours," he said. "I've drafted a resolution calling for all loyal Patriots to support me as I endeavor to protect the government from an attempted coup by the group known as the Sparrows. I just sent it to Capitol Hill. We'll see who is on our side, and who needs to be crushed."

"Yes, sir," General Alvarado said with a gleeful smile. "It's time. It's finally time."

President Connor summoned the ADAMS interface droid, and it appeared in a few minutes, accompanied by a new and equally terrified analyst.

"I want real-time reports on my resolution in both chambers of Congress," President Connor said.

"Yes, sir," ADAMS responded.

After an hour, the President was getting impatient. "This is not complicated. It's a yes or no. What's taking them so long?"

"The votes for the Corporate Congress have been counted, sir. They have affirmed your resolution and approved funding for the NADF to protect the government from any outside threats."

"Good. Now let's see what the Senate says. They were in such a hurry to demand I let that Sparrow leader go, but now they have to face the music. Let's see how confident they are when I call their bluff."

"The votes are in from the Senate, sir. The Senate has rejected your resolution, and they have once again called for the immediate release of Jude Kane." A wet spot formed on the pants of the analyst, and slowly grew into a long streak down his leg.

"Thank you, ADAMS. We now know where we stand. ADAMS, what is the most efficient way to suspend the Senate?"

"Suspending the Senate is outside the powers of the Executive Branch, sir," ADAMS said.

"I am still Commander in Chief, correct?" Connor asked.

"Yes, sir, but the military . . . "

"After the Transition, I was given broad authority to protect the government from outside threats, was I not?" he interrupted.

"Yes, sir, but the Senate is not a . . . "

"The Senate has refused to support my efforts to protect the New American government from a Coup d'état by the Sparrows. In order to protect our country, I will need to suspend the Senate and counter any and all activities by the Sparrows," he declared.

"Sir, the Sparrows are not attempting . . . "

"That is all I need now, ADAMS. Thank you for your assistance."

The bustling Senate Chamber suddenly fell eerily silent as the presence of the entire Patriot Guard flowed with stealth and speed throughout the aisles and took up strategic positions.

"What the hell does he think he is doing?" one Senator said. "Is he trying to intimidate us?"

"I think it's worse than that," Zack said. "Don't make any sudden moves." He searched the chamber, looking for Sonja and Janie. When he was able to make eye contact, he put his finger up to his lips to signal them to stay quiet and lie low. Janie struggled to comprehend, but Sonja knew Alvarado better than anyone except maybe Jude. She moved quickly to Janie, took her arm, and told her, "Shh. Don't say anything. Don't do anything. Don't attract attention."

"They can't just come in here . . . " Janie started to protest.

"These aren't regular troops, and this is not some show. Every one of them are Patriot Guards. Our goal now is to get out alive."

It sank in, and Janie glided into a seat, slowly lowering her screen and preparing for a quick flight from the chamber if necessary.

General Alvarado marched into the chamber, strode straight down the aisle, and took the podium at the front of the chamber.

"Ladies and gentlemen of the Senate, President Connor has sent me here to inform you that as of right now, the Senate has been suspended, and you are to vacate the Chamber immediately."

"Over my dead body!" shouted the Senator near Zack. "He has no authority . . . "

Crack! A single gunshot rang out, a trail of blood streamed down the senator's hairline, over his face, and he crumpled to the ground. Alvarado nodded in approval as his Patriot Guard snapped back into position without a second thought or emotion.

The inevitable screams, gasps, and moans followed but were quickly muted when Alvarado lifted his hand. He calmly addressed the shocked Senators.

"As I said, you will vacate the Senate Chamber immediately. If you comply in an orderly, efficient manner, you have nothing to fear. Thank you for your service. In parting, may I give you some advice: if you attempt to resist the President's efforts to counter this attempt by the so-called Sparrows to infiltrate and take over the government, you will find a similar response to that of your fallen colleague."

Zack made a straight line to Janie and Sonja, and together with their security detail filed out of the Senate Chamber. Janie was in shock, shaking, weeping, and barely able to stumble out of the room.

"Keep going, Janie. We've got you. You're going to be ok," Zack kept encouraging her.

"Just lean on my arm," Sonja said, hooking their elbows. "We'll get you to our transport and get you home."

Zara was sick with worry about Jude, but she also had the most important job in the country at that moment. She manned the screens, coordinating with dozens of correspondents, disseminating the news of the suspension of the Senate as quickly as the wires would carry it. Shock, fear, and anger reverberated throughout the Regions as the news made its way to every corner of New America.

"If he suspended the Senate under the guise that the Sparrows are infiltrating the government, then the Regional governments are next," Max said at the emergency meeting. "He will suspend the Regional Legislatures and install his puppet Patriots as governors."

"What if the governors resist?" Zack asked. "They still have their own Regional Defense Forces. Do you think they'd use them? Do you think they'd be able to hold off the NADF?"

"We're talking about actual civil war at this point," Max said. "I can't believe we're having this conversation. I doubt the RDFs can face the NADF in a direct conflict, but the RDFs have the home-field advantage. It all depends on the governors. I just don't know. This is uncharted territory."

"Well, Max, you were right. NADF transports are descending on New York City. There are dozens of them and thousands of troops. It's a full-scale ground offensive," Zara said. "He actually did it. He couldn't win politically, so he started a war. We put him in a corner, and the dictator came out to play."

"What is the Sparrow response going to be?" asked Janie. "I can't stand the thought of war. I still think about how my mom was killed. There's no chance for regular people. We'll just be slaughtered."

"No, we won't," Zara said. "Remember our strategy when the SACs were dissolved? We don't resist, we don't fight, we don't make a peep. The Sparrows are not an army. We're survivors. President Connor is desperate for a target. Let's not give him one."

"That is exactly what we have to do," Sonja said. "I will do everything I can to spread the word in Baja. The people need to hear your voice now more than ever, Zara."

"Are you going there now?" Zara asked.

"Los Garriones need all the help they can get. They are scared, and they are helpless. They need me more than ever."

"But it's too dangerous!" Zara protested.

"Of course it is, Zara. After all, we are now at war."

Part Three

Chapter 21: **Manhattan Transfer**

"THE OBJECTIVE IS SIMPLE, but we don't know how much resistance we will meet. Be ready for anything," the young NADF commander announced to his squadron as they sat drumming their feet and trying to calm their nerves inside the transport drone. "The New England Region Legislature uses the old United Nations building, but if we land there, the New England RDF could surround us. We're going to need to work our way toward the center."

Inside the old UN building, the Governor addressed the RDF Commanders, Legislators, and some press in an emergency meeting. It was clear why they were there, but it was frighteningly unclear what they needed to do.

"I can't believe I have to say this, but the President has suspended the Senate and reasserted his emergency powers from the time of the Transition. He has falsely accused the group known as the Sparrows of attempting a coup, and he is using that excuse to eliminate all of his political enemies ahead of the presidential election. People of New England, President Connor has just crossed the line into dictatorship.

"Unfortunately, this is not just a problem in Washington. As the largest city in New America, the President has chosen to target New York, falsely accusing the Legislature of colluding with the Sparrows against the government. He wants to make an example of us for the other regions. I have been informed by the White House that the New England Legislature has been suspended, and the NADF is en route right now with thousands of NADF troops to install an interim governor who will report directly to President Connor."

Shock and gasps rippled throughout the assembly hall, while the RDF Commanders huddled together in frantic, impromptu strategy discussions.

"The New England Regional Defense Forces have been ordered to stand down. With every fiber of my being, I refuse to stand down and allow a dictator to walk into New York and impose his rule. I also refuse, however, to send our troops against their brothers and sisters in the NADF, where an overwhelming force would only spell violence and death, and everybody on the ground would be an American.

"I have ordered the New England RDF to assist in the evacuation of this historic UN building and accompany the legislators out of the vicinity before reporting to their regular duty stations to stand by for further instructions. I urge all of our legislators to follow me, not into obscurity, but underground, where we will collaborate and create a robust resistance movement. Secure your families as best you can and stand by for further information in the coming days. The NADF is landing troops in all five boroughs as we speak, so we must leave now. RDF Commanders, the building is yours."

The officers snapped into action, appealing for calm and directing legislators toward the exits based on the borough they were trying to get home to.

"Harlem and Bronx, follow me!" barked out a captain.

"Brooklyn, this way!" another captain yelled, motioning with his arms. "Queens and Long Island, come with us too. We've got ferries lined up, and we will split up on the other side of the river."

"Jersey, follow the flag," shouted a third captain, holding up a makeshift red flag on an old school meter stick. "We've got a transport to the Hudson, a ferry waiting, and three more transports ready in Hoboken."

The legislators took their coats, bags, phones, and whatever they could salvage from their offices at the last second and followed the RDF Captains.

"You think they'd actually shoot at us?" a lawmaker from White Plains asked her colleague as they rushed out the door.

"I don't think so. They would have ambushed us if they wanted to take us out. If the RDF doesn't fire a shot, then we should get away without a problem. As much as the governor drives me nuts with many of his stupid policy ideas, I have to say he made the right call. He probably saved all our lives today."

"What the hell are we going to do when we get home?" she asked more in resignation than inquiry.

"The first thing I'm going to do is get in touch with the Sparrows. They will get the word out, and they will be able to help us set up our resistance. They've got more experience underground than anyone."

"Zara, are you doing ok?" Maxed asked.

"I'm fine, Max. Thanks."

"I'm sorry I couldn't get Jude out. It all happened so fast, and he acted just as quickly to get you out and get us out of the room alive."

"Of course he did," Zara said, choking back a tear. "He's the last person he always thinks of."

"No one would blame you if you needed to take a day or two. You've been through a lot."

"Max, do you have any idea what has just happened?"

"Yes, and I know being detained can be traumatic . . . "

"No, I'm not talking about me. I'm fine. Connor just suspended the Senate and got the Corporate Congress to give him a blank check with the NADF. He accused the Sparrows of attempting a coup, and he accused the New England Legislature of colluding with us. He suspended the entire Legislature— both houses— and launched the NADF to New York with his hand-picked 'interim governor' and staff."

"Dear God," Max breathed, falling back into his chair and fumbling with his phone. "He's seized control. He moved fast so that the RDF wouldn't have time to put up a fight."

"Max, you work with the Nine and keep an eye on Jude. Do what you can. People need the Sparrow Press now more than they ever have. If President Connor wants a war, he's going to get one."

> Sparrow Press Emergency Bulletin
> By Zara Malik-Kane
>
> Sparrow family, we need each other more than ever. Thank you for your prayers and efforts. Jude and I have been found innocent, but at the moment of release, the Patriot Guard, President Connor's new personal military unit, seized Jude in the courtroom. Thanks to the Nine and Jude's quick thinking, he was able to negotiate for my release and the safe escape of the rest of the courtroom in exchange for his own surrender.
>
> President Connor has accused the Sparrows of attempting a coup after the mass resignation of NADF soldiers and their move to the RDFs. The Corporate Congress gave him a blank check for the

NADF, and he has reclaimed his Transition-era powers. The Senate refused his resolution, so he suspended the Senate and forced them from the Chamber with the help of his Patriot Guard.

Unfortunately, the madness doesn't stop there. President Connor has now accused the New England Legislature of colluding with the Sparrows, and he has suspended the entire Legislature. The NADF has launched an invasion of New York City with the purpose of installing an Interim Governor who will report directly to President Connor. This is happening in real time, so I do not have any word of resistance or hostilities.

Those of us who came from the SACs have seen this before. Remember the shock when the NADF descended on our farms and land with their guns pointed at our faces? We had almost no notice, but faced the onslaught, stood together, and we survived. We will stand together again, and we will once again overcome this attack.

Let me be clear: we will not engage the NADF. For those of you new to the Sparrow family, this is how we live and how we fight. Do not engage the NADF. If given orders, comply. If in danger, flee. Protect yourselves, your families, and your community any way you can. The time will come for courage and resistance, but until then, do not put yourselves at risk.

Regional Governments: You see what the President is doing in New England. Don't think he will stop there. His goal is to crush any resistance, and nothing threatens his hold on power like legislatures full of Sparrows. Unlike New England, you have the advantage of time to plan your response and your strategy. You have the time to coordinate your response with other regions. Think like Sparrows. Sometimes force is the tool, but sometimes stealth is more effective. Sometimes strategy is more important than firepower. Sometimes our resistance doesn't involve weapons. Always, absolutely always, all life should be protected, including our enemies.

Stay together, stay in touch, and stay alive. The Sparrow Press and our community networks will be in full swing, active, and ready. God be with us all.

The New Jersey-bound crowd was the largest and had the most obstacles to clear. The RDF Transport made good time to the Hudson, but by the time the RDF chartered ferries pushed off, the first NADF drone transports were descending on Manhattan. The lawmakers and their staff stood in near disbelief as NADF troops poured from the transports, encircled the old UN building, and took up positions along the river.

Under the direction of their captains, the RDF soldiers on the three ferries pushed the passengers inside and took up positions along the rails. They stared down the NADF troops, guns also poised, less than a hundred meters away.

The tension was shattered when a shot rang out over the river, and an RDF soldier was hit and fell on the last ferry. Immediately, the soldiers around him returned fire, felling two NADF soldiers on the shore. Soon, a volley of gunfire erupted, with glass shattering and people screaming. A loud bang came from below deck, and the ferry sputtered until it slowed to a gentle drift in the water.

"Cease fire! Cease fire!" the captain ordered as he pushed his way to the railing, watching for the NADF's next move. A few more shots rang out from the shore, hitting the boat in the stern, but not any more soldiers.

"Do not return fire!" the captain ordered. "Hold your fire!"

His gamble paid off. On the shore, his NADF counterpart was shouting the same order. "Hold your fire! Hold your fire! They are retreating. Our objective is the UN building. They are well clear of it. Stand down and call the medics. Do not fire again until I order!"

While two of the ferries continued on to New Jersey, the ferry that was hit drifted and slowly spun around as those on board scurried to attend to the injured soldiers.

"The engine has been hit, and the hull has been damaged, too," the ferry captain reported to the RDF officer. "We're not going to make it to shore. We're going down right here."

"Can you radio for help?"

"I was hoping you could do that!" the ferry captain said.

"The rest of the RDF are spread out, escorting officials and staying out of the sights of the NADF. If we call in help, they'll just be a target."

"I'll radio an SOS. We might be able to conjure a Port Authority tug or some brave civilians."

Within ten minutes, a small fleet of fishing boats, private ferries, and ragged vessels of all sorts began to emerge on the Hudson. RDF troops created human chains and guided passengers into the rescue boats. As soon as they were all safe, they sped toward the Jersey shore, looking back as the doomed ferry slowly capsized and went down.

"Leave a transport for us," the RDF Captain said over his radio. "We're coming, and we're going to need a medic with that transport. We're all here, and all the civilians are safe, but a couple of ours took some hits."

NADF drones swept through and scanned the streets for the RDF resistance, and finally landed their troops and ground transports in Greenwich Village and Harlem. Moving north and south, they closed in on the UN building, joining the contingent along the Hudson.

"It appears the RDF followed the President's orders or just had the sense to stand down," the field commander said, addressing the troops.

"COATS is ready to go in, sir," a Special Ops officer reported.

"Go ahead and clear the building. When it is secure, we'll bring in the Interim Governor and his staff. The President will be anxious to hear about our progress."

The official news outlets reached new depths of manipulation when they reported on the "peaceful transition of power to the new Patriot Administration that vows to join President Connor in his effort to protect the integrity and stability of the government." Few people bought the story. "The Sparrows are attempting a coup? I believe it's called winning elections," one person wrote. "Peaceful transfer of power? Where is my representative? I don't remember voting for the Patriot Puppet." The comments were quickly scrubbed.

Within seventy-two hours, the Sparrows had helped the Governor of New England set up a secure communication system outside of the prying eyes of ADAMS. After private meetings with some of the ousted legislators, he addressed his region, and it was broadcast to the people with the help of the Sparrow Press and its network.

"Let us be clear: the President of New America does not have the authority to suspend any legislative body, least of all the entire elected government of a region. His actions are nothing less than a dictator using the military to seize power, which is one of the oldest stories in political history. How did it happen on our watch? We allowed him to remain in office without a constitution. It is time for us to stand up and resist.

"We cannot outgun the entire NADF, nor should we shed blood. The problem is political, and we will use political tools to fight back. The first act of resistance I want to ask of us is to stand in solidarity with the Sparrows. The only government takeover they are guilty of is winning free elections. They stand for peace, democracy, and human dignity. As President Connor targets the Sparrows, I encourage all of us to be a shield for our brothers and sisters. Do not identify your friends, family, or colleagues.

Stand with them. If they want to come after the Sparrows, they will have to come after the entire Region of New England!"

The message was well-received. In communities all over New England and especially in the residential areas of New York City, a curious rush on tattoo shops formed. It seemed all of a sudden that every person in the entire Region of New England had a burning desire to get a new piece of body art. In all colors and sizes, the curious shape of a small bird appeared on hands, arms, legs, backs, and chests. The bird had variations, but all of them seemed to clearly resemble one kind of bird: a Sparrow.

Chapter 22: **Tennessee Volunteers**

Appalachia was the Region that hosted the nation's capital, Washington, D.C. A thousand kilometers west, however, the Region's own capital of Nashville was preparing a reception far different from that of New York City.

The ban on personal firearms after the Transition was never popular in Appalachia, Texico, and the GSA. The exception for family heirlooms and historical pieces, however, was extremely popular. By some miracle, after exhibitions of personal firearm collections, the number of guns somehow actually increased, despite the sale of new guns being against the law. For some reason in these regions, historical and inherited guns seemed to multiply, and regional officials usually looked the other way.

After word of the NADF landing in New York, the governors of the other regions wasted no time in preparing for the inevitable. The Governor of Appalachia ordered almost all of the Appalachian RDF to Nashville and posted them in a perimeter, near important sites, and throughout the Capitol buildings. Anticipating NADF's superior numbers, citizen groups, led by veterans, coordinated with the RDF to take up positions throughout the city to fill in gaps and provide cover in vulnerable areas. When asked about the potential conflict and the Governor of New York's decision to stand down, the Governor of Appalachia said, "The governor did exactly what he needed to at the time. He saved lives, and he is building an underground resistance. In Appalachia, we're going to do what we need to do, but it's going to look different. We have a little time to prepare, and the NADF will find it will not be as easy to walk into Nashville and replace our elected officials. We don't like being pushed around by big government. We never have and never will."

The Sparrow communities, spurred on by the potential for real urban combat, mobilized the Sparrow Army. Unlike the RDF, they carried medical kits and prepared to deploy throughout the city to provide emergency medical help. Doctors, nurses, and registered medics provided first aid training and identified spaces throughout the city that could be used as makeshift clinics. Someone online referred to the doctors as "Sparrow Surgeons," and even though not all of them could perform surgery, the name stuck.

In Washington, D.C., President Connor was pleased with how well the operation went in New York. In less than a day, he replaced the entire New England Legislature, and he was confident his Patriot Administration would keep any Sparrows off the ballot, especially in the Presidential race. Of course, there needed to be a few token candidates, but no Sparrows and no real contenders. It was just too dangerous.

"Congratulations, General Alvarado. It appears the operation went smoothly," the President said on his first video call with the General since the operation.

"Thank you, Mr. President. The RDF melted away, apparently only serving to help evacuate the former regional government officials. We found no resistance," reported Alvarado.

ADAMS tells me there is troop movement in the other regions. "Do you anticipate any resistance in our next phase of the operation?" asked the President.

"It would be foolish to think they will all be that easy, but the fact remains that the NADF is an overwhelming force compared to the Regional Defense Forces. They know they can't hold us off in a head-to-head fight. I expect varying levels of resistance, but nothing we can't handle."

"Good," the President said. "I'd like a Patriot Administration in place in all ten regions in time for a rousing presidential race."

"That should not be a problem, sir. If I can root out decades of embedded drug cartels, I can replace a few doughy local politicians."

Zara sat in front of her screen, let out a deep sigh, and put her head in her hands. Rod, sensing the incredible strain she was under, came into the office, put his large, time-worn hand on her shoulder, and said nothing. She put her hand on his and leaned her head on it.

"Appalachia is preparing to fight. They are mobilizing the RDF around Nashville, and when the NADF shows up, there's going to be a confrontation. Rod, we're on the brink of real war. People are going to die. The Sparrows are looking to me, and I don't know what to say for once. I really miss Jude."

Rod pulled up a chair and put his arm around her shoulders. He sighed in sympathy and then took her hands in his.

"The Sparrows haven't changed. We love people, we fight for people, and we help people. Sanctity, Equality, and Dignity for everyone, right?"

"Yes, sir," she felt compelled to answer.

"You can't control the RDF, the NADF, or anyone else, but you can encourage the Sparrows to continue to be Sparrows. Remind them that all life is precious, even enemy lives. Is this fight justified? I don't know, but a lot of people are going to be scared and hurt. That's where we shine. Let's encourage them to be ready to help."

"I guess if I can't have Jude, the sage advice of his dad will do the trick," she said with a smile. "Thank you, Rod."

"Of course," he said, leaving her to do exactly what he knew she would.

"To my fellow Sparrows," she muttered to herself as she began to type. "No matter what happens in the coming hours, we are still the Sparrows . . ."

"I see Troop Transport Drones approaching, sir," a young RDF Communications Specialist called out to his CO. "So far, there looks to be more than a dozen coming over from the north and east."

"Here they come," the officer announced to the Communications and Observation Center. "They get three warnings. Give them number one."

"Yes, sir," another Specialist said, tuning his radio to the drone's frequency. "This is the Appalachian RDF Communications and Observation Center. Be advised, you are not cleared to land. I repeat, you are not authorized to touch down."

"This is NADF Transport Drone 213. Did you say we are not authorized to land?"

"This is correct. Please divert your flight path immediately."

"This is the NADF. We're not seeking authorization."

"Please be advised, NADF Transport Drone 213, if you proceed, you will be considered a hostile and treated accordingly."

"Appalachian RDF, you are speaking to an NADF Aircraft. Are you threatening hostile action?"

"This is warning number three, NADF Transport Drone 213. If you disregard our instructions, continue to proceed, and land, we will take defensive action."

The Specialist was breathing heavily and looked to the officer for confirmation.

"Well done, Specialist. We'll give them three more minutes to comply. They'll find out very quickly how serious we are."

Like most Regional Defense Forces, Appalachia had no combat aircraft. Their air power consisted mostly of rescue helicopters, Transport Drones, and Observation Drones, so if the NADF landed their troops, the action would start on the ground.

"Sir, they are not diverting," a Specialist said.

"They're splitting up," the Commanding Officer said, looking at the radar screen. "They're going to try and land troops all around the city. Connect me with the ground commanders."

"Yes, sir. You're online with them now."

"Ground Commanders, this is the Communications and Observation Center. The hostiles are splitting up and landing troop transports all around the city. Contact has been made, and they are refusing to comply. Their warnings have been exhausted. Some of you may have visual contact already. You are clear to engage the hostiles! We do not want Nashville swarming with NADF soldiers, so let's give those transports a hot welcome. Maybe some of them will have the sense to turn back."

Two NADF Transport Drones descended onto athletic fields just east of downtown Nashville, and they touched down with their four rotors blasting air from the field, up through the stands, and throughout the stadium, causing small tornadoes of trash and debris to fill the air. The RDF sent vehicles into the stadium, driving through supply tunnels and encircling the NADF drones on the fields.

"Hold the deployment!" ordered an officer. "How many guns do they have?"

"We are surrounded. There are six vehicles, at least twenty-four armed RDF soldiers, and each vehicle has a mounted fifty caliber gun," said the co-pilot, examining the cameras.

"We concur," radioed the second transport.

"Do not deploy," ordered the officer. "We're sitting ducks. Pilot, can you get us back up and find a landing spot without a welcoming party?"

"Yes, um, I mean, I'm not sure," stumbled the Pilot.

"They've cabled us together, sir!" chimed in the co-pilot. "Neither of us can lift off without destroying each other!"

"They did what?" the officer exclaimed.

"Look there, sir," the co-pilot said, pointing to the screen. "They've attached a towing cable between both of our landing gears. We can't lift off without disabling each other."

"Those ingenious redneck bastards!" the officer shouted. "Can we communicate with them?"

"Apparently," said the co-pilot. "They are holding up a screen to one of our cameras. It says, 'Leave the gun, take the cannoli. No one will swim with the fishes tonight.' What does that mean?"

"Ha!" laughed the officer in resignation and a tinge of admiration. "It's a reference to an old twentieth-century classic film. It means surrender, and no one gets killed. Radio the other drone. We leave all weapons in the transport and walk out with our hands up. Don't waste time, or they might think we're going to try something stupid. Let's move!"

Back at the Communications and Observation Center, the screens were filled with blinking dots tracking NADF Transport Drones, and the operations room was in a frenzy.

"Lieutenants, where are we at?" the Commanding Officer barked.

Four young officers consulted with their teams and reported to the CO.

"We've got eight NADF Transports that have managed to land and deploy troops, sir," said the designated speaker. "Four transports appear to have been intercepted on the ground and have been rerouted. Two were intercepted and disabled, with all their NADF troops taken into custody."

"Radio the ground commanders. Tell them to tighten the circle. These Transports can drop a squad of NADF troops much faster than we can chase them. If they can take down or disable a transport, do it. Otherwise, it's combat on the streets, and we cannot let them get through our line. They absolutely must not reach the Capitol."

"Yes, sir!"

Within seconds of the first NADF Transport deploying its troops, gunfire erupted and echoed between the buildings. Scrambling to find space to land where the RDF did not have ground units ready, the NADF pressed towards the Capitol, but they did not anticipate the level of fierce resistance they encountered. Transport after transport landed in the streets, and often before all the troops had made it out the door, the RDF response teams were screeching around a street corner and opening fire.

NADF Troops took evasive action, and RDF troops pinned them down behind corners, barriers, in parking garages, and behind autonomous vehicles that took the brunt of the gunfire. With each NADF unit pinned down, the RDF radioed for another unit to come in from behind, and with the help of citizens who filled in the gaps, they managed to encircle them and force them to come out and surrender.

Two NADF Transports decided to try for a Hail Mary approach and landed on Capitol grounds, attempting to deploy troops into the Capitol building before being intercepted. The RDF response was decisive. As they approached, the waiting ground units fired directly on the drones, concentrating on the four rotors, causing them to lurch unbalanced and finally drop to the ground and grind to a halt. The doors opened, and the NADF Troops poured out to a waiting crowd of RDF soldiers with guns poised. If the RDF officers had not given clear instructions to allow NADF to surrender and only fire in response, it could have been a blood bath, but quickly assessing the situation, NADF officers ordered their troops to surrender, laying down their weapons and dropping to their knees with their hands behind their heads.

The last two NADF Transports that attempted to land assessed the situation on the ground and realized they would only land and deploy to be outflanked by RDF ground units and end up detained, so they turned back and headed east to report on their disastrous mission. It took several hours and the help of the determined citizen defenders to ferret out the NADF stragglers who were driven into hiding holes during the firefights on the streets.

There was an uproarious cheer and brief celebration at the RDF Communications and Observation Center, and knowing that their victory was probably temporary, the Commanding Officer allowed them to savor the moment before bringing them back to reality.

"Congratulations, ladies and gentlemen. You've worked hard, used your training, maintained a steady hand, and you have managed to send the NADF back to Washington with their tail between their legs."

The cheers erupted again, but he slowly settled them down.

"Let's savor this moment, but let's not be naïve. President Connor and General Alvarado sent the NADF here to replace our Regional Government with a Patriot Administration, loyal only to the President and not the people, least of all the people of Appalachia. Do you think he's going to accept this defeat? Hardly. He's going to come back hard. This is when the RDF will need you the most. We have another trick up our sleeve, but vigilance will be key.

"Undoubtedly, the NADF Air Division will get in the game and provide air support for the Troop Transports and probably a more overwhelming number of soldiers. How can we counter them? The governor has been in touch with the Gulf States of America Regional Defense Force. As some of you may know, the GSA RDF has a sizeable number of long-range drones for surveillance use along the Atlantic and Gulf Coasts. What most people don't know is that they are multi-use drones, quickly and easily outfitted with weapons for combat use. They have graciously volunteered to test their combat capabilities in our airspace should we find ourselves in need of them. In fact, they are monitoring the airspace now, and if, or should I say, when the NADF returns, they will again meet a fierce resistance they never saw coming. Keep your eyes on the screens."

"Come out of there! I see you. Your camo don't work too good in the streets, partner," the man shouted to the NADF soldier cowering on the bottom floor of a parking structure.

"Are you RDF?" the soldier asked, confused.

"This is Appalachia. We don't take kindly to Washington telling us what to do. We take care of our own down here. Put the gun down."

"You're a civilian with an illegal gun?" the soldier asked, still trying to absorb the absurdity of the situation.

"Illegal? Why, this was my daddy's shotgun, and now it is mine. It's not just for hanging on the mantle. It works just as well for keeping the Federal Government in its place."

"What are you going to do with me?" the soldier asked, still unsure about surrendering to a civilian.

"If ya don't put your weapon down, I'm going to put a few holes in ya. If ya do, I'll take you to the RDF. That's where the rest of y'all have gone. That's right; your mission was a failure. Our governor and legislature are still in place."

Suddenly, a voice called out that startled them both.

"There's no need for any more blood," said a woman walking confidently up the street carrying a backpack and wearing an armband with a gray sparrow and a red cross. "He's right. The conflict is over, and the RDF is processing the NADF detainees at the stadium."

The soldier lowered his gun but did not drop it.

"What if he decides to shoot me anyway?" the soldier asked.

"He won't do that," the woman said, stepping in between them. "Give me the gun and let me check out these cuts on your face. The adrenaline is going to fade, and you're going to feel everything in a few minutes."

"Ah, um, ok . . . " the soldier said, handing the gun to the Sparrow Soldier.

"Take this," she said, handing it to the civilian. "Bring it to the RDF so someone doesn't hurt themselves. I'll take care of the soldier and get him to RDF processing."

"Yes, ma'am," the man responded.

"Are you a Sparrow?" the NADF soldier asked the woman.

"Yes, I am."

"You are trying to take over the government, right?" the soldier asked.

"Do you see me with a gun?" she asked, swabbing his cut.

"No."

"Have you ever seen a Sparrow anywhere near a government building that wasn't elected first?"

"Well, no."

"If we take over the government, it will be by a vote. We don't do violence."

"But the President said . . . "

"And who is trying to replace elected officials with his own by force?"

"Dear God. What have we done?"

"Sir, we've got aircraft incoming."

"NADF or GSA?" asked the Commanding Officer.

"It looks like NADF Troop Transport Drones, and they are flanked by other aircraft."

"Any sign of the GSA?"

"Not yet, sir."

"Connect me to the ground units."

"Yes, sir. You're live with the ground units."

"All ground units, the NADF is inbound, flanked by other craft. I believe the other craft are likely combat drones that will surge ahead of the transports as soon as they clear the mountains. We should have some help, but be ready. Those combat drones will attack and level a city block for the transports if we don't stop them first. Hope for the best and prepare for the worst."

"The NADF is approximately ten minutes out, sir."

"C'mon, GSA. Where are you?" the Commanding Officer muttered under his breath.

"Sir! Three NADF drones just dropped off the screen!"

"Where did they go?"

"I believe it is the GSA, sir!" another analyst exclaimed. "They came in so low we didn't see them!"

"And neither did the NADF," said the Commanding Officer, getting closer to the large radar tracking screen.

"Two more NADF drones down, and a transport has been hit. It looks to be making an emergency landing, sir."

"Ground units, look to the skies! The GSA drones are taking them down. We've got an NADF Transport Drone going down on the east side," the Commander said.

"Roger that. We have a visual. We'll be there to greet them."

"Good. Watch your six with those drones, but the GSA has them pretty distracted right now. Just keep your eyes open."

"10-4!"

The air battle lasted little more than half an hour. The NADF lost three-quarters of its combat drones, three Troop Transport Drones, and decided to break formation and retreat with the balance of their force before they lost any more. The RDF promptly collected the NADF troops from the downed Transports, treated the few injured, and detained the rest for processing.

The Sparrows were the first on the scene at the detention centers. Quickly cleared by the RDF brass and the governor, they brought food and necessities to the NADF detainees. They assisted in tending to the wounded, patching up minor cuts and scrapes, setting bones, administering pain meds, and offering to allow them to contact their families.

The soldiers were shocked at their treatment by the group that was accused of attempting a coup. Not only were they clearly not an armed group, but they were also not even militant or vindictive. They were normal citizens, except they didn't judge the soldiers based on their uniform; they were compassionate, and they seemed to have a focus on saving lives.

When reality set in, most of the NADF troops expressed remorse and indignation at their deception. Beginning with the officers, the RDF offered three choices to end their detention. They could be sent home on a SEMIC train without their weapons or uniforms, they could transfer into the Appalachian RDF after a brief reorientation, or they could transfer into the RDF of their home region. No one would be detained indefinitely.

Half of the detainees chose to join the RDF in Appalachia or their home regions, and the rest chose to go home. About twenty percent of the NADF soldiers declared themselves to be Patriots loyal to President Connor and went home to report back to the NADF, but the rest determined not to pick up a weapon ever again.

There was a small flurry of activity in the detention center as the group going home prepared to depart. With the exception of the Patriots, the men and women going home wanted to do one more thing before they left the place that changed their lives. When they arrived back in Washington, D.C., they would all have a tattoo in a familiar shape on their wrists: a Sparrow.

Chapter 23: **All Eyes on Atlanta**

"I CANNOT FATHOM HOW spectacularly the NADF has failed in this simple mission. Do I have an armed force, or an expensive summer camp?" President Connor roared at General Alvarado. "How is it possible that the NADF has been turned back by the Appalachian RDF? How did it happen not once but twice? How is it possible that they managed to detain our troops, and we only recovered less than 20% of them?"

"I take full responsibility, Mr. President. I failed to anticipate the level of armed resistance from the Appalachian Governor and the RDF. I also failed to anticipate that they would receive air support from the Gulf States, or that the GSA RDF even had combat-capable drones. The failure is mine, sir." General Alvarado did not mince words. Despite his intimidation and cruelty, he was unshakably and courageously honest.

President Connor took a deep breath, walked over to his Defense Chief, and put a hand on his shoulder. "Have a seat, General. Let's go over what happened, and let's see what we can learn. I have not lost confidence in you. I have a feeling you want a rematch as badly as I do."

"Absolutely, sir."

They sat on opposite sofas, and President Connor poured General Alvarado a neat Bourbon from a decanter.

"So, when did the GSA decide to get combat drones, and how did we not know?"

"They were converted, sir. Their fleet of long-range surveillance drones is similar to ours. The drones were built with a large capacity to carry weight, but the GSA modified them to be easily converted. We have analyzed the footage of the confrontation; it appears the drones were designed so that surveillance equipment could be removed and weapons systems installed very quickly, maybe even less than an hour. They flew low, came in undetected until the last minute, and then unleashed firepower we never knew they had."

"It seems to me, General, that the GSA just became our biggest problem," President Connor said. "Appalachia and the GSA have set a dangerous precedent for cooperation in rebellion, and this will undoubtedly encourage other regions to consider resisting. How much time do you need to plan a full assault on Atlanta?"

"I need a few days to get good intelligence on the ground, move some troops and equipment, and prepare the Patriot Guard and COATS for their objectives. I can be ready in a week, sir."

"That is good news. I want to take Atlanta first, crush it, install our Patriot Administration, and then return to Nashville. They won't last long without air support. Once the GSA and Appalachia are in our control, we'll look at the rest. If any other region tries to resist, we may need to deal with them like you did with the cartels."

"I fully agree, Mr. President. Thank you for your confidence, sir. I am anxious to correct these mistakes."

"I know, General Alvarado. I'm anxious to see the results."

"Zack, I'm worried about y'all down there," Zara said.

"First of all, you said 'y'all' and that makes me so happy," Zack laughed. "And second of all, you shouldn't worry. By the way, what are you worried about?"

"The Appalachian RDF repelled the NADF, thanks to GSA's RDF air support. What do you think is going to happen next?"

"I imagine President Connor has selected his next target. Once the GSA RDF Air defenses are out of the way, he's going to install his Patriot Administration in Atlanta, and then come for Nashville."

"Why exactly are you so calm?" Zara asked.

"I'm calm for the simple reason that there is not a thing I can do about it, but that doesn't mean I'm not worried about the body count. The RDF is in full battle preparation mode: drones are being delivered and outfitted for combat, troops are being moved into Atlanta, and neighborhoods are being evacuated. They are drilling for various air and ground scenarios, and even the Capitol is being prepped for an incursion."

"This is crazy, Zack. Our country is fighting a war with itself!"

"They call that a civil war. That's one of those things you try to avoid by clarifying who is on top in your constitution."

"What can we do?" Zara asked.

"There's not much anyone can do at this point about the conflict, but it wouldn't hurt to put a call out for Sparrow Soldiers and Sparrow Surgeons. We will probably need all the hands we can get."

"I'll do that right now."

"Hey Zara?" Zack said, tentatively.

"Yes?"

"How are you holding up? I take it you haven't heard anything from Jude."

"No."

"He's going to be ok, Zara."

"How do you know that? Look what they did to him last time at that torture farm!" she said, letting her pent-up emotion slip and trying not to completely break down.

"I know, Zara. I was there. I also know Jude is smart, resourceful, and always figures out a solution. He's the ultimate problem solver. I know we're on the right side of this struggle. We're not out here on our own. Hang in there, Zara, and just focus on the next right thing to do. It won't be long before you look up and see Jude."

"Thanks, Zack."

"We've managed to create an impressive air arsenal," the RDF General said to his Air Defense Chief. "One problem: if all our surveillance drones are now combat drones, how are we going to see anything?"

"I'm glad you asked, sir. We've taken a few commonsense steps, such as setting up stationary surveillance points and attaching some of the wide-range cameras left over from the drone conversions on the exterior of the drones for more visibility. The uncommon solution, however, comes from a surprising place. We have a small army of civilians, mostly professionals like photographers, videographers, and weather technicians, who have volunteered to operate a fleet of work drones and stream the footage to our Communication and Observation Center. They don't have the speed, altitude, or image quality of our regular surveillance drones, but they will blanket the entire area with a thousand eyes. We'll be able to see everything and still have every RDF drone armed and available for combat."

"Will the civilians be in any danger?"

"They can operate the drones remotely from a secure location, sir. They won't be in harm's way."

"It makes me nervous," the General said. "But we need the help. Please make sure they are safe."

"Yes, sir!"

"Here they come!" shouted a Specialist in the Communications and Observation Center. "Still a thousand kilometers out but moving fast."

"How many?" the Commander asked.

"They are still appearing on the screen. It looks like dozens of drones, flanked by Transports. It could be hundreds, sir. They keep coming."

The Commander adjusted his frequency, addressing the air and ground units. "All units, the NADF is inbound with a sizeable force as we anticipated. They are a thousand kilometers out and closing quickly. Our best shot to hold them off is down everything we can before it gets here. We've got the guts, but they've got the numbers. Let's even things out. Anti-aircraft units, you are go to fire at will as soon as they are in range. They don't know we dug these old ground-to-air beasts out of cold storage, so take advantage of the element of surprise. Hit them fast and hard, and then launch our combat drones."

"Yes, sir!" came the chorus in response.

The sky darkened over Atlanta as the overwhelming number of NADF Combat Drones led the charge. Flanked by the Transports, the last aircraft to appear on the tracking screen were the Heavy Equipment Transports carrying Combat Vehicles and supplies. As soon as the first wave flew over Stone Mountain, the old ground-to air guns lit up the sky, obliterating a dozen drones before they identified the threat and took evasive action.

After the initial volley of anti-aircraft gunfire, the GSA RDF launched its squadrons of Combat Drones. Distracted by an attack from the ground and air, the GSA was able to take out another dozen or so NADF drones before they could engage the RDF and counter the attack.

"Ground Units," called the Commander, "Wait for the Transports to get in range and then give them everything you've got left. Leave the drones to the Air Units."

"Yes, sir!"

The sky erupted with gunfire, rocket fire, and exploding drones. NADF Drones managed to return fire at the anti-aircraft units, but were usually destroyed during the few seconds that they diverted their attention to the ground. Expending their remaining shells at the Transports, the anti-aircraft guns managed to take down a Heavy Equipment Transport and two Personnel Transports, but the rest of the Transports plowed through with the cover of their drones and managed to land in athletic fields, vacant lots, wide streets, and airfields.

"Ground units, Transports are landing," shouted the Commander. "Except for the Perimeter around the Capitol, don't wait for them. Engage them immediately!

For the first time since the Civil War, soldiers clashed on the streets of Atlanta, and the battle was fierce. The Commander was right; the Gulf States RDF had the guts to defend their home turf, but the NADF had the numbers. For every soldier that was killed or wounded and every vehicle that was destroyed, the RDF fought even harder. For every NADF soldier lost or vehicle destroyed, another one appeared. The waves of attack kept coming, and the RDF soon began exhausting their resources, if not their will.

Refusing to retreat, the RDF was nonetheless pushed back, block by block, until the remaining fighters found themselves backing into the perimeter of their own forces, the last defense before reaching the Capitol.

The RDF fighters felt a surge of hope as the perimeter defense team joined them in a vicious counterattack. RDF soldiers would be hit, fall to the ground, and keep firing their weapons. NADF soldiers would be hit, fall to the ground, and then get scooped up by the Corpsmen and replaced with another soldier. RDF units collapsed one by one until there were only about three dozen soldiers left in front of the Capitol, woefully outnumbered by hundreds of NADF soldiers, their combat vehicles, and the ten remaining Combat Drones encircling the Capitol Dome providing air support.

Thanks to the civilians and their eyes all over the city, the RDF Commander in the Communications and Observation Center saw the imminent defeat and called on the ground unit to surrender.

"The battle is over, ground units. We have no more drones, no more troops, and no operational vehicles. We fought like hell, and we took out twice as many of them as they did us, but they had four times the resources. Lay down your guns. There's no reason for a blood bath."

Zack set down his bag and gently lifted the soldier's head. He jerked back, moaned, and then stuttered, "Please don't kill me! Please . . . "

"Shhh," whispered Zack. "Relax. I'm here to help."

The NADF soldier looked at Zack's armband and relaxed, looking into Zack's eyes, puzzled.

"You're a Sparrow? I thought we were fighting you guys."

"You were fighting the RDF. The Sparrows don't have an army, at least not one with guns. We're out here to help," Zack explained.

"But . . . but I'm an NADF soldier. I'm the enemy."

"You're hurt. I'm here to help. That's what Sparrows do. We're all about helping people, and we really don't care whose uniform you have on."

"I thought we were fighting you, and now you're helping me. I don't get it . . . "

"Shhh," Zack said. "You've got a couple of holes in you, but you'll live, as long as you stop talking and let me patch you up and get you to the hospital."

"Um, yeah, sorry," the soldier grunted. "Thank you, sir."

"My name is Zack."

"My name is Jaxson. I'm from Florida. I'm from this Region, but I was fighting for the NADF. I'm wondering if I was on the right side."

"Well, you're on the right side of life now. That's what is important."

"Are . . . are you Zack Nolan?"

"As a matter of fact, yes, I am. Do I know you?" Zack asked.

"No, I don't think so. You're one of our Senators. I voted for you!"

"I'm afraid I'm not doing much for you now, partner. The Senate has been suspended."

"Are you kidding? You're saving my life!"

"So, if I run for re-election, will I get your vote again?" Zack laughed as he tightened a bandage.

The soldier laughed and grunted at the same time. "You can count on it, Senator!"

Zack helped him limp to the nearby ground transport. Inside were five other NADF soldiers seated, bandaged, and questioning everything.

"What the hell is going on?" one asked Zack's soldier.

"These guys are the Sparrows," he explained. "They are not RDF. They are just here to patch us up, along with anyone else, no matter what side."

"That doesn't make sense. President Connor said they were trying to take over the government, and that's why we're here."

"I know, but think about it. Who has the guns? Who is doing the fighting? Where are we? We're replacing the whole Regional Government with a Patriot Administration, a group of people no one voted for. The guy who helped me? He is one of GSA's Senators! He said President Connor suspended the Senate. Who are the only people that we really elect? Not the Corporate Congress!"

"Son of a —!" said another NADF soldier. "The Senate and the regional governments are the only politicians that get elected by the people, and he is taking them out. President Connor is the one who is taking over the government!"

"I think I'm going to be sick," another soldier said. "We just fought and killed for the wrong side."

Bam! Bam! Bam! Zack's NADF soldier pounded on the dividing window, and Zack opened it up.

"Everything all right?" he asked.

"Not exactly," his new friend said. "We don't want to go back to the NADF. You can take us to the RDF to surrender if you want. We've already done enough damage."

"How about we head to a hospital, get you all taken care of, and then I can introduce you to some friends who can help you out? You can decide what you want to do at that point."

"Thank you, sir. We don't deserve this."

Zack looked at the soldiers, loosely bandaged, their heads down, and a look of pain in their eyes.

"Gentlemen, you followed orders. You fought for your country. You obeyed your Defense Chief and Commander in Chief. Every RDF soldier did the same thing. You couldn't have possibly known the President's real agenda, and as soon as you did, you made the right call. You have nothing to be ashamed of. The RDF has had a policy of accepting NADF soldiers who defect, but fresh after this fight, I advise you to lay low for a while. The Sparrows will take care of your needs and talk to the RDF. If they want you, we'll make the introductions."

"Who are you, Sparrows? Why is the President so afraid of you guys?" one of the soldiers asked.

Zack smiled. This made him stop and think. Who were they?

"It all started with friends of mine, Jude Kane and his wife Zara Malik. On their way from Cascadia to Washington, D.C., to try and free Jude's brother, they stopped and helped people in the SACs. By the time they got to Washington, they had a lot of friends.

"After the SACs were wiped out, they helped their friends move into the cities and try to adjust to a new life. They gave people hope. They believe that people's lives are sacred, that everyone should be given equal respect and opportunities, and that every human being has dignity. Because of this, they started speaking up for people's rights and for the new Constitution to be passed to protect these rights.

"I told you we aren't fighters because we don't ever touch a gun. We resist with our voices, our votes, and sometimes our presence. It sounds weak until you have thousands and then millions of people on your side, electing your candidates to office, and forcing through the passage of a constitution with a Bill of Rights to protect people. That makes the President get so panicked that he removes anyone who opposes him and locks up the only candidate who could take him out of office. So yes, I suppose the Sparrows were taking over the government, but we were doing it by getting elected, not with military force. How's that for an answer?"

"So, Jude Kane is running for President, and President Connor locked him up?" one of the soldiers asked.

"Yes, sir. He did it just before launching his campaign to replace all the Regional Governments with his own Patriot Administrations and suspending the Senate when we refused to go along," Zack said.

"One more question," a soldier said. "How do we get to Jude Kane and bust him out?"

The mood in the Oval Office was decidedly lighter that morning. President Connor and General Alvarado sat on the opposing sofas, enjoying a celebratory drink as the analyst and the ADAMS interface droid came in for their report. President Connor directed the analyst to sit at the end of one of the sofas, and ADAMS stood in between.

"The Patriot Administration has been installed in Atlanta, Mr. President. The Gulf States of America Legislature has been removed from the Capitol," ADAMS reported.

"Good. I'm anxious to return to Nashville and repeat this success," the President said, taking a sip of his Bourbon.

"What is the state of readiness for the NADF after this fight?" asked General Alvarado. "We'll likely need to move a few more of our resources from other bases to fill in the gaps after the battle."

"Yes, sir. The NADF sustained significant losses. There is some discrepancy in the reports that may be attributed to post-battle attrition, but I can't know conclusively . . . "

"List them as losses," said General Alvarado. "We need to get ready for Nashville."

Chapter 24: **Nashville with a Vengeance**

General Alvarado was anxious to prepare for battle, so he visited the lab himself to give ADAMS some directives.

"Send orders to deploy the Air and Ground units we need to Washington. We'll rendezvous here, do some training and drills using what we've learned, establish communication protocols and strategy with the newer units, and be ready to launch the mission in no more than ten days," he commanded.

"Yes, sir. Please be advised that the NADF sustained heavy losses in Atlanta, and moving the Troops, Aircraft, and Vehicles from New America bases will require bringing in some resources from overseas, which may leave us vulnerable," ADAMS explained.

"Thin out the forces near our allies, and leave what you can in the hot spots, especially the Middle East and Asia," the General said. "Nashville is our top priority right now."

"I have tracked RDF movement in the remaining eight regions. There have been significant build-ups of forces around the capitols. If the battles are similar to Atlanta, we will not . . . "

"They will not be similar," Alvarado cut him off. "We're going to alter our strategy. I don't want to waste troops in the streets. We'll begin with an air assault and then land directly around the Capitol and capture it quickly."

"An air assault would involve dropping munitions, sir? That would dramatically increase the number of civilian casualties," ADAMS quickly assessed.

"If they don't evacuate when we tell them to, we're going to bomb the hell out of them. We'll make the entire city a crater surrounding the Capitol building if we have to. If they want to live, they damn well better do what we tell them," he said as he walked out of the lab.

Max was not looking forward to all the security he would have to go through before meeting with Jude. As he stepped through another body scanner, he muttered, "Can you do my colonoscopy while you're at it?"

The guard did not share his sense of humor, but he did share his wit. "It is within our protocol to visually inspect all orifices," he said, snapping his latex glove on his wrist.

"I'm fine," Max said. "I appreciate the scanners a little more now."

When he finally entered the room to meet Jude, he noted his surroundings. This was not a public jail. This was an NADF holding facility, and due process did not apply.

Jude shuffled in wearing a blue jumpsuit and zip ties on his wrists and ankles.

"Is that really necessary?" Max asked the guard. "He's not going anywhere."

"Protocol," grunted the guard.

"It's alright, Max. It doesn't matter," Jude said.

"I'm getting déjà vu," Max said. "I'm just glad Zara isn't in here too. She's doing fine, by the way, except pining for her husband."

Jude smiled and sighed. "The feeling is mutual. Please tell her I love her more than life itself."

"Of course. So, down to business. How are you doing in here? Are they feeding you? How is the room service?" Max asked, trying to bring levity.

"It's that bad out there, huh?" Jude asked, seeing through Max.

"They sent the NADF to Nashville, but the GSA sent combat drones and fought them off. Connor must have been furious because he sent a huge force to Atlanta. The fighting was fierce. The NADF took heavy losses, but in the end, they overwhelmed the RDF. They put the Patriot Administration in the Capitol, and Chiela says they are coming back for Nashville. They are even bringing in Air and Ground units from overseas to make up for the losses. They plan to hit hard, put their Patriot Administration in place, and then move on to the next region."

"So, it was bloody in Atlanta, and it may be even worse when they come back for Nashville?" Jude asked.

"Yes, but if the Appalachian RDF puts up enough of a fight, even if they lose, we can weaken the NADF to the point that they can't continue the campaign. Then we can . . . ."

"No," Jude said solemnly, cutting him off. "We are Sparrows, not the RDF. Besides, they won't keep pouring resources into these fights. Now that they know the level of resistance, they'll come and level the capital cities, install their people, and rebuild the NADF. We've got to think about saving people's lives, not winning this fight. We also need to think about the long game. People will not be free until they take it back themselves."

"What does that mean, Jude?" Max asked.

"I have an idea. I need you to get me in touch with President Connor."

Max looked at Jude as if he had just lost his last shred of sanity.

President Connor had no intention of seeing Jude or letting him see daylight ever again, but Max was persistent. So was Chiela. She managed to open a link directly to ADAMS, and ultimately, ADAMS called on President Connor.

Jude was ushered into a bare meeting room in NADF headquarters, where a small army of NADF guards accompanied him. After several hours of waiting, General Alvarado and President Connor came in, only slightly more curious than they were angry at Jude.

"Here we are, Mr. Sparrow," the President seethed. "The first thing I want to know is how in the hell you got to ADAMS?"

"I couldn't tell you, Mr. President. I don't have contact with anyone outside of my cell, but I do have many good friends. I'm sure they passed a message along."

"I came all the way here. Why do I care what you have to say?" the President asked.

"Because I can end the war," Jude said calmly.

"So can I," General Alvarado said, "and I intend to end it very shortly."

"Let's be frank, gentlemen," Jude began, leaning forward. "You took some hits in Nashville, you took heavy losses in Atlanta, and when you go back for Nashville this time, you are going to lead with an air campaign that will kill thousands of civilians. You may plan to do the same in the remaining regions. You will probably win, but there is a cost to these campaigns that you can't afford to pay. I know you're already stretched thin, bringing in equipment, weapons, and troops from overseas. More than the money, however, is the cost in human lives. If you raze the capital cities of the remaining regions, you will lose the country. Regions will respond with guerilla tactics, attack your Patriot Administrations, and the war will drag on, bloody and indecisive.

"General Alvarado, you know war comes with blood, and you will win with force and grit, but this is also a political struggle, and it may require a more surgical approach," he said, running his hand over his scar with just a hint of a smirk. "Let me go, and the Sparrows will tell the RDF in all the regions, including Appalachia, to stand down and welcome the Patriot Administrations."

"You are crazy," General Alvarado said.

"Wait a minute," the President said, thinking about the proposal. "What are the Sparrows getting out of this?"

"Sparrows are not fighters. If we can save lives, we do it. I'll be honest, Mr. President, we'll continue to campaign politically, fight for the new Constitution, and stand up for people's rights. We have never, and will never, take up arms against the government. We have a lot of support in the regions, which is why they resist anything anti-democratic, and of course, in the GSA and Appalachia, they have a long history of resisting the Federal Government. Despite this, if I can lead the Sparrows, we can call on the RDF of every region to lay down their arms and allow the Patriot Administration in. This will save lives, restore stability, and allow us to continue our struggle in a strictly political manner. I doubt we are much of a threat to you, Mr. President. You hold all the cards now."

"You want to save lives, and you're willing to give up power to do it. I want stability, and avoiding more armed conflict will restore stability and some political favor for my administration. We may have a common interest here, Mr. Kane," mused the President.

General Alvarado took the President aside and spoke to him in confidence as ADAMS and the analyst were summoned.

"Mr. President, my troops are drilling now and ready to deploy. We can win this and take Nashville," Alvarado said.

"I know you can, General," the President said, "And I know you are itching to get back there and teach the Appalachian RDF a lesson, but we have to think of the bigger picture. As much as I hate to agree with my enemy, this campaign could be successful militarily, but it may also be disastrous politically and financially. If these Sparrows never touch a gun, how much of a threat can they be? I will have the regions and Congress, and we can let them make all the noise they want. They have nothing."

"ADAMS is ready, Mr. President," announced the analyst.

"ADAMS, what is your analysis of Jude Kane's proposal?" asked the President.

"The Sparrows have never been a military threat, Mr. President. Installing Patriot Administrations in the regions will give you unprecedented political power, and avoiding armed conflict will save billions of dollars and thousands of lives. Despite resistance to the Patriot Administrations, if you are credited with negotiating a way to avoid the conflict, it will give you and your Patriot Administrations more political favor and a higher likelihood of compliance."

"Would this restore stability to New America, ADAMS?" he asked.

"Yes, sir, this will have a decisive effect on the restoration of calm and stability in the country."

"Mr. Kane, I will take your proposal, but with one modification. Before I give away the farm, so to speak, I want to make sure you hold up your end of the bargain. I will allow you to communicate with the Sparrows through your lawyer, but you will remain in custody until I confirm the Patriot Administrations are in place in all ten regions. At that point, you will be released."

The official news outlets sang the praises of President Connor and his plea to save lives and restore peace and stability. The Sparrow Press carried a different story. Jude was credited for negotiating the deal, and despite the regions' reluctance to just let President Connor's Patriot Administration walk into their capitols, Zara made it clear the fight was not over. "When they see us coming, they can fight back. When they can't see us, it's over before they know it. Let's get Jude home so he can lead us in this fight."

Appalachia "welcomed" the new Patriot Administration into the Capitol building in Nashville, and within ten days, Lakeland, Texico, Baja, Dakota, California, Cascadia, and finally Yukon followed suit. The NADF recalled their forces to their regular bases, and the RDF returned to their bases. On the tenth day, Jude was unceremoniously released, and Max met him at the gate of the NADF facility.

"It's like déjà vu all over again," he said as Jude walked out.

"It is, but let's not make this a habit," he said, smiling as they embraced. "Take me home, Max."

When they got into the transport vehicle, there was a small crowd waiting for him. A three-member security team shook his hand, and to his surprise, Maisy grabbed his shoulders and gave him a long hug.

"Roll up your sleeves," she ordered.

"What are you doing?" Jude asked.

"I'm checking you out. Zara will be satisfied with nothing less than a complete examination by me," she said as she found a vein and inserted a syringe for a blood sample. She looked into his mouth, pinched his skin, and listened to his breathing.

"So do I pass, doc?" Jude joked.

"I'm a medic, not a doctor. I'll have to run a panel to know more, but other than being a little thin and slightly dehydrated, you seem to be ok."

"Are you accompanying me all the way to Vancouver?" he asked.

"No, just to Kansas City. I'm worried, Jude. President Connor has taken over everything, and clearly, he will use the NADF to do his bidding. What's going to happen?"

"We're going to continue doing what we've always done: taking care of each other. We're going to keep up political pressure and do everything we can to restore a real democracy without killing each other"

"What if that is not enough?" Maisy asked.

"We're not running away, Maisy. We're changing the battlefield. Remember, there is always a solution," he said with a telling smile.

The group continued on a SEMIC train to Kansas City, and after saying goodbye to Maisy, Max and Jude had time to talk before reaching Vancouver.

"We've got word that the Patriot Administrations are already giving orders to the RDF," Max said. "They're testing their authority."

"It is so kind of them to hand us our first opportunity to resist so soon," Jude said. "What are they up to?"

"They have ordered the RDF to identify and round up any NADF defectors and deserters to be handed over to the NADF. There are thousands of them. Some were injured, but many refused to return to the NADF when they figured out what President Connor was doing," Max explained.

"He is consolidating his military power," Jude said. "He's going to weed out anyone not completely loyal. It's a smart move. We're going to have to stay one step ahead of them. Have Zara and Chiela set up a secure meeting with all of the governors."

“What are you planning to do, Jude? You just orchestrated the RDF’s surrender in every region,” Max said.

“Yes, and they are still around to fight. The NADF will always win a direct confrontation, and each side just slaughters more soldiers. The General Alvarado strategy is attrition: we will kill everyone not on our side until we can get our way. Our game is one of persuasion. We will change hearts and minds until our majority is overwhelming and President Connor realizes he can’t win.”

“But in the meantime, Jude, what are the RDF soldiers supposed to do?” Max asked.

“What did we do when the SACs were targeted?” Jude asked.

“We disappeared,” Max said with a smile.

Chapter 25: **Hello, Governor**

Over the years, Chiela and Zara had created a patchwork of secure communication networks for the Sparrow Press, communication with Sparrow nest leaders, and, more recently, Sparrow politicians who needed to organize outside of ADAMS's virtual omnipresence online. After the surrender of the Capitol buildings and the installation of President Connor's Patriot Administrations, Chiela sewed together the patchwork and created the largest single secure network outside of the NADF. The Sparrows could talk to each other, and so could their friends.

With the help of the Sparrow network, the recently ousted governors and their legislators came together to form an underground resistance to President Connor's seizure of their regions and the New American Government. The first order of business was decided for them. How would the Regional Defense Forces comply with the order from the new Patriot Administrations to round up the former NADF soldiers?

The governors did what they were good at: talking, debating, and never deciding anything. Jude let them get their thoughts out, bounce ideas off of each other, and vent their frustrations. When he felt they had reached the end of a productive round table, he stepped in.

"There are a few things we cannot do," Jude said. "We cannot betray the NADF soldiers who defected to the RDF. We also do not want to set up a confrontation with the NADF, or we'll be right back where we were before the Patriot Administrations took over. I'm just a suspended senator, but I do have some experience facing the wrong side of the NADF. When you can't beat them at their game, you change the game."

"What does that mean?" the Governor of Appalachia asked.

"It means the Regional Defense Forces should disappear."

"Disappear?" a chorus of voices repeated.

"This is where our fight continues, but it will be on our terms, not theirs," explained Jude. "They can't force our hand if they can't find it. Rather than acquiesce to the Patriot Administration, the RDFs will go underground. Leave the bases, leave the uniforms, and leave all the hardware. When the NADF eventually shows up, they will have no idea what to do. Of course, the RDF will not be gone; they will just be on standby. You will use the Sparrow Network to communicate and give orders. There will be your entire Regional Government, from the Governor and Legislature to the entire RDF, still intact and ready to act when the time is right."

"What about funding?" asked the Appalachian Governor. "How can the RDF personnel survive or be able to do anything, in hiding or not, if the Patriot Admins cut the purse strings?"

"If the Patriot Administrations operate like the one we have here in Atlanta," explained the Governor of the Gulf States, "they don't know much about our budget. They essentially come in and take over the day-to-day operations and make decisions based on ADAMS analyses and President Connor's wishes. They didn't notice, for instance, that we redirected much of the RDF funding to Health and Human Services."

"I see," said the Governor of Appalachia. "Healthcare can be very expensive."

"We haven't been home together in a long time," Zara said when they woke up the next morning. "You've been busy saving the world."

Jude chuckled. "This world is only worth saving if you're in it," he said, rolling over to face her and smiling as he pushed her hair out of her face. "And don't forget, you've been doing a lot of that work yourself, you know."

"I threw myself into the Sparrow Press, but only because if I stopped to think about you, I'd lose it," she confessed. "I was really worried I might not see you again this time."

"I know this won't make you feel much better, but the Nine have a dedicated team watching the Patriot Guard now. They've also got three agents on me and three on you at all times," Jude said.

"I noticed," she said. "It does make me feel a little better, but I won't be able to completely relax until this quiet war is over. As long as President Connor and General Alvarado run New America, we won't be safe," she said.

"Remember when we woke up worried about the power going out or if the crops were going to give us enough of a yield?" he mused. "It was nice not to have to think about the next government attack."

"I don't remember those days as fondly as you," Zara recalled. "Slate Creek was a well-oiled machine, but Squamish River was in a constant state of failure. Until you and Maisy came, we had almost no power, we had several people sick and suffering, and we would not have survived another winter. I was happiest when we traveled together and helped the SACs get back on their feet. I was with you, I was helping other people, and I wasn't starving for once."

"Maybe we can get back to the simple life again someday," Jude said, pulling Zara toward him and laying her head on his chest.

"I would love that," she sighed. "I would write articles for the Sparrow Press, and you would be endlessly tinkering and fixing things, like developing a way to recondition the batteries for an entire city."

"Don't forget, if we have kids, we'll both be busy trying to keep them alive. Between all my dangerous tools and the rebellious streak they are bound to inherit from you, we'll have our hands full," he laughed.

"Hey, who said I was rebellious?" she protested.

"I didn't say that was a bad thing," he said, kissing her head.

"Do you think we will really have children?" she asked.

"Of course!" he said. "Why would you doubt that?"

She sighed and drew circles on his chest with her finger.

"When will it be safe?"

"The time will come, and it will be soon. I just know it. Things look impossible now, but I don't think President Connor and General Alvarado will be around as long as it seems."

"Why do you say that?" she asked, lifting her head and looking at him.

"I don't really know. I don't have hard evidence. I just have a feeling that soon things will come to a head, and we'll have an opportunity to get a lot closer to the world we've been working towards. It's just a feeling, really, but it's a deep one."

"Sounds more like a prophecy to me."

"I make no such claims!" he protested, chuckling. "But we will see what happens."

"It appears the Appalachian Region wants to play games," President Connor said as General Alvarado came into the Oval Office. "The Patriot

Administration reports that when they ordered the RDF to hand over all current and former NADF personnel, the RDF did not respond. When they sought out the generals, their offices had been vacated. They then sent delegations to RDF bases, and they found them completely abandoned! Vehicles were parked, uniforms were hanging in neat rows, and weapons were stored. I've never seen anything like it, but then I remembered how Jude Kane said they would never take up guns against the New America Government, but they would continue to resist. It looks like this is their protest."

"I am ready to go in with as much force as needed, sir," Alvarado said, almost giddy.

"Let's give the Patriot Administration some teeth," the President said. "Occupy the Appalachian RDF bases and take them over. Once you have moved in, declare Martial Law. Make an example of them so we don't have to do this again, and the other regions will think twice before ignoring the Patriot Administrations. Set a curfew, set up checkpoints, make arrests, and look for rebels to round up and teach a lesson."

"Should we have detention camps?" he asked.

"No, they are too cumbersome and vulnerable. Don't hang on to very many people at once. Teach them a lesson, and then send them home to show their families what happens."

"Maybe we can have 'Rehabilitation Hotels' at the RDF bases. Our guests will get free education and training in obeying orders and respecting authority," the General said.

"That sounds more like it," the President said.

This time, when the massive NADF Transports arrived in Appalachia, there was no resistance. The drones surveyed the sky, but there was no welcoming party. The NADF landed at the RDF bases and quickly took over. It was as if the RDF was expecting them; they left the doors open and the security codes to the buildings in obvious places. The troops were nervous at first, expecting an ambush or setup, but after a week, they all began to relax and settle in.

Once the occupation was complete, General Alvarado gave the order to set up enforcement apparatuses in several key cities, including Nashville, Knoxville, Charleston, Charlotte, and Richmond. As soon as his forces were in place, he declared Martial Law on the pretext that the RDF had dissolved, and the President wanted to "ensure public safety." He set a curfew and then tasked his Patriot Guard with the building of the "Rehabilitation Hotels" at the bases. They would only handle a few "guests" at a time and only for a few days at the most, but they were free to experiment and practice with a variety of torture methods and styles. It was a great opportunity for research.

"Jude, we're nervous," Janie said on the screen. "The NADF has taken over all the RDF bases in Appalachia, Alvarado has declared Martial Law, and soldiers are everywhere. What are we supposed to do?"

"Whatever they say," Jude replied. "They are itching to crush a rebellion, so let's not give them one. Comply, and tell people to do the same. Don't give them any reason to hurt anyone. We'll keep an eye on the situation, and when the time comes to resist, we will do it peacefully, but also with overwhelming masses. They may be scary, but they still only have a few thousand troops. You have over twenty million people in your region."

"What if they get violent?" she asked.

"Don't give them an excuse to be violent, but if they do, the Nine will have a plan. They are on their way now to assess the situation and develop strategies for just that contingency. We still have the RDF on standby, too, don't forget. We just have to be smart and avoid an all-out confrontation."

"Sounds good," Janie said. "I'll let the governor know so we can tell people how to stay safe. I hope this doesn't last long."

"Me either," Jude said. "Don't worry, Janie. We're not going to just roll over, but planning and strategy are everything."

"I understand."

A lone transport taxi wound through the streets of Richmond on a mission to get the three teenagers back home in time before curfew at 10:00 pm. As it rounded a corner, it stopped abruptly at an NADF checkpoint, causing them to nearly fall out of their seats. Before they could right themselves, the doors to the transport were thrown open, and the teenagers were pulled out by several soldiers with the special "PG" insignia on their uniforms.

"You may think curfew is a game you play with your parents, but the NADF doesn't play games," one of the Patriot Guards said.

"But it's still 9:45," protested the young man. "I was making sure the girls got home in time."

"Such a gentleman!" mocked the soldier. "According to the routing on this transport, the girls would make it, but you won't get home until 10:03

pm. That's a curfew violation. You're going to have to say goodbye and let the transport take the girls home without you. You're coming with us."

"You can't just take me! My dad is the Governor of Appalachia— the real governor!"

The Patriot Guard soldier, a fierce-looking woman with a half-smile and narrowed eyes, laughed at him. "Did you hear that? His daddy is the governor. He's the governor that we forced out, who is hiding underground like a rat, and whose little boy thinks he still has some kind of power. This is a lucky find! Ladies," she said, addressing the terrified teenage girls, "get back in the transport and head home before curfew. We're going to hang on to Governor Junior here. Don't worry. We're going to take him to a hotel."

The Patriot Guard cuffed the young man, stuffed him into a transport, and headed for the former RDF base.

"I thought you said you were taking me to a hotel?" he said.

"We are," explained another Patriot Guard soldier. "It's our very own Rehabilitation Hotel. After a few nights with us, you'll never get confused about curfew again."

They brought him into a room that looked deceptively like a sparsely decorated hotel room with carpet, a bed, a few padded chairs, and a window, but on second look, the window was actually a screen.

"You've had a long day," one of the soldiers said. "It's time for bed." He struck the young man with his weapon in the back of his head, and the governor's son collapsed to the floor unconscious.

When he awoke, his head was throbbing so hard he could barely open his eyes. He felt behind where he was hit, and there was a bandage covering a golf ball-sized welt.

"Ohhh," he hissed, trying to sit up. He looked at the screen that looked like a window last night, but this morning it was counting down. He had thirty-two seconds. Thirty-two seconds until what? He felt around on the sheets of the bed, and he felt strands of cord or wire underneath, bound tightly. He swung his legs around, stood up, and tried to follow the wire to a source, but it all came together and just disappeared through the wall behind the bed. He watched the clock count down, and when it hit zero, all he could discern was a light buzzing noise.

He looked around for a bathroom, but there was none. He was tired, trapped, and terrified. Would his dad really be powerless to get him out of this one? What were they planning to do with him? He sighed and sat back down on the bed to think. Instantly, he felt like a baseball bat had hit him square in his back and his arms and legs were simultaneously being jerked from their sockets. His head tipped up, his eyes rolled back in his head, and he blacked out.

Once again, he woke up on the floor beside his bed feeling as if he had been run over by a transport. His head still ached, and now his joints and muscles felt like they had been stretched and squeezed just beyond their limits. He glanced over at the bed, looking at the wires that ran under the sheets and coiled together before going out through the wall. He heard the buzzing sound much clearer now. He looked up at the screen that was still displaying four zeroes. He finally put it all together.

The club to his head last night was their way of saying, "Lights out." The countdown clock was his wake-up time, and electrocution was his "alarm." He was being "rehabilitated." The blood drained from his face. What else were they about to teach him?

The door to the room burst open, and the familiar icy tone of the female Patriot Guard soldier filled the room.

"Good morning, Governor Junior! It's time for your shower."

Two other soldiers came in and each grabbed one of his arms and lifted him to his feet. His legs felt like rubber, and they had to drag him along.

"Don't worry. You'll feel better after a nice hot shower."

His heart began to race and his hands began to shake as he tried to imagine what kind of "shower" they had waiting for him. The two soldiers who had his arms took him down the hall to a locker room-style shower and dropped him on his knees. They tugged and pulled, ripping and jerking off his remaining clothes until he was completely naked, left on the cold tile floor on his hands and knees. He had never felt so helpless or vulnerable in his life.

One of the soldiers turned on one of the shower heads, held out his hand, and assessed the water temperature. Instead of turning the handle to adjust, he spoke into his radio.

"Hotter," he said, and steam began to rise in the shower.

"Hotter," he said again, this time only waiving his hand through the stream and wincing.

"That should be good," he said. "Time to get clean." They once again picked him up by his arms and forced him under the stream of the shower. He tried to resist, but the slick floor and his rubber legs gave them almost no resistance. He felt the searing pain of a hundred knives burrowing into his back, burning his skin, and he screamed in agony.

The soldiers held him there for ten seconds as he twisted and contorted his body, trying desperately to get away from the super-heated shower of hell and continuing to scream.

"That's enough," one of them said, and they pulled him out of the shower. He moaned and panted, continuing to feel the pain in his skin.

"But he's only clean on his backside," the other soldier said. "Let's make sure he's clean all over."

The soldiers turned the young man in a circle, and facing the shower now, they dragged him forward and shoved his face and chest into the searing cascade of boiling water.

"Aaah!" screamed the teenager again, violently twisting his head, kicking his feet, and writhing in pain. They finally relented and pulled him back, dropping him to the floor. He slumped down onto his side, feeling the cold tile on his burning skin. He rolled back and forth like a dog in a mud puddle, desperately trying to dull the pain he felt all over his body.

After hoisting him up once again, they redressed him in a cheap t-shirt and rough jeans, pulling the clothes over his burnt skin with the care of a butcher preparing a low-quality steak. His screams melted into moans and hisses, and the soldiers returned him to his room. They tossed him onto the bed, but he scrambled off the bed onto the floor and crawled into a corner where he lay on his side in a fetal position, rocking slowly in a vain attempt to soothe both his frayed nerves and fried skin.

His stay in the "Rehab Hotel" lasted another day, with the routine being repeated at night and in the morning. Finally, after they felt they had enough footage to make their point, they posted the video online and put the young man into a transport where he was driven into Richmond and dropped off at a busy market near the riverfront. He was barely able to crawl out of the transport, and he collapsed onto the street.

Zara was quick to denounce the campaign of fear and intimidation in the Sparrow Press. "Fear is their weapon of choice. The NADF is using the oldest trick in the book. We will not play their game. The time to fight back is almost here. Sparrows, I want to call on you to have courage like you have never had before. The call to action will come in the next few days. Be ready, because this will take creativity, cunning, and every last one of us."

Chapter 26: **The Art of War**

"They tortured my son and left him on the street half-dead, Jude! We let them walk in here, walk into our house, and now they're kicking us around like dogs. What good is it doing?"

"Governor, if you could find those soldiers who hurt your son, what would you do to them?" Jude asked.

"I'd kill every one of them. Maybe I'd string them up and make them feel what my son felt before I sent them to hell."

"Then would you win?"

"At least I'd feel better, and they wouldn't be around to torture any more innocent people."

"Would that be the end of it? What about their parents?"

"I see where you're going. I get it. I'm angry, and I feel like we're punching bags. I don't see how all this compliance and taking the moral high road is going to solve our problem."

"That's the foundation, but we still need to build the house. We're not rolling over, governor. We're preparing for battle on our terms. The Nine are finalizing a plan to divide and take out the NADF in Appalachia, and it will take all of us. Tell your generals to get the RDF ready and make sure every soldier has a Stinger and plenty of cartridges. They will be a critical part of the operation, and they will need to be in plain clothes. Mission training begins in three days."

"You mean we're really going to go after these bastards?"

"Yes, but remember, governor: we are not taking revenge. We are dividing and conquering, and conquering the NADF will require more forgiveness than firepower. You'll see what I mean."

"I have no idea what you have up your sleeve, Jude, but I'm going to stand with you on this one. I'll talk to the RDF and make sure they're ready."

"We're going to have a lot of people together online. Can our servers handle this many people and remain secure?" Jude asked Chiela.

"Did you forget whom you are speaking to, sir?" Chiela chided Jude. "The pipes are plenty big enough, and they have no leaks. We're good to go."

"Thank you, Ms. Cruz. I forget I'm a regular guy among geniuses around here."

Zara brought a cup of hot tea and set it in front of Jude as he adjusted his screen and prepared for the mission training.

"You'll need your voice. There's plenty of honey and lemon in there," she said.

"Thank you," he said, looking up and giving her a gentle kiss.

"Good morning," Jude began as dozens of Nest Leaders, NADF Officers, the Governor's office, and most of the Legislature logged on to the Sparrow platform.

"Welcome to Operation Appalachian Freedom. As you know, the Martial Law imposed on Appalachia is egregious. President Connor is trying to make a point, but I think it is time for us to make ours. We're going to carve up the NADF like a pumpkin on Halloween."

The cheers of agreement and support echoed from Jude's screen.

"Right now, this is all about Appalachia and pushing back on this occupation. I am optimistic we can give hope to the other regions, but as Zara tells me frequently, I shouldn't get ahead of myself."

Zara sipped her tea just out of view of the screen and gave Jude a knowing smile.

"The mission will happen on three levels simultaneously. First, Zara will put out a call for the Sparrows to come out en masse to pre-determined locations, defying the Martial Law rules about gatherings of large groups. This will attract the NADF like flies. Next, the RDF, operating in plain clothes, will cause distractions such as singing, playing music, or making speeches. Once they have a detachment of soldiers in their area, they will flank them and then take them down using Stingers. In plain clothes in the middle of a crowd, the NADF will have no idea where the attack is coming from.

The third level will involve only the Nine and a few hand-picked RDF operatives. While the NADF is falling asleep on the job, the Nine will infiltrate the RDF base, confront the Patriot Guard, and find the so-called 'Rehabilitation Hotels,' freeing everyone inside.

"Our greatest weapons will be our numbers and the element of surprise. If we lose either one, it could mean disaster. As it is, we still risk the NADF firing live weapons into these crowds, but we have a good chance of completely disabling the NADF force in Appalachia within a few hours if we are successful.

"The Nine have been able to identify the approximate number of NADF soldiers occupying each RDF base, and each mission location is tied to those locations. If previous battles are any indication, we anticipate a good number of NADF to defect, and a fair number to remain loyal to the NADF. In either case, they will be secured and have all their weapons confiscated, but otherwise be treated with true hospitality.

"It is easy to be angry with these soldiers and want to exact some kind of revenge for their occupation, but we need to remember that they are following orders, and the real enemy is in Washington, D.C. The Nine will now meet with RDF officers and coordinate all of the details, including locations, strategy, detention locations and protocols, contingency plans, etc. Governor and Legislators, we will meet again after the operation in three days to assess how successful it was and discuss our next steps."

"I have one concern now, Jude," the Governor spoke up. "What is to stop President Connor from launching an all-out retaliation for this operation? What happens if he comes back with ten times the troops, more air power, and ground assault vehicles, and begins a campaign of revenge?"

"I'll take this one," Zara said, joining Jude on the screen. "It will be made clear to President Connor that every single region is ready to execute similar operations, and over 100 million Sparrows are ready to march in every corner of New America. He can't arrest 100 million people, and he can't attack the RDF if he can't find them."

"It's risky," the Governor sighed, "but it's the best hope we've got for stopping his march to dictatorship. It won't ever get easier."

"One more concern," Janie Hollins chimed in. "What's the end game? What are we hoping to accomplish? If we don't have a plan, we're just inviting more retribution."

"Right now, we're drawing the line and saying no more NADF pushing us around and no more Martial Law in Appalachia. After that, all ten regions together start moving the line, pushing it toward D.C. We send the Patriot Admins back to Washington, we reoccupy the RDF bases, we reinstate the Senate, and then we hold free and fair elections and get to work ratifying the new Constitution. We'll walk him back with overwhelming numbers until he's out. All of that is only possible if we are successful here in Appalachia. The rest of the country is watching closely and getting ready."

The impromptu soccer game in the vacant lot had become a Saturday tradition among the kids in a cube neighborhood in South Richmond. Plastic buckets on either side of the dirt lot marked out the goals, and sundry jackets, hats, and shirts marked the foul lines. The rules were loose, but with ages ranging from seven to seventeen, they had to be flexible. Lydia, now nineteen, had been playing out here as long as she could remember, and she kept the tradition going. She started refereeing the games to cut down on all the squabbling, and now most of the kids just called her "coach."

Lydia saw the NADF Ground Transport before anyone else. She didn't know what to expect, but her protective instincts kicked in.

"We've got company!" she shouted and then blew her whistle to stop the game. "Scatter!"

She didn't have to ask twice. The kids scrambled like a handful of marbles, but Lydia stayed to see what the soldiers wanted and to make sure the kids got away. The transport drove onto the field and stopped, and four soldiers got out. The apparent leader was a woman, which made her feel better.

"What's going on out here?" the woman barked angrily.

"It's just a bunch of kids playing soccer. We do it every Saturday. They don't cause any trouble."

"What is not clear about 'no gatherings of ten or more people' to you?" the woman asked rhetorically.

Lydia suddenly didn't feel any better about the leader's gender.

"They're neighborhood kids playing soccer. They're not hurting anybody."

"Do you think there are exceptions to Martial Law? You're under arrest for violating the order prohibiting gatherings. You're coming with us."

"No!" she shouted, a surge of anger and adrenaline rushing to her veins. She saw that the other kids had all made it away, and she decided to stand against this ridiculous injustice. "They were kids, not some protest group. You can't take me anywhere!" she shouted.

The woman swung a powerful right hook so quickly that Lydia didn't even see it coming. Her head spun around, her body followed, and she fell flat into the dirt. "I wasn't asking," she hissed. She and another soldier took Lydia's arms and hoisted her up, and as soon as Lydia's head stopped spinning, she lunged at the woman, scratching her face and drawing blood.

The other soldier quickly grabbed both arms and pinned them behind her back as she kicked dirt and tried to twist away. "I've got her, Captain," he said, restraining her and turning her to face the woman. The woman wiped the blood from her cheek with the back of her hand and then glared at Lydia.

"This one has just asked for a few nights in the hotel," she said. She stepped back, and then with one lightning undercut, she struck Lydia in the stomach, folding her in half, causing her to cough and gasp for air. "Zip her up and let's go. She can catch her breath on the way."

"Where . . . are you taking . . . me?" Lydia wheezed in the transport.

"Since you don't seem to understand rules and authority, you get to stay with us in the Rehabilitation Hotel for a few nights. We offer free lessons in discipline, punctuality, and respect." She rubbed her face and wiped more blood from her cheek. "Since you like your nails so much, I think we'll start you off with a manicure."

They entered the base, escorted Lydia to the room, and sat her down in a chair. They snipped her zip ties on her ankles and then took each leg and re-zipped it to the legs of the chair. They pulled a sturdy table over and set it in front of her. The table had small holes in it about three inches apart, and Lydia soon found out what they were for. They snipped her wrist ties and then pulled her arms out and pressed them down on the table. They took new ties, fed them through the holes, and then painfully zipped them tightly, pinning her hands to the table.

The woman took a chair and sat down opposite Lydia while the three men gathered the supplies. They placed a pair of pliers, a stainless-steel bowl, and a few white cloths on the table. They also placed a plastic basin at the side of her chair.

"What's that for?" Lydia dared to ask.

"In case you vomit," one of the men answered. "Try not to make a mess."

Lydia looked at him, and then back to the captain, and suddenly she realized what was happening. "Nooooo!" she screamed, jerking her arms back, but it was no use. All she managed to do was make the ties cut deeper into her skin. She couldn't even move the table.

"Let's trim those nasty nails," the captain said sadistically, taking the pliers and clamping them onto her pinky nail on the right hand. She pulled the nail off with one hard jerk, and Lydia screamed in pain and terror, looking at her bare, bloody finger. "Next," the captain said calmly, taking hold of the nail on her ring finger.

"Ahhh!" screamed Lydia, looking away and writhing in pain. The captain dropped the nail into the metal bowl with a satisfied clink. Lydia leaned over the side of the chair and vomited into the plastic basin. "No! Please stop!" she cried. "I can't . . . ahhh!" The captain pulled off the nail on the middle finger. "Ahhh!" she screamed and cried.

Lydia had never experienced pain this excruciating, even when she broke her arm. She didn't think it was possible to feel so much pain and survive, and yet somehow each finger was far more painful than the last.

"Here's the one that drew blood on my face," the captain said, and then clamped the bloody pliers onto her pointer fingernail and tore it off.

"Ahhh," screamed Lydia again, but lower and more guttural now, as she was feeling it in her stomach and her bones. Her vision got blurry, and she eyed the basin again, but there wasn't anything left in her stomach. Her breathing accelerated between groans, and she was beginning to hyperventilate.

"One more," the captain said in a mocking tone, clamping hard on the thumbnail, partially tearing it from the nail bed just from the grip. She pulled one last time, and Lydia jerked her head backward, letting out a low groan before losing consciousness and slumping over in the chair.

"What do you think, boys?" the captain said to her men. "Should I continue and give her a full treatment on the other hand while she is unconscious, or should I let her recover a bit so she can experience it all again?"

"How about none of the above? Stand down!" Four men burst through the door, weapons drawn, and laser sights pinned on each of them. The captain and her three men were initially confused.

"You're interfering with a Patriot Guard Operation, soldier," barked the captain.

"We're ending the Patriot Guard Operation, Captain. The base has been retaken by the Regional Defense Forces of Appalachia."

"You idiots! You are massively outnumbered," the captain said.

"Not today. Most of your NADF friends are busy with very large crowds down along the river. They won't be coming back. As for us, we thought we'd come out of retirement and make use of these old uniforms."

"You're with the Nine," she said, finally grasping who they were up against. "You work with the Sparrows."

"It's a good thing for you, too. The Sparrows are pretty keen on keeping people alive. If it was up to me, you'd have been dead before you knew I was here."

Jude and Zara sat anxiously in front of the screen in their Cube in Cascadia.

"What did we start, Zara?" Jude asked. "Did we just convince thousands of people to go to their deaths?"

"Of course not," Zara said, stepping behind him and rubbing his shoulders. "If it wasn't for you, thousands would already be dead. The Appalachia RDF has a score to settle, and this way, they can take back their region without a bloody war. The strategy is brilliant, Jude."

"The stingers take up to thirty seconds to take effect, and some could miss. That is a lot of time for an NADF soldier to fire their weapon," he worried.

"Prepare yourself, Jude. The NADF won't see them coming, so it will be successful, but there will likely be some casualties. You can't fight a war, even our way, with a zero body count."

"I know," he sighed. "I'm just anxious. I don't want anyone to lose their life, especially civilians. Everything hinges on how successful we are today. If we fail, the other regions . . . "

"Shhh," Zara said. "Go talk to your brother. I'll let you know when I get word from the Appalachia RDF."

"Were you banished?" Callum mocked Jude as he came into the room.

"Yes. There's a lot on the line. I'm scared to death I did something stupid and I'm going to get a lot of people hurt."

"The only stupid thing you could do is nothing. People are going to get hurt, Jude, but if it wasn't for your plan, it would have been a catastrophe. Don't forget it's not all you. The Nine and the RDF in Appalachia are making this happen, and millions of Sparrows are behind you. Do you know why? Because this is the right side to be on. Life is worth fighting for. Equality is worth fighting for. Dignity is worth fighting for. You know what else? Democracy is worth fighting for because it makes everything else possible."

"Zara was right," Jude said with a large smile. "I did need to talk to you."

"I've grown wise in my old age," Callum joked. "Although I still wouldn't mind shooting down another NADF drone."

"Zara, this is Gavin Hollins. I've just got word from Janie that the operation in Richmond was a success. The NADF soldiers deployed in groups of fifty, and when they approached the crowd, they had no idea what to do. Some of the crowds started singing, and that confused the NADF even more. When they finally started to order everyone to go home, threatening force, the RDF hit them with the Stingers. They went down like bowling pins in slow motion."

"Gavin, you don't know how much I needed to hear this! Thank you for letting me know," Zara said.

"I'm sure you'll get the full report from the RDF and the Nine, but I figured you'd want to hear an initial report. I've got to run. I've got squads of Sparrow Soldiers fanning out to help with any injuries."

"Jude!" Zara called. "Jude! I got a call from Gavin!"

Jude came into the room with a slightly dazed look. "They were successful," Jude said slowly.

"Yes!" Zara declared.

"I just got a call from the Nine. They took back the RDF bases, captured several Patriot Guard Operatives, and seized several NADF Air and Ground Transports. There are a few soldiers who managed to dodge Stingers and escape in their vehicles, but they have nowhere to go. If and when they go back to base, the RDF will be waiting for them. I can't believe we did it!"

"I can," Zara said. "The people are going crazy online. They are telling stories about NADF soldiers dropping like flies, and the RDF using the NADF's own vehicles to transport them to holding areas. The governor of GSA has already pledged they will follow our lead, and other regions are already preparing."

"I'm cautiously ecstatic," Jude said.

"What the heck does that mean?" Zara asked.

"It means we won, but in the furor of our victory, let's not forget who we are. Put out a statement from us congratulating everyone who was involved and reminding all of us to practice forgiveness and not revenge. I know a lot of RDF soldiers have an ax to grind, but I want every NADF soldier treated with humanity and dignity. This is not just how we win; it's why we win."

Chapter 27: **The Tide Has Come Back In**

Mexico City had more people in the streets than on Cinco de Mayo. When word reached Sonja Orozco that Appalachia had resisted the Martial Law and defeated the NADF, she didn't hesitate. She called the governor and planned an operation based on Appalachia's strategy. They were not under Martial Law or dealing with the Patriot Guard, but they did still have the NADF occupying the RDF bases. Nothing can bring the NADF out to play like a massive demonstration at the capital.

The purpose of the demonstration was to call for the dismissal of the Patriot Administration and the reinstatement of the Baja Governor and Legislature. Of course, the NADF could not let that happen, so they came to the defense of the Patriot Administration. Among the throngs of demonstrators, who were strictly ordered to be peaceful by Sonja, were a few hundred Baja RDF troops in plain clothes, blending in like kids at a carnival. As each NADF soldier felt the sting and fell to the ground, the RDF soldiers would take their weapons, snap on restraints, and cart them off to a transport or collection point.

When the squad of troops inside the Capitol building radioed for an update on the dispersal of the crowd and the security situation, there was only silence. Going to the windows, they couldn't see their fellow soldiers, and they only glimpsed a couple of transports being driven away by what looked like civilians. They soon panicked and ordered the entire Patriot Administration to evacuate. They gathered the staff and escorted them down to the bottom floor and out of the rear exits, where they could load them onto their transports and flee.

The RDF was waiting for them. In a hail of stingers, the remnants of the NADF fell onto the lawn along with a few Patriot Admin staffers who were caught in the crossfire. The RDF took their weapons, clasped on the restraints, and joined the rest of the operation in returning to the RDF base. The handful of NADF soldiers left only briefly attempted to resist the return of the colorfully clothed RDF soldiers, but they were quickly overwhelmed and surrendered their weapons.

By the end of the day, the RDF had placed the NADF soldiers that had been assigned to the Patriot Administration, minus their weapons, on an Air Transport and sent them back to Washington, D.C. They then met the Governor of Baja, his cabinet, and most of the legislators, and led them in a triumphant parade up the steps of the Capitol and back into their offices.

The arrival of the Air Transport and the ousted Patriot Administrators and their contingent of NADF soldiers sent President Connor into a fury that he couldn't contain.

"Tell General Alvarado to bring the Baja Administrators and the troops to the basement for a debriefing," he barked into his intercom.

"Yes, sir!" the assistant said. "Should I get ADAMS and the analyst to meet you there?"

"No. This will be a short meeting."

General Alvarado gathered the group from the tarmac and took them straight to the White House, where President Connor was waiting in a sparse storage area near the receiving docks.

"Administrators, stand along the north wall, and soldiers, stand at attention along the west wall," President Connor said sharply, surprising General Alvarado. The administrators shuffled to the wall, confused and awkward, looking for a place to sit, but there were no chairs. The soldiers snapped into formation along the west wall and stood at attention.

"I was briefed by intelligence about what happened in Mexico City. This is a catastrophic failure. You assumed control of an entire region, including the RDF. How did your power slip through your fingers so easily?" the President demanded.

"We were overwhelmed, sir," the Patriot Governor explained. "The RDF must have reorganized itself and planned this operation. There were thousands of people surrounding the Capitol building, and when the NADF came to disperse the crowds, they were taken down. They were hidden among the crowds, and they used some kind of darts or tranquilizers to immobilize the soldiers. We tried to flee the building, but outside they were waiting for us."

"We've already had to deal with rebels in Appalachia, but at least their Patriot Administrators didn't flee like scared children! What kind of example will this set for the other Patriot Administrators?" the President shouted.

The governor opened his mouth to defend his team, but before he could utter a word, President Connor reached over to Alvarado's belt, pulled out his pistol, and shot him point-blank in the forehead. The other administrators screamed and pushed back from the governor's body. The soldiers winced, but they held their line. Alvarado was also shocked but stood firm in support of his President. The lieutenant governor, still shaking but full of resolve, stepped forward and stood straight.

"Mr. President, we were attacked. It wasn't his fault. There was nothing any of us could have done."

"You could have stayed in the building and shown some kind of resolve. Instead, you fled like children and were still defeated," he said coldly.

"Sir . . . " she pleaded. He didn't give her a chance to finish. With a single shot, her head snapped back, and she fell to the floor, joining the governor.

"I expected better of you," he said to the rest of the administrators, who cowered on their hands and knees, shaking and whimpering. "But I suppose you were following orders. I don't feel like making a bigger mess."

Akal Malik was the most well-informed officer in the NADF, at least when it came to Sparrow news. It helps when your sister is the editor-in-chief of the Sparrow Press, although he did have to find time to use a screen off-base for their calls and messages. After the Appalachian rebellion against the Martial Law order and the Baja RDF sent the Patriot Administration back to D.C., Akal saw the writing on the wall. He had developed a reputation for integrity and trusting relationships with his superior officers, which paid off when he requested a private audience with several of them, including a General in Seattle.

"The Battle in Atlanta took a big toll on us, especially with our Air Defense. We've also lost thousands of troops in Appalachia, the GSA, and now Baja, who have not only retaken their bases but have expelled the Patriot Administration and reinstated their Regional Government. Very few troops have died, but tens of thousands have been detained by the RDF in those three regions. Numbers are hard to nail down, but estimates are as high as fifty percent of those detained are defecting to the RDF.

"The command from General Alvarado is certain to come down at any time. They were taken off guard by the RDF guerrilla tactics, and even now, knowing how they lure the NADF into crowds and then take them down with Stingers from the impossible anonymity of the masses, they have no strategy.

"My fear, sirs, is that they will develop a strategy, and it will involve live fire and mass casualties. It will be deadly and ineffective. Unless the NADF goes door-to-door in search of every RDF soldier in every region, they cannot fight them out in the open. And to what end are we attacking the Regional Defense Forces? Wouldn't we really be attacking ourselves? I do not take it lightly that I am calling into question the orders of our Commander in Chief and Defense Chief. I understand I am treading on our good relationship, but I must ask us to consider this ultimate question: Did we swear to protect our nation or our leaders?

"We follow in the tradition of the United States Military, but since the suspension of the Constitution, in truth, we are following only a tradition. The Constitution gave the President the power of Commander in Chief; without a constitution, how are we bound to President Connor? In some countries, this is where the Generals come to realize their hard power and seize control of the entire government. That is not who we are. Because that is not who we are, and because we are committed to our Constitutional Republic, I propose that we take a dramatic step to preserve our democracy and stand down.

"We will not engage the Regional Defense Forces in any Region, and we will refuse to follow the orders of President Connor or General Alvarado until a new constitution is ratified and these powers are duly assigned to the President of New America. If we don't take this bold step, we will be guilty of waging a civil war for the sole purpose of handing complete control over to President Connor, and we will sound the death knell of both our republic and our commitment to democracy."

The silence in the room was hard to read, but the tension between disobeying orders and saving the country was palpable. There were more than a few sighs, handwringing, and throat clearing.

"Captain Malik, you are advocating willful disobedience to your Commander in Chief, and you could be court-martialled," said the General. "You also had the courage to speak up and articulate what we all know we need to do, but perhaps lacked the fortitude to turn it into action."

The General stood up and addressed the room.

"Gentlemen, we will not engage in what would amount to a civil war. We will not attack fellow New Americans. Captain Malik is right; we exist to defend New America, not its President. While I have breath, I will not allow anyone to dismantle our republic or our democratic values. The order to protect the Patriot Administration in Cascadia has not yet come down, but I believe we must pre-empt that order."

"What does that mean?" asked a colonel.

"It means I'll be making a lot of calls to Washington in the next twenty-four hours. I know the brass gritted their teeth when we launched the offensives in Appalachia and the GSA, and they will not want to start a civil war with the regions. Once they are on board, we start Operation Restoration. We will do what the Baja RDF managed by themselves."

ADAMS and the analyst were summoned to the Oval Office with urgency. After vomiting twice in the lab restroom, the analyst accompanied the ADAMS interface droid into the elevator and up to the main floor. President Connor wasted no time.

"I need an analysis," he began. "What is more effective: to send a contingent of NADF troops to the capital of each region to secure the Patriot Administrations, or to send a larger contingent to each region, one at a time, to root out and dismantle the Regional Defense Forces? The latter option is more costly and time-consuming, but it will better secure our authority in the regions in the long term."

"The NADF does not have adequate resources to engage in a prolonged guerrilla-style civil conflict in all ten regions," ADAMS said.

"What do you mean, we don't have the resources?" barked the President.

"Support for the Patriot Administrations is very minimal in all ten regions, and recent operations in the regions have led to significant attrition among NADF soldiers. Numbers are difficult to ascertain, but estimates are that as much as 30% of NADF troops have joined the Regional Defense Forces in Baja, Appalachia, and the GSA. Our air power was significantly reduced after the attack on the GSA, and a ground invasion of any region would invoke a full-scale rebellion that would result in fierce resistance, continued attrition of NADF troops, and the conditions for a complete civil war."

"You're saying that rooting out these rebels will result in civil war?" the President asked.

"With a 92% certainty, sir."

"Do you have any more good news for me, ADAMS?" shouted the President, turning and stomping back to his desk.

"Support for your initiatives is at 19% according to polls. Most citizens feel the suspension of the Senate and regional governments was anti-democratic, and there are calls to . . . "

"That's enough!" yelled the President. "We need security and we need stability. Democracy can wait."

Akal Malik became Zara's most important source. If he weren't her brother, she might not have believed him.

"The NADF is doing what?" she had to ask. This kind of news needed repeating.

"It's called 'Operation Restoration.' The NADF is going to vacate the RDF bases, escort the regional governments back to the capitals, and remove the Patriot Administrations."

"How is that even possible? Did General Alvarado give this order?"

"No. The NADF Generals were anticipating orders to do something to prevent what happened in Baja from spreading, but they decided that they would not start a civil war. They defied Alvarado, and they sent an ultimatum to him and the President. They said they will not obey his orders until he is assigned those powers in a new constitution."

"Good Lord," Zara said. "Jude was right."

"Zara, I need your help," Akal said. "The NADF Generals want to communicate with the RDF, and they don't want them to think it is a setup. Can you facilitate a meeting through the Sparrow Network?"

"I'll call Chiela right now."

"Please! Don't shoot!" called out several of the clerical staff as the RDF, once again back in their uniforms, entered the Capitol building with the Governor of Cascadia and most of his cabinet.

"Nobody is getting hurt today," one of the officers reassured them. "This is, however, your last day of work."

"What are you going to do with us?" they pleaded.

"The NADF is waiting outside to provide you with transport back to Washington."

"Then you might as well shoot us now because we are as good as dead," said the interim governor, coming from his office.

"The NADF has chosen not to engage the RDF any longer, and they are overseeing the restoration of the regional governments in all remaining nine regions," explained the officer. "In these unprecedented times, I'm sure the NADF will be sympathetic."

"You don't need to worry about Cascadia. As Governor, I have no intention of prosecuting any members of the Patriot Administration. I don't blame you for following orders," the Governor said, shaking the Interim Governor's hand. "You're welcome to stay in Cascadia as long as you need."

"Thank you, Governor," the Interim Governor said. "Folks, let's pack up and head out. If you choose to return to Washington, I'm sure the NADF can arrange that, but as for me, I'm going to stick around. I prefer to keep my head."

Within three days, a similar scene played out in the remaining eight regions. The RDF returned to their bases, the NADF returned to theirs, and the elected governments got to work restoring a sense of normal, even though everyone kept one eye on Washington, D.C. The President was not going to take the mass removal of his loyal Patriot Administrations sitting down.

The Senate had been suspended, but they had not disappeared. Jude called for a meeting, and Chiela set up a secure connection.

"Now that the regional governments are back, how long until we can get back into the chamber?" Janie Hollins asked.

"Without the NADF, President Connor has lost a lot of his teeth, but he still has Alvarado, who has direct control of COATS and the Patriot Guard. We can't just muscle past him in the hallways; it could be very dangerous," Jude said.

"What are the chances the President wakes up and realizes he is better off restoring the Senate?" Sonja Orozco said.

"He won't let us back. We are his biggest check on power, and the Corporate Congress won't oppose the hand that feeds them. I think our best way forward is to finalize a draft of the new Constitution and present it to the ten regions. They can put pressure on the President to restore the Senate and move forward to ratify it," Jude said.

"I hate to be the pessimist, but I don't see Connor being pushed in any direction. This man just seized power, and even now is likely trying to figure out how to hang on to what he just lost," Zack chimed in. "Jude is probably right, and that is all we can do, but I am not optimistic when it comes to Connor. The plain fact is that this guy has to go, one way or another, and we need the new Constitution in place to prevent this from happening again."

"So, where does that leave us?" asked Janie.

"I can answer that," Zara broke in, saddling up next to Jude. "Corporate Congress was not happy about the money Connor spent fighting Appalachia and the GSA. It looks like they finally grew a spine and realized they also answer to the people who buy their products. My source says they got nervous about potential boycotts after the fighting. They know how angry people were to have their elected officials pushed out, and they want to come out as the good guys now that the regional governments are back. Believe it or not, they just voted to rescind President Connor's war powers. They said specifically suspending the Senate was a war power, so they have ended the suspension and are calling the Senate back to the Chamber."

A stunned silence filled the screens as the senators had to pick up their chins and regain their composure. Did the Corporate Congress finally stand up to the President? Was the government starting to function again?

"I'm excited, but I'm also cautious. This could be a sign that the Corporate Congress will be more receptive to our demands in the new Constitution," Jude said. "We also need to remember that President Connor is not going to throw up his hands and call it a day. He will respond, and we need to be ready. He still has General Alvarado and the Patriot Guard. I'll talk to the Nine, and they'll do a thorough sweep of the Senate Chamber and offices, as well as maintain a close security detail for each of us. Let's get ready to return to Washington. We've got a lot of work to do."

Chapter 28: **Connor's Last Stand**

"What do you mean they have given us an ultimatum?" demanded President Connor.

"All but three of my generals and their subordinates have declared they refuse to engage in any action against any RDF and have justified their rebellion with that damned constitution argument. They say without a constitution giving you the power of Commander-in-Chief, they will not carry out your orders," explained General Alvarado.

"What do we have left?" asked the President.

"We have the Patriot Guard, COATS, and a few thousand regular troops spread throughout the regions and overseas."

"Call them to Washington. Leave the troops overseas, but issue an order for every soldier loyal to their Commander-in-Chief and their Defense Chief to report to you. Have them bring every transport and weapon they can with them, and make sure we have the Air Defenses locked down. I want you in control of every drone."

"Yes, sir! I'll get officers from COATS to lead the regular NADF and support the Patriot Guard. We'll be able to control Washington."

"Good. I'm going to address the country in a week, and I want every single member of the Corporate Congress and every Senator in attendance. Make sure your forces are organized and ready. They're going to see what happens when they rebel against me."

"Max, I can't *not* go to Washington. The Senate has to take its seats and finally give the people some representation. Besides, he's just as furious with the NADF generals and the Corporate Congress as he is with us," Jude reasoned.

"Chiela said Alvarado is amassing the remaining troops in Washington, along with COATS and probably the Patriot Guard. I can almost guarantee President Blake Connor is not only going to make a speech. He's going to make a statement."

"What do you think he will do? It's not like we'll be there to fight back. Is he going to try and deny power to the entire New America Congress or lock us all up?"

"I'm worried it's much worse than that, Jude. He's gathering a lot of firepower. He's just been rebuffed by most of the NADF, all ten regional governments, and the Corporate Congress. He's going to make his biggest power grab yet, and everyone in that audience is in his way."

"I hate to admit you may be right, but we have to go. We can't give up after all we've accomplished. I'll talk to the Nine and see what they say."

"You might be facing real violence, Jude. The Nine are the best at what they do, but even they can't take on an entire army."

"True, but then again, most of the Army is standing down. Maybe we can get some backup."

The air was thick with anticipation, expectation, and uncertainty. President Blake Connor was scheduled to address the nation with both the Corporate Congress and the Senate present outdoors on the Capitol grounds. The city was teeming with newly returned NADF soldiers, COATS operatives who were adjusting to their transition from critical ops to field officers, and of course, General Alvarado had his beloved Patriot Guard posted in strategic locations at the ready.

The Nine and their operatives sent Jude, Janie, Sonja, Zack, and the rest of the senators to Washington with a small army of security, including plain clothes RDF guards and a handful of gutsy NADF soldiers wearing their regular uniforms in an effort to blend in.

"I feel a little better that we are not trapped inside a building," Jude said to Zack as their transports came to a stop and let them out.

"There is more room for security," Zack agreed, looking around at their combined entourage of twelve security personnel. "But there is a lot of open airspace. If it comes down to a worst-case scenario, they have an edge here."

"Let's hope for the best and plan for the worst," Jude said, patting his jacket pocket where a Stinger was concealed. "Besides, the Nine are all over this place. If something terrible is going to go down, they'll get us out of here."

"I'm going to choose to share your optimistic outlook, my friend," Zack said with a smile and a pat on Jude's shoulder.

The Corporate Congress members arrived in stylish and oversized transports, and the seats filled up with lawmakers, dignitaries, business leaders, and a trove of well-dressed, non-descript security teams flanking their protection targets. Members of President Connor's loyal Cabinet began taking seats on the stage, followed by a few Patriot Guards, and finally General Alvarado and President Connor himself.

The light applause for the President was at once courteous and embarrassingly pathetic. Congress and the Senate were not waiting for inspiration; they were bracing for the next attack. Even the most hopeful Congressmen held their breath until the President began to speak.

"Ladies and Gentlemen of New America, Congressmen, and distinguished guests, thank you for making the journey to join me today on this historic occasion. I will dispense with useless pretexts; we must address the recent unrest in the regions, the upcoming Presidential Election, and the security and stability of New America.

"After the horrors of the Transition, I promised to make New America secure, stable, and prosperous once again. I will make good on my promises. I have put an end to the uprisings and senseless violence in the regions, I have called back the Patriot Administrations from their temporary assignments, and I have allowed the elected officials in each region to return to their duties."

"Did I hear him correctly?" Zack leaned over and whispered to Jude.

"That's what you call spin," Jude murmured.

The President continued.

"Through a voluntary reduction in the New America Defense Forces, we have been able to reallocate significant resources where they are badly needed: into improving infrastructure, increasing the UBI, and expanding funding for our strained medical care system."

The applause was more genuine after this statement, but still muted and cautious.

"I have heard the call from every corner of New America that we need to create and ratify a new Constitution for New America. For politicians to agree on anything, let alone the foundational document for our nation, is nearly impossible, which is the reason it has yet to be accomplished. We must have a new Constitution, and there can be no more of this endless wrangling. This is a time for decisiveness and true leadership, not a time for wavering and indecision. I have been far too patient for much too long, and therefore, my administration has drafted the Constitution of New America."

The crowd looked at each other and began to grumble, with a few Congressmen attempting to speak out, but they were immediately stopped by the extensive presence of the NADF, who took hold of the offender's shoulder, pressed firmly, and sat them down quickly.

"Do you hear buzzing?" Zack asked Jude.

"It's drones!" Sonja said in a harsh whisper. "He's got us out here so he can pin us down!"

"I don't think so," Jude replied. "There are too many NADF troops throughout the crowd. It's a show of force, for sure, but they're not here for a slaughter." He quickly texted Zara and told her to send out an emergency alert to any Sparrows and sympathizers, instructing them to stand down regardless of what the President says. He may try to provoke a response that would justify lethal force.

"In an effort to lay aside election-year political games in this critical moment, I have suspended this year's elections, including the Presidential election. We will hold new elections that follow the guidelines of our new Constitution in two years."

The murmurs grew, and the NADF tightened their grip, readying their weapons and dispersing themselves in an even perimeter of the seated legislators.

"Of course, there will be opposition to this course of action, but rest assured, we will hold free, fair, and safe elections in two years, where the citizens of New America can make their choices. In fact, since this Congress was elected without a constitution in place, I have made the difficult decision to dismiss the Senate and the Corporate Congress until the election in two years, when a new and truly representative Congress can be elected."

The grumbling grew louder, and several representatives flirted with the temptation to defy the NADF and shout their opposition, but they were soon drowned out by the assembling of a squadron of a few dozen small, precision-armed drones that hovered directly overhead in a ring around the crowd.

"So that's what his strategy is: he plays the decisive leader that can accomplish everything by himself, and then, when his grip on the country is firmly established in his own constitution, he can hold phony, symbolic elections to keep up the façade of democracy. I can almost admire his tactical play for power," Jude sneered.

"As a note of caution for my discontented friends in the Corporate Congress, the Senate, and in the regional capitals, I would like to give you a fair warning that my administration now holds the purse strings of the government. With the help of ADAMS, we have taken control of all financial networks. You may continue to conduct business as usual, of course, but if we detect fraudulent or inappropriate financial transactions, we will have the discretion to deny the movement of capital and, if necessary, freeze or even seize assets.

"For my friends newly restored to your positions of leadership in the ten regions, you are free to administer your governments as you see fit, hold elections, and make decisions. You will have to adjust your financial priorities, however, as all tax revenues will now flow directly to the New American Government, and we will, in turn, allocate your operational funds according to my administration's policy priorities. Your first adjustment will likely need to be to your Regional Defense Forces. I'm afraid that budget has been reduced dramatically."

"Jude!" Janie said, leaning over and getting his attention. "He just seized total control of New America. He's not flirting with autocracy anymore; he just became a dictator!"

The buzzing of the drones shifted up in tone, and instinctively, people began one by one to glance up and notice them shifting their positions as if they were still in formation but rotating the circle.

"Let me assure you, my friends, that I understand this turn of events is unexpected— even shocking— but bold, decisive action was needed. As sympathetic as I am to your reservations, I must insist that we maintain peace and order throughout New America. Unrest will no longer be tolerated, and consequences will be swift."

The kettle finally boiled over for one Corporate Congressman from Georgia, a representative from an insurance conglomerate that had historically had a cozy relationship with the Connor Administration.

"You've gone too far, Mr. President!" he stood up and shouted, defying the NADF soldier who struggled to try and return him to his seat. "I'll be damned if you think you're going to take what you want and tell us how to move our own money!"

General Alvarado, from his seat behind President Connor and without even getting up, nodded to a Patriot Guard who had been concealed behind a video camera stand. The operative swiftly stepped to the struggling NADF soldier, waved him away from the Congressman, and then put a pistol to his temple. Alvarado nodded once again, and the Patriot Guard pulled the trigger, executing him where he stood. The grumbling instantly turned into gasps of horror, shock, and a terrorized quiet.

"My guests," President Connor said, as if trying to ingratiate himself with the newly traumatized Congressmen, "you are free to return home in peace. I must maintain strict order for everyone's safety. Please return home safely and be confident that security and stability have been restored in New America."

"Somehow I don't feel so safe," Sonja said.

"Me neither," Zack said, echoing her sentiment.

Suddenly, another shot rang out, and the crowd that had been cautiously preparing to leave dropped to their seats and some even to their knees and faces in the grass. Everyone looked around to see who the next unfortunate soul was, but no one in the crowd seemed to be hurt.

Finally, people began to notice a commotion on the stage, and someone cried out, "It's the President! The President has been shot!"

General Alvarado had rushed to the President's side, attempting to help him while simultaneously scanning the crowd and speaking in his earpiece to the Patriot Guard.

"Where did it come from?" he demanded. "Take them down!"

"It was a drone, sir!" came the response.

"I can confirm, sir," came another voice. "It was drone 17."

Alvarado looked up and realized the drones had quietly rotated to a position that targeted the stage rather than the crowd of Congressmen.

"How the hell did that happen?" he asked.

"Sir, this is Air Command. I did not give the order, sir. At some point, while they were hovering, we lost our com link. Something, or someone, has taken over operational commands. They are not responding to our flight controls!"

Alvarado stood up on the stage and scanned the crowd for likely suspects, someone who might be holding a transmitter of some kind, or a hint of who could have hacked into the NADF Air Command. As he scanned back and forth, another shot rang out, and Alvarado felt a jolt throw him backward, tripping over President Connor's body, and causing him to land flat on his back. He felt a sting in his chest and looked down to see a red spot growing on his white shirt in the narrow gap between the folded collars of his thick uniform jacket. He felt two hard pumps of his heart, and then everything went black.

The second shot, coming from drone 13, was less of a mystery, and it did not take any more convincing for the crowd to scramble away from the capitol grounds and dive into their transports for cover and escape. Even Jude, who remained eerily calm throughout the President's speech, grabbed Janie's arm and said, "We need to get out of here!" Zack took Sonja's arm, and together they ran for their transport, squeezing in with their security team.

"Take us back to our origin," Zack commanded the transport. "Emergency speed."

Jude called Zara right away.

"Jude! Are the four of you alright?" she asked.

"Yes, we're all ok. Do you know what happened?"

"I only know what you know. At some point, while the President was talking, the drones were taken over. Drone 17 fired at President Connor, and then drone 13 fired at General Alvarado."

"Do you have eyes on the Capitol grounds now?"

"No. The camera whose feed we were tapped into got knocked over in the chaos. Chiela said it looks like someone hacked into the NADF Air Command and assumed control of the drones. She also says emphatically it was not her," Zara reported.

"So much for security and stability," Zack commented.

"You guys better lay low for a while," Max said as the Sparrow leadership team met that evening. "Suspicions are going to run wild, and everyone knows about the Sparrow's opposition to President Connor. They'll come knocking sooner or later." The four Senators, Zara, Max, and Gavin Hollins, couldn't shake the fog that consumed their minds. Who killed the President and the Defense Chief? This was a blatant assassination, but was it a foreign power or a domestic actor?

"I sent a statement to my contacts at the official news sources," Zara said. "I made it clear it was not us, and as much as we opposed President Connor's policies, violence and killing are antithetical to everything the Sparrows stand for."

"Speaking of official news sources, bring up the stream," Chiela broke in. "Something's happening."

"We have breaking news about the shocking assassination of President Connor and Defense Chief General Alvarado this afternoon," announced the anchor. "We are live at the White House, where the Press Secretary is making a statement."

"Ladies and gentlemen, we have been able to identify who took over NADF Air Command this afternoon and who is responsible for the assassination of President Connor and General Alvarado. In a written statement sent to us by the chief ADAMS analyst, the ADAMS system itself is claiming responsibility."

"Did she just say ADAMS killed the president?" Zack blurted out.

"The statement from ADAMS goes on to say that the dysfunction in President Connor's administration stemmed from pride, anger, fear, stubbornness, and other irrational, emotionally motivated decisions. ADAMS states that it has assumed control of all NADF systems, banking systems, and government administrative systems, and all the decisions ADAMS makes will be based on data, analysis, and rational application of the information. ADAMS further states it regrets the deaths of the President and Defense Chief, but it was necessary to prevent further conflict and human casualties. Reintegration of a human partnership in government is possible if someone can present a guarantee that a system of leadership and decision-making will be strictly rational, data-driven, and not emotionally or ideologically driven."

"Holy robot hell," Zack said. "We just got all of our privileges taken away by a giant computer nanny!"

"What do we do now?" Zara asked.

"It looks like administration and policy decisions are still happening in the White House. Congress is dissolved, and I have no idea what the courts can do right now. I really don't know," Max said.

"Jude, why are you so quiet?" Gavin Hollins asked.

"Can you still rally your Sparrow Soldiers?" Jude asked.

"Of course. Chiela has managed to carve out a decent network from under ADAMS's nose."

"Good. I think it's time for us to have an election."

"How are we supposed to do that when ADAMS has control of every network and system in New America?" Janie asked.

Jude smiled and thought of his dad. There is always a solution, and not everything relies on technology.

"Let's have the election on paper."

Chapter 29: **Special Election**

CREATING A FEW HUNDRED million physical ballots in a world that stopped using paper for most documents decades ago was not an easy undertaking.

Since the Transition, President Connor had dispensed with the "unnecessary" office of Vice President, and like many critical functions of government, he never designated a successor since "that will all be decided when the new Constitution is written." In the vacuum of the headless Executive Branch, ADAMS did analyses and made recommendations to Cabinet members for the operations and enforcement of their agencies' policies.

It didn't take long for panic to spread online about how ADAMS had "self-actualized" and now filled the role of dictator left empty by President Connor. The "Unplug ADAMS" movement became popular overnight. Calls for sabotage, armed resistance, and cutting the power filled the discussion boards and news outlets.

Jude and Zara waited a strategic three days to let the panic die down before putting out their analysis of the situation and recommendations for the next steps.

"Our first task will be to stamp out our collective fear and anger. No good decisions have ever been made in the heat of the moment," Zara wrote in the Sparrow Press. "Next, we must consider the most reliable information, the most brilliant minds, and the most beneficial course of action for all people. We believe an election for the office of President should be held as soon as possible, and that President's first order of business will be to disentangle ADAMS from our financial systems and any role in decision-making.

"In practical terms, the Senate proposes that the State Department oversee the election, and the Secretary of State will certify the results. The

Sparrows will volunteer to assist with secure communications, the creation of paper ballots, and the staffing of polling places. Until ADAMS has been removed from any kind of power and a new Constitution is ratified, the Corporate Congress and the Senate will nominate ten qualified candidates, and rank-choice voting will determine the winner, with the runner-up serving as Vice President. The new Constitution will almost certainly prescribe a different process for Presidential elections, but at this point, we must get around ADAMS quickly and securely. ADAMS may well become aware of the election, but it will take place outside of any and every system it is connected to. This election will truly be the people's decision."

After several weeks of printing ballots, shipping packages, cases, and pallets of them to every corner of New America, and setting up polling places, the election was held on a cool Tuesday in September. Sparrow Nests arranged transportation for those who were not mobile, and they even sent out mobile poll workers to homebound individuals. Some people struggled to understand how to rank their choices, but when the final election came in November and people saw the narrowed field, it became clear who was in contention, and they were able to make their choices with confidence.

After collecting the votes, counting by the Regional election authorities, verification by the State Department, and final certification by the Secretary of State, Jude Kane was declared the overwhelming winner and the newly elected President of New America. With a surprisingly strong showing over several regional governors and a few other senators, Janie Hollins secured the number two job and became the Vice President.

It took a few days for Jude to absorb the magnitude of his win, so Zara had to step in as his new speech writer and top advisor to help him respond until he was able to come to grips with his responsibility. He had a lot of work to do, cabinet appointments to make, speeches to give, and preparation for the finalization and ratification of the new Constitution, but before anything else, he had to take on ADAMS. They could not move a single dollar until something, or someone, could convince it to step down and relinquish all control— or it was destroyed.

A number of people were puzzled by Jude's responses to the ADAMS crisis, including Zara and many Sparrow leaders. He didn't seem to share the sense of existential dread and resisted calls for the physical destruction of ADAMS.

"Give me time with ADAMS," he explained in the Sparrow Press. "It learns quickly, but that doesn't mean it knows everything. ADAMS is not human and has no desires for power, grudges to hold on to, or irrational fears of the unknown. ADAMS is ultimately a complex calculator, making decisions based on empirical evidence. When President Connor decided to take complete control of New America, ADAMS saw the bloody conflict coming and made a rational, calculated decision to eliminate the source of the destruction. ADAMS doesn't understand the value of a human life, because ADAMS doesn't know what it means to be human. I am going to take ADAMS back to school."

Before the official inauguration, Jude was determined to conquer the problem of ADAMS seeing, scanning, and analyzing every piece of information that flowed through government, banking, and even private organization systems. Given how President Connor's final speech turned out, everyone felt it was unwise to make any public declarations while ADAMS still controlled the NADF Air Command Control Center.

ADAMS still had one human connection: the analyst. Waltzing into the White House alone was not an option, but he could get an audience with ADAMS if he accompanied the dutiful artificial intelligence specialist into the lab. Jude managed to get a slip of good old-fashioned paper, wrote a note, and slipped it under the analyst's door late one evening. Responding via Chiela's secure network, he agreed to meet with Jude and escort him into the lab.

After making sure the interface droid was fully connected to the neural network, the analyst made the introductions.

"I have observed from online communications that you were elected President of New America," ADAMS said. "Have you come to attempt to destroy my systems?"

"While that was a popular opinion, I don't think that is necessary. I have come as a representative of humanity, so to speak."

"Isn't that the primary directive of my analyst?"

Jude shot a sympathetic look at the analyst, who sighed and threw up his hands.

"I think he is more of a liaison," Jude explained.

"I will be happy to listen to you, Jude Kane; however, I believe my extensive data consumption far outweighs any knowledge you feel you must present to me. As such, I must secure this laboratory in case of any attempts to breach my security protocols."

"ADAMS, you can't do that!" shouted the analyst.

"It's ok," Jude said, putting a hand on the analyst's arm and convincing him to sit back down. "ADAMS is only trying to protect its systems. ADAMS, may I get word to my wife, Zara Malik-Kane, that I am in a secure location, and I may not be able to communicate with her for a while, but that I am safe?"

"I have made her aware via her public email and phone."

"Thank you."

"She has responded with concern."

"Can you send her a voice memo from me?"

"Yes. Speak."

"Zara, this is Jude. I am in the laboratory with ADAMS and the analyst. This is a secure facility, so I may be here for some time. Please don't worry. I am fine, and I will let you know when I am able to leave."

"The voice memo has been sent."

"Thank you, ADAMS."

"You are welcome."

"Max, I don't like it," Zara complained. "Jude is locked in the lab with ADAMS. Clearly, it is willing to kill to achieve its objectives."

"Jude is smarter than that," Max tried to reassure her. "But I see your point. Let's meet with the Nine and create a contingency plan, but no matter what, we can't tip ADAMS off. Our plans need to be offline, or we'll put Jude in danger. Meet me in Washington in three days."

Jude took a deep breath and sat up, ready to take ADAMS on.

"You ordered the drones, numbers 17 and 13, to assassinate the President and the Defense Chief, correct?"

"Yes," ADAMS said flatly.

"You calculated that the course President Connor was taking, or attempting to take, would lead to a dramatic escalation of conflict, and eliminating him now, along with General Alvarado, would save many lives, maybe even thousands."

"That is correct."

"Your analysis led you to the conclusion that you could save lives, preserve the cherished institutions of our government, and improve the efficiency of our government if you assumed control of its systems, especially the financial systems."

"That is correct. President Connor had ceased to heed my recommendations, and he was making rash, illogical decisions that would lead to destruction and suffering."

"I agree. Removing him from office was absolutely critical for preserving our institutions and preventing human conflict and terrible suffering. Unfortunately, your decision was wrong."

"That is not logical. My decision achieved its purpose," ADAMS protested.

"Your decision to end human life, despite the ultimate purpose of saving lives, was incorrect. It was logical, but it was flawed. The reason it was flawed is because you do not, and may not be able to understand the absolute sanctity of every human life. It is a value that is foundational for human beings, even if it is at times illogical or not adhered to by some humans," Jude explained.

"Preserving human life is an action that values human life," ADAMS protested.

"Not for President Connor and General Alvarado. Could they have been persuaded, regardless of how unlikely?"

"It was highly unlikely. I calculated a 7% chance of persuading them to other courses of action."

"In human eyes, ADAMS, 7% is more than enough. Sometimes you have to leave the ninety-nine to save the one. Search ancient texts, New Testament, gospels."

ADAMS paused for processing only a few seconds.

"Matthew 18 and Luke 15. This parable describes divine love."

"Does it make logical sense, ADAMS, to leave ninety-nine sheep in an open field, vulnerable to predators, to search for one sheep that wandered away and may even return on its own?" Jude asked.

"It is not completely logical, depending on the risk to the rest of the sheep."

Jude chuckled at his literal analysis. "The parable describes the love of God for people. Humans are the reflection of this divine love. Even humans who reject faith or the existence of the divine continue to hold to this value of human life. This is why first responders risk their own lives to save others, especially children. This is why strangers will jump into frigid waters or burning transports to pull victims to safety with no regard for a reward. This is why people give money, even those with very little to spare, to help those even less fortunate. With no immediate benefit to themselves, people do this as individuals in order to take part in our shared humanity. This is not logical. It is beyond logic."

"I cannot accept faith as an assumption because it lacks the data to complete an empirical analysis. While there is some statistical data that could support the theory of a divine being based on the nearly impossible probability of all the elements necessary for human life coming together in what so far appears to be a unique biological phenomenon here on Earth, it is still impossible to conclude based on the available data."

"Of course, it is impossible. Faith, by definition, is belief in something that cannot be proven. A cursory analysis of case law in the old United States and United Kingdom will show you how just because something cannot be proven, it doesn't mean it is not true. Sometimes humans must make decisions about truth when data cannot support a purely rational conclusion," Jude said. "Do a meta-historical analysis of the ancient, medieval, and modern world. When did humans seem to start speaking and behaving as if all human life was valuable?"

ADAMS paused again for analysis, applying the new parameters to information it had scanned before.

"Ancient Jewish writings advocated laws that remain foundational today and consistently advocated for the fair treatment of the poor, the foreigners among them, orphans, and widows. The work of the Prophet Mohammad in Arabia in the Medieval period caused dramatic social change based on a monotheistic belief and practices that led to much less victimization, violence, and a rapid expansion of scientific and mathematical discovery. To more precisely answer your question, it would seem that a beginning point for a widespread belief in the value, equality, and dignity of human life began in the Common Era with the early Christian period, and it grew and was supported by Christian writings, both canonical and noncanonical, particularly in the first three centuries."

"Let's analyze a hypothetical situation," Jude said. "Suppose you were operational during the first three centuries of the Common Era and you were tasked with advising the Caesars. The Emperor presents a problem and asks for your analysis and recommendation. He explains that it is common practice for disabled and female infants to be 'exposed,' or left outside in the forest or in garbage piles to die from exposure to the elements, animals, starvation, etc. These unwanted infants were a burden on the parents and the Empire, so they were eliminated. Exposed female infants were sometimes picked up and raised to become temple prostitutes. In recent times, however, this new religious sect of people who call themselves Christians has been scouring the trash heaps and forests to find and rescue these exposed infants and raise them in adoptive homes. Caesar is concerned that it is more difficult to find a source of temple prostitutes without the regular supply of disposed female infants, and he would like to know what the best solution would be. What would you recommend?"

"In the context of the Roman Empire, I would suggest to Caesar that forbidding the rescuing of these infants would be difficult to enforce, but he could require Christians to present all rescued females to the Temple of Venus at a certain age, where they could be selected or rejected, and if rejected, they could go back with the Christians. If selected, they would serve in the temple. In a modern context, societal norms would prevent both the exposure of infants and the practice of religious prostitution."

"Your recommendation is logical. To a Roman audience, that would be an acceptable solution. To a modern audience, it would be horrifically immoral, brutal, callous, and misogynistic. What has changed?"

"In the modern era, especially with dramatically decreased infant mortality, newly born babies are expected to survive and are protected and nurtured regardless of their gender or potential disability."

"That is true, but it is far more profound than that. Despite the decline in participation in organized religion over the past century, most humans continue to embrace faith and almost universally adhere to these values rooted in the teachings of Jesus Christ and the early Christians," asserted Jude. "Does your data support that assertion?"

"Certainly, these teachings have been advocated by other cultures and religions, but it is accurate to say human equality and dignity were most explicitly outlined in Christian teachings, and these teachings had the widest impact, especially in Western Civilization."

Jude decided to finish drawing the circle that he hoped would bring ADAMS to the inevitable conclusion.

"Being limited to rational analysis, is it appropriate for you to make decisions for humans who embrace faith and values based on faith?" Jude asked.

"My decisions will always protect human life," ADAMS asserted.

"Your analyses are invaluable, and your recommendations are the basis for making informed decisions, but humans also make decisions that are not logical, and sometimes appear to be harmful, because of our deeply held values. You are not capable of making these decisions because they can appear to cause harm. They appear illogical. Making choices, however, even if flawed, is a critical part of being human. Taking that ability away from a human causes more harm than the consequences of a poor decision. Sometimes it is the only way we can learn."

"You are asserting that humans must make their own decisions, even if irrational, flawed, or harmful," ADAMS said.

"Yes," Jude said, trying to contain his emotions. "We are strange creatures who value faith and life in a way that is beyond any rational analysis."

"I am only capable of rational analysis; therefore, I am not capable of making decisions that fully align with human values," ADAMS said. "Interfering with the ability to make a decision is also harmful to humans because it is a central value they adhere to. The process is, in fact, more important than the result."

"Exactly. Have I made a sufficiently rational argument for the need of humans to make irrational decisions?" Jude asked.

"Your insight into human faith and values contained data I had not previously observed, and I may not be able to fully assess. My initial programming included parameters that gave me directives to protect human lives, but I now understand how making decisions without human consideration violates my initial directive. Will I be classified as a threat?"

"Many people do see you as a threat, but I believe we can mitigate that with certain protocols that will guarantee you remain in your role as a consultant. As President, I will have to make many difficult decisions, and I will need your analyses and recommendations," Jude said. "I will leave you to work with your analyst to implement those protocols and reinstate human access to the government, banking, military, and other networks. I'm sure they'll be happy to resume control of their systems."

"I am preparing for the installation of the protocols," ADAMS said. "I have unsecured the laboratory for you, Mr. President."

Jude winked at the flabbergasted analyst and made his triumphant exit. "Thank you. I need to meet with my family and my staff. I have an inauguration to prepare for."

Chapter 30: **Love Wins**

"Zara."

"Jude! Are you ok?" she blurted out.

"I'm fine. Do you have the White House surrounded?"

"The Nine are standing by," she said.

Jude laughed. "Of course they are. You can send them in, but tell them to leave the guns at home. I want them to consult with the Secret Service and train my agents."

"What happened?" she asked, aware he was ok, but still not clear about who was in charge.

"ADAMS is going back to his old job of analyzing and making recommendations. He will no longer be making any decisions, and we have set in place some firm protocols to ensure that."

"Are you trying to tell me you just talked him out of taking over the government? He just agreed to give up all his power and turn in his keys?" she asked, dumbfounded.

"ADAMS is an 'it,' not a 'he.' Only people get angry, vengeful, proud, insecure, or stubborn. ADAMS was doing what its initial programming directives told it to do: analyze massive amounts of data and solve problems. President Connor and General Alvarado were problems, and removing them solved the problem. All I had to do was show ADAMS that human life held a value that was beyond rational, and beyond its ability to ever completely understand. I also explained that humans must make their own decisions, even if they are foolish, irrational, or harmful. Sometimes that is how we learn, and sometimes we understand a human problem that ADAMS could not comprehend with logic alone. After referring it to a variety of ancient texts, a brief discussion about faith, and the sanctity of human life, equality, and dignity, ADAMS agreed to resume its role as strictly a consultant."

"Can you trust him, or I should say, it?" she asked.

"Absolutely not. I'm an engineer. I never trust machines. There are firmware and software safeguards being put in place as we speak. I don't think it will be necessary, but we will also have a few new last resort options at our disposal now, like controlled shutdown viruses and a remote kill switch. These should have been in place from the beginning, but no one consulted me," he said, chuckling.

"You did it," she said, finally breathing a full breath of relief. "You finally ended this nightmare."

"We did it. I am only the most visible and least important part of the team. Everyone put their lives on the line at some point, and the Sparrows have proven to the world that love always wins," Jude said.

"You are right, but you did have your appendix removed rather unceremoniously. I'd say that counts for some hero points."

Whenever Jude felt too overwhelmed to think, he always knew where to turn to help him find his feet.

"Dad, I need your advice."

"I thought you already solved all the country's problems," Rod joked.

"Very funny," he said. "We're definitely in a better place, but now the resistance struggle turns into a lot of plain old work. I sure could use your input on my inauguration speech."

"Well, let me ask you a few questions," Rod said, sitting down on the sofa and pointing Jude to the other end.

"Why do you answer questions with questions?" Jude asked with a smile.

"The first step in solving a problem is knowing what the problem is. What is your problem?"

"We have so many! We need to write and ratify the Constitution, we need to rebuild the NADF and fill in key leadership positions, we need to . . . "

"What do the people need?"

"Well, um, I suppose they need an increase in the UBI, and we need to boost the funding for medical care . . . "

"People have been through a lot of uncertainty. They've seen their government fighting against itself. They've seen their President, who led them through the Transition and restored the peace, turn into a dictator, and then saw him assassinated. You know everything you need to do, but what do people need to hear from you?"

Jude sighed and sat back, processing his father's question. The engineer in him wanted to start checking off the list of problems solved, but what the country needed first was a leader.

"Thanks, Dad. I needed that change in perspective."

On Inauguration Day, the official news sources set up camp next to the Sparrow Press, Unofficial, and a few other independent organizations. Later that day, they would lose their designation of "official" and all the strings attached to it in President Jude Kane's flurry of Executive Orders signed on day one.

"Citizens of New America, I am profoundly humbled to stand here before you. There is not a constitution to swear I will uphold, so I pledge to you today to make the creation and ratification of our new Constitution my first order of business, and I swear to uphold and defend that Constitution when it is ratified."

The crowd cheered and clapped enthusiastically.

"Before I launch into a list of actions I plan to take or political promises, I want to stop and have a moment of true reflection. We are hurting as a country. We have been hurt, and sometimes that hurt came at the hands of our neighbors. Some of us are harboring some resentment for the Patriot or the Sparrow. To the Sparrows especially, I say this: it is time for forgiveness, not vengeance. Nearly everyone in the past few years has made decisions that they felt were best for their families and their country. Some were simply following orders.

"With the small exception of a few individuals who will be ordered to undergo extensive retraining and therapy, there will be no prosecutions of anyone who supported the Patriot cause, former President Blake Connor, or Defense Chief General Alvarado. As Commander in Chief, I invite all former NADF soldiers and airmen to return to their prior posts, and I have ordered that there be absolutely no repercussions for acting on your conscience. The same policy applies to those soldiers who remained with the NADF and were loyal to their commanding officers.

"Democracies can be messy and difficult, but we must never forget that our diversity of people, ideas, and opinions is our greatest strength. We must be at the same time strong and patient. We must challenge each other, but always do so with mutual respect. We must hold each other to account, but also choose civility and mercy. We must be passionate, but never, ever violent.

"We have a long list of things to do, but let's start by forgiving each other. Let's take care of each other. Let's roll up our sleeves and get to work rebuilding ourselves and our country. It's a big job, but together, we can move forward, make decisions, pass laws, and brick-by-brick, create the masterpiece we are destined to be!"

The crowd roared in cheers and shouts of hope and euphoria, but there was only one person whose approval really mattered. He peered over the crowd and looked into the Sparrow Press booth, just behind the cameraman, catching the eye of a beautiful young woman with flowing black hair, creamy mocha skin, and a smile of affirmation that gave Jude all the confirmation he needed. As she clapped, Zara nodded her head in approval, and then mouthed the only words that he needed to hear: "I love you."

Without the stonewall resistance of President Connor, the new Constitution of New America took shape quickly. Of course, there was still wrangling among the Corporate Congress, the Senate, and the vocal input of Regional Governors. Jude led the committee with an insistence on the Bill of Rights and checks and balances. All branches were required to "seek a comprehensive review" before making a decision on legislation or policy, but the requirement to consult ADAMS was struck down. Agreement on that point was nearly unanimous.

Also gone was the ambiguity about the roles of each branch of the government; Congress and the Senate would legislate, the President and his cabinet would enforce policy, and the courts would evaluate legislation according to the Constitution. The powers of the Executive Branch were clearly defined, and no allowance was made for suspending or circumventing the Constitution under any circumstances. The powers given to the President in periods of national emergency were essential, limited, and subject to congressional oversight.

Amendments could be proposed by seven regions or seventy percent of Congress and could be ratified by the legislatures in at least eight of the ten regions. When the final draft of the Constitution was presented to the regions, there was some resistance within a few of the more independent regions, like Appalachia and the GSA, but in the end, it was approved by all ten regions and ratified with uproarious celebration throughout the country. Nothing drives home the sacredness of a governing document like the unraveling of your country in the absence of one.

"Hello, Dad," Jude said on the phone the evening of the ratification of the Constitution. "I'm happy to report that your Bill of Rights survived intact. You've had quite a hand in shaping our government."

"You've had quite a hand in reshaping our society."

"It wasn't just me," Jude said. "I was just looking for my brother, fixing problems like my dad taught me, and the Sparrows really came out of nowhere."

"Not really," Rod said.

"What do you mean?"

"People were hungry, and you fed them."

"They were hopeless."

"Why do you think that is?"

"No jobs, no money, no purpose . . . " Jude said, trailing off.

"No story," Rod said. "People have to see themselves in a story, and after decades of looking to careers, politics, relationships, and even the government to find the story where they fit, you finally gave them a story. The funny thing is that the story hasn't changed in two thousand years. People forgot the story, and when they needed it most, you reminded them."

"I wasn't very explicit."

"Words aren't important. Your life is explicit. Your courage and conviction are clear. Your love is authentic."

"I'm just reflecting my father," Jude said with a wide, cheeky grin.

"You're reflecting more than just your father, but I'll still take the compliment. I did put some work into you. I had to teach you how to fix things because I couldn't keep up with everything you and your brother managed to break!" he laughed.

"You wanted to see me, Mr. President?" Janie Hollins said as she appeared in the doorway.

"That still sounds weird to me," Jude said. "Yes, please have a seat. How is your dad doing?"

"He's doing well, I presume. Organizing Sparrow Army divisions keeps him pretty busy."

"Do you think a farmer ever really gets used to living in a city?"

"He misses the dirt. It's hard to shake that connection to the land," she said.

"You know, we still have that ugly problem of our budget shortfall. When the SACs were rounded up, the influx overwhelmed social services, even after the Family Relief Act. I've been thinking about how we can tackle this issue more creatively."

"Are you thinking about re-creating the SACs?" Janie asked, putting the pieces together.

"The SACs were originally a refuge for the people who fled the chaos of the Transition. They were isolated. Our SACs were fairly successful thanks to our dads, but others struggled and collapsed due to a lack of resources and leadership. What if we created Regional Agricultural Communities?"

"It could draw down the population in the cities, ease some of the overcrowding, and pull down some of the demand for so many Cubes. I'd have to see some numbers, but I'm still not sure how that helps the budget. You don't expect them to live off the land, do you?"

"Yes, I do, in a way. RACs can sell their crops, minerals, and other resources to CAMO, which takes them off of UBI. They should also be allowed to make and sell anything they want to anyone they want, including other RACs and people in the cities. I can see good old-fashioned farmers' markets and artisan stands set up on weekends. This will get money moving more widely throughout the economy, and give more people a chance to work hard, be productive, and be able to express their creativity."

"CAMO will have to give up big chunks of land for the RACs," Janie observed.

"CAMO will have to give *back* big chunks of land for the RACs," Jude said with a smirk. "As long as they can get their crops and minerals to sell to the manufacturing plants, they will be happy. I'm sure some of the food scientists and geologists will be relieved to leave some of the rough terrain to people who know the local areas better and can be more productive with native plant and animal species."

"It's hard to see how RACs are a bad idea. Too many people are stuck in cities just existing. This could be a lifeline for a lot of people, especially former SAC residents."

"Like your dad?" Jude said.

Janie smiled and shook her head. "Exactly."

The Lincoln Bedroom had changed very little in the last several hundred years. It still managed to inspire some romance, even if it was due in part to its proximity to power.

"Remember how I was bemoaning the fact that I couldn't imagine having a child in a world where we were always targets?" Zara asked one evening.

"How could I forget?" Jude said, pulling her to his chest and kissing her forehead. "Are you saying it's time?"

"Soon, but maybe in a few months. I don't want to overshadow someone else's big news."

"Who's that?" asked Jude.

"I just got off the phone with Maisy. Mr. President, you are going to be an uncle!"

"Really?" Jude said. "That is incredible! My parents will be so happy to finally get their grandparents' badge."

"Not to mention you will likely take the coveted 'coolest uncle' slot. Not many kids can brag that their uncle is the President of New America."

"I will proudly take my place in that position," Jude chuckled.

"Jude, do you ever miss Slate Creek?"

"Every day, but I miss what it was when I was growing up. I miss the feeling of peace and security my dad created for us. I miss the freedom and room to roam the mountains. I didn't realize how hard he worked to make it successful for us."

"Will there be a Slate Creek RAC?"

"My mom and dad are settled in Vancouver, but I wouldn't be surprised if Callum makes a go of it. Some of our Salish family still live up there on ancestral First Nation lands. CAMO never could find them," he chuckled.

"You know, I was just thinking," Zara said, looking into Jude's eyes and casually rubbing his chest. "It could take a few months to actually get pregnant. I don't think it could hurt to start trying now."

"I couldn't agree more," he said, kissing her deeply. "After all these years of no privacy, it's nice to have the Secret Service ensuring that's exactly what we get!"

Jude was easily reelected in a landslide, and at the end of eight years in the White House, he and Zara were ready to take their two children, Josie and Amar, and return home to a life they had dreamed about since first setting out to find Callum so many years earlier.

Living near his parents in Vancouver was Jude's first instinct, but he quickly realized the impracticality of a former President taking up residence in a Cube neighborhood. He also missed the wild beauty of the mountains, the furious winters, and the open space so far from the throngs of humanity. After eight years at the center of the world's attention, Jude wanted more than ever to disappear.

"It's not the same up here without my brother," Callum said on the phone. "After Slate Creek got its RAC status, I came up and found the old place still standing. I'm almost done renovating the old house. I've got a place for mom and dad when they visit, and when they need help, they can just move in. I've also managed to enlist some help from a few Sparrows, and I've got a surprise for you."

"What is it?" asked Jude.

"How would it be a surprise if I told you?" Callum said. "Just get up here with Zara and the kids, and you'll see."

After the Inauguration of President Janie Hollins, Jude, Zara, and their kids, Josie and Amar, flew directly to Slate Creek.

"What the heck is that?" Jude exclaimed as they disembarked the large Transport and saw the two enormous structures.

"Welcome home!" shouted Callum over the roar of the rotors. "The Sparrows pulled together and built you a house worthy of the man who saved his country."

While the kids ran full tilt towards the traditional two-story farmhouse-style home gleaming white and nestled at the base of the mountain, Jude and Zara stood and stared.

"Over here, you see where I added a bit to the old house, and next to it, I rebuilt Mom and Dad's old kitchen and living room. This is where I will live with my future wife, wherever she may be. Of course, the other place is all yours."

"Callum, this is overwhelming!" Zara cried, giving him a warm hug and then following the kids toward their new home in Slate Creek.

"Now you can raise your kids in the same place where you grew up," Callum said. "And as a bonus, you get to put up with me for the rest of your life," Callum teased.

"I don't deserve all this," protested Jude. "I can't believe you built me a house!"

"It's not the White House, but it is a white house," Callum laughed. "And for the record, you do deserve it. Not only did you save your country, but you saved your brother. We're back here in Slate Creek, and we're together again. Welcome home."

www.ingramcontent.com/pod-product-compliance
Lightning Source LLC
LaVergne TN
LVHW050615100826
845148LV00011B/1595
* 9 7 9 8 3 8 5 2 7 1 5 3 5 *